Home Light Burning

Also by
Jim H. Ainsworth

Biscuits Across the Brazos
Rivers Flow
Rivers Crossing
Rivers Ebb

Home Light Burning

A Novel Based on Actual Facts and Events

Jim H. Ainsworth

SUNSTONE
PRESS

SANTA FE

Sunstone books may be purchased for educational, business, or sales promotional use. For information please write:
Special Markets Department, Sunstone Press,
P.O. Box 2321, Santa Fe, New Mexico 87504-2321.

Book design • Vicki Ahl
Body typeface • Franklin Gothic Book
Printed on acid free paper

Library of Congress Cataloging-in-Publication Data

Ainsworth, Jim H.
  Home light burning : a novel based on actual facts and events / by Jim H. Ainsworth.
      p. cm.
  ISBN 978-0-86534-745-8 (pbk. : alk. paper)
  1. Texas--Fiction. I. Title.
  PS3601.I57H66 2010
  813'.6--dc22
                                        2009044447

WWW.SUNSTONEPRESS.COM
SUNSTONE PRESS / POST OFFICE BOX 2321 / SANTA FE, NM 87504-2321 /USA
(505) 988-4418 / ORDERS ONLY (800) 243-5644 / FAX (505) 988-1025

IN MEMORY OF HY AND LEV.
Thanks for facing life head-on
and leaving behind stories worth repeating.

Acknowledgements

THANKS TO ALL THE FOLKS WHO HELPED ME. You know who you are. And thanks to all who have read my other books and taken the time to write me and say so. I know who you are.

A Few Words

AN EXPLANATION IS NEEDED, I THINK. THIS IS A work of fiction based on real events. I occasionally had to fill in the blanks with stories or descriptions of what might have happened or what I think happened. A few characters came from my imagination as did all of the dialogue, though I have a pretty good idea of the dialect. It isn't the things that I made up that worry me, but the things that I know happened. I had trouble believing some events—until I found proof. If you find some event or scene highly unlikely to have happened, I humbly ask you to suspend your doubts until the end. After you read the last page, I will provide proof of the events that seemed most doubtful to me.

1

PRIVATES LEV AND HY RIVERS RODE OUT OF the sugarcane fields and stopped to wait for the rest of the 19th Texas Cavalry on the banks of Yellow Bayou, a marshy arm off the Atchafalaya River that jutted into Old Oaks Plantation. Hy found the place peaceful when they stepped off their horses—a little like Texas and home, but Lev did not like the heavy air, weeds high enough to hide a mounted man, and plentiful poison oak. After crossing the wide Atchafalaya horseback, he no longer liked any body of water wide or deep enough to make a horse have to swim. "Why do they call it Yellow Bayou?"

Hy pointed down the meandering bayou as the setting sun splashed across the water. "Water looks kinda yellow when the sun hits it just right. Guess that's the reason."

Lev looked down the bayou past the turtles sunning on drift logs, but just saw muddy ... or bloody. He had spent the day afoot in head-high weeds, picking off Yankees foolish enough to show themselves on the decks of the Union's Brown Water Navy vessels. He followed orders, but it had seemed a little like plucking squirrels out of trees. He had almost grown accustomed to cavalry skirmishes that pitted man against man, horse against horse, but sniping from the cover of rocks and weeds made him more melancholy than usual.

The spring smells of new grass and water beginning to

stagnate were soon conquered by the odor of horses and thousands of unwashed men gathering around campfires as the rest of the 19th and Taylor's army arrived. Hy spread his bedroll close to the bayou and was soon lulled to sleep by the sounds of water lapping against the bayou bank. Lev lay awake, studying the murky water. The constant etching of water against dead cypress stumps had formed knotty gnarled appendages that seemed to move with each ripple. Lev imagined them as dead sentinels rising out of the river mud to take their revenge. When moss hanging from tall cypress trees cast flickering moonlight shadows across the sentinels, Lev surrendered to his imagination and moved toward higher ground. He stopped at the picket line to untie Handler and led him toward the sugarcane fields a few yards west of the water. He knew the horse would stay with him, but hobbled him in case something spooked him during the night.

Thinking of moccasins and copperheads, he looped a grass rope around his bedroll. He was closer to the sugarcane fields than the bayou now, and the smells of sugarcane and dry switch grass calmed him. He lay on his back, stared at the moon, and considered what was coming tomorrow. Colonel Parsons had told them that Yankees would be trying to cross the bayou and the river on their way to Baton Rouge come morning. He rolled on his side and studied the future battlefield. Demanding and resolute floodwaters had formed deep and narrow creeks on the side of the bayou. Soldiers had dug the creeks deeper and used the dirt to make three rows of earthen breastworks. A good place for infantry to take a stand, but treacherous for mounted soldiers. The sugarcane fields were cumbersome for men horseback, but Lev hoped to fight from there. Handler would give him an advantage. Thinking about the coming fight kept Lev awake most of the night. Hy slept like he was in bed at home.

As night settled two days later, the fields of Old Oaks Plantation had been transformed into a battlefield and then abandoned like a spurned lover that had not served her purpose well. The Confederates had failed to keep federals from crossing the river. Now, the green fields of spring, the sugarcane fields, had turned black from fire, the ground almost bare from the stomping of horses and men. The fighting field, pockmarked with cannon holes and littered with hastily built breastworks, horse carcasses, broken wagons and firearms, bled with curling spirals of smoke from dying fires and scattered pieces of smoldering lead. Dark blotches scarred the once-green pasture and swarming flies marked the only distinction between burned spots and puddles of still-moist blood.

At full dark on the second day, the sounds of pain, cries for help, the squeals of dying horses, and the noisy retreat of cavalry gave way to the sounds of lapping water again. Squirrels barked from the tall trees, and birds sang again. Yellow Bayou had not surrendered. Nature was forgetting the violence and had begun to heal.

The smell of warm blood and burning hair awakened Lev. He wondered if it was his own blood and hair. That might explain why he could not feel his legs. He did not remember where he was—even his name had burned itself to ashes and a slight breeze had blown away the smoke. In his mind's eye, he could see jumbled letters that might have been his name—or his life—drift away in the wind. Maybe you don't have a name in hell. Probably don't need one. There was some pain above his waist, though he could not locate exactly where. His arms would move, but they refused his instructions to search where it hurt. Opening his eyes was out of the question. He did not want to see legs that he could not move. He drifted back to wherever he had been.

A horse's squeal brought him back to semi-consciousness. The pain below his waist was unbearable, but welcome—it meant something was down there. Something or someone was rolling a huge weight across the bottom part of his body, alternately grunting and squealing with each infliction of pain, as if it enjoyed hurting him. Lucifer was surely dragging him into hell. Lev had always imagined meeting the devil on two good legs. He would lose a battle with the dark angel, of course, but had hoped the bastard would give him a sporting chance. He never expected to be immobile—never expected to be afraid to open his eyes. Another crushing move like the last one would break both ankles. Ankles. He still had two and they had feeling. The short sense of elation was enough to make him open one eye.

Handler. The name came to Lev in his own guttural whisper followed by a groaning whinny that turned into a squeal—a horse's voice. He had named the bay Handler because he handled so well. The horse was lying on top of Lev's legs, trying to get up, but Handler was lying against one side of a steep ravine, almost upside down. Each failed effort to rise brought excruciating pain to Lev. When Handler tried to rise again, Lev pulled his legs out, shivering with relief.

He pulled himself up enough to reach the horse's neck with one unsteady hand. "Easy boy. You hurt?" Handler was so smart that Lev imagined a sarcastic reply. *Hell, no, I ain't hurt. This laying down and not getting up is a natural thing for us horses to do.* Lev had always talked to Handler like an old friend until the other soldiers began to notice. After that, their man-horse conversations turned to gestures, touches, and eye contact. When Lev and Handler signed on to the Texas Cavalry, the horse was easier to talk to than anyone, even brother Hy.

Sweat made the blood bay's body look bloody all over, and Lev's fingers felt warm blood as he stroked the gelding's neck. The smell made him gag. Horse's blood had a distinctive, overpowering, hot odor that reminded him of the water in his mother's black pot on chicken-killing days. A steamy odor of guts and singed feathers. When a horse bled enough to smell like that, it usually meant he was losing his battle to live. Another squeal and deep groan from

Handler. Lev knew he needed to put the horse out of pain, but his carbine was in the scabbard under the horse and his Navy Colt was missing from its holster.

He located the source of the pain above his waist. The strain of trying to get out from under the horse forced blood out of a hole in his chest. He didn't want to, but he made himself look down at the growing dark stain on his shirt. The bloody stench might have been as much his as Handler's. He imagined that he could see the blood push out from the hole in his shirt each time his heart took a beat. Judging by the pain, the bullet had cracked or gone through a rib. He tried to feel his back to see if it had gone clean through, but he could not reach it. Hell had not taken him yet, but it was close. He lay back to ease the pain and die.

With closed eyes and short breaths, Lev tried to thwart the sense of panic and hopelessness that threatened him by reconstructing what was left of his memory. Red River Campaign ... sometime in May 1864. Texas and Louisiana had plenty of cotton and Lincoln needed it for idle Northern textile mills. He also wanted Louisiana and Texas secured to thwart possible French intervention into the war through the Texas coast. The president had sent Major General Nathaniel Banks, his strongest rival in the upcoming presidential election, to secure the Red, Atchafalaya and Mississippi rivers. Confederate General Richard Taylor, son of former president Zachary Taylor, despite having less than half the soldiers, had been regularly whipping the Yankees and sinking their Brown Water Navy vessels. Lev and Hy's horse company, Burford's 19th Texas Cavalry, had joined Parson's Brigade at Yellow Bayou, Louisiana to support General Taylor. They served as sharpshooters along the banks of the bayous and the Atchafalaya and skirmished Union troops in horseback engagements. At Crump's Corner, fifteen hundred Confederate Cavalry had shocked five thousand Federals by fighting them to a draw.

At Yellow Bayou, superior force finally won and the Confederacy had been unable to keep the Union Army from crossing the river. Lev's first serious injury since the war began came with his first bitter taste of defeat. Feeling that his mounted regiment was invincible had kept despair at bay … until now.

He tried to survey the battlefield without moving anything except his eyes. He could not remember how, but he had been shot in the part of the battlefield that he had planned to avoid. He was in one of the trenches and could not see east or west. A small mound of dirt kept him from seeing more than a few inches past his boots. It was painful, but he managed to turn his head to the west. A pair of dead eyes met him. The shock brought more pain to his neck and chest. The eyes held a startled look, frozen in time. They belonged to a bigheaded horse that had probably been a mottled-gray, but was now almost white. He was old by the look of him and his coat was dull. Underfed and wormy. The dirt pile and a horse on each side hid Lev well. That explained why brother Hy and the 19th had ridden off and left him—unless they were all dead. It explained why the Yankees had not returned to finish him off or take him to a hospital tent as a prisoner. Even the Federals had enough decency to do that for a wounded Confederate.

His nose and ears told him more than his eyes could. Smoldering fires, dried blood and the occasional squeal or groan of another horse dying told him the battle was over. There were no human voices—no sounds of wagons being pulled or of horses walking. Out of options, Lev did what he always had when forced into a corner. Some things stick in a man's mind more than others. He didn't understand that, just accepted it as fact. He closed his eyes and went to his place of safety—a place he had not visited since he was a boy.

2

THE PLACE WAS ALWAYS THE SAME—A MUD AND stick hut with grass-thatched roof, a fire burning. In winter, the fire was in the stone fireplace or on the earth floor. In summer, it was just outside the door. A pot of coffee and a pot of beans with a slab of bacon were usually cooking in one place or the other. The story was always the same, too. Lev's grandfather, Jim Rivers, sat in his straight-backed chair. Jim could not pronounce his squaw's Choctaw name, so she consented to being called Armelia. She tended the fire, nodding occasionally and smiling as the story unfolded. Lev first heard the story with his ear pressed against his grandfather's chest, listening to the old man's heartbeat harmonize with the words. As he grew older, he progressed to Papa Jim's knee, and finally, the floor.

Lev was young again, on the floor, picking at the bark on Papa Jim's twig chair while the story was repeated. It soothed him somehow, made him feel warm and safe—strong like the rawhide binding that held the twig chair together.

Lev's great-grandfather, also named Levin, had fought in America's first war. Jim Rivers always finished his story the same way. "Your great grandpa Levin swore and be-damned that a man could will himself to die then come back to life—just by getting his heart to slow down. My daddy did it once, too. Woulda bled to death from being stabbed, otherwise."

As a boy, Lev practiced the techniques his grandfather and grandmother had taught him, imagined that he could make his heart beat slower, but never really knew if he could. He lost interest in slowing his pulse until the war—put it aside as a boyhood thing. Now, he would find out if what his grandfather had said was true.

Lev heard himself screaming as Lucifer burned his chest, branding him as his own. The searing pain and the smell brought him back to the trenches at Yellow Bayou. Brother Hy Rivers stood above him, his boot planted on the left side of Lev's chest, pressing something like hot coals just under Lev's right nipple. Lev tried to raise his arms to push away whatever was burning him, but found his wrists bound to wooden stakes.

"Don't move, little brother. Just a second more." Hy removed the hot iron and stepped back. "Sorry about the pain, but had to plug that hole." He returned the flat iron to the fire and began daubing the seared flesh with something black. The smell, a mixture of smoldering pig manure and burning flesh caused Lev to retch.

He turned his head to keep from drowning in his own vomit. There was little to cough up, but Lev tried to spit out the taste. "Damn. You trying to kill me?"

Hy frowned as he removed a wad of chewing tobacco from his jaw and layered it onto the black muck. He laid a pair of clean legless longhandles across the wound and tied the arms to each of Lev's arms. He spit out what was left of the chewing tobacco. "When you can raise up, I got another pair to wrap around you. Should stay put as long as you don't go walking around." Hy drew a Bowie knife from a scabbard opposite his pistol holster and cut the rawhide from Lev's wrists.

Lev winced as he looked at the old flat iron in the fire. He was reluctant to move anything other than his head. Talking hurt like hell, but he needed to prove he was alive and that Hy had really come back. "Where did you find this concoction?"

"Farmhouse up the road. Found that black shit in the barn, the iron setting on an old ironing board in the house, and two pairs of longjohns hanging on the clothesline."

"What was wrong with heating your knife instead of that flat iron? Damn thing will leave a scar as wide as my leg."

"I needed the handle. Besides, the knife would barely cover that big hole. Would have had to burn you twice if I had used it."

"Any idea what that black shit is?"

"Figure they use it to doctor hogs. There was a hog pen by the barn."

"If the stink don't kill me, hog filth probably will."

The matching lines that ran from the top of Hy's cheekbones to his jawbones deepened as his gaunt face grew solemn. "Better just worry about that bullet. It's still in there."

Lev studied his brother's face under a month's worth of rusty beard. He was twenty-eight, six years older than Lev, but three years of war had made him look nearer to forty than thirty. Weight loss had made his cheekbones more prominent. The wavy lines that ran from the top of his cheekbones to his jawbones were deeper. Old-timers called it the Rivers line, since all the Rivers men had it. People said they looked alike but Lev could not see why. Lev had his mother's black hair, and Hy's was the color of red oak leaves in the fall. Neither had looked in a mirror in a long time. Lev knew he was skinny, but wondered if he had aged as much as his brother. "How long I been here?"

"Day and a half. When you didn't show up, I came looking. Hadn't been for Handler squealing, I might not have found you in that hole you're in."

Lev glanced over at Handler—dead. "You have to shoot him?"

"Nope. Died before I could." He reached down to touch the gelding's forelock. "Never saw a horse as good in a fight as this old boy. I saw him knock down two horses and run over at least three Yankees during the fight. My dun won't even bump into a man, much less another horse."

Lev winced as he turned toward Handler. "Should never have brought him into this hell."

"Twenty buck bonus for having your own horse was hard to pass up. Besides, I think he probably saved your life."

"How?"

"He's got a ditch down the side of his jaw. Probably dug by the same bullet that hit you. Slowed it down some, I imagine."

Lev did not see how a bullet with such a trajectory could have hit him, but the possibility eased his pain a little. Minie-balls usually tore a man's insides beyond repair.

Hy looked toward his dun. "You had anything to eat?"

"Had a little tad of hardtack in my pocket. Swallered a little chewing tobacco. You got any water?"

Hy took a canteen from his saddle and held it to Lev's lips. Lev washed it around in his mouth before swallowing. "Probably need to get away from this open field."

"How you plan on doing that without bleeding to death?"

"Might be able to ride in a day or two if I had a horse. Rather die from riding than from a bluecoat bullet. And anything beats a prison camp."

Hy looked out over the battlefield to avoid his brother's eyes. "Lev, the way I see it, you're supposed to be dead. Need to see if I can find you a hospital. Blood ain't coming out, but you may be bleeding inside. Don't see how you stayed alive with that big hole in you."

Lev shook his head. "You reneging on our agreement? We don't get captured alive and we don't go to any damn hospital—even if one of us has to shoot the other. We both seen the inside of those hellhole hospitals. Rather die out here in one piece than let a sawbones butcher cut me up."

Hy knelt and propped an arm on his knee so he could look into his brother's eyes. "I ain't backing out on a damned thing. It's your call." He stood and looked in all directions. "Guess we gonna have to stay here till that bullet does whatever it's gonna do. I still can't believe you didn't bleed to death. That was a hell of a hole I closed up."

"Burned up, you mean."

Hy pointed a thumb toward his horse. "Confederate family down the road gave me a few slices of smoked beef and some pickled eggs. We'll camp here for a few days till you can travel. You're pretty well hid. I'll just prowl around in the woods during daylight and see about you at night. I'll leave my canteen and the food."

"A few days, my ass. I ain't laying here between two dead horses for a few days. The stink is already bad enough to gag a maggot."

Hy walked to the edge of the woods and returned with Lev's Colt and carbine and a sack full of grub. He laid them beside his brother. He offered a small bottle of whiskey, but Lev shook it off. It seemed that the bullet had stalled his fondness for whiskey. Hy was already walking back to his horse. "Need to do some scouting."

Nausea gone, Lev had slept most of the day when Hy returned at nightfall. He was hungry—a good sign, he reckoned. Hy handed him two fried peach pies that were still warm. Lev grinned. "We eatin' high on the hog tonight. You getting all this stuff from the same folks?"

"Nope. Spreading it around. I made a circle around here. Don't want to call attention."

Propped against Handler's stiff body, Lev put the dead smell out of his mind as he relished the pies and studied the tree line. "Just a matter of time till they find one or both of us."

"I reckoned that already. Look yonder at my dun." Hy seldom named his horses. Just called them by color.

Lev strained to see. "What's that behind him?"

"Think they call it a travois. Made it out of green limbs. Think you can ride in it if I pad it with some saddle blankets and such?"

"Where we going?"

Hy dropped to one knee and picked up a clod. "I got permission from a captain to come back and find you. Said if I found you alive and wounded, we should head home. They can't take care of any more wounded men. Said the Boys in Gray lost more than four hundred men here ... over sixty of our boys in Parson's brigade. He says the war is lost."

"Captain Haley?"

Hy tossed away the clod. "No. Haley took a bullet. They took him away. From what I saw, he's finished. Met this officer on the road. His arm was in a sling. Didn't catch his name."

"So you left our outfit and ran across a wounded captain on the road back to find me?"

"I know what you're thinking, but I didn't just run off. There just wasn't anybody with rank to ask in the Nineteenth." Hy handed a canteen to his brother as if it were a peace offering. "That's fresh milk. Milked the cow myself."

Lev put the warm milk to his lips, licked them, turned up the canteen and drained most of it. He grinned as he lowered it. "Damn, that's good. How far away from home you figure we are?"

"Bout four hundred miles. Be there in less than a month."

Lev studied the travois. "That damned contraption is gonna kick up more dust and make more noise than a team pulling a wagon. Shoulda got us a little cart or wagon."

"Hate to steal a man's wagon. Figured we would travel at night and stick close to the woods when we can."

Lev felt a rush of energy from the pies and milk. "Noticed you got my saddle off Handler. You already rounded up the blankets to pad that damn thing?"

Hy grinned. "Saddle and all your gear already stashed over by the dun. Got us some clean clothes, too."

Lev laid back. "We'll leave at dark tomorrow night—head toward Texas and home. When we get behind Yankee lines, we'll ask the first Graycoat we see the whereabouts of our outfit. If we don't see any, we just keep going till we wind up somewhere. If we learn where our outfit is, we go to 'em. Agreed?"

Hy was already walking toward the dun.

3

LEV HEARD THE HORSE BEFORE HE SPOTTED her as daylight filtered through the trees. They had camped in the woods in a small gully covered with brush and weeds and she was on the edge of a meadow several yards away. The horse was tied to a tree limb and had paced long enough to stomp down a trail. Lev nudged his brother and pointed. "Wonder who that little filly belongs to?"

Hy rose to one elbow and tried to focus sleepy eyes. He pulled his scattergun closer. "Don't know, but she's too damn close to suit me. Best just to keep still till the rider comes back and goes on about his business."

Lev kept staring. The filly was copper-colored with no noticeable markings other than a small strip of white on her back ankle. "I figure she's just under fifteen hands, don't you? Just right."

"Not much to look at. Never liked that color horse. Looks jittery the way she's pacing. Skinny, too."

Lev continued to study her. "Been tied too long. Look at the ground under her and the way she's worked up a sweat. Bound to be thirsty."

"How the hell you know that?"

Lev winced as he pulled on his boots. "Think I'll just sneak around and see if I can find her owner."

Hy sat up and whispered a little louder. "The hell you say.

We been staying out of sight for four days now and you want to risk being seen to get a horse a drink? Besides that, you walk; you bleed."

"Don't think I been bleeding. I'd be dead by now if I was bleeding inside and there ain't been any outside since you burned the hole. If riding in that damn contraption ain't killed me, walking a few feet sure as hell won't."

Lev studied the horse more. "I think you been trying to see if you can knock me out of that damned sling, anyway. Bumped into every tree between here and Yellow Bayou."

Hy took offense. "We can always travel down main roads and stay out of the trees. You rather be bumped or shot at?" Lev ignored the question as Hy looked in the direction of home. "How far you figure we been?"

"My guess is no more than forty or fifty miles. It's slow going pulling that damn travois. If we run on to some Federals, we'll just have to sit there and let 'em shoot us. The dun can't run with that thing behind him."

Hy rose to a squat and looked at the horse. "What are you thinking?"

Lev winced as he stood, but managed a few steps toward the clearing. "Think I can ride a horse if I had one, and I aim to have that one."

Out in the open, Lev felt burned skin resisting but stepped directly toward the horse. She shied and whinnied, then eased to a low, rumbling nicker from deep in her throat as Lev put a hand under her muzzle and scratched between her ears. "Shhhh, easy, girl." He eased his palm between the filly's eyes. "Not a cavalry saddle, but those are U. S. saddlebags, and the horse carries a Yankee brand."

Hy carried his sawed-off shotgun as he made a wider circle around the tree. "Think I found her rider. Come over here."

Lev caught the smell before he saw the body in the weeds.

The large man lay crumpled in a fetal position, his pants down around his ankles. "Damn. No wonder the horse is nervous. That old boy is about to get rank. Reckon he was a just a real fat man or he swoll up when he died?"

Hy pointed with the shotgun. "Lotsa fat and a little swelling. No sign of a wound that I can see and I ain't interested in looking too much closer. Fat enough to choke his heart down when he stopped to do his business." Hy nodded toward a small clearing in the woods. "Probably trying to make it to that little outhouse."

Lev looked through the trees. A worn path led to a small outhouse beside Beulah Land Baptist Church, a long narrow whitewashed plank building set deep in the woods.

"He was sure nuff all beef—plumb to the hock. Don't see how that little filly carried him. From the looks of things, he got real sick before he died." The two brothers stared at each other, waiting for one to say what needed to be said.

"Probably stole the horse from some dead soldier. He ain't got no more use for her, and we do. Don't look like the horse is worth much, anyway ... being skinny like that."

Lev already had the horse untied. He put a finger in the backside of her mouth and felt her gums and teeth, and then bared her lips to see. "I make her out to be coming three." She pulled back, looking for an escape. Lev held her bit by the shank and stared directly into her eyes. Her wild eyes darted between Lev and Hy and the dead man before settling on Lev. "Easy girl. I ain't up to no bronc ride."

Hy started back across the meadow to saddle the dun. "You putting one of them hexes on her? Better let me try her out before you get on her. You ride the dun."

Lev eased closer to the filly, rubbed her neck and shoulder, mumbling conversation that Hy could not make out. "Nope. I'll ride this one." With his left hand, he grabbed a handful of mane and pulled it back and forth before putting his right hand on the saddle horn. He pulled her head around and mounted in one smooth motion, grunting a little with the sharp pain. By the time Hy returned with the dun, Lev and the mare had dragged the body into the churchyard and had begun to drag limbs to cover it.

Hy held his nose with one hand and went through the dead man's pockets with the other. He pocketed the meager findings and began to gather rocks for more cover. "Why didn't you leave him in the weeds?"

"Come Sunday, folks will be sure to find him before church. The man provided us with a horse and little traveling money. We owe him a debt."

Hy nodded as he examined their handiwork. "We stole from dead men before and didn't bother to bury none of them."

"They was trying to kill us. This one wasn't."

"You pull up his pants, too?"

"How would you like to be found dead with your pants down?"

"Reckon I wouldn't, especially on Sunday."

Lev felt good to be mounted again, as if he drew strength from the horse. His calmness transferred to the filly. He brought her neck gently around until her nose touched each boot.

"Yank's neck is limber enough for her to kiss her own ass."

"Yank ain't a proper name for a mare."

"He have anything in his pockets worth having?"

Hy held up a small wad of bills. "A little Confederate paper and a few coins. Small bottle of what looks like home-growed whiskey."

"This saddle and saddlebags are a damn sight better than mine. I'll empty mine and leave them here."

4

AFTER THE INITIAL SURGE OF STRENGTH AND sense of well-being that came from riding a horse instead of being pulled like an invalid, Lev started to focus on the bullet. He imagined it ripping his internal organs and filling his body with blood. After running out of supplies, they ate what they could kill or steal and drank mostly from stagnant puddles or creeks when they could not find a cistern or well. When they camped, Lev searched for the bullet with his hands, figuring it would eventually work its way to his skin. When he slept, he searched for it with his mind, trying to locate the source of the pain. He was able to slow down his heartbeat almost at will now, thinking that it might keep bleeding at bay. The worry wore him down.

He felt better when they crossed the Sabine into Texas. They bathed in the river and filled their bellies and canteens. They had been traveling for a week, camping in the woods at night and taking to main roads as they felt distance grow between themselves and Yankees. No sign of any Confederates. They had used the sun for a guide, heading northwest as steadily as they could. They got lost once in heavy timber when clouds covered the sun.

Three days past the river, it started to rain just after they broke camp and rode away without breakfast. Drizzle had prevented a fire. Hy stopped the dun and turned in his saddle to look back at

Lev. Water dripped off the brim of his hat. "How long you figure on going without eating?"

Lev rode beside him. "You ain't got any rations left?"

"If you mean that stringy squirrel meat, no. I mean a real breakfast. A hot one. I never liked riding in the rain and there ain't no officers telling us we got to keep going. And you, you look like death warmed over. We need to get somewhere in the dry."

"Just like to keep moving since we got inside Texas. Feels like home and a warm bed are just around the next bend."

"Well, they ain't. Shoulda stopped in Nacogdoches last night. Sign back there said we're in Cherokee County. Any idea how far it is to Rusk?"

"Figured we would have seen it by now."

"Might be a doctor there. Damn sure would have been one in Nacogdoches."

Out of habit, Lev stuck two fingers in his vest pocket looking for the makings to roll a cigarette. He found none. "You feel that bad?"

"Me? Hell, I been riding in front for a hundred miles to keep from stepping on you when you fall off your horse."

They rode for another hour before they saw movement near a small building nestled in a little copse of pines. Black clouds made the day dark as night as they stopped in front of the box-and-strip building. A sign dangled on the porch. Good Samaritan Inn. They stepped down at the hitching rail, loosened their cinches and let their horses drink their fill from the water trough. They wound wet reins over the rail twice. Lev hung a spur rowel and stumbled as he stepped on the porch. Several boards were missing. "Watch your step. This porch has probably killed better men than me."

Lev peeked through the road grime covering the poured glass part of the front door. He used his sleeve to wipe away cobwebs coated with red dust and the door squeaked open from the pressure. Sparse light from a single candle filtered onto the porch from inside.

Hy had one boot on the first porch step when he flinched. He drew his pistol and aimed at a dark form on the corner of the porch. A big black man leaned against a corner post, just out of the wetness. He wore a black rabbit fur hat with a flimsy brim, chaps turned black from blood and grease, a black muslin shirt, and black cavalry boots. Hammered-tin conchas ran down each leg and outlined the pockets of his Mexican chaps. The barrel of a belly gun hid just behind the buckle of his wide gunbelt. The man also carried a long-barreled revolver on one hip and a large knife on the other. The shotgun cradled in the crook of his arm pointed in Lev's general direction.

He seemed unperturbed at having Hy's pistol trained on him. "What are you peckerwoods lookin' at?"

Hy was flustered that he had not seen the man until he moved. "We lookin' at a nigger like to got himself shot. Still could if he don't get a civil tongue in his head."

The man moved away from the post and stood straight. Lev eased his hand toward his pistol as he looked over his shoulder. "You carrying enough hardware to load a man down. Expecting trouble?"

"Always expect trouble when a couple of no-count spitwads show up where they ain't wanted."

Lev turned to face the man. "I got nothing against the colored, but I didn't insult you and I expect civil behavior in return."

Hy pulled back the hammer of his pistol to remind the man it was pointed at him. "Lev here is carrying a bullet that has him a little indisposed. Else he would have already whacked your insolent mouth or put a bullet between those black eyes for pointing that scattergun in his direction."

The man did not move.

Hy took a step forward. "You aiming to shoot that damn

scattergun or you just gonna stand there smelling like the ass-end of a dead skunk?"

The man spat on the boardwalk before moving the shotgun away.

Hy eased the hammer forward, but kept his eyes on the man as he followed Lev through the door. He paused before closing it. "My apologies for an ill disposition. I have not had my breakfast." The man still stared with hate-filled eyes, making Hy regret the apology. "You boys ought to wear lighter colors. Might keep you from getting shot."

Their eyes were slow to adjust to the sparse light provided by the flickering candle. The air was close and humid and tasted as bad as it smelled. A mixture of human sweat, stale whiskey, cigarette butts, chewed tobacco, and spoiled food came to rest on the back of Lev's tongue. It burned a little as it went down his throat. A bar was on the right, four tables on the left. A small apothecary occupied a corner next to the bar in front of a stairway. A wood cook stove sat in the center of the back wall. A cast iron skillet and pot sat beside each other on the stove, both crusted with something rust-colored. A dipper handle curled over the top of the pot.

A stringy-haired woman moved sawdust on the wood floor with a broom. A tall, lean man with heavy eyebrows and green eyes stood in front of two shelves of liquor bottles and glasses, palms pushing down on the bar, his face expressionless. A cigarette hung loosely from the corner of his mouth. Used to older bartenders who leaned toward softness, Lev thought this man seemed out of place. He pointed an index finger toward the ceiling and turned it in a circle. "Any doctors around here?"

"Only one we had died a while back. Somebody sick?" The cigarette dangled with each word, its smoke causing the bartender to squint. The voice was mellow and deep. The reply conveyed little to determine the man's mood, but he seemed confident, almost overbearing. Lev felt a strange twinge of envy as he compared his emaciated and filthy appearance to the man's well-fed look and confident manner of speaking. The bartender had a way about him that probably drew other people in, but Lev did not like him. He wondered why the man was not fighting in the war.

Lev sensed a slight movement from the floor at the corner of the bar. An animal different than any Lev had ever seen stared at him. A low rumbling growl came from behind its bared teeth and seemed to crawl across the floor toward Lev's leg. The thing looked like a cross between a big lizard and a hairless coyote. Lev detected a sulfurous odor. Neither Lev nor Hy approved of dogs inside, especially a place where people ate.

The bartender seemed to be enjoying their discomfort. "Don't worry none about the dog. He don't bother nobody less I tell him to."

"Don't usually worry too much about dogs, but that thing looks more like a inbred coyote with a bad case of mange." Lev glanced at Hy as if he did not see him, looked up at the ceiling, turned and left as abruptly as he had entered, abandoning his bewildered brother in the middle of the room. On the porch, he checked for the black man and his shotgun. Finding him gone, he wondered if he had ever been there at all. He dodged the missing boards and unwound Yank's reins. He was already mounted when Hy walked out on the porch.

———————————

From the corner of the building, she had watched them from black shade provided by a thick stand of tall pines. They interested her—the men and their horses—especially the way they had handled Anderson Bonner, a man looking for a reason to kill any white man.

She had an eye for horseflesh and considered the trait to carry over to men. The mare looked familiar, but she could not place it yet. Most men who passed through rode poorly fed, ungainly beasts with big heads and plodding hooves dressed in worn out saddles, fighting bits ill-suited to their mouths. These men rode good horses that stepped lightly and alertly, suggesting that they could move in any direction with grace and speed. The horses' ears pointed forward, alert to all movements but frightened by none. Their gear was well worn and worn well. A hickory stick a little shorter than an ax handle was tied behind each saddle cantle. One carried a carbine in a scabbard, the other a shotgun. The scabbards were covered in wooly sheepskin to keep them from galling the horses.

Pistols and knives sat on them like appendages attached by an unseen force. Hats bigger than most of the local farmers wore. Neckrags that had been jaunty before they faded. Small feet surrounded by worn-out boots with tall tops and floppy mule ear pulls. Long angular faces with sharp lines that reminded her of the small carvings old men whittled from pieces of soft pine. They appeared as ghosts of themselves, searching for a way back to former lives. Soldiers without uniforms.

She liked the way they carried themselves. Something about they way they mounted and dismounted—the way they walked. Confident but wary. But one was hurt—she could see that.

———————

Hy stood on the porch, resisting returning to the dun. "What's your hurry? We need something to eat and maybe a place to lay down out of this wet."

Lev seemed unnerved as he looked up at the sign. "This ain't the place. First time I've been under roof in a long time. Felt like I was gonna smother in there. Ain't nothing stinks as much or looks as bad as a saloon in the daytime. Thought we were looking for a doctor, anyway."

"It was that ugly, stinking dog, wasn't it? Grandma's superstitions again."

———————

"Don't want to spend no time under a roof with a thing that claims to be a dog, but looks like the devil's own son. It's a bad omen." Lev felt a hand on his right leg and reflexively grabbed it.

When he saw her, he was embarrassed at his nervousness. A young girl, her hand caught, looked up at him. Lev thought her face was dirty at first, because it was the color of the wet red mud on the road. Small white lines crept away from eyes that had probably seen too much sun. Her thick coarse hair was rust-colored and unruly curls had been pulled back and tied with braided strands of horsehair. Her pine needle scent cleansed the smell of the bar from his head.

She stared at the hand holding her wrist. "Understand you need a doctor."

Lev released her. He was wary, trying to recall what Grandmother Armelia had said about redheaded women encountered on the trail. He believed it was a bad sign, but it might have been good. "You know where one is?"

"My daddy was the town doctor here since before I was born. Died right inside there." She pointed toward The Good Samaritan.

"We're sorry about that, but don't reckon your daddy can help us much now."

"No, but I can. Been doctoring since I could read. Daddy taught me everything. He was in a lot of pain for a long time before he died. I did most of his patient work."

Hy looked at his brother and winked. "Where do you do your doctoring?"

"Right in there." Her eyes darted almost imperceptibly toward The Good Samaritan. "I keep a couple of rooms out back. Do everything from pulling teeth to setting broken limbs. That little drugstore in the corner is mine. I been known to barber, too."

Lev eased Yank back a few steps. "Never seen a woman barber. Well, ma'am, we could use a haircut and shave, but just ain't got the time. Much obliged."

The girl pointed to Lev's chest. "You're giving a little to that right side. From the smell, you been putting some sort of nasty poultice on an injury. Best guess is you been shot."

Hy laughed out loud. "So far, she's smarter than any of them army doctors."

Lev eased forward to look closer at the girl. "Say you're right. What would do you with a man been shot in the chest?"

"How long ago was it?"

Lev figured. "Best I can recollect, it was a little over two weeks ago. We been traveling for the better part of twelve days."

"Carrying that bullet and riding?"

Lev winced as he felt the bullet stab him. "It was either that or walk."

"Main thing to worry about now is being nasty like you are. You need to get that hog poultice off, clean the wound ... and yourself. I'll know more after I examine it."

Lev sniffed himself without meaning to. "Well ma'am, it ain't that I don't appreciate it, but you don't look old enough to be a doctor."

Hy interrupted. "What's the harm, Lev? Ain't no doctor here. Seems like she's the next best thing."

"My daddy said I had the gift. Even the Caddos come into town to see me. They call me medicine woman."

Lev took off his hat and ran his fingers through his black hair. "You seem mighty anxious to help us out, ma'am. Why would you care about two strangers?"

She looked toward the saloon and lowered her voice. "I need the money. Trying to get away from this saloon to my own place."

"Didn't your daddy practice here?"

"No." She pointed down the street. "See that burned out spot? That was our house."

"Lost your daddy and your house?"

She inclined her head toward the saloon. "Lots of places

burned around here lately. Daddy left this world owing a big bill to Filson in there—plus a few other folks in this town. I've paid just about everybody but him."

Hy looked toward the saloon door. "Filson the big barkeep?"

She nodded.

Lev stepped off the mare. "We ain't got enough between us to pay off much debt, but I guess it can't hurt for you to take a look. Ain't saying we'll stay, but where could we get a good bath, a hot meal and a bed if we decided to?"

"I got a room out back with tubs and beds. You can throw the horses in with mine. I got a shed you can put your saddles under. Horses won't be in the dry, but they'll be well fed."

Lev loosened his cinch again and retied to the rail. "Let's see about that bath first. We'll leave the horses here till we decide."

When they reached the corner of the building, they heard a whinny coming from deeper in the piney woods. A white horse walked the perimeter of a small corral made by nailing boards to pine trees. Two strands of cotton rope served as a gate.

Hy whistled under his breath. "What's that?"

"That—is the best horse in Cherokee County."

The brothers smirked as they stared at the barrel-bodied horse with white, curly hair. "That's your horse? Sorry, but I thought it was a big sheep."

"His name is Sheep, for obvious reasons. Follow me, and I'll show you your room." She extended a hand. "My name is Olivia, Olivia Brand."

Hy took her hand. "Hiram Griffin Rivers. Call me Hy. This is my little brother Levin. Call him Lev."

She stared at the dark spot on Lev's shirt, wrinkling her nose. "You got a clean shirt? If you don't, I can wash that one."

"Got spare outfits in our saddlebags, but they a long way from being clean."

She led them across a narrow back porch to a large room.

Washtubs sat on each side of the wood stove in the center of the room. Four single beds were pushed against one wall. A dressing screen stood in one corner beside two cane-bottom chairs with towels draped across their backs. The stove was cold. "Too hot for an inside fire. It'll take me a while to get hot water going outside."

Hy touched her sleeve as she started to go. "Miz Brand, my brother here can go for days without eating, but I'd like to sit myself down to a hot meal." He smiled as he inclined his head in Lev's direction. "If he was a better hunter, I wouldn't be so hungry."

She looked toward the door that connected her rooms to the bar. "Filson won't allow me to feed you in here. Says it takes away his business. They don't cook breakfast in there, but dinner should be ready in a couple of hours. Supper will be what's left from dinner. If I was you, I'd bathe first. You'll have time."

Lev was looking up at the ceiling and taking deep breaths trying to get used to being inside again. When his look found one of the beds, Olivia's voice faded for him. He sat on the bed and took off his boots. His socks were full of holes and filthy. When he looked up to see if Olivia had noticed, she was gone.

5

HY WAS STANDING IN THE DOORWAY LOOKING toward the back yard when Lev awoke. "How long I been asleep? Seems like the sight of that bed just pulled me over and knocked me out."

"Slept the day away. I already fed and watered the horses."

"You unsaddle?"

"Not yet. I know how you feel about having a horse at the ready." Hy looked toward the back yard. "Come over here."

Lev looked over Hy's shoulder. He had slept well past sundown and the back yard was illuminated only by firelight. Olivia, wearing only bloomers and a blouse, walked barefoot on a bed of pine needles as she tended two fires. One fire warmed a cauldron of water; the other licked at a black pot hanging from a metal tripod. She worked the black pot contents with a long hickory stick, pulling and dunking shirts, pants, socks and longhandles. Clothes were already hanging on a rope strung between the fires. "Them our clothes?"

Hy nodded. "Except for the dress. I fell off asleep for a while, too. She must have sneaked in and took everything except what we got on. Even the clothes rolled up in our bedrolls."

"Barely remember taking mine off when I laid down." They were both barefoot and dressed only in longhandles. Their gunbelts hung on two pegs under their hats.

The girl spoke to them without looking up from her work. "Step out here and wet a finger in that cauldron. May be a little hot for a bath, but it's hard to keep it right when you sleep all day. Wish you had bathed first. I'll have to wash those bedclothes again."

Lev stepped away from the door and stuck his head out the window off the porch. "We ain't exactly dressed. Any of our belongings dry enough to put on?"

She turned to face them and their sucked-in breaths could be heard above the crackle of the fires. She looked different than before. Maybe it was the firelight; maybe it was a bath and clean clothes. She had looked fifteen that morning, dressed like a boy. Now she looked thirty. "You got dry clothes, but you sure ain't putting 'em on without bathing. You boys strip down, throw those dirty clothes out the back door and I'll wash the whole kit and caboodle for a dime. Strip the bedclothes and toss them out, too."

Lev knelt again and spoke through the window. "How we gonna work this, ma'am? There ain't nothing in here for us to cover up with and we need to get out there and get some water for our baths."

"Don't put yourself out. My job to haul water for bathing. No extra cost. You get behind that screen in there and I'll bring in the water. You can strip down and throw the dirty underwear and socks over the screen."

Hy walked out into the yard, picked up a bucket and dipped it into the cauldron. Olivia picked up another. Lev wrestled it away from her and began dipping. "Much obliged, Ma'am, but we do can our own water hauling. Just turn your head."

Lev felt the bullet after one bucket, but kept hauling water. They were naked to the waist and starting to drop the bottom halves when the girl entered without knocking. She lightly touched the burn on Lev's chest. "That's exactly the shape of the iron I use for laundry." She wrinkled her nose. "Hope that smell is the medicine."

Lev looked at Hy. "Smelled like that when Hy put it on me. Don't think it's going bad."

She smiled, showing white, but slightly crooked teeth. "Smells like hog lard that's gone bad, though. You don't look much like a hog." Before he could protest, she began cleaning off the rancid grease with a wet rag. "Don't want all that nasty-smelling stuff to get in your bathwater, do you? After you bathe, just leave your shirt off and I'll put a clean poultice on. The early wash is almost dry."

She stripped the beds and carried the sheets and pillowcases outside. Lev propped a chair under the door handle before pulling off the longhandles. Hy threw their dirty clothes through the porch window, settled into the tub, and picked up a bar of soap. "Wonder if she bathed right out there in the yard while we were asleep? She reminds me of Hester."

"Every pretty woman reminds you of Hester."

Olivia placed a set of clean clothes on the windowsill just as Lev poured the contents of the rinse bucket over his head. Dressed, dried and feeling somehow stronger, they carried their tubs to the woods and emptied them. Olivia had covered her bloomers with a dress and was sitting on the porch when they returned. The dying fires cast dancing shadows across her and the clothes still on the drying line. Both men examined the expression of sadness on the face they had only glanced at in the daylight. Her nose was a little too sharp and her face a little too long, but her almond-shaped earth-colored eyes sparkled and her skin looked softer and baby-smooth in firelight. Her unruly hair was pulled back into pigtails and was just beginning to resist with frizzing as it dried.

She met their stares with her own curiosity. "You boys slept through the only good meal they serve in the bar. Expect you're hungry, but I need to do some doctoring before you go eat."

Hy put his hand on the door leading to the bar. "You gonna need me for that? I might just go in the bar and wait."

Olivia held up a fist and opened it. A rabbit's foot swayed from a leather string wrapped around her index finger. "This yours?"

Hy smiled. "It's Lev's. Our grandma is full-blood Choctaw. Superstitious. Gave us both one when we left to fight. Lost mine. Lev don't believe in taking no unnecessary chances on that sorta thing."

Lev's face warmed a little as she dropped the rabbit's foot into his open palm. He motioned for Hy to go ahead without him. "Go on. This may not be pretty."

Hy turned at the door. "You know anything about the surly colored man wears all that artillery?"

Olivia nodded. "Name's Anderson Bonner. Carries a grudge every bit as heavy as all those weapons. Folks around here say his cabin is full of white scalps."

Hy put a hand on the door handle. "He's dangerous then?"

"Like a rattlesnake."

When Hy left, Olivia went into the other room and returned with a doctor's bag and a pan smeared with white paste on one side and brown paste on the other. "Sit here on the edge of the porch, Lev." She dipped two fingers in the brown paste and gently applied it to the burn.

Lev's eyes watered as he sniffed it. "What is that?"

"A balsam. Daddy's own recipe. Made out of pine and other plant resins. It stinks a little, but it's mainly to hold the poultice in place." She dipped and applied until the burn was well covered. "The stinging will stop when I apply the poultice. You ain't gonna cry on me, are you?"

Lev looked at her and smiled. "Your eyes are watering, too."

She wiped the sticky balsam from her hand, dipped her fingers into the white paste, and applied it over the balsam until it was well covered. "Starting to feel better? This is my recipe. A little bran, starch, and meal. I put in a little clove to make it smell better."

"Sure beats that hog lard."

"Stand up and lift your arms, please."

Lev stood as she unrolled thin muslin and began wrapping it around his chest. He could feel the hair on her arms reaching up to tickle the hair under his. He took a deep breath as she tied off the muslin. She smelled of ribbon-cane syrup, evergreen, and pine smoke. "You must not have used the same soap we did."

"I got my own recipe for soap, too." She looked up into his eyes. "Feeling better?"

They studied each other for an instant before he reached for his shirt. "Yes, ma'am. Looks like your daddy taught you good. I'm much obliged."

"You go get yourself some food. You're thin as a rail. Never saw a man that needed meat on his bones more. Nothing but a rib rack."

They walked back inside and met Hy coming back from the bar, bringing the smell of whiskey with him. He seemed impatient and irritable as he spoke to Lev. "You about ready to eat?" He turned toward Olivia. "We'd be much obliged if you would eat with us, Ma'am."

Olivia lit a lamp with a small candle and sat down in one of the chairs. "No thanks, I don't go in there unless I have to."

Hy sat down on the edge of one of the beds. "Don't blame you for that. That bartender fella talks sweet as pie, but I get the feeling he's insulting me with every word. He a friend of yours?"

She looked afraid to answer. "Daddy thought he was our friend. Now, I just owe him a lot of money."

Filson walked into the room without knocking as if he had heard himself being discussed. He stopped when he saw Hy sitting on the bed and Lev buttoning his shirt. Sarcasm drenched his words. "Am I interrupting something?"

Olivia rose from the chair. "I've asked you to knock more than once."

A strong smell of lilac water and talcum powder reminded Lev of the swamp water they had patrolled in Louisiana. The combination caused a reflexive gag. He walked over to the peg where his gun and hat were hanging. He noticed that Filson had added a belly gun to his waistband. Filson took his time looking around the room. "Just came in to see if you can help out tonight."

Olivia kept her eyes down. "Doing what?"

"Pouring drinks if I get behind. Customers don't like the old lady doing it." He turned toward Lev. "You men staying the night, are you? I got a livery stable down the street where you can board your horses."

Lev leaned against the wall. The sharp pain from his chest made him feel vulnerable and weak. "Much obliged. We'll keep that in mind if we decide to stay."

There was a nervous pause as Hy rose. Filson turned on his heel and left without getting an answer from Olivia.

Lev eased away from the wall. "Ain't none of my business, but this man Filson don't look like no bartender I ever saw."

Olivia took a deep breath as she took Lev's hat from the wall peg. "Are you boys real soldiers? Don't see any sabers or uniforms."

Hy touched the scabbard that held his knife. "We never was much good with them sabers ... bad to get in the way ... noisy, too. We swapped ours for these Bowie knives."

"Are those ax handles behind your cantles?"

The questions made Lev wary and he remained quiet.

Hy answered. "Some of our boys ran out of ammunition in our first fight. Took to using rifle butts. They're poor weapons, likely to break, and hard to come by. Those hickory clubs are easier to swing. Easier to replace, too."

Lev nodded. "Clubs are quiet... and don't need reloading." He took a seat in a cane-bottom chair. There was bitterness in his voice. "Tell the truth, we stole about everything we got, even the hats and revolvers. Most of it came from dead men."

"Can you can use those pistols?"

"I've seen Yankee captives questioned less."

Olivia smiled. "Sorry. My daddy always said curiosity killed the cat. Why no uniforms?"

"Never really had a whole uniform. Nothing much left of what they gave us when we signed on. We just wore what we could find. Mounted men can scout around for goods. Most of the foot soldiers are barefoot and near naked. We're probably better outfitted than we were when we signed on." Lev strapped on his gunbelt. "Filson holding the debt over you?"

Her lips firmed. "I do whatever is required to live around here. That includes laundry, bathwater, cleanup, slopping hogs, a little cooking. And, of course, doctoring and apothecary." She looked in the direction of the bar. "Nothing else."

Olivia opened the back door. "You boys go fill your bellies. Filson don't like you coming through my place, so best go around. You know where to bunk. I stay upstairs, so I'll be down in the morning to collect what you owe me."

As they rounded the corner of the building to head for the front entrance, Lev turned back. "Forgot something. You go on; I'll catch up."

Olivia answered his polite knock and stood in the doorway without speaking. Her silence made him forget his mission for a few seconds. She put an impatient hand on her hip. "Cat got your tongue?"

"Uh, no. We just seemed to forget the real reason we stayed here."

"And what is that?"

"The bullet."

"Still feel it?"

"Sure do."

"You didn't mention it one time when I was tending to your burn."

"You're the doctor. Figured you'd get around to it."

She stepped out onto the porch and looked at the moving

clouds that were breaking up to make room for the moon. "My daddy would have already had you on the table and the bullet would likely be in a spittoon."

"Can you do that?"

"I've taken out my share of bullets. But I have seen more men die from cutting on them than from bullets. You're not bleeding— inside or out—so my guess is the bullet fractured and is nestled in there somewhere. If it was me, I wouldn't take it out until it started to move or really hurt. It may even work its way to the skin and come out on its own."

6

IT WAS WOODSTOVE DARK AS LEV STEPPED OUT
of the bed of pine needles and into mud as he approached Yank.
He fretted a little over her wet saddle and the small hole she had
dug in the mud. Nothing to be done about it now. He checked the
porch for the black man before dodging the missing porch boards
and walking through the door for the second time. Hy was by the
stove, looking into the pot that had been there that morning. Filson
stuck his head out of the back room and glanced at the mud trail
left by their boots. "Help you, gents?"

Hy pulled out the dipper and sniffed. "Did this used to be
stew?"

Filson wiped at the bar with a dirty rag. "Was stew at noon,
stew at supper. Ain't good enough for you boys, I got hogs would
love to have it."

Hy raised his eyebrows. "How much for two bowls with some
cornbread or biscuits?"

"Two bits for the both of you. Ain't no cornbread left. Might be
part of a bread loaf back there somewhere. Baked yesterday. Two
coppers extra."

Lev made his way toward a table.

Hy dug in his pocket and laid a Confederate half dollar on the
counter. "Anything to drink?"

The bartender stared at the coin. "That's Confederate."

Hy's eyes slanted and grew cold. "I reckon this is Texas and Texas is still a Confederate state." He moved the half dollar closer to Filson. "Where I come from, that kinda talk could get a man shot. Now, do you or don't you have anything to drink?"

Filson smiled and picked up the coin. "Got warm beer and fresh whiskey."

"I already had some of that green whiskey. No buttermilk or sweet milk?"

"You see a cow around here anywhere?"

Hy turned toward Lev and smiled. "I don't see no damn squirrels or possums around here, either, but one or the other sure as hell died in that stew pot over there."

Filson was a bigger man than Hy or Lev with the body of a man who knew how to use it. He studied Hy from boots to hat, smiling from bottom to top. "You boys mighty particular for strangers coming in a man's place."

"You this rude to all your customers, or did you just single us out for special treatment?"

Lev moved the table enough to scrape the floor and gave Hy a look that said shut up. Hy shrugged. "We'll have two bowls of that stew, what's left of that bread, and two cups of coffee. Guess you got coffee."

Filson's green eyes locked into Hy's blues as he inclined his head toward the coffee pot on the stove. "Help yourself. May be a little too strong for you buttermilk boys."

Hy picked up his change and sat beside Lev. "Damned if he ain't a surly bastard. Man owns a place of business needs to treat customers better. Took our money quick enough."

Lev looked around the room. "Best to let it go. We don't need any more attention than we already got in a strange place. He knows folks here; we don't. How much of that fat man's money we got left?"

"Enough to get home."

"Need to save enough to pay the woman."

Filson stepped to a side door and hollered something that they could not make out. The cowed woman they had seen sweeping before appeared with two bowls. Her skin was chalky and her scalp showed through thin graying red hair. She dipped the bowls full of stew, dropped a spoon in each bowl and set them on the table. "Help yourself to one of them cups on the post over there if you want coffee."

Lev stood. "Much obliged." He pulled down two cups, shook a spider out of one and dust out of both before pouring two cups of thick, black coffee. The stew was thick too, barely warm and hard to swallow.

Hy tried to wash it down with a sip of coffee. "Guess I forgot what coffee tasted like. Used to like it." He put down his cup, glanced at Filson, and walked outside to get a canteen. Two men were inspecting the brand on the mare when he stepped off the porch. They wore a smattering of Confederate colors, but neither was in complete uniform. "Help you boys?"

The shorter of the two men looked up from rubbing the brand. "That's a Union brand and them's U. S. saddlebags."

Hy ignored the statement as he unwound the canteen strap from his saddle horn. He held the canteen with his left hand and moved his right closer to his pistol. "Guess you boys are old friends of mine. Sorry I didn't recognize you right off. Mind reminding me of your names?"

Their faces showed confusion. "We ain't never seed you before today."

Hy shook his head and looked down. "Well, where I come from, only old friends ask how a man comes about owning his horse." He touched the pistol butt. "Otherwise, a man could take it the wrong way."

The taller man stared at Hy's holstered Colt. "We Home

Guard, friend. It's our job to ask questions."

Hy smiled. "That right? My brother Jacob enlisted in the Shiloh Home Guard in sixty-one. Same time I enlisted in the cavalry. He'd be about thirty-six now. Pretty old man, I reckon. I thought Home Guard was just for old men. Now, what is it exactly you need to know about this horse?"

"Need to know where you come by a Union horse. For all we know, you a Yankee spy."

Hy laughed. "Now why would a spy come riding into a Texas town on a horse carrying a Yankee brand and Yankee saddlebags?" Hy took a deep breath and smiled into their vacant eyes. "Listen, boys, I'm having myself some fine squirrel stew inside. My brother always been better with horses than me. Why don't you come inside this friendly establishment and he'll tell you more'n you want to know about that little copper filly."

Hy jerked a thumb toward the two men following him through the bar's door. "These here fellas want to know how you came by your horse and them Union saddlebags. They're Home Guard and think we're Yankee spies."

Lev examined the butternut and gray on the men. He moved his chair closer to the wall and Hy's chair scraped the floor as he moved it to Lev's left. The truth seemed better than any option Lev could think of. "We found his owner dead. I'm carrying a Yankee bullet and needed a ride. My horse was shot out from under me at Yellow Bayou."

The two men stood staring, not sure how to answer. "You do look kinda peaked."

Hy pointed toward another table and chairs. "Drag up a chair. I'm getting a crick in my neck trying to look up at you."

They dragged two chairs closer and sat down. Each put a hand on his pistol. "We lookin' for deserters, too. How come you boys didn't stay with your company?"

Hy's expression changed. "Deserter is not a word my brother

and me take kindly to, gentlemen. How many battles you boys been in?"

The two men exchanged looks and squirmed in their seats. "We been lookin' out for things back here. Plenty dangerous what with dealing with deserters and Yankees to watch out for at ever turn. Niggers are gettin' restless, too. We think they been settin' fires."

Lev looked toward the door. "We met a dark feller on the porch when we rode in this morning. Looks like the type to set fires."

Tall Home Guard frowned at the mention of Anderson Bonner. "Bonner's one of a kind. His own mama said he was born pissed off and got worse. Hates anything white. Thinks the man who owned his mama is his daddy. The old woman said it wasn't so, but it stirred up a lot of hate in Bonner."

"What's he do? Sure ain't no field hand."

"Works for Filson over there."

"Slave?"

"Nope. Filson freed him."

"Must stick in his craw to work for a white man."

Short Home Guard laughed. "Keeps him in bullets and gives him cover for doing other bad deeds." Tall Home Guard gave his friend a look that implied he had said enough.

Hy took another bite of his stew and a drink from his canteen before handing it to Lev. He looked toward the bar. "How bout that bread I paid for?"

Filson walked through the door behind the bar and returned pulling the woman by her arm. He twisted her wrist until she dropped to her knees. "You deaf? Cut two slices off that old bread loaf and get it out here."

Lev looked at the two men with a question in his eyes. Tall Home Guard spoke softly. "Filson's hard on his old lady. She's mean as he is, though. Riles him on purpose."

Short Home Guard grinned. "Treats that dog-from-hell better than his old lady."

Mention of the dog got Lev's attention. "What kinda animal is that? If it wadn't so tall, it would look like somebody took a sharp skinning knife to one of them gators we saw in Louisiana."

"All we know is it's a bloodsucker. When he turns it loose, the chicken count around here thins out. Kills goats, too. We know it's him, cause he sucks the blood right out of 'em."

Lev continued questioning the willing boy. "So where did it come from and why don't somebody shoot it?"

The boy whispered. "Have to shoot Filson first. Folks around here say it come from two creatures from hell what fell in love. I figure it's some sort of inbred coyote-dog thing."

Hy watched the woman shuffle out. "That really his wife? Looks a lot older."

Short Home Guard chuckled. "Filson wears a woman out pretty quick. She was a real looker when they first got here. Think he's tryin' to run her off and get him a new 'un. Y'all seen that conjure woman out back? He's got his sights set on her."

The woman walked to the table and dropped a slice of bread in each bowl. Lev looked up at her. Her face was defiant, but her eyes held fear. "Much obliged, ma'am." He turned toward the men. "You boys seem to be fighting age."

Hy took another sip of the bitter coffee. "Course, it's none of our business how you serve the cause."

Lev felt the room closing in on him. He leaned in closer and looked at each man for several seconds. "But understand we all done answering questions ... especially from a couple of wet-behind-the-ears-boys trying to act like our betters."

The two men looked at each other. The tall one turned toward Filson. "Filson, send us over a bottle of that rotgut and four glasses. We gonna have a drink with these two men." He put out a hand toward Hy. "Name's Jerry Yost."

Lev shook the offered hand but did not give his name. The introductions stopped there.

Filson set a bottle of clear whiskey on the table and Short Home Guard poured a shot in each glass. Hy and Lev lifted their glasses as if saluting the men. Hy winced at the taste, but found it smoother than the drink he had earlier. An hour later, the bar was full of drinkers and card players, and the bottle was three quarters empty.

Short Home Guard stood. "Got to see a man about a horse." The taller one followed him out to the alley behind the building. The woman opened the door after them as if to follow, but Filson pulled her back. "You know damn well where they going. Always trying to get a look at what other men got to offer, ain't you?"

She cowered. "I was going out to get your damn dog."

"Goddam whoredog slut."

Hy and Lev had risen to leave and Hy started toward Filson, but Lev grabbed an arm and pulled him toward the door. Filson hollered after them. "Where in hell you going?"

Hy answered. "Didn't know we was obliged to account for our comin's and goin's."

"You ain't goin' anywhere before you pay for that bottle of whiskey."

Forced calmness kept Lev's voice guttural. "Them Home Guard boys ordered that bottle. We had one shot each. They drank the rest. You need to be collecting from them."

Filson laid a scattergun on the counter. "Them boys gone. Bottle's gone. I'll take a dollar each—Federal."

Hy put a hand on his Colt. "You ain't taking shit, you surly bastard. We ain't paying for no damn whiskey we didn't order or drink."

Lev surveyed the room as he put a hand on Hy's gun arm. "Give him his two dollars. We ain't known around here and people likely to take his word against ours."

"Hell, Lev, that green whiskey goes for ten dollars a barrel."

The bar became silent as Lev looked each patron in the eye.

He found no sympathy.

Hy stared with cold eyes before he stalked to the bar and slammed down two dollars Confederate. "You'll take Confederate or nothing." He stared at Filson and the scattergun until Lev called him.

Dark-faced, they walked backwards toward the door until Filson stopped them again. He pointed toward the porch. "Paid for the whiskey, now we need to collect for that mare you stole."

7

LEV AND HY LOOKED AROUND THE ROOM TO see if the other drinkers were supporting Filson. Nobody looked up. The Home Guard soldiers walked back into the room. Yost pointed toward the porch. "Recognized that mare you're riding right off. Belongs to Luther Hathaway."

Lev caught the eye of one of the patrons who seemed sympathetic. The man confirmed what Yost had said. "He's right, mister, mare's name is Blue."

Hy was not convinced. "Blue? That mare ain't nowhere close to blue."

The man looked toward Filson before deciding to continue. "Called her Blue because she hates blue uniforms. Yankee soldiers abused her pretty bad when she was just a filly. Killed her mama, too."

The man seemed ready to tell the complete story when Filson ran out of patience. "Luther Hathaway was a big fat man. Did regular business in timber, horses and about anything else could be traded over in Louisiana and East Texas. Wouldn't ride nothing else but his boy's horse after the boy was killed."

Lev felt like a mouse caught in a trap. He looked at Hy before turning back to the sympathetic bar patron. "The man we found dead was fat, sure enough. If he's got family around here, we'll return the horse to him and pay for her use."

Filson laughed. "His son was Luther's only family and Yankees killed him. Man would have to kill Luther to get that horse away from him. Reckon the sheriff will be wanting to ask you boys about that."

Hy tried to read Lev's mind as they moved a step apart and put their hands on their pistols. He nodded toward the two Home Guard soldiers and spoke to everyone in the room. "Like we told these boys, we found the man dead. Anybody says otherwise is a damn liar likely to feel the barrel of my pistol across his head."

Filson eased his hand closer to the shotgun on the bar. "You just leave the money for the horse and you boys can go on your way. Sheriff don't have to know nothing."

Lev's eyes were red. "And how much you figure the horse is worth?"

"Fifty dollars seems fair. She's a fine mare as I recall."

Lev and Hy pulled their pistols at the same time. Hy trained his on Filson and Lev pointed his at the Home Guards. Filson put both hands in the air. "Easy does it, boys." He pointed a thumb over his shoulder at the door to Olivia's quarters. A shotgun barrel peeked through a crack in the open door, trained on Lev. A black hand eased the door open to reveal the man who had been standing on the porch. His almost perfect blackness, interrupted only with tiny eye-slits that revealed cream-colored pupils, made him seem bigger and more threatening.

Filson smiled. "My boy, Bonner. Handy with a scattergun. Ease them pistols up on the bar."

Hy sidestepped to his right and put Filson between himself and Bonner. He pulled back the hammer of the pistol and aimed at Filson's head. Olivia's feminine voice drew every eye in the room. She had a revolver pressed against Bonner's neck. "Drop the shotgun, Bonner." She wore a big straw sombrero and a pair of men's pants and boots. Her too-big pants were held up with a cotton rope.

Bonner leaned down to place the shotgun on the floor as Hy advanced toward Filson in long strides. Filson rushed to grab the scattergun and point it, but was frozen by the steadily advancing barrel of Hy's pistol. His fingers touched the stock just as the cold barrel of Hy's revolver pressed against his forehead.

Hy nudged the barrel forward enough to make Filson stretch his neck. "You owe me two dollars and an apology."

The bartender's mellow voice cracked. "I don't owe you shit and I ain't never said I'm sorry to any man."

Hy tapped the gun barrel against Filson's head in a steady cadence that emphasized every word. "Then you can say you're sorry to the devil, friend, cause I'm sending you to hell."

Lev swept the room with his gun, looking for the dog. "Rest easy, boys. Hands on the table. Unless you intend to smoke your hardware, don't reach for 'em. This don't have to get any worse than it already is."

Hy felt a need to explain. "You boys and this barkeep are goddam thieves."

The stringy-haired woman came through the back door, leading the hairless lizard-dog on a leash made of grass rope with a loop tied in the end. The dog's spine and ribs were visible as it stretched waist-high to the woman. When it saw that Filson was being threatened, it growled, bared its teeth, and charged against the leash. Lev pointed his pistol toward the dog. "You want that thing to live, better get ahold of it."

She dropped the loop over a brass hook that appeared to have been put there for the purpose. The dog lunged, but the rope held. The woman, oblivious to the dog's howling, stared at the pistol barrel against her husband's head. She did not move toward him, just stared at Hy's Colt as if it were a long lost friend. Her eyes flicked back and forth from the gun to Hy's eyes and her tongue darted out of her mouth as she seemed to silently plead for him to pull the trigger.

With the thumb of his free hand, Hy pushed Filson's nose enough to cut off his air. "Now, I'll take that apology for your rude behavior."

"That'll be a cold day in hell."

Hy pulled the trigger.

8

THE SOUND AND ACRID SMELL OF GUNSMOKE made the room feel as if it were about to explode into the street. Eyes of patrons widened as they fought their natural inclination to run. A few rose from their seats, afraid to remain standing, afraid to leave. As the sound of gunfire subsided, heavy breathing seemed to make the walls expand. The few seconds of silence stretched for a frozen minute.

"Son-of-a-bitch." Filson screamed as he dropped to one knee and examined the hole as blood oozed from his boot. "Goddamn you."

Hy put the pistol against Filson's forehead again. "Now you gonna have to apologize twice."

"Go ahead and shoot."

Hy pulled back the hammer again. "Send word if they really do have cold days in hell."

"Hy!" Lev walked backward toward the door. "We got our money. Let's go."

Hy stared at Filson for a few seconds before swatting the side of his face with the gun barrel. He picked up the scattergun and walked toward Lev. He paused to survey the shocked faces in the barroom. They made him feel like some sort of vicious animal. "You men saw this man try to cheat us. Damn lucky we didn't kill him." He unloaded both scatterguns, dropped them and kicked them across the floor. "We ain't even taking the guns."

Olivia came through the bar and stood beside Lev. "Better take those Home Guard pistols and Bonner's."

Lev glanced at her in confusion. "Lay 'em on the table, boys. Butt first. We'll leave these just a ways down the road. We ain't thieves." They backed out of the room together. Olivia's sheep-horse was waiting.

Lev felt a twinge from the bullet as he mounted and turned the mare. Her back hoof made a sucking sound in the mud. He heard a confused rooster crow as if it were dawn instead of night. Two bad signs.

They rode hard past the town square and threw the guns in the yard of the Cumberland Presbyterian Church. Neither the mare nor the dun could catch Sheep, but Lev finally shouted loud enough for Olivia to grant his request to stop just outside of town. Hy and Lev and both their horses were covered in mud from Sheep's hooves.

Lev was breathing hard. "Miz Brand, what are you aiming to do?"

"I'm going with you."

"No ma'am. I can't allow that. The way we gonna have to travel now ain't fit for a woman."

Olivia's voice was high, brittle and quivering. "You need me. I know this country. I know places to hide ... people who can help."

Lev squirmed in his saddle as he shook his head.

"You owe me, dammit! One of you would be full of lead if I hadn't got up behind Bonner. Now you gonna ride off and leave me to deal with it? You damn well better follow me unless you want to make this your permanent home." She turned Sheep and squeezed him into a run.

They ran the horses till they frothed and gasped for breath. The smoke from their lungs and their grunting blended with the smoky mist rising from the recent rain as they wound deeper and deeper into the piney woods. Branches had scratched their faces when they stopped at an abandoned barn. From Yank's back, Lev pulled the door open and they rode inside. The smell of mildewed hay mixed with stagnant water from a puddle in the floor. Part of the barn's roof and several sideboards had either rotted or blown away.

Lev stepped down. "Where are we?"

Olivia ignored the question as she scraped straw with her boots to clear a spot for a fire. With flint, steel and tinder, she had one going in a matter of minutes. "I got coffee and some provisions in my knapsack."

Lev was using dry straw to wipe off the horses when he noticed the fire. He and Hy had done without fires most nights on the trail because it took so long to start one. Olivia appeared to be as able with flint and tinder as she was with doctoring. It irritated him. "Think it's safe to build that fire?"

"If I hadn't, I wouldn't have built it."

"It ain't cold and we ain't cooking. Why take the chance?"

"I like a fire and coffee of a night. If they come after us, it will be morning."

Lev and Hy were squatted by the fire sipping coffee and staring into the flames when Olivia took two ducking bags off her horse and tossed a bag to each brother. They breathed a deep sigh when they saw their clean clothes inside. She unrolled her bedroll and lay down by the fire. "A thank-you might have been nice."

Lev stared into his coffee. "Just trying to make our way through the country. Now we done stole a horse and people think we killed that fat man."

Olivia seemed surprised. "How many men do you think you killed in the war?"

Hy did not turn toward her. Lev straightened his bedroll and stretched out. He stared at the cracks in the barn roof a few minutes before answering a question he had never been asked, never considered. "Only a fool would try to keep a count of such a thing and only a liar would tell you he knew."

Lev's heart had been set on a good night's sleep in Olivia's rented room and he was angry for having been robbed of it. Hy soon snored but Lev gave up on sleep just before dawn. They left without breakfast, following Olivia to a small meadow with sparse grass and water. Lev and Hy paced while the horses grazed in predawn light. Olivia kept silent until they stepped into their stirrups. "I can lead you out of here, but I need to know where you want to go."

Lev looked at Hy. "Our best chance of keeping away from the law is back with our company."

Hy's eyebrows rose. "How we gonna find 'em?"

She turned Sheep to face them. "Where were you heading before you decided to stop in Rusk?"

Hy waved a hand in a general northwestern direction. "Home."

"And where is that?"

"Ever hear of Ellis or Navarro County?"

"Went to Waxahachie once when my mama was still alive. Seems like it took about five days by wagon. Staying away from the roads will slow us down some, but we'll still travel faster than that wagon did."

Lev rode the mare forward, then backed her up. "Not going as far as Waxahachie. Just a place south of there and out away from things on Chambers Creek. It's about on the Ellis and Navarro county line."

Hy had reloaded his Colt and was checking his scattergun. "You figure there's a posse after us?"

Olivia shook her head. "I doubt they could get one up to chase down anybody that would shoot Filson. He may come himself, but he'll take a while to heal. Lots of people would pat you on the back for shooting him. Those two Home Guard boys may be coming, though, and they'll bring Bonner with them. They're just itching for a fight and ain't got anything else to do. Bonner kills white folks for pleasure."

Lev looked toward Rusk. "If he hates whites so much, how come he works for Filson?"

"Filson provides him with ammunition and the means to keep from real work. He likes settling Filson's grudges with whites. He'd work for you just as quick. He hates Filson as much as the next white man, maybe a little more."

Lev reached into his pocket and pulled out all the money he had. He offered it to her. "Take what we owe you and go back. They won't blame you for what we did."

"I know what I'm doing. It was no accident that I was saddled and ready to ride. I need you and you need me."

Hy reached across and put his hand on her saddle horn. "I been thinking about that. How come you were all saddled up when we came out of that saloon? It was like you knew what was gonna happen."

"I didn't know. But I've seen Filson and them boys pull that whiskey stunt more than once." She squinted as if her eyes were burning with memories. "I've saddled up more than once, waiting for the right man to call Filson to task for cheating him. Always disappointed—until now."

"How did you know we would?"

"Didn't. But I knew that Filson was pushing you two a little harder than usual, and it was bothering you boys a lot more. Plus the horse upped the ante."

Lev squeezed the mare. "We have to ride."

They broke into a fast walk through heavy piney woods with Olivia riding between them. Lev reached down to stroke the mare's neck. "Is what they said about this little mare true?"

"I've heard stories about Luther Hathaway and his copper mare a long time. Everybody in these parts knows about her."

Lev considered the signs he had ignored when taking the

horse. "What about the blue thing? That true, too?"

Olivia told the story as it had been told to her. Hathaway's son and three of his older cowboys had been delivering a herd of horses to the Confederate Army, including the filly and her mother, when Yankees stopped them and requisitioned the horses. Hathaway's son resisted and was shot. The other three hands were forced to deliver the remaining horses to a Federal camp. When Yankee soldiers tried to separate the filly from her mother, the mare fought so hard that a trigger-happy soldier who had been kicked shot the mother in front of her filly.

"The Yankees turned the cowboys loose and they came home without Hathaway's horses or his son. They did have a pocketful of money and an order for more horses, though."

Lev scoffed. "Damn Federals had the nerve to order more horses after killing his son?"

"Officers who placed the order didn't know the boy had been shot. Hathaway was mad as hell. The boy was his whole life. He did business with both sides before the killing, but turned on Yankees afterward. Gathered up a bunch of gunmen to deliver the horses and offered a bounty on the man who shot his son."

Lev was having trouble putting the pieces together. "So how did he get this horse back?"

Olivia looked at the gentle horse nodding along under Lev. "Hard to believe, but they said this little filly was meaner than her mother. Kicked, fought and bit every soldier that came close to her. Kicked one soldier in the head and bit a chunk out of another's shoulder. "

Lev looked between the mare's nodding ears. "I expect she just gave as good as she got. Beatings probably explain her hating blue."

Hy looked at the mare. "That and seeing Bluebellies kill her mama."

Olivia continued. "Yankees gave up and sold her to an

unlucky horse trainer. He got her calmed enough to lead off about the time Hathaway and his bunch arrived. Hathaway recognized his own horse and shot the horse trader without asking questions. Yankee soldiers let Hathaway believe he had killed the right man. The gunmen knew better, but they let the old man believe he had avenged his son's death."

Hy pointed at Lev. "Told you Yank was no name for a filly. You gonna call her Blue?"

Lev was hesitant. "People will think me a fool to name a penny-colored horse Blue."

Olivia laughed. "Her real name is Butternut. Folks just started calling her Blue when she bit a chunk out of a Yankee prisoner when Hathaway was up by Nacogdoches and the story got around. Hathaway called her Butter."

Hy laughed. "Butter is bound to be confused. Take care she don't throw you and bite off an ear."

When they stopped to let the horses drink, Lev asked the question that bothered him. "Why didn't you just leave Filson, run away?"

"He warned me not to. I wasn't so much afraid of his killing me, just what he would do instead of killing me. He's threatened me with that dog more than once."

9

THEY RODE AT A STEADY PACE, BUT NEVER faster than a long trot. At twilight, they stopped beside a small pool that looked clean enough to drink from. Hy and Lev pulled the horses' bridles off and loosened their cinches to let them blow, but Olivia stood in her stirrups and searched the area. Not seeming to find what she was looking for, she rode around the pool bank. Lev pulled a piece of hardtack from his saddlebag. "Where you going?" When she did not answer, he shouted again. "You don't need to be running off by yourself."

She turned in her saddle. "You never needed to be by yourself? I'll be back."

Lev's face darkened a little. Hy chuckled as he watched her ride away. "You noticed the way she sits in that saddle? Reminds me of my Hester."

"You already said that."

"We'll be home in a few days. What are we gonna do about her?"

"What do you mean?"

"You forgetting I got a wife and son at home? We can't just waltz in on Mama and Hester with a crib girl."

"She ain't no crib girl."

"Maybe she ain't no sporting woman, but you know Filson was using her. She set us up to kill him for her."

"She took care of us when she didn't have to."

Hy smiled. "Well, hell. You already smitten with her, ain't you? You forgetting that you got Mary Ann waiting for you?"

"Mary Ann is just your wife's sister. I never promised her anything or asked her to wait." Lev stepped back and looked across the small pool. "And I ain't carried away with this woman. Just figure I owe her a debt."

"Still don't answer what we gonna do with her."

"We ain't gonna do nothing. She's a strong woman used to taking care of herself. She'll let us know what she wants to do before we get home."

"Don't count on it. I think she just intends to stick with us."

"She's a damn resourceful woman. Don't know if I ever saw one could come up with things a man needs as quick as she can."

The next morning, coffee was boiling and Lev and Hy were laughing for the first time in a long time when Olivia returned from her morning ritual, her face still moist from washing. Her shirt was crinkly from having been washed and wadded into her knapsack to dry, but she showed few other negative effects from rough traveling. She stopped and studied them for a few seconds. "You both look different when you laugh. Figured a smile would crack your faces."

Lev rose to his feet, feeling guilty. He should have had her horse saddled when she returned, a fair exchange for her changing his poultice. "Just some old stories about our folks."

She stuffed her other shirt into the bag. "Maybe I'll meet them one day. I suppose you boys are starting to recognize the country we're traveling in now."

"We've pretty much known where we were since we came out of those tall pines."

"How close?"

"Should be two more camps. Then arrive about high noon the next day."

"Guess it will be great to embrace your family again. I envy you."

The brothers stared into their coffee cups.

"Did I say something wrong?" Neither replied as Olivia applied the last of the poultice to Lev's wound. "This is healing well. You won't be needing my ministrations after today."

Lev stiffened his chest as she wrapped the thin muslin around him. "Where will I go next time I need doctoring?"

She smiled as she rolled the last of the muslin and put it into her doctor's bag. "Depends on how close you are to where I settle. I liked Waxahachie. I expect to go on there and try to find a doctor I can work for."

"There's a doctor in Dresden. That's about a half-day's ride from our place. I could take you there and introduce you. Besides, you can't go to Waxahachie alone—at least, not yet. There's talk of slaves on the loose and some of these Home Guard boys are even dangerous for a woman traveling alone."

"I might just get you to do that." She turned toward Hy, sitting on his saddle blanket, staring into the fire. "Thinking of home?"

"Just trying to imagine what it's gonna be like ... seeing my wife and boy after all this time. He was still on all fours last time I saw him. Guess he would be four by now, walking on two feet."

"What are their names?"

"Who?"

"Your wife and baby, of course."

Hy stared into the fire for a few more seconds before answering. "Hester Matilda's the wife ... Otho Penne's the boy." Hy grimaced as he said the name. "I was off working cattle for a feller when he came. She named him that awful name after some of her people just to spite me for not being there."

"Does she write often?"

Hy looked confused, as if the question would not process with his clouded thoughts.

She softened her tone. "Do you boys read and write?"

"Oh, we can read and write as well as the next man; our mama saw to that, but we don't get many letters in the cavalry. We move too quick and never know where we're gonna be."

"Didn't you ever write her?"

Hy tossed a twig into the fire. "I wrote once, but the letter wore itself out in my pocket before we got to a place to mail it. When we were not fighting or traveling, Lev and me was always scouting around for provisions. Figure that scouting was what kept us alive." He looked up at Lev. "To tell the truth, I been trying to remember what Hester looks like for about two days. She just got kinda blurry—sorta angel-like. I can remember Mama and Papa, but I can't seem to remember her."

Lev sat down beside his brother. "You mean you didn't see both of 'em when Captain Watson sent some of you married boys home to look for deserters? That was less than a year ago."

"She was gone to her parents when I got back home. By the time I got word to her, she had to travel through rough country to get to me. Left the boy at home."

"But you told me that you did see her."

Hy frowned at his brother. "I saw her, but it was dark ... and I was a little drunk. I didn't know she was coming till she got there."

Lev smiled at Olivia. "Ain't sure we can ever go back to being civilized again."

Olivia reached into her knapsack and pulled out a pair of scissors and a comb. "You boys find yourselves a place to bathe good before we camp tomorrow night and I'll send you home looking civilized—even if you ain't."

They came upon an abandoned well late the next day and made camp early. They drew water and bathed standing up as Olivia waited behind an old farmhouse. They built a big fire for light and Olivia went to work on their hair. She snapped her scissors twice to announce she was finished and stood back to survey her handiwork. Lev combed his hair and studied the stranger staring back at him from Olivia's small, broken mirror. He looked deep into the stranger's eyes and did not recognize what he saw. Lev touched the back of his neck, reacting to the cool feeling left by missing hair.

Hy broke his trance. "You about through primping? Let that mirror see what a handsome face looks like for a change." Lev handed him the mirror and Hy stared at his own wavy reflection. A little tic developed along his lower lip as he studied himself. He made a clicking sound with his tongue to stop it. He saw a stranger in that mirror, too. Olivia ran her comb through Hy's trimmed beard and hair. She returned the mirror to her knapsack and sat down by the fire. "You two could be twins except for the coloring."

Hy snickered. "Papa always said he stole me from a bitch wolf's litter. I'm the only redhead in the bunch."

Lev's mind was on home. "Think our sisters are still home?"

"I bet the girls are, but I figure the old man is still gone."

Olivia walked away a few feet to brush off the clippings from her shirt and pants. "You say the old man is gone? You mean your daddy doesn't live at home?"

Lev answered her. "It's a long story. One you probably just as soon not hear."

10

OLIVIA STARTED ASKING QUESTIONS ABOUT THE countryside and their family as soon as they broke camp the next morning. "We might as well pass the time talking. If your daddy is not at home, where is he?"

Lev talked above the creak of saddle leather and the hooves of Butter and Sheep. "Daddy's always been a traveling man of sorts. Likes to go different places. Guess when he came here from the Carolinas, he just couldn't get rid of the urge."

"So you boys didn't grow up around here?"

Hy took the question. "Lev has lived here since he was about thirteen. I spent most of my boy years south and west of here—Liberty County, Gonzales, Dewitt—anywhere Papa thought he could claim or buy land cheap. He liked unsettled places. Figured he could get a head start if things were a little less than civilized. He'd claim him some land, then run for some kinda judge or the like."

"Is he a lawyer?"

"Naw. Mama's daddy taught him to read and write late in life. Studied the law some. I was seventeen when Mama yanked us up from Dewitt County and brought us back to East Texas."

"Why did she leave?"

"Said she was tired of Papa dragging her to wild places. She hates uncivilized behavior, liquor, and all the things that go with it."

Hy whistled "John Brown's Body" as if it were a signal for

Lev to pick up the story. Lev's voice had a somber tone. "Our older brother, William, was killed when we lived out in Dewitt County."

"How old was he?"

Quieter now. "William was nineteen."

Hy urged him on. "Go ahead and air all the dirty laundry."

"We had a sister, just between Hy and me in age. She was just fifteen when she decides to marry this man named J. Creed Taylor. Mama has a fit—says she's too young and this old boy and his whole family are too rough. William, well, he was Mama's favorite and he got mad at anything that made her mad."

"What was her name?"

"Mama's name is Rachael."

"I meant your sister."

"Her name is Eliza Jane, after Papa's sister."

"Unusual for a girl that young to go against her parents."

"Eliza Jane is headstrong. Well, she defies all of us and sneaks off and marries the Taylor boy. We don't see her for several months, but William makes it his business to run into her new husband ever chance he gets. The law has to pull 'em apart more'n once. Papa and William was at Clinton one night, listening to political speeches. Papa liked that kind of thing. William runs into our brother-in-law and starts up again."

"Starts up?"

Lev pushed back his hat and looked south, as if he were trying to look at Clinton—to see what happened there. "Well, William stabs J. Creed Taylor in the heart. Kills him dead."

"My God, I thought your brother was the one killed."

Hy picked it up. "Sheriff locked up William and chained him in his cell. Somebody broke in and killed him that night. We had hardly set down after burying William before Papa strapped on his pistol and tied a shotgun to his horse. Said he aimed to kill the ones responsible."

"Where is your sister during this time?"

"Mama's just as stubborn as Eliza Jane was wild. She wasn't speaking to her after she married the Taylor boy. After William killed her husband, Eliza Jane wouldn't have anything to do with the rest of us. Mama said she lost two children and she wasn't about to lose any more—or her husband. Warned Papa that if he went off looking for a fight, she would pack us up and leave him."

"So that's when you all came back here?"

Lev chuckled. "Not exactly. Papa wasn't about to let Mama threaten him. He rode off, bound for vengeance. Turns out that Eliza Jane's dead husband was named for his uncle and that uncle is the head of a real big family that was all meaner than cur dogs. They went to hunting Papa instead of the other way around." Lev seemed surprised when his voice softened with the memories. "He didn't know which one of 'em to kill and couldn't kill 'em all. When he came back without his revenge, we were gone. Mama's not a woman to trifle with. She didn't like it out there to start with. Says East Texas is the only place she's been able to put down roots."

"So your Papa is still out there?"

"No. He had a right smart of land out there around Clinton and on the Guadalupe River. It took him a while to sell it. Then he followed us back here, but it was too late. Mama had already settled on her family's old place and figured out she could make do without him. Us boys was big enough to do work around the place. We made out riding horses for other folks. The girls kept a good garden and some milk cows."

"So where is he?"

Hy answered. "Last we heard, he's always lived not more than a day's ride from us, but he can't stay still. Buys one place, sells another. Likely to saddle up without notice and be gone for a month or more. He shows up in the yard for supper ever once in a while. He and Mama are civil, but she says he has to prove he can stay in one place before she'll take him back for good."

Lev pointed his right hand in the direction of home. "Mama

used to come out on the porch at night with her lantern. She'd point off in some direction and say that Papa was out there tonight. She did it for Obedience and Minerva, our little sisters. Those girls always thought their papa was watching them every night when they went to bed."

Hy looked at his brother. "You always thought that, too."

Lev awakened before dawn to the sound of Olivia's saddle being thrown on Sheep's back. He feigned sleep, watching through squinted eyes as she straightened the blanket and pulled her cinches tight. He closed his eyes as she quietly mounted and sat motionless in the saddle to ponder them. When she turned away, he rose. "You not gonna say goodbye?"

She stopped and dropped her head a long time before turning Sheep to face him. A rooster crowed in the distance. "Always thought the two of you were heavy sleepers."

He pulled on his boots and ran his hand through his hair before putting on his hat. He picked up his shirt and began tucking it in as he walked toward her. "I been watching you get up and go off by yourself every morning. You never needed your horse before."

She lifted her head and seemed to be focused on one abandoned star left in the still-dark sky. "I figure I've nursed you two young whelps right to your mama's front door. I intend to turn off here and head toward Waxahachie."

"Thought we agreed it ain't safe for a woman to be traveling alone in this part of the country."

"I'm not just any woman. You boys should know by now that I can take care of myself."

"Ain't saying you can't, but why not give this Dresden doctor a chance first? You can sleep at our place tonight and I'll take you there tomorrow."

She shook her head emphatically. "I'm not walking in on a woman who is a complete stranger to me and asking to spend the night—especially looking the way I do."

"What's wrong with the way you look?" Lev grinned. "I've come to enjoy watching you get up every morning."

She suppressed a grin, causing a slight quiver to her lips. "You say we can be there by noon? Suppose it won't hurt to at least meet your family. Your mother sounds like a woman worth meeting."

11

It was just past noon when they saw the little house nestled in a bend of Chambers Creek. A dozen or so mixed cattle and two milk cows grazed the meadow between the riders and the house. Cedar boards and batten, darkened and streaked from humidity but not yet turned to gray, provided backdrop for a deep porch that stretched across the front under a pitched roof of rusted tin. Stone intended for the front of the house lay in a neglected pile in the front yard, weeds and grass trying to reclaim it for the earth.

A small shotgun cabin of chinked logs on the north and a lean-to barn with a small rail corral on the south flanked the house. From the looks of it, the cabin predated the house by many years. The creek just behind the house was sheltered by ash and box elder. Honey locusts, bois d'arcs and willow trees made a natural fence along the creek bank south of the house.

From habitual wariness that had kept them alive during three years of war, Lev and Hy stopped their horses before they could be seen from any of the buildings. Olivia gave Lev a questioning look. He turned away from her as he dismounted and swept the landscape. It did not seem like home, just another place where danger could lurk.

June bugs buzzed in the still air as Hy and Lev watched. Hy spoke. "Something don't seem right. Nobody about."

The door slammed on the porch and Rachael Rivers stepped outside as if she had sensed their presence. Lev had not seen his mother in almost three years. Her once-black hair, now mostly white, contrasted sharply with her dark skin as she squinted her eyes against the noonday sun. She wore her hair as she always had, pulled tight across her long face and tied back in a bun with a black ribbon. Her eyes were hooded and set deep and the skin around them was darker than the rest of her face. At first glance, those eyes made the thin, slightly stooped woman seem almost menacing.

The expression in those eyes betrayed her, though. They reflected the trouble she had seen and her determination to face more. Resigned to her past and future lot in life—frightened, but defiant. She put a hand across her eyebrows to shield her eyes from the sun as the boys walked toward her. When she recognized her sons, she put both hands to her throat and breathed deeply. Never a woman to show her emotions, she waited for their greeting.

Lev put a hand on the bois d'arc hitching rail in front of the house. The bark was still fresh, the wood yellow, and sticky resin still seeped. He looked at the black residue on his hand before winding Butter's reins around the rail twice. His voice croaked. "Mama. You recognize your own sons?"

Rachael dropped her hands, lifted her apron to absently dab at them. She stepped off the porch and walked toward Lev. "I don't see my son for over three years and that's all he's got to say." Her voice always carried a slight quiver as if she were about to cry.

Lev opened his arms and awkwardly hugged her. Hy tied the dun to the rail and took his mother in his arms as if she were a long lost sweetheart.

She looked over his shoulder at the sheep-like horse and woman astride him. Olivia had hung back a respectable distance. "Who's that?"

Hy rushed out an answer before Lev could. "That's Miz Brand.

She's the doctor that saved Lev's life. We had to run from some Yankees, and she came along to keep him from dying."

Lev frowned at his brother as Rachael examined him from head to foot. "Where are you hurt and where is Alfred?"

"Alfred's part of the Nineteenth went over to Arkansas, we hear. Probably a good thing. Me and Hy had a bad fight at Yellow Bayou. That's over in Louisiana." He turned to signal Olivia to come to the house and faced his mother with a somber face. "They killed Old Handler, Mama."

"That's a shame. I know you set a store by that horse."

They all turned as the door slammed and Hester walked out, belly bulging. Hy stared at his wife as she used her hands to check the condition of her long auburn hair. "Why, Hy." She took a deep breath, lightly brushing an invisible hair from her freckled cheek, at a loss for words. "I declare. I never expected..."

Hy ignored the steps and leaped on the porch to embrace her, taking care not to touch her stomach. When he released her, he looked down. "I never expected, either. How could this be?"

Her face red, she looked at Lev and Rachael. "Shut up, fool. You forgetting you were home six months ago?"

Lev laughed. "Looks like he took a night or two off from hunting them deserters. Must 'uv been drunker than he admitted to me." Lev beckoned his sister-in-law with open arms.

She stepped into his embrace and whispered in his ear. "You can shut your filthy mouth, too." Hugging Hester always lifted Lev's spirits, but left him confused. He envied Hy his near-perfect wife.

Otho came out of the house and looked up at his father. Hy dropped to his knees and put a hand on the boy's head. "I'm your daddy, Son." Otho looked toward his mother for confirmation.

Hester wiped at her eyes with the hem of her apron and snuffed as Olivia stopped Sheep just short of the group. She looked toward Hy before speaking to Olivia. "Hello. My fool of a husband has got the manners of a boar hog. My name is Hester and that's our little boy, Otho."

Olivia touched the brim of her straw sombrero. "My apologies for butting in on your family, Hester. A fine looking boy. My name is Olivia Brand."

"If you'd care to light down from that horse, we can go on the porch and maybe draw you some cool water from the well to wash up and have a cool drink. I imagine you're all tuckered out from traveling. How far have you come with these two no-count boys?"

Olivia stepped down from Sheep and looped his reins on the rail between Butter and the dun as she gave Lev a look that told him to answer.

"We stopped in a little town a few days east of here when I about died from Hy's nursing and asked around about a doctor. We was lucky to find Olivia. Her daddy was a doctor and he taught her real good." He paused to look Olivia in the eyes. "Reckon she saved my life."

Rachael stepped forward and took Olivia's hand. "You have my eternal gratitude, Miz Brand. I am Rachael Rivers and I raised my boys to have better manners. War undoes everything a mother tries to do."

Olivia smiled. "I'm afraid Lev has exaggerated my role. I just kept a bad situation from getting any worse."

Rachael examined Lev again. "You never said where you were shot." Without waiting for an answer, she touched Olivia's arm. "I have forgotten my own manners. Y'all must be starving. We just had our dinner, but I expect I can find some ribbon cane syrup and some sausage and biscuits that can be warmed up. I promise to do better for supper. Then Lev can tell me where he got shot."

Lev looked around the yard and toward the house. "Speaking of biscuits, where's Minnie and Obe?"

A forced smile crossed Rachael's face. "Obedience married last summer and moved off to Waxahachie. Minnie's around here somewhere. Probably gathering firewood. She'll be proud that you boys are here to eat her biscuits again." Rachael's mind seemed to drift. "Alfred wanted to be in your outfit. I told him to find you boys."

Lev looked at Hy as he spoke to his mother. "Wish you could have talked him out of enlisting. Hell, he's barely old enough to make a hand around here."

Rachael wrung her hands as if Alfred had just escaped their grasp. "He was nineteen when he left. Be twenty now. Soldiers came by here and shamed him into it, I think."

Hy put his hand on his mother's shoulder. "We'll get to looking for him soon as we can, Mama."

Lev was sopping the last of the ribbon cane syrup from his plate when Minnie walked in with a bundle of firewood in her arms. "Mama, whose horses ...?"

She dropped the wood and ran to Lev. She caught him before he could rise from his chair and they almost fell as she wrapped her arms around his neck and plopped herself into his lap. "Well, little girl, you still make a mighty fine biscuit. Best I ever ate, even when they're left from breakfast."

12

LEV PUSHED HIS CHAIR BACK FROM THE SUPPER table that night. Rachael's questions about the war were wearing on him. "Some of the boys lost their horses and had to walk. Once we got in Louisiana, me and Hy barely knew where we was half the time. Swamps and heavy timber and bottomland around there." They had pushed back plates cleaned from a supper of hominy, pork tenderloin, cornbread and beans. Lev felt guilt with each bite. He had noticed the paucity of his mother's smokehouse and cupboard.

"You and your horse got shot, Lev. I want to know about that."

Hy looked at his brother. "Mama, we ain't heroes." Hy tousled Otho's hair and looked at Hester's stomach. "I got a wife and family to think about."

Rachael pressed on. "Five sons is too many to send off to war. Nobody expects a mother to give up all her sons. Tried to get Alfred to stay home. He's just a boy." She paused and studied the age in Lev's expression. "Course you were, too, Lev. How much longer do you think it will go on?"

"I never put a number to it back then, but I didn't think it would last this long."

"Is it true we're losing? That the Yankees are going to come and take away our land and property, burn everything in sight?"

"We're just horse soldiers, Mama. We don't get told much

except when to fight, but there's rumors. So far, we been keeping 'em out of Texas."

The night was cool enough to sit in the parlor with hand fans and the windows open. Rachael sat in a dark corner so that she could study her sons in the dim lantern and candlelight without her scrutiny being noticed. She could not decide what was marring her happiness at seeing them home alive. She watched their hands and feet fidget as they studied the ceiling as if it were going to fall on them. Then she knew. It was their eyes—they seemed to change with each blink—going from warm to cold, happiness to sadness, comfort to wariness, even from love to cruelty. In spite of her best efforts, the war had made them their father's sons—made them uncivilized and violent. She wondered what it was doing to Alfred.

Lev interrupted her reverie. "What do you hear from Archie and Jacob?"

"Your brothers are better to write than either one of you. Jacob drops by every once in a while. The Home Guard sends him off in all directions. Mostly protecting Confederate widows and orphans and taking them food and provisions. Archie, when he writes, talks more about his horse and the weather than the things his mother needs to know. Still don't see why you boys couldn't have stayed together."

Hy clicked his fork against his plate. "We all asked to go in the same cavalry, but Parson's twelfth said they had to have at least one of us and Arch drew the short straw. The twelfth is mostly younger boys. By rights, they should have taken Lev, too."

"Well, at least it's good to have you boys home to stay."

Hy glanced at Lev. "Mama, we ain't home for good. We got to go back."

Rachael pulled a string of thread from her lap. "Oh. I just thought, with Lev hurt and all ..."

Lev broke in. "Fact is, I plan on taking Olivia over to Dresden tomorrow and then going over to the courthouse in Corsicana to see if I can get information on where the nineteenth is."

"Why Dresden?"

"Is Doc Robinson still there?"

"As far as I know."

Lev nodded toward Olivia. "I told Olivia that he might be able to put her medical studying to good use."

They moved to the porch when Minnie brought out her guitar and Lev's fiddle. Lev had to be coaxed, but he finally began playing *Home, Sweet Home*. As the sounds of night in the country mingled with the sounds of her children playing, Rachael finally sang along with *Sweet By and By* in a firm voice that quivered just the right amount on the high notes, making a yodeling sound that made Hy's skin tingle and the hair stand on the back of his neck in a flood of sweet memories. "Mama knows how to bring the Lord down to the porch, don't she?"

Rachael dragged out an old green canvas cot and made Lev a bed on the front porch. Hy slept with Hester and Otho in the back bedroom and Olivia slept with Minnie. Minnie crouched by the open window and cajoled Lev to scoot his cot close so that they could talk like old times. Olivia feigned sleep as she listened. They giggled when they heard Hy pick up his son and place him on the pallet at the foot of their bed. They stopped giggling and smiled when the bed began to squeak.

Lev was awakened from sound sleep by his mother's hand on his shoulder. "Get up son. Time for church."

He rose on one elbow. "Church? Is today Sunday?"

They put it off until they were having corn coffee after Minnie's eggs and biscuits. Lev put down an empty cup and met Rachael's gaze. "Mama, me and Hy sorta lost track of time. We barely know what month it is anymore. Plumb forgot what day it was."

"I just told you it was Sunday."

"I know, Mama, but we got to spend our time finding out about our outfits today. They may think we deserted. You see?"

Rachael stared. "It's the Lord's Day."

"Mama, me and Hy don't feel right going into the House of the Lord just now. After all the things we had to do, I ain't sure the Man Upstairs would want us mixing in with the good folks doing their worshiping."

"That's war. You think the Good Lord don't know that?"

"I planned on going down to the courthouse in Corsicana to see if there's news from the Nineteenth. Maybe drop Olivia off at Dresden on the way."

"Won't do you any good. The courthouse is closed on Sunday and you think Dr. Robinson's gonna work on the Sabbath?"

Hy tried to salvage his brother. "It's the only day we got, Mama. You say a prayer for us."

"You think I don't pray for all five of my boys every Sunday ... every night? I was just thinking that maybe you might go down and get your sins washed away while you was home." She rose and picked up her sons' plates, cups and saucers as if she were dismissing them from her life.

Lev was tying Butter and Sheep to the back of the buckboard when Hester stepped down the porch steps. Pregnancy looked good on her. Lev had always thought of his brother's wife as the best wife a man could have. Sebastian had always referred to his daughter-in-law as a pretty package—a "pure and good-humored woman", he had said.

Lev turned and smiled at her and she squeezed his arm. "Tell me to go about my business, but I have to ask."

Lev smiled. "Go about your business."

"I see the way you look at Olivia. Can't say I blame you. I like her myself."

"She just helped us out a lot. Nothing more than that."

"You're a fool if you think that. You know I'm asking for Mary Ann's sake. She's got her heart set on having you."

Lev stiffened a little. "Listen, Hester ..."

She put a hand on his arm to stop him. "Don't say anything. You don't have to. Just don't go by to see her on your way back. Let me tell her. If she sees you, it will hurt more."

Minnie and Olivia chattered like schoolgirls most of the way to Dresden. Rachael, choosing to ignore the fact that Olivia had traveled several days with her sons, insisted that Minnie go along as chaperone. "It will make a better impression on the doctor ... since you insist on bothering the man on Sunday." It made sense and Minnie really wanted to miss church and go.

They stopped the buckboard in front of a blacksmith shop in downtown Dresden. The blacksmith was pounding a hot horseshoe into shape on his anvil. Lev sat in the buckboard spring seat and waited for the pounding to stop. The blacksmith recognized Minnie as he lifted the horse's leg and snugged it between his knees. "Well, me wee Rivers girl. What would you be doing so far from home?"

Minnie smiled. "Hey, Captain Rutherford. This is my brother Lev, home from the war. And this is our friend, Olivia Brand. She's a doctor ... almost."

They waited as Captain Rutherford measured the shoe, took horseshoe nails from his mouth and drove them into the hoof wall. He smoothed his handiwork with a file before taking his money from a grateful rider and walking to the buckboard. "I don't usually work on the Lord's Day, but I think He will forgive me for helping out a stranger in need."

He extended a hand toward Lev. "Minnie has told me about you, Lev."

Lev accepted the large hand, still warm and gritty from the forge and bellows. "Much obliged. We're looking for Doc Robinson."

They found the house just on the outskirts of town. The imposing two-story had a front porch on both levels. Olivia touched the reins in Lev's hands enough to signal the wagon horse to stop. "I think I may have made a mistake. Better get on Sheep and head to Waxahachie."

"Why?"

"Something about that huge house worries me. He must be a big man around here. My daddy was a doctor, but he was always one of the poorest people in town."

"Reckon this doctor is important enough. They say he named the town after some medical town in Germany. Owns the grocery store and the drugstore, too. But I hear he's a fair man, not likely to put his nose in the air."

Olivia shook her head. "That's a big house."

"Papa said he had eight or nine kids. Needs a big house." Lev touched a rein to the horse's rump and drove on.

Two hours later, they were standing in Olivia's new bedroom behind the apothecary in downtown Dresden. Dr. Robinson and his family had welcomed Olivia like a savior. He showed her around his home and insisted on driving her back into town in his buggy, as if he were afraid she might decide not to stay. When Lev took Sheep to unsaddle him and turn him loose in a lot behind the drugstore, the doctor seemed disappointed when he returned. He seemed anxious for Lev and Minnie to leave, but they stubbornly waited him out. When the doctor finally drove away, Lev and Olivia stood on the deserted street in front of the apothecary as Minnie politely waited on the buckboard, just out of earshot.

Left alone with Olivia for the first time since the night they met, Lev was out of words. "Well, this worked out just fine. Says you can have the run of the apothecary. No telling what kind of potions you'll be coming up with by the time I come back."

"You coming back?"

Lev looked a little surprised. "Course I'm coming back. Why wouldn't I?"

Her eyes narrowed as she glanced down the street toward Minnie and then down the deserted street the other way. "You have a nice family. I really like Hester and Minnie ... and your mama, of course. They told me about Mary Ann."

"Everybody gets into my business."

"I told you I've seen more things than most women my age. It's made me a little hard, but a good judge of men. I judge you and your brother to be good ones and I thank you for all you have done." Lev was about to speak, but she put a hand on his chest to stop him. "That wound is just about well. You'll get cured of me, too."

"Cured? I don't know ..."

She stopped him as she removed his hat and touched his lips with her own. Withdrawing, she touched two fingers where her lips had been. "Hear me out. This needs to be said." She put his hat back on pulled it down. "We both know what stands between us. A man like you is strong-willed on everything except women. You won't ever be able to deal with my past life. I'm not going to lie to you and I'm not going to tell you the truth, because neither would do any good."

"Maybe you're a good judge, but you could be wrong about me."

"I'm not. It would hang like a specter over our bed and our lives, and you know it. Even if you and Hy had killed Filson and set fire to my entire life back in Rusk, it would still rise up out of the flames to haunt us." She pushed him gently toward Minnie and the buckboard. "Stop by to see Mary Ann on the way home."

He reached into his pocket. "I hate to leave you all alone here in this strange place." He made an awkward attempt at embracing her, but succeeded only in putting a hand on each elbow. He stepped back and held out a closed fist. "Hold out your hand." Lev dropped his rabbit's foot into her open palm and closed her fingers around it. "You keep this. Ain't brought me much luck up to now."

She looked at the good luck charm and smiled. "Dr. Robinson showed me where he keeps a rifle and a handgun. Says there's a preacher and his family about two doors down and the family that helps with the grocery right next to me." They stepped off the boardwalk into the street, rutted from wagon tracks. She waved him away as her eyes began to glisten. "I've been alone for a long time. There's worse things."

Lev pulled her to him and spoke into the sweet scent of her hair. "By God, but you're the most resourceful woman I ever met." He turned and walked toward the buckboard.

Lev stopped at the courthouse in Corsicana and visited with some wounded veterans and older men who had served in the Mexican war. Like useless remnants of another time, they sat on hard benches downtown on Sundays and most other days, ruminating about how the country would go to hell if the Yankees won. They were full of information that Lev had no use for, but had only rumors about the 19th.

It was dark when they stopped at Ransom and Edeline House's farm on the way back. Mary Ann and Hester's parents greeted them warmly, inquiring about the war, Hester and grandson Otho. They said that Mary Ann had gone to Sunday night church with some of their neighbors. Lev never got off the spring seat. "We need to get on home. See if Hy's found news about the Nineteenth and Alfred. Tell Mary Ann I stopped by."

13

MINNIE'S CHEERFUL CHATTERING SUCCUMBED to the rhythmic sound of tree frogs and a welcome cool breeze. Her head bobbed on Lev's shoulder in time with the movement of the buckboard. The creak of wagon wheels and whippoorwill calls made Lev's despondency deeper. He had been away from fighting just long enough to despise going back and was displeased with himself for getting soft so quickly. They were within shouting distance of the house when he saw a man mounted on a big Morgan horse stopped in the middle of the road. Lev recognized the dark outline and smiled. He made no effort to stop the plodding wagon horse until the big man moved directly into its path. Lev clicked his tongue, slapped the reins and headed straight for him. Minnie lifted her head and sat taut on the seat when the wagon lurched.

The big man's right hand was busy holding a shotgun and he had trouble getting his horse settled with just his left on the reins. "You aim to run over me?"

Lev laughed at the sound of the familiar voice. "Man's got to expect that when he puts his horse in the middle of the road on a dark night."

"Heard tell you was back. Where's your brother?"

"Got four brothers."

"The one deserted with you."

The tone made Lev's smile disappear as he moved one hand

to his pistol without replying. He looked beyond the man who had blocked his path as moonlight crept through the post oaks that lined the deep sand road. Water, wagons and horses had made the trail as deep as some creeks.

"Sorry, Lev, but I got orders to take you boys in. You come with me now and I'll come back for Hy. I got a horse tied back over in them woods you can ride. You just let Minnie go on to the house with the wagon and you get on down."

Lev was incredulous. "You serious, Wade?"

"Times is different, Lev. Old days is gone. We got brother fighting brother and friend against friend."

"What's that got to do with your trying to arrest me and Hy?" It was too dark to see clearly, but Lev's memory filled in the details of the man's chiseled features, his lean muscled frame. Wade Monroe had been his best friend once. They had played together as boys, courted Hester and Mary Ann in the same wagon many times. When Hester had chosen Hy over Wade, there were serious trouble and some threats made by Wade. Lev had chosen his brother's side, of course, but had always expected his friendship with Wade to rekindle when tempers cooled.

Wade's voice was strained. "Just send Minnie to the house, Lev. Ain't no use in her having to see this."

Lev took a deep breath. "I hear this is dangerous country these days, what with no-count lawmen running things. Ain't sending my sister off in the buckboard by herself. Be better if you get on out of the way while I take her home. Then me and you can talk about whatever subjects come into your head, Wade."

Wade Monroe was a man ladies just naturally took to. Even Minnie seemed mesmerized by his presence. On the night that Hester married Hy, Wade had stood outside their wedding cabin and fired his pistol, shouting for Hy to come outside and be killed for stealing his woman. Before Hy could get dressed and step outside, Sebastian had put a shotgun barrel under Wade's chin and led him away from the honeymoon cabin. They never saw him again—until now. Wade stepped down from the horse. He seemed to stand taller. Still easier on the eyes than Hy—even Hester had said as much. Lev's respect for his sister-in-law deepened. Wade cast a deferential glance toward Minnie as he pointed at Lev. "Home Guard says they's questions about you and Hy."

"You Home Guard these days?"

"Deputy Sheriff." Wade turned at a shuffling of leaves behind him.

The sound came from behind a huge post oak a few yards down the road. The man sat erect in his saddle as his horse jumped the ditch and landed on light feet. A colt landed seconds behind the mare the man was riding. Lev could not make out the mare's color in the filtered moonlight, only that she was dark and might be black. The colt trotting alongside looked midnight blue in the sparse light. The mare's head remained low and her ears bobbed back and forth as she started toward them in a fox trot. She moved like she was walking on water, as if the slightest hesitation or firm contact with the ground might cause her to sink and drown. The colt trotted alongside without need of a lead rope. The canopy of trees had kept the road dry and full of deep, filtered sand. Such sand usually creates a cloud of dust, but the horse's contact with the ground was so slight and so quick that only little puffs trailed behind her hooves.

Lev smiled. He had seen the old man at woods' edge before he spoke to Wade. He could not make out his features, but he knew who he was by the way he sat the horse. As he drew closer, Lev noticed some changes in his father. When Lev last saw him, Sebastian Rivers had black hair so thick that a permanent sweatband crease caused it to jut out and over his ears as if trying to protect them from the elements. Now, Lev could not make out any hair and wondered if his father had lost it all.

Sebastian stopped on Minnie's side, reached up to the

spring seat and locked fingers with his daughter. Looking at Lev, he touched his hat brim. "Son." Sebastian had a way of looking into a man's eyes as if he were searching his soul.

Lev repeated the ritual motion. "Papa. What happened to your hair?"

Sebastian lifted his hat to reveal gray-streaked black hair that looked as if it had been cut with a dull ax. Long strands stood up at the crown, presiding over clumps of various lengths that stopped abruptly just above the sweatband of his hat. "What happens when you fall asleep in the chair while a drunk barber wields a pair of scissors. It was getting hot, so I told McCulloch to trim it close. He may have gone a little overboard. Be glad when my hat fits again."

"Who's McCulloch?"

A gray man and his gray horse appeared out of the tree moon shadows as if the sound of his name had caused him to materialize. Sebastian pointed the fingers of his right hand at the man. "McCulloch, my cook. Used to call him cook and barber, but I'm taking away the barber title."

The old man eased down from the saddle, bowed, and made a sweeping gesture with his hat, revealing white hair cut in the same fashion as Sebastian's. His movements on the ground were jerky and Lev noticed a tremor when he shook his hand. His remount appeared as one unbroken movement without struggle, spasm or tic. The tremor disappeared when he picked up the reins. A mounted McCulloch erased a decade from the old man Lev had seen on the ground.

Sebastian inclined his head toward the old man. "McCulloch here is as good a man as I have ever seen with horses—just bunged up so bad he can't ride the young stock anymore. But not worth a damn as a barber when he's drinking."

Lev liked the old man at once. "You any kin to General Ben McCulloch?"

"My nephew. I rode with John Henry Brown when he took the

general's body from Pea Ridge back home to Austin."

Still staring at Lev, Sebastian raised his eyebrows enough to call the old man's story into question.

Wade had watched it all with growing impatience. He remounted. Sebastian seemed to notice Wade for the first time. He stared at him until Wade shifted in his saddle. "You still here, Mister Monroe?" He emphasized the first part of the name, knowing it would irritate Wade.

"I got business with Lev and Hy."

"What business?"

"Home Guard says they got questions."

"You got this notion you part of the Confederate Army, Wade. You need to get over it. You just a man tends to errands the sheriff feels like he's too good for. Now get on home."

Lev could not chase away the empathy he felt for his old friend. Sebastian had never approved of their friendship and judged Wade Monroe to be worthless as a boy and as a man. Wade dug both heels into the Morgan and rode close enough for the horse to push against Sebastian's mare. He leaned over and grabbed a handful of the mare's mane. "You ain't talking to no drunk kid this time, Mister Rivers. I'd kill any man tries to point a scattergun at me now."

Sebastian's eyes slanted. "That so? My recollection is I told you not to show up here again."

"You aiming to get in my way of taking Lev in?"

Sebastian inclined his head in Lev's direction. "Go ahead."

Wade glanced toward the woods. Sebastian let his reins lie across the mare's neck, crossed his forearms and leaned back a little. The shift was just enough to make the leather groan. "If you waiting for them colored boys you brought along to do your dirty work ... they ain't coming."

"What did you do to 'em?"

"Not hurt. They got a little uppity and we had to hog-tie 'em over by that tree where you got that horse staked out. Take 'em on home as you leave. Don't want to have to fool with 'em in the morning." Sebastian squeezed the mare just enough to push away the bigger Morgan.

Wade pointed a finger at Lev. "We ain't done."

Sebastian watched as Wade headed in the direction of the men he had brought with him. "Hate to think I might have that man as a half-assed relative."

Lev stared at Wade's outline as it disappeared into the woods. "How's that?"

"Couldn't have Hester, so he set his sights on her sister. He aims to marry Mary Ann."

Lev seemed not to hear his father as he clucked at the wagon horse and moved toward the lantern that Rachael was softly swinging on the front porch. It was too dark for Lev to see his mother's expression as she stood on the porch, staring down at his father. Sebastian had ridden beside the back wheel of the wagon, figuring that Lev could provide him entrance to his wife's yard. McCulloch stayed in the shadows and waited. Lev was relieved when Minnie broke what seemed to be a stalemate by jumping down from the wagon and trotting toward the outhouse. Lev stepped down and led the wagon horse to the small barn, feeling like the small boy who used to exercise extra caution to keep a team of horses or mules from running over him when he un-harnessed them. He unhitched the wagon tongue and had begun to hang the harness when he heard their first words drift though the rising dew.

Rachael looked over Sebastian's head and spoke as if communicating to the wind. "I was beginning to get worried."

"Our boy can take care of himself."

"I was worried about Minnie."

"He can take care of her, too."

"I suppose that Olivia Brand found herself a place to live over in Dresden."

"Don't know anything about anybody named Brand."

"What got ahold of your hair?"

Sebastian lifted his hat. "It'll grow back."

"What did Wade Monroe want? Came to my door brazen as a banty rooster."

"Just a man been given too much authority and too little brains. He thinks he's some sorta Confederate law. Tries to think up ways he can settle old grudges he gathered up in the life he had before he put on that badge." This met with silence, as if Sebastian had spoken more than his allotted words. He tried again. "Where did Hy get off to?"

"Hester got the boy to sleep so Hy and her could go walking down by the creek. They took a blanket and a basket and was gonna have supper on the creek bank." She lifted her chin in that direction. "Here they come now."

Separated only for brief periods since enlisting, the two brothers came together like pup siblings on the way back to the house. Hester hooked an arm under each of their elbows and brought them back like bounty. She poked Lev slightly. "Tell me."

"Tell you what?"

"Did you stop by to see Mary Ann or not?"

"I did."

She pinched his arm just behind his elbow. "Well?"

Lev shrugged. "She was out with Wade Monroe."

Hester's face paled. "She don't care a fig for Wade. If she was with him, Mary Ann was just being polite, I expect. He keeps asking."

"Seems to have his heart set on getting him one of Ransom House's daughters, don't he?"

Hester flushed. "Wade Monroe ain't never gonna be part of this family or the House family."

She smiled when she saw her father-in-law. "Hello, Mister Rivers."

Sebastian used the excuse to do what he had wanted to since his arrival. He dismounted, removed his hat and took Hester in his arms. He was not embarrassed to come into contact with the grandchild inside her. He loved Hester as much as he loved his daughters, and hugging her came easier to him than hugging them because she made it easy. "Having babies looks good on you, girl."

He reached behind her and clasped Hy's hand and shook it. Rachael hung her lantern from a nail in a porch post. Her reflection revealed a slight softening as she saw her husband shake hands with their son as he hugged his wife. "It's late, but I guess we could set a spell."

Sebastian stood in the yard, holding his reins, while the rest took to the porch.

Lev looked toward McCulloch, still mounted and standing in the shadows. "He really kin to General Ben McCulloch?"

Sebastian shrugged.

"We all heard about John Henry Brown bringing the general's body back from Arkansas to Austin. Major Brown passed within twenty feet of Hy and me when he rode through. Took the time to say a word or two about Handler and Hy's dun. He knows Colonel Parsons, commander of our brigade. Can't recall seeing that old man with him, though."

Sebastian twirled his reins. "Reckon it don't matter either way. I hear you lost Handler. Most men never own a horse half as good. John Henry Brown probably recognized a good horse when he saw one. "

Sebastian stayed close to his horse, waiting for in invitation to join them on the porch. When none came, he gestured for the old man to come forward and watched with admiration as McCulloch rode his gray horse toward them. "Don't know if the old man is really kin to Ben McCulloch or even knows John Henry Brown. Only thing I know for sure is that he knows more about horses than anybody I ever run across."

Rachael bristled slightly as the old man approached, put off a little at Sebastian's quick reversion to his former role as head of her house. McCulloch dismounted and leaned against the hitching rail as if he were afraid to get too far away from his horse or too close to Rachael. Sebastian broke the uncomfortable silence. "I heard that Parsons admired good horses and horsemen. I sent five good horses and five good boys who could ride the hair off 'em to this war. If I thought I could still make a hand, I'd go myself. You boys think it's too late?"

Lev shook his head. "The news don't seem too good, but the news we get ain't usually reliable."

Sebastian inclined his head in McCulloch's direction. "We hear it's all but over. So far, you boys, Parsons and John Henry Brown been keeping the goddam Yankees out of Texas. That may be the best we can hope for." The words had barely left Sebastian's mouth when he saw Rachael rise from her porch rocker. His taking of the Lord's name in vain had ended what could have been a splendid evening.

14

LEV OPENED ONE EYE WHEN HE HEARD A rooster crow. He jumped a little at the pair of eyes that greeted him. Ears perked, the little dog sat back on his haunches as if waiting for Lev's eyes to open. He smiled and wagged his tail when they did. His compact body was covered in short hair splotched black and white. Lev touched the top of the dog's head. "Boy, is that you?"

Minnie stepped out on the porch and yawned. "That's him."

"Where's he been?" The dog had been a sickly runt pup, not expected to live, when Lev left for the war.

"Stays wherever Papa tells him to. Says he's still your dog when you come to claim him."

Lev had shut Boy from his memory, figuring that he had died. He pushed his legs over the side of the cot and touched the dog's face. Boy sat quietly and kept his tongue to himself as Lev cupped the dog's face in his palm. Lev saw his former peaceful self in Boy's eyes, giving him hope that he might return there someday.

Sebastian and McCulloch slept in the barn and had their breakfast on the porch. Otho insisted on sitting on his grandfather's lap. Lev and Hy wolfed down their food, uncomfortable having breakfast at their mother's table while their father ate outside. By good daylight, Hy and Lev had said their goodbyes and the men were mounted. Rachael walked up to Butter and put a hand on Lev's knee. "Look out for Alfred if you can, Son."

Minnie knelt to hold Boy as they rode two abreast toward Waxahachie with Sebastian and McCulloch in front. Both had said they knew people there who could tell them how to reconnect to the 19th. Just after noon, they were leaning against a hitching rail talking to Emory Rogers, a man about the same age as Sebastian.

"Part of Parsons' Brigade, are you? The Hell Yelpers. Well, keep yelling at the sons-of-bitches."

Sebastian swelled a little. "What's the latest on the war, Emory?"

"South is in bad shape. If your sons find their outfit, it's likely they'll be dismounted. Can't provision for the horses. Lots of cavalry boys already walking."

Hy shook his head. "Horses are the only things that kept us from starving. Colonel Parsons knows that. He won't dismount us."

"He may not have a choice. It's bad. Lee's on the run in Virginia and a merciless, murdering general named William T. Sherman is marching toward Atlanta ... burning everything in his path."

"Any idea where we can find Colonel Parsons?"

"Nope. Commands shifts so often I can't keep up. Which company of the 19th?"

"Company C."

Rogers reached into a shirt pocket and reviewed some notes written in tiny script. "Word is Colonel Burford resigned after Yellow Bayou. Let's see ... Nineteenth, Company C looks to be under Colonel Ben Watson now. In and out of Texas, Arkansas and Louisiana. Watson is a Waxahachie boy. From reports I get, most of the Texas Cavalry regiments are likely to be back in Arkansas, patrolling the Arkansas and Mississippi to keep Federals out of Texas."

Lev and Hy experienced a sudden, intense need to reconnect to the 19th — to find their little brother. They knew that it might be now or never and did not want the war's end finding them sitting near home in Texas. Their bellies were full; they had replenished their ammunition, and their horses had rested. Arkansas was all they needed to hear. They tried to ignore Louisiana. Both never wanted to see another swamp.

They became soldiers again as they rode away. It took more than two months, but they finally found the 19th on the banks of the Arkansas River. They presented themselves to Colonel Watson at his tent and explained their absence.

The colonel stared at them a long time without speaking, finally turning his glance toward the river. "Colonel Parsons said you boys would be back if you were alive." He looked at Lev. "You still riding that blood bay?"

"No, sir. Shot out from under me."

"I never saw him in battle, but Colonel Parsons regaled me with stories about what a jumper and bumper he was. Swore the damn horse knew what he was fighting for."

Lev thought about the stories of Butter and her hatred of blue uniforms. Maybe Handler hated them, too. The brothers waited for desertion to come up. When it did not, an emboldened Lev asked the question. "Sir, our mama's after us pretty hard for news about our little brother. His name is Alfred Rivers."

"He mounted as well as you boys?"

"Papa would have sent him off on a good horse."

"If he's mounted good, he's probably in Arkansas. If not, he's probably walking around on the Texas-Louisiana border, taking potshots at Yankees on the water and in the swamps."

The brigade spent the next few months monitoring Yankee troop movements close to the Federal garrison at Pine Bluff, Arkansas. Hy and Lev foraged for themselves and others, firing their weapons only at wild game. No word of Alfred.

William Steele, a native of New York, replaced Parsons as brigade commander in October of 1864. The new commander received orders to march south toward Louisiana. Hy and Lev felt swamp fever coming over them, but they diverted toward Texas and camped in Nacogdoches. Close to Rusk, Lev and Hy thought of Filson for the first time in months and chanced a nighttime visit to The Good Samaritan Inn. They found it closed—no sign of Filson, wounded or dead.

When supplies and rations ran short again, the men were sure they would be dismounted. With Parsons gone, nobody to fight, and a constant flow of news of Federal victories, morale sank. Hy and Lev resolved to find Alfred and ride home if they started to take away their horses, but spirits rose when Parsons returned to command the 12th and 19th in April of 1865. He made a speech that brought forth rebel yells. The old commander resolved to fight as long as the breath of a single Yankee miscreant polluted the air of their Sunny South.

Hy and Lev were feeding their horses corn just after Parson's speech when they sensed someone watching. His flowing beard was turning white but the hooded, intelligent, beseeching eyes could not be mistaken. After a stay at home to recover from illness, forty-five-year-old John Henry Brown was back commanding the Third Frontier District of the Texas Militia. He got right to the point. "I spoke to Colonel Parsons and I have a proposition for you. You know my position with the Texas Militia?"

"We do."

"Word has reached us of a possible Yankee invasion at the southern tip of Texas. Colonels Barrett and Branson, in violation of a gentlemen's agreement, intend to cross our sacred border. To further insult us, they are leading the Sixty-Second US Colored Infantry. I intend to lead the Texas Militia and whoever will join us. We plan to stop them."

Brown paused long enough to study their blank expressions. "We have kept the rascals out for the duration, and it's a matter of Lone Star pride that they not get in during the final days of the war. I have need of good men with good horses."

Lev ran his palm down Butter's shoulder and picked up a front hoof. John Henry Brown was obviously an intelligent, well-spoken man, but his plan made no sense. "How far you going?"

"To the Rio Grande—about five hundred miles. Good men with good horses could make it in less than three weeks. Colonel Parsons has granted you permission to accompany me if you so desire. We plan to reconnoiter with Colonel Rip Ford and will be under his command."

Lev looked at his brother and got an assenting nod. "How many of our boys you taking?"

John Henry Brown smiled. "You are the only two from the Nineteenth. Most of your fellows are poorly mounted and just want to go home."

Lev leaned against Butter, crossed his arms and sighed deeply. "We was thinking of home, too. We got a younger brother we need to find."

Commander Brown nodded. "I will not make a promise I cannot keep, gentlemen. Finding your brother is not our mission, but I will do all in my power to help when we return."

Hy shrugged as he looked at Lev. "If you think we can make a hand at this, I guess we can try to help. Things around here sure starting to work on us."

"I warn you that it may be only for Texas pride that we fight. This war is nearly over. General Lee has surrendered. They may have whipped the South, but we can damn sure keep them out of Texas." He extended a firm handshake to each brother. "It is an historic time, gentlemen."

The fighting had already commenced when they arrived at a place called Palmito Ranch on May 13, 1865. Yankees had destroyed all of the supplies at the Confederate camp. The Rivers brothers and John Henry Brown's Texas Militia joined Colonel Ford and pushed back the invasion to Boca Chica—a symbolic and empty Confederate victory. Native Americans, Negroes, Mexicans and Whites all fought in this, the last battle of the Civil War.

Commander Brown approached them as Lev and Hy were packing provisions in their saddlebags and bedrolls to return home. "I am in your debt, gentlemen."

Hy shrugged. "Wasn't much of a fight for horse soldiers."

"No, sir. It was not. However, I can't help but feel that those Yankees were intimidated by a few hell yelps from good Texas horsemen. We won a victory."

Lev stepped into a stirrup and mounted. "Is it over or not?"

"It was over when we started down here."

"Are we dismissed or do we need to find our outfit to muster out?"

"I believe that Colonel Parsons has already disbanded your regiment. I have permission to formally dismiss you, your horses and weapons."

They shook hands and Lev and Hy turned their horses north. John Henry Brown called them back. He put a hand on Butter's neck and leaned into her as if he needed support. "Men, the aftermath of this war will continue for many years. I don't believe I can tolerate what is about to happen to our beloved state. With Lincoln killed, the North is going to take even more revenge. I plan to emigrate to Mexico."

Lev leaned down to look John Henry Brown in the eyes. He could not believe his ears. "Mexico? Our daddy fought to run the Mexicans out of Texas. Can't see our family going down there to join 'em now. You really think it will be worse in Texas than in Mexico?"

Commander Brown nodded. "You'll likely have to take an oath to the people you have been fighting for four years. It won't just be the military that will make life hell for Confederate soldiers, but scalawags from all corners of the north will besiege our state like locusts. Helpless slaves will be let loose on a society that is not prepared to absorb them. Confederate soldiers will be reduced to the lowest rung of society."

Hy's expression was doubtful. "We ain't never been really soldiers, sir. All we know is horses and a little about cattle. Maybe we can manage to stay out of their way."

Brown shook his head. "I hope you are right, but I think not. Your beloved Parsons agrees with me. By now, Colonel Parsons has told his men to meet him at the Falls of the Little Brazos within sixty days if they want to go with us to Mexico. It would be an honor to have you join us there."

Lev was taken aback. The war was over and the men he admired most were leaving the country. "We got lots of family in Texas. We'll have to talk it over with them."

"Bring them with you, of course. Mine is coming with me. If not, prepare yourselves to protect them constantly. Texas is going to run with more blood than it did during the war; most of it will be ours, and it will be against the law for us to fight back."

The brothers knew that their mother would never leave her beloved East Texas. Even Sebastian would balk at running off to another country, especially a country he had fought against. He would stay and deal with whatever came his way. Lev tipped his hat toward John Henry Brown. "Much obliged, Sir. We will consider your kind offer. It has been a pleasure to serve under you."

Colonel Parsons disbanded his regiment in Sterling, Texas. The 19th was no more. The Confederacy was no more.

15

THEY BEGAN TO SEE WHAT JOHN HENRY BROWN had meant as they headed home. They passed many Confederate soldiers. Most were afoot ... all ragged, some crippled, walking on crutches made of hickory or oak limbs with the bark still intact. Many were out of their heads and lost. Most had no shoes. All had a look of defeat. A few had rumors of Yankee invasions of Texas to pass on. "They're coming by boat from Galveston and from Arkansas and Louisiana by land. The sons-of-bitches ain't done with us yet." The brothers' trip to the Rio Grande now seemed wasted.

Two days away from home, they fell silent around their campfire. They had let traveling toward home take priority over hunting for food. John Henry Brown had provisioned them with some coffee, but no pot to boil it in. They had boiled it a tin cup at a time, but having to spit out grounds made it almost not worth the effort. Lev tossed his into the fire as if he were striking a malevolent force. He had not slept in two days. The weather had been hot and humid during the day with little relief at night. The morning brought a blanket of fog and mist, as if God were following them, replacing the misery of war with miserable weather. Hungry and weak, Lev gasped for a good breath, but could not seem to draw the heavy air to his lungs. For the first time in months, he thought he felt the bullet move.

Hy saddled the dun. "You gonna saddle up or did you decide to take the day off?"

Lev picked up Butter's wet blanket. The smell of his own body repulsed him as he rose. The smell of a wet horse blanket was usually familiar, even comforting, to Lev, but this blanket reeked as it mixed with a dead possum that had turned rank during the night. They had not stopped to camp until well past dark, and had not seen a stagnant pool a few yards from their bedrolls. A water moccasin boldly plopped into the water, slithered a few feet, and then turned with its head above water as if it were watching him—daring him. A bad sign. Lev felt the hair on the back of his neck stand up. He had forgotten to place a horsehair rope around his bedroll to keep snakes away. He swatted a horsefly on Butter's shoulder and pulled back a palm full of blood. Gnats swarmed to the corner of the horse's eyes and around her nose. Lev swallowed hard as he saw Hy's lips moving, but the banter seemed far away and in a foreign language, one he did not want to hear spoken.

They had barely departed when he saw them passing in the woods beside the road. Four men dressed in various combinations of blue uniforms. Butter rolled her eyes and pinned her ears at the sight. Two black soldiers were led by two whites. Hy had seen them, too. Neither said anything until the men turned onto the road behind them and began following.

Hy glanced over his shoulder. "You think we made that long trip to the river to keep 'em out and they was up here all the time?"

"Might be Federals, but them old boys are likely just scavengers and nothing but trouble. Them uniforms don't match or fit. The colored ones got their sabers on backwards. I figure they're playing both sides against the middle."

"Hold up there, Johnny Reb." A tall, thin man with yellow, pointed teeth spoke. The skin on his face looked paper-thin, as if it had been stretched too tautly over his cheekbones. Pain-filled desperation filled his eyes.

The black soldiers rested their rifles across their saddles and stayed put as the two leaders approached. The second white man looked to be out of the same womb as the first, just a year or two later. Lev's skin crawled and Butter squealed and kicked when the man touched her brand. The man moved back. "Touchy bitch, ain't she? We just patrollin' these parts, on the lookout for Rebs what run off with Federal horses and supplies." He pointed toward the encircled U. S. on the saddlebags. "Looks like we found you boys taking things don't belong to you."

The smell of the man brought deep revulsion to Lev's throat that threatened to overflow.

"We ain't holdin' no grudges, though. You boys just turn over them two horses and them weapons, we'll let you keep whatever else you carryin' off and let you go on home."

Hy looked back at the black soldiers, sabers backward and hats cocked, gun barrels leaned in his direction. High and mighty. "Soldiers, my ass. Them two damn sure ain't soldiers. Doubt you are, either."

The younger brother made an exaggerated roll of his shoulders. He spoke with a nasal voice that raked across Lev's frayed nerves and seemed to press on the bullet inside him. "Them two niggers got authority to recover Union property. Guess you boys ain't heard that county jails fillin' up quick with Reb soldiers already. We ain't aimin' to take you off to jail, just takin' what rightfully belongs to the Union."

Hy smiled. "Now we surely do appreciate that, but could we see some kind of proof of your authority to take what's rightfully ours?"

The brothers' expressions changed as they stared at each other, then looked toward the black soldiers. When the younger brother beside Lev turned, he felt the barrel of Lev's cocked Colt pressed against his Adam's apple. "Hellfire, boy, you crazy? They's four of us agin' two of you."

Lev's eyes were red and burning. He used his pistol barrel to rake off the man's hat and grabbed a handful of matted, greasy hair. "Right now, it's just you and me, Shithole."

The black soldiers trained their weapons on Lev. The reluctant older white man shook his head as if in pain and pointed his pistol at Hy. "Them niggers ain't likely to miss. I give the word, they'll blow both you boys off them hosses." The saliva in his mouth had dried and his speech was thick. Despair was in his eyes. Lev almost felt sorry for the man. This was clearly the younger brother's idea.

Lev yanked the matted hair of the younger brother. "Doubt them boys could hit the broadside of a barn sitting on them horses. Either way, the top of your head comes off."

"You shoot me, they'll kill you for sure."

"Only thing for sure is that you won't never know it." Lev pushed the barrel hard under the man's chin, enough to lift his jawbone. He felt a surge of hatred so strong that he almost hoped they would fire just to give him a reason to pull the trigger.

The man's head was jerked back so tautly that he could not turn it toward his brother, but his eyes darted sideways. The other brother squirmed in his saddle, keeping his gun on Hy. "What you want me to do?"

Lev eased the barrel off enough for the man to speak. His voice came out in sharp slivers. "Give us the weapons and we'll be on our way. You keep your horses."

Lev wanted it to be over. "Only thing you might walk away with is your asses. You tell those sons-of-bitches to head on down the road easy-like. Stay on the road where we can see 'em. When they're out of sight, I'll turn you loose."

"You crazy. You can't kill us all."

"One might live, maybe two, but you won't be one of 'em."

The man cut his eyes toward his brother again. "Do what he says. If I ain't there straightaway, come ahuntin'."

The older brother moved his pistol away from Hy's head and

pointed it toward the sky, nodding to the black soldiers as he rode toward them. Lev pulled the handful of hair hard as he shouted to the departing men. "Leave them guns and horses. Ain't aiming to be ambushed."

The departing brother turned. "The hell, you say. That ain't part of it." He saw nothing but angry determination as he looked from Lev to Hy. "Look, boys, we don't mean you no harm. It's just that this war has done starved us out. I got kids that need food."

Hy had drawn his pistol and trained it on the older brother. "Shoulda thought of that before you pointed them guns at us. Dismount and throw 'em on the ground or start shootin' 'em. Don't make me no never-mind which one it is. Just as soon kill all four of you thieving bastards."

The older brother flinched when he heard the clanking sound of the black men's weapons hitting the ground. They dismounted and stood by their horses. He shook his head and followed suit. Hy rode close to him. "Now you get on down the road behind them boys. You as much as turn your head, I'll blow it off. When you're out of sight, we'll turn this other moron loose."

The walking men were almost over a small knoll in the road before Hy disarmed the younger brother. Lev kicked him off his horse. Butter, teeth bared, tried to take a chunk out of his blue-uniformed shoulder. The man fell down trying to escape the mare's wrath. When he rose, Lev's hickory stick struck him in the teeth. The man rose to his knees, spitting blood and a yellow tooth. Lev dismounted and drew back the stick.

Hy rode closer. "You aim to kill him?"

"Butter would do it if I let her. He's the worst kind of damned road trash. Vermin. Killing him now will probably save him from killing somebody else down the line. He put them other boys up to this."

"Suit yourself. He's the bad apple in the barrel for sure."

Lev's jaw tightened before he released the hammer and

holstered his pistol. His hard breathing startled him. Hy and Lev stared at each other as the man struggled to his feet and stumbled down the road. Hy stuck the thieves' pistols in saddle pommels and saddlebags and the rifles and shotguns in scabbards as Lev tied the horses nose to tail. Each led two as they headed toward home. Lev's irritability had eased some with the exertion, but he still felt the bullet. In all those years of fighting, he had never wanted to kill a man—until today ... and the war was over. John Henry Brown may have been right about Texas flowing red with blood.

16

RACHAEL HAD STOOD ON THE PORCH WITH HER lantern each night since the war's end. Her patience was rewarded as she saw two of her sons lead four horses into her yard. Hy left the dun untied and in charge of his two horses as he dismounted and ran to the house. He almost bumped into Hester as he jumped the steps and landed on the front porch. She was holding Kaletta, their six-month-old daughter. Otho was asleep. Hy stepped back at first, almost irritated that a child he had never seen was occupying space he had dreamed of for months. Hester smiled and locked his gaze as she handed the child to him. "Meet Kaletta. We call her Kat."

He was awkward until Hester pulled back the blanket and he caught the sweet scent and sight of his sleeping daughter. "Kat, huh. One of these days, I'm gonna name one of our younguns."

Hester looked into Hy's tired eyes. "I felt you coming hours ago."

Sebastian appeared from the woods as if he had been waiting for his sons' arrival. His hair had turned white and grown long enough to reach beneath his hat and pester his ears. Its fine whiteness quivered enough in the slight breeze to give him a ghostly quality as he rode toward them. McCullough remained at the edge of the trees. Lev and Rachael waited in awkward silence while Hester rubbed Hy's bearded face with all her fingers and moaned into his parted lips with happiness.

Lev dismounted stiffly, feeling suddenly old and alone. He looped Butter's reins over the hitching rail and walked up the steps to his mother. The light from her lantern revealed a deep struggle between sadness and joy. He hugged her and looked over her shoulder at Sebastian. His father's gaze had always been direct and challenging. Not now. In the sparse light from stars and a quarter-moon, he saw his father shake his head and look away. He felt the wetness of tears on his shoulder and heard his mother's deep sigh. He knew. "It's Alfred, isn't it?"

Sebastian looked toward the family plot. "They brought him home a few days after you boys left. Said a damned gun blew up in his face."

They walked out to the family burial plot under a small copse of scrub oaks on a little hill just beyond the house. Sebastian had fenced it with bois d'arc posts and rails. He had exacted a promise from Rachael to bury him there when he finished the small enclosure around two of her infant siblings. They never expected to bury one of their own there. Now there were three flat bois d'arc markers, two gray and one still yellow, all carved with names and dates. Lev noticed that the skin on his mother's hand had gone slack and spotted as she patted the dirt on her son's grave. "I wish that William could be here with his brother." Sebastian flinched at the opening of the old wound.

Hats in hand, Lev and Hy listened to the wind sift through the trees, shifting leaves on willows and hackberries and awakening the fluttering of cottonwoods by Chambers Creek. They tried to think of something to say to their mother—an apology, of sorts, for not looking out for their younger brother. They did not notice when Sebastian walked away. Lev flinched a little as he felt a nudge against his lower leg. Boy was looking up at him.

When they returned to the house, Sebastian had untied the captured horses and had them strung in a line. He and McCulloch were studying them, talking more to themselves than to each other. Sebastian leaned his arms over one saddle. "Hope you boys didn't buy them horses. Pretty sorry lot. I figure the gear is worth more than they are."

Exhausted, Lev led Butter toward the barn. "Nope. Took 'em off some old boys who tried to steal ours."

Sebastian nodded. "Was they wearing Yankee uniforms?"

"They were. A couple of colored boys and two white-trash brothers."

"There's a sorry lot of men around here picking up them uniforms from somewhere. Mostly deserters from both sides—white vermin that round up a few freed slaves and start preying on innocent folks and soldiers coming home."

Hy, still arm in arm with Hester, stepped off the porch and spoke to his father. "We heard the North is gonna make it hard on us."

Sebastian's eyes slanted and grew cold. "Yanks ain't had time to get here in force, but I expect it'll get worse before it gets better. We'll need to get rid of them horses and saddles right away. The Union has already started putting a few people into our law enforcement."

"What people?"

"Lots of folks coming out of their holes, pretending they were union sympathizers all along. Nothing they'd like better than to put some Confederate boys in jail."

———

Word of Alfred and the return of Hy and Lev reached other Rivers children and they began to arrive by wagon. Some brought their families; some came alone. When six of the ten siblings finally gathered, Rachael softened enough to allow Sebastian to help her organize a big dinner-on-the-ground. She had been rationing her food for months in anticipation of just such an occasion. Jacob, Hy, Lev, and Arch—the soldiers, accepted hugs from the women and stares from the children with joyless equanimity. Everyone seemed surprised that they had returned alive. Hy and Lev studied their brothers as if they were meeting for the first time, searching each set of eyes to see if the boy they had known was behind the wary and pained expressions, the reflected memories of war. Alfred's memory walked the gathering, a touch here, a gesture there, like a ghost.

The next day, the men gathered wood and hauled water while the women began peeling potatoes and onions and shucking corn for a stew. When the men finished building a fire under Rachael's cast iron pot, they moved away from women's work to whittle and smoke. Boy stretched his small body on the sand just outside an invisible circle around the family, content to place his head between his paws and patiently watch Lev and Sebastian for a signal to enter the circle.

He licked his lips as Rachael dropped cubed beef from her smokehouse into the warm water in the pot and let it come to a boil. Minnie and Obedience stoked the fire, stirred the beginnings of broth, and added the vegetables. The smell wafted over the yard and lifted spirits. The feeling of joy colliding with pain forced Rachael to find her rocker and sit. The women exchanged looks of surprise and concern because Rachael never took off her cloak of authority, never rested.

She watched her sons, especially Lev. He and Alfred had been hers. Sebastian had taken the others. Now death had taken Alfred. And Lev had returned, but not as the son she knew. The softness seemed to have left his thoughtful eyes, replaced with something she could not identify. Had he not been hers, she would have thought she was watching a stranger—one who frightened her.

Sebastian had saved two bottles of home brew for the occasion, but decided not to chance Rachael's ire. Besides, indulging did not seem right with Alfred buried a few yards away, the mound on his grave still not settled. He stared at the sons he had last known as boys, wondering how he could establish new relationships with the men who had known terror and violence that even he had not experienced. Fighting Mexicans was different than fighting Yankees, somehow. Victory in the Texas Revolution had been sweet, but defeat in this war was bitter. He wanted to talk about these things, but he sensed that his sons did not.

He settled for a study of the faces of the new men in the family. Obedience had married a man named Ferdinand Naron. He wondered what the hell kind of name it was and what kind of man wore it. The man was dressed like a merchant, round and smooth of face. His vested wool suit was too tight and he looked hot inside it. Sitting among the long faced-sharp-angled Rivers sons, he reminded Sebastian of a pig awaiting slaughter. But he seemed a good fit for Obedience. She looked like a bastard child among her siblings, with a round face and body and pale complexion. Ferdinand seemed anxious to take his wife and leave her hardscrabble, prone-to-violence family. Minnie had invited Ben Parks, a man who repeatedly asked for her hand. Sebastian was sure that Minnie would eventually say yes because Ben was just like her brothers, only bigger and louder.

The brothers thought the occasion should be joyous, but could not figure out what should be celebrated. They had not expected to return home defeated, not expected to lose a brother. But it was more than that. Each had expected to be battle-hardened, but this hardness was supposed to be composed of valor, of elation and confidence and courage, not this cold emptiness and wariness that often turned into palpable fear in sweat-soaked dreams. Dreams of the men they had killed and those that had tried to kill them, of mutilated bodies, of horses that had died under their saddles, of snakes and swamps. The reasons had been clear once, but not so much now.

When Minnie brought out her guitar and her father's fiddle, Sebastian glanced at Rachael as he refused to play, as if playing the fiddle would mean he had been forgiven, and he had not. When Lev picked up the fiddle and Minnie strummed the guitar, Arch produced a bottle of whiskey. The music and whiskey changed the mood enough to rekindle old memories, old feelings, especially when Rachael was persuaded to sing. Arch's bottle survived one pass among the brothers and brothers-in-law and Sebastian. When McCulloch turned up the empty bottle and drained only a drop, they laughed. Sebastian and McCulloch found stumps to sit on, but the brothers mostly stood or paced, searching for some connecting threads from their shared past to start weaving new relationships in a new life, studiously avoiding talk of the war or its likely aftermath. The conversation stayed on horses, cattle, whose-kid-is-that, and the weather.

The music was interrupted when Hester's parents arrived at dusk with Mary Ann. Lev put out a hand to help her out of the buggy. She hesitated before taking his hand, an expression of contentment, but not joy, on her face. A smile flickered, but did not emerge, as she stepped from the wagon and faced him for the first time in many years. She left her hand in his and held his gaze, calmly waiting for him to speak. He avoided her eyes, but kept hold of her hand. She studied his changed face and expression, the hardness that had found a home there—and she seemed to understand. She had changed too, but not as much. The girl Lev had known was skinny, flat of chest, with sharp cheekbones on a too-long face. He had never thought of her as pretty—until now. She was still slight of form, but her face was fuller, her eyes soft. She looked at him with unabashed longing and compassion, as if she was offering to take in and store the pain of his war years until he could be civilized again. Finally, she spoke. "It's good to have you home for good."

Lev could think of no reply. He stood looking into her soft eyes, bathing in the compassion and understanding that nestled there. It was like a balm for his soul. She seemed to know what he needed and stood silently by the buggy so that he could take it. They stood that way until Hester tapped him on the shoulder. "Daddy won't mind a bit if you give her a hug. You're like one of the family." He would have been irritated by an interruption from anyone other than his beloved Hester. He smiled and took Mary Ann awkwardly into his arms.

When it was time to serve the stew, Mary Ann filled his bowl and brought his cornbread to a ragged quilt she had thrown on a patch of grass a little away from the others. They ate together, speaking only a few words. She seemed to understand his need for silence. She persuaded him to play his fiddle again after supper and he and Minnie played until Ransom House insisted on taking his wife and daughter home.

Hester touched her father's elbow. "Just one more tune before you go, Papa." She took the fiddle out of Lev's hands and handed it to Sebastian, asking him to play his special waltz. With Hy, she coaxed Lev and Mary Ann onto the dusty dance floor, and then left them to waltz alone. Lev stood board-stiff and held her at arm's length at first, remembering the steps that Eliza Jane had taught him years before. He wondered where his rebellious sister was and if she still blamed them all for what William had done. For the first time, he seemed to understand the depth of despair she must have felt when her brother killed her husband.

His fingers brought him back as they, on their own, seemed to remember Mary Ann's fingers. He drew her closer and pressed his hand softly against the small of her back. Lev felt the first real surge of warmth in his blood since the day he had left Olivia in Dresden. Olivia. Like other life pleasures, he had shuttered the memory somewhere, hoping to open the shutters when the war was over. He relaxed a little, surprised to really feel the music from his father's fiddle and his sister's guitar as he and Mary Ann floated across the hard dance floor, raising minute trails of dust in the starlight.

Rachael folded her arms across her chest as they watched Ransom and Edeline House drive away with Mary Ann. She supposed she would be pleased if Lev chose Mary Ann for his wife. If she was anything like Hester, she could possibly cleanse the violence from Lev's soul and Rachael could share the tender, loving son she once had with his new wife. When the buggy was out of sight, she turned back toward the porch and her eyes involuntarily met her husband's. Sebastian had been watching her. She still could not look into his eyes without seeing William's violent death replayed there. She could not bear the shame of what William had done to Eliza Jane's wild husband. The revenge taken on her son, however, would always be associated with Sebastian—almost as if he had killed William himself. She had not seen Eliza Jane since the killings. Rachael had lost a daughter and a son in two swift plunges of a knife.

She muttered to herself more than anyone who might be listening. "I had hoped that word would reach Lucy and she and Frank would come." Unlike her rebellious younger sister, Lucy Elizabeth had married attorney Frank Blair, a genteel, yet brave, educated man—a former sheriff—the type of son-in-law Rachael wanted for her daughters. Clinton was at least three days away by wagon and she supposed that it was too far to bring four children.

17

THE DARK SPOT ON LEV'S SHIRT WAS EXPANDING. A small stream of blood made its way through his protesting fingers, and then trickled to a stop. He heard himself cry out as he awakened. Glad that he had chosen to sleep in the barn, he lay back on the tattered quilt he had used for a pillow and reconstructed the dream. His grandfather had been there, gently coaxing him to slow down his heartbeat and the loss of blood. Olivia had come from the shadows with bandages, issuing urgent instructions to Sebastian and Hy. She could not seem to see Papa Jim. Lev could not recall her words, but the blood flow had slowed to a trickle when she arrived out of the misty recesses created by his dream. He lay back and tried to remember the rest, but the sound of saddle leather and approaching horses chased the dream away.

Boy watched through a crack in the barn siding, growling. Lev quieted the dog and pulled on his pants and boots before peeking. He could make out four mounted men in the dawn light. He recognized the backward sabers and cocked hats of the men who had tried to rob them the day before. The young white brother spat through the space left by a missing tooth. The three flanked Wade Monroe as he spoke to Sebastian and Hy. "Things is different now, old man. South done lost the war. Best thing for Confederate soldiers to do is return any property they took. And Rebs ain't allowed to have weapons." Lev still could not believe that his old friend was determined to be an enemy.

Sebastian leaned against the hitching rail with his arms crossed, squinting into the morning sun, wishing it were at his back. Hy, shirtless and barefoot, had taken time to strap on his holster. Tender-footed, he shifted from one foot to the other as Wade demanded return of the horses and weapons they had taken. Hy had always thought that Sebastian had expected him to kill or at least punish Wade for trying to ruin his wedding night, but Hy had felt flush with victory back then. He had won the hand of his lovely Hester over a man that all women seemed to desire. He was comfortable letting his father deal with his old rival. Sebastian was handling the situation by remaining silent.

Wade turned toward Hy. "Where's your brother? He got them stolen horses and guns?"

Hy looked beyond the mounted men toward the trees along the banks of Chambers Creek. "My little brother ain't quite used to sleeping inside after all those years with nothing but sky to look up to." Hy allowed a small grin to cross his face. "Ain't got a pretty wife like mine to lay beside him."

Wade wrenched his jawbone and looked toward the barn. It was hard for Hy not to admire the cut of the man. No wonder Hester had fancied him. "Lev's probably camped on the creek. Spect he'll be walking up anytime." Hy pointed toward Wade's gun hand. "Best keep them hands where he can see 'em ... else, he might get the idea that you boys mean us harm. War left my little brother a little crazy, you know. Shoots anything that moves" ... he looked directly toward the uniformed men ... "especially if it's blue." Everyone except Wade looked toward the creek.

Sebastian moved away from the hitching rail. "Lev's always been pretty good with a long gun and blue uniforms might cause him to forget the war's over."

Unperturbed, Wade stared at the house, hoping for a glimpse of Hester. The younger brother stretched his long neck in all directions as he flicked his tongue between the unfamiliar space left by the missing tooth. Lev got the message and walked out the back of the barn and toward the woods to get behind them, Boy following. Sebastian caught sight of him. He spoke loudly to capture Wade's attention. "Last time you was here, you was all about defending the South. Now, you on the other side. Or was you on the wrong side of this fight all along? People around here find out you been spying for the North all this time, your life won't be worth a plug nickel."

Wade looked past Sebastian toward the porch window. "Your kind ain't running things around here anymore. It's a new day, Mister Rivers."

"Not around here, it ain't. I know them two colored boys. Who's the white road trash you drug up with you?"

The bottom half of the younger brother's face was bruised from Lev's club. He narrowed his eyes as he stared at the bold old man, but said nothing.

Wade seemed suddenly ashamed of his followers. "Them's Yankee soldiers. Indians call them niggers buffalo soldiers."

"The hell you say. Them two boys and that white-trash old boy you got slithering along behind you never saw a uniform till they stole the ones they wearing." Recognition flickered in Sebastian's expression as he looked at the white brother. "Don't they call you Rattle?"

The brother flinched. "Ain't my name."

Sebastian saw Lev approach from the creek trees, rifle in hand. He spoke loudly to Wade again. "You come around here a while back accusing my boys of being deserters. Now you calling us thieves." Sebastian took a step to his right as Hy moved left. "Me or Hy shoulda killed you the night you came around shootin' off your damn gun on the night of the wedding. Woulda saved the folks around here a lotta trouble. Now get the hell off my property."

Wade turned to see Lev standing behind them as he

answered Sebastian. His voice was calm and deliberate. "Hell, this ain't your property. Don't even live on it. You just hiding behind the old woman's skirts." Rachael stiffened as she pushed open the door and stepped out on the porch. Wade flinched at her glare. "No disrespect meant, Miss Rachael."

Wade heard the click of the hammer before he saw the pistol appear in Hy's hand. "That's by God enough. Don't ever let mention of my mama escape from your dirty mouth again, Wade Monroe. This here is Rivers land. You set foot on it again, you'll die on it. I'll see to it myself. Same goes for that inbred trash you brought with you."

Lev stepped forward enough to look closely at his old friend, trying to look behind the dead eyes and derisive expression to see the boy he once knew. He saw nothing. "How come you taking up with this trash against us, Wade?"

Wade looked down at his old friend. Lev thought he recognized his boyhood friend for a second, but he disappeared as quickly as he had appeared. "Got a job to do, Lev. I aim to do it. You and Hy shouldn't ought to have taken up thieving."

Hate and disgust rising, Lev turned toward Rattle and poked his ribs with the rifle barrel. "You a slow learner, ain't you, boy. Shoulda killed you when you tried to rob me the first time."

Rattle looked down at Lev and smiled, showing the space between tobacco-stained teeth. "May be that I get a chance at killin' you first."

Wade backed his horse away from the drawn guns. When he was fairly safe from a sure pistol shot, he turned again. "You and your kind's days are numbered. They gonna be more Yankee soldiers than you can count around here any day. We'll be back for them horses and guns." He turned and rode away.

Hy spat into the dirt and spoke to Sebastian. "Guess you was right about shooting that horse's ass before. He's gonna keep troubling us till we do."

_____

Lev leaned his rifle against the porch. "Guess the older brother lost his taste for stealing. Didn't appear to be cut out for it. That younger one is mean as a snake. Dumber than a stump, too."

Sebastian showed disgust by making a clicking sound with his teeth and spitting. "That old boy would cut a baby's throat for a quarter. They call him Rattle." He noted their puzzled looks. "Always figured it was because his brain rattles around in his head, but he does have a snaky look about him, don't he."

Hy looked toward his father. "How you reckon they come up with new horses and guns so quick?"

"Scavengers been gathering around here like buzzards for months, just waiting for the war to be over so they could pick over our bones. They got plenty of horses and guns."

Lev thought of John Henry Brown's warning. "Who are these scavengers?"

"People with money, mostly. They come from up North to buy our land and anything else worth having cheap. There's local Unionists, too. They been outcasts for the duration and now they're ready for revenge."

Hy thought his father was exaggerating. "That don't explain these old boys in our yard. Wade ain't rich and them others are near starved."

Lev agreed. "Besides, people around here ain't gonna sell out."

Sebastian was insulted by their doubts. "You boys been gone too long. I ain't got a single friend that ain't behind on a note or his taxes. These scavengers will buy those notes or take the land for back taxes."

Hy was still not convinced. "Them old boys that tried to rob us ain't even good thieves. They ain't got a pot to piss in or a window to throw it out of."

It was starting to sink in with Lev. "But they did come up with better horses and new guns."

Sebastian was emphatic. "Damn right. Them old boys and the likes of Wade Monroe are just tools. The scavengers are rounding 'em up just like they do horses. People with big heads like Wade, poor white folks, deserters, slaves turned loose without any way to feed themselves ... they do the dirty work. The real thieves are wearing clean suits in town somewhere. They're inside the banks and courthouses."

The confrontation ruined everyone's appetite except Hy's. He ate breakfast inside with Hester while Sebastian ate on the porch with Lev and McCulloch. Lev looked over his plate of eggs at his father. "Wade and that bunch had to ride right by where I left those horses. Guess you moved 'em."

Sebastian forked a slice of salt pork. "We took 'em down the creek and pulled a tree branch along our tracks. A good tracker could have found them by now, but those fools couldn't track a herd of cattle through snow. They'll be back with help, but they won't come until they find some good men. Figure that'll take a coupla days."

Lev looked at McCulloch and his father, feeling that they both expected a solution from him. "You know any buyers around here?"

"Too risky. Come right back on you if you sell 'em within a day's ride. But McCulloch and me know some buyers looking for horses west of here."

Lev did not like where this was going. "You and McCulloch want to take 'em out west, you're welcome to whatever they bring."

Sebastian stared at his son as if he was meeting him for the first time as a man. "Yours and Hy's horses. You took 'em. You sell 'em."

McCulloch poured a little coffee into his saucer. "I know the buyers and how to find 'em. Your daddy has got other business, but I'll go with you if you don't mind the company."

Sebastian nodded. "I'll cover your tracks and try to lead 'em another direction if they decide to follow."

After breakfast, Lev retrieved the guns he had wrapped in old bed sheets and buried under straw in the barn. McCulloch packed them on the pack mule that had appeared during the night. Rachael was irritated that he had to leave. She looked over his shoulder at Sebastian as Lev hugged her goodbye. "Don't see why you can't just give those horses and saddles up. You just been here two days. Don't seem worth it."

Sebastian stared at his boots while Lev answered. "Guess it don't make much sense, but these old boys are bad actors, Mama. Give that Rattle feller a gun, he's likely to turn around and shoot you with it. Besides, losing their horses and guns is likely the only punishment they're gonna get for stealing."

Hester hugged Lev warmly and whispered in his ear. "Thanks for not taking away my man again."

Hy seemed a little uncomfortable with the arrangement, but it was decided that he and Sebastian would stay and take care of the women. "Lev's right, Mama. Give them old boys what they want, they'll be back to take the clothes off our backs in no time."

Lev saw the pack mule as another mouth to feed, preferring to load supplies and the weapons on one of the other horses. McCulloch was set on taking the mule. "Never pack anything on an untested horse unless you can afford to lose it." McCulloch continued tying knots as Lev shrugged. Impatient to leave now that goodbyes had been said, he squirmed in his saddle as McCulloch made another circle around the mule before checking his own rigging. He led the mule away without speaking and Lev followed. He turned back only once. Boy was sitting beside Sebastian, looking up for permission to follow Lev. Hester and Hy were arm in arm on the porch. Hy stepped off the porch as if he expected Lev to beckon him to follow. The brothers had been inseparable for four years. Lev, feeling as if he was leaving part of himself behind, touched the brim of his hat and turned away.

Lev knew that he was a poor and impatient tracker, but was

surprised to have seen no sign of the horses until he heard them whinny to the mule and their horses. They were in a small meadow surrounded on four sides by timber and three sides by a sharp bend in Chambers Creek. Trees along the creek provided a natural fence, but the horses stayed because they had little reason to wander. A donkey was there to keep them at home if one decided to cross the creek or venture into the woods.

Lev now understood how his father seemed to magically appear whenever anyone approached Rachael's house. Camped in the creek bed, Sebastian and McCulloch could see anyone approaching the house from either direction without being seen. Even a campfire behind the bend would be hidden from passersby. Silt had deposited on one side of the creek, making tall dunes. Boot tracks and the remains of many campfires said that Sebastian and McCulloch had been there a long time. A dilapidated log shack stood just beyond the creek bend. Water stains breast high to a horse on the logs showed a history of rising waters.

"You and Papa been living here all this time?"

"One or both of us stays here most of the time. Anybody coming up that road to your mama's has got to pass through me or your daddy."

"We heard he had built himself a nice place up by Red Oak."

"True enough. Got land there and a little house over by Dresden, too. Both places gone to seed since you boys went off to war and couldn't look out for the womenfolk."

The mention of Dresden reminded him of Olivia. Why was her name never mentioned during the family gathering? Surely Minnie had kept up with her. He had tried to crowd her out of his thoughts during those last months of the war, and had almost succeeded. He had intended, only as a courtesy, to drop in on her at Dresden to see how she was faring. He owed her that.

Surprised that he had never run across it in his childhood wanderings, Lev stepped off his horse and peeked inside the small cabin. Bugs and other vermin scattered. The black dirt floor was hard and cracked, not trampled and swept smooth like dirt floors in an occupied house. A few weeds that did not require sunlight stubbornly stuck up through the cracks. He bumped his head coming out the low door when he heard approaching horses. He was embarrassed to have let his guard down.

McCulloch had already tied the horses in a string and was waiting outside. "They say that some early settler built this little cabin. Covered by vines and brush when we found it. Guess the builder didn't know about creeks getting out in East Texas. Slave family lived here later. It ain't fit to sleep in, but it keeps our saddles and gear dry and we take to it when the weather gets fierce enough. You about ready?"

McCulloch handed Lev a single lead rope that had been looped through two rope halters so that the horses could be led side-by-side. The old man had saddled all the horses except one. "One of them saddles was too worn out to bother with."

Lev figured it belonged to the reluctant older brother. "These buyers we're going to see—they know you?" McCulloch led his horses and the mule west, either not hearing or ignoring the question. Lev regretted asking it.

18

THEY HEADED ALMOST DUE WEST AND LEV'S somber mood lifted a little with each mile traveled. McCulloch was a man of few words, but seemed to know exactly where he was going. Lev was content to let him lead and was grateful for silence. The confrontation with horse thieves had unnerved him and left him feeling like the fighting would never stop. The home he had known was now a strange place, threatened by the same people he had been fighting for four years. Only now, he could not legally fight back.

Fighting in heavy timber and swampland had left him feeling trapped and confined, almost unable to breathe. Only three days into the ride, he felt the air grow lighter, giving him a sense of well-being. He had never been this far west. A man could see out here, and he could breathe. There was a lot to see, and he liked what he saw. Maybe John Henry Brown and Colonel Parsons should have considered the Texas frontier rather than Mexico.

They had not seen a person in three days when McCulloch stopped and motioned for Lev to bring his horses alongside. The old man looked up in the hills. Lev had been surprised by the hills, having always thought of the frontier as mostly flat plains. There was plenty of flat land, but there were also little canyons gouged out of the rocky plains by centuries of flowing water. The Indians were watering their horses downstream on the Leon River, directly in the path that McCulloch wanted to follow. Lev had no experience with Indians. He sat perfectly still, studying their horses and finding them wanting. They were not leading or driving a remuda and there were no women or children, so he assumed they were a hunting or scouting party. He could not see how they were armed and could make out little of their appearance from this distance. "Comanches?"

"Most likely. Could be Kiowa. Can't tell from here. Indians is Indians. They'll all kill you and steal everything you got."

Lev smiled. "My grandmother was a full-blood Choctaw."

McCulloch looked down at his saddle horn, his expression blank. "Maybe you could ride up there and tell them old boys that. Probably just let us pass. Indian courtesy and all."

Lev ignored the slight. "We close to any help?"

"I figure we're in Palo Pinto County by now. Sebastian calls it Eastland County, but it ain't got a courthouse yet."

"Papa buy any land out here?"

McCulloch seemed irritated by the question as he studied the Indians. "Did once. Sold it. These here Indians are a bad turn of events. Wouldn't worry much except we're leading vulture bait behind us. We must look like a treasure of easy pickin's."

Lev was unnerved. Used to fighting white men, he had never faced an adversary who did not understand the rules of warfare. He knew that the horses they were leading would not only attract the Indians, but would make it impossible to escape or fight effectively. "They're out of rifle range. You know this country well enough to find us a place to hole up and maybe pick 'em off if they come after us?"

McCulloch's hand trembled a little as he studied the Indians. "We're not too far from Blair's fort. I was planning on staying out of those cedar breaks and traveling along the river, but we'll be easy prey there, in plain sight. Only way now is to untie these horses and push them through the cedars just over that ridge."

Lev studied the rock hill on the other side of the Leon with cedar trees thicker then Louisiana swampland. The plan seemed foolhardy to Lev and his expression showed it. "You planning on us driving these horses up that hill, through them little trees?"

McCulloch pulled on his mustache. "Indians only like the breaks when they in there first. Seems the best way to get to the fort without riding straight at 'em."

Lev shook his head. "How you know some more ain't in the trees?"

"Hard to keep a horse from rubbing up against a tree or two and I ain't seen any limbs quiver. Course, they could be in there afoot." He looked at Lev and saw the skepticism. "There's more open country on the other side and a farmhouse between here and Blair's fort. Might work. If it don't, we'll just turn the horses loose and make a break to save ourselves. They ain't mounted well enough to catch us."

"Any soldiers or people at Blair's fort?"

"Not likely, but the horse buyers your Papa and me know frequent the place pretty regular. They use the area around the fort as a place to gather cattle." McCulloch inclined his head toward the Indians. "Most likely, them Indians are starving or close to it. They're interested in horsemeat more than us. Ever ride in cedar breaks?"

"Nope. Never seen any till now." The small cedar trees running up the slope of the hill looked harmless enough.

"That little hill is mostly slippery rock. See that big bald spot on top? Fix on that before we head out. You won't be able to see a damn thing once we ride in. Cedar trees are just tall enough to keep you blind." McCulloch stepped down and started tying stirrups to saddle horns. "Don't leave anything hanging loose that a cedar limb can get between. It will either tear it up or drag your horse down."

They tied off all the stirrups, tightened flank girths and

remounted. "It's tight in there. That horse of yours afraid of having to rub up against trees?"

Lev shook his head. "Be better for me and Butter to lead the way and you push from behind." McCulloch hesitated, but turned the horses loose. Butter hit the cedars like a buffalo bull, creating a din of cracking and popping. Lev felt his shirtsleeves being torn and was grateful for the loan of his father's leggings as the cedar limbs scratched along both legs. He could almost see over the tops of the cedars, but not quite—just enough to make a man feel trapped and blind. Butter never hesitated. Lev looked behind to see if McCulloch and the horses were following, but could see only the mule, ears backed and bucking as his load dragged across cedar limbs. Lev had the same feeling he had experienced in the swamps of Louisiana. Butter broke small limbs like they were kindling, leaving a trail for the horses being pushed by McCulloch from behind. As they entered an area of solid rock near the top, the horse clawed for traction, causing sparks to fly from her shoes. She led the horses to the bald knoll and over it.

When Lev saw a clearing on the other side, he pushed forward with his stirrups, signaling Butter to stop, but felt surprising reluctance, as the mare seemed ready for an all out run. Lev let her run when he saw two small buildings on the open prairie. They headed for them at full speed. He turned to see the mule, McCulloch and the four horses close behind. No sign of Indians. McCulloch waved him on. They drove past the abandoned house and barn at full speed, headed for Blair's Fort.

The wind was brisk and felt good on Lev's face. It felt good just to see. He had never really let Butter run all out for a distance. The little mare took to running just as she took to cedar breaks and bumping. Lev felt the brim of his hat flopping in the wind as he turned to check for pursuers. They were not being followed, but he let Butter keep up the pace until they passed through the open gate at the fort. McCulloch pushed the mule and other horses in behind him.

They dismounted, closed the gate, and checked the horses for injury. There was some hide missing, but nothing that would not heal in a few days. Lev ran his hand over Butter, then over the saddle and equipment. A fifteen-minute run through the cedars had put two years of normal wear and tear on his saddle and chaps. They checked the fence's perimeter before unsaddling and turning the horses loose. Twelve log cabins had been built in the square. The remains of scattered campfires showed that the fort had been occupied recently.

McCulloch kicked some coals. "Used to be eight families here. They stayed together as protection from the Indians."

"Why'd they leave?"

"War being lost, hard times, who knows? Military forts will probably be re-occupied soon. Maybe they didn't feel the need for it anymore."

"I don't see no horse buyers."

"They're never gone from here more than a couple of days. They'll be back."

Dried beef in their stomachs, McCulloch threw his bedroll on a small cedar bed he found in one of the cabins and Lev camped close to a gun hole in the fort wall. He was up and down all night, peeking through, expecting Indians to scale the fence at any time. At dawn, they built a fire for heating canned tomatoes and coffee, wishing for eggs and ham. Lev ventured outside long enough to kill a rabbit. He was growing impatient to see the buyers and wanted to take the horses on to Palo Pinto. McCulloch was roasting the rabbit over an open fire when they heard horses approaching from the west just before sunset.

Lev climbed to a gun turret and watched them. "You able to recognize these cattle buyers Papa talks about?"

McCulloch turned the rabbit on the wooden spit he had

carved. "Should be a short fella setting his horse good. Gets way up in his hat."

The lead rider fit McCulloch's description including a hat that seemed to engulf his whole head. Lev kept watching until the man's jug ears were discernible. The two men following wore boots that reached their knees, hats big as sombreros, and batwing chaps of thick cowhide. The men looked spent and weary, but kept a steady pace as they bent their heads against the strong wind. Their saddles looked light and were without adornments other than big horns for holding roped cattle. One carried a long riata, and the other a long grass rope. The jug-eared leader had a short grass rope thrown over his saddle horn. Lev admired the way they traveled, the way they looked, as he opened the gate and watched them enter the fort.

The leader barely acknowledged Lev and McCulloch as he headed straight for the horses. When he had rubbed his hand over the skinned places and picked up their hooves, he motioned to his two men. They took saddles and blankets from rails where McCulloch and Lev had placed them to dry and began saddling the horses. "You're missing a saddle. Saddles are harder to come by than horses these days."

McCulloch explained. "Hap, one saddle just wasn't worth the trip."

"I see the others took a whipping coming through the breaks."

"Couldn't be avoided. Either had to push 'em through hard or give 'em to the heatherns."

Hap finally turned toward Lev and extended his hand. "Hap Hopkins. You must be Sebastian Rivers' boy."

Lev shook the man's small, callused, stubby-fingered hand. "Yes, sir. Lev Rivers."

Hap examined Lev from boots to hat. "You handle a horse as good as your daddy?"

"Not yet."

Hap laughed. "We're getting up a herd to take down to Louisiana. I hear you know that country."

Lev smiled. "Know more about it than I care to. I was lost most of the time I was there. Had to have a compass to find my way back to Texas."

"We just about got enough cattle to drive to New Orleans. Most of the smart cattlemen seem to be heading north and west with their herds, so we're going south and east."

"Who's gonna buy 'em down there? Thought the Yankees were the only ones with money."

"There'll be Yankee soldiers there, all right, with Union money. Won't bring as much as up north, but we won't lose as many on the trip. Won't need as many men." Hap pulled a spectacle case out of a shirt pocket and opened it. "Course, I never been accused of being smart. It's rough work. Wild cows—wild country. Need men who can handle horses and cattle on the plains and in heavy timber. Your daddy seems to think you can."

"You offering me a job?"

"Pays thirty dollars a month and found. You bring along that little mare, there'll be a bonus of another twenty when we deliver the cattle. You can have yourself a high time in New Orleans with that much money."

Lev calculated the possible total pay in his mind and wondered if his father had set him up for this job. "Mister Hopkins, I been home a total of less than a week in more than four years. I'd have to think on it." He hated the way his words came out.

"Take all the time you need. We'll be leaving at first light." Hap sat the spectacles on his nose and slipped the earpieces over his ears. "Now, about these horses—not up to Sebastian's standards."

They haggled a little as Hap began listing the shortcomings of the small remuda as the two cowboys put them through their paces. To salvage his father's reputation, Lev explained how they had come by the horses. Hap made an offer of a hundred dollars for the horses, tack and guns. Lev winced. An hour later they settled on one-fifty for the horses and tack with Lev keeping the guns.

Lev settled into his bedroll early and thought about Louisiana swamps, Mary Ann, Hy and Hester, his mother, scavengers in East Texas, and Olivia. He wondered if Sebastian had a reason for sending him off on a long cattle drive. Hap Hopkins and his two cowboys impressed him. They lived the type of life he wanted to live. They were good at what they did. He loved the country he had passed through to get here—except for the cedar breaks. He loved being able to see the horizon and to breathe lighter air. The sky was bigger and he heard it got even bigger in the Panhandle to the north. If the herd had been heading north, he would have gone. But it wasn't. And he hated low country and swamps.

19

HE WATCHED THEM LEAVE IN THE EARLY
DAWN. Hap and his men were well- provisioned and shared
bacon, sourdough bread and beans with Lev and McCulloch. Lev
felt like a small boy who had shirked a task his father had asked
him to perform. As he checked the guns packed on the mule, he
understood why McCulloch had insisted on bringing it. When he
asked McCulloch to confirm his decision about not joining the drive,
the old man only said that the trip would be rough and dangerous.
"Roping cattle in cedar breaks and driving them into low country is
fraught with inconveniences that are more than some men could
bear." The words made Lev feel worse as they headed toward
home.

McCulloch took a different trail when they reached the Leon.
Lev assumed he was avoiding the Indians and the cedar breaks and
said nothing. When he had recognized nothing by late afternoon,
he screwed up the courage to ask McCulloch about their route.

McCulloch held up his horse. His hand was steady as he
pointed in a direction that seemed northwest to Lev. "I know a good
place to camp tonight. Safer than out in the open."

Lev followed McCulloch across flat prairie most of the day.
In late afternoon, the land's monotony changed abruptly as they
entered cedar breaks. Lev could see only a few feet in any direction
and was surprised, even irritated, to find himself in a deep ravine

with high cliffs on either side. He had not seen hills on the horizon, so it seemed as if they had stepped on Earth's tongue, been swallowed, and now were traveling down its throat. A deep, winding creek ran beside them and McCulloch seemed to be following its path. The hillsides were almost solid with cedars, interrupted only with sparse mesquites that seemed to grow out of rock. The area around the creek bed had sprouted a few scrub oaks and cacti. There were signs of cattle or buffalo. Lev was not sure which.

As they followed the winding creek, Lev noticed tree trunks, buried cedar posts, and rocks that had been painted red and blue. He wanted to ask McCulloch about them, but the old man rode several yards ahead and stayed out of earshot. Just keeping him in sight was becoming more difficult as the breaks thickened. Lev could hear McCulloch's horse, but the old man appeared and disappeared like an apparition. The close quarters worked on Lev. He could only see up and the hills seemed to be turning into mountains. Air seemed inadequate and heat was starting to get to him when he rounded a bend and heard a gust of wind shaking the leaves as it traveled down the creek.

A welcome breeze struck him as a trail became visible around the curve and buildings came into view—a small unfinished cabin, a barn with a corral. A little washout that held creek water seemed unnatural, man-made to Lev. As they rode across a shallow portion of the creek, a dugout against one rocky hill proclaimed itself as the original shelter for settlers who might have lived there once. Lev looked around for people, but the signs were of abandonment, not recent use. McCulloch stopped in the open area. Lev eased closer, unsure if the old man was hard-of-hearing or just heard what he chose to. "This place belong to somebody you know?"

"Belongs to your daddy."

"Thought you said he sold his land out here."

"Sold the land he bought. This was his homestead. Expect nobody's noticed he's been gone awhile." He paused to study Lev's expression. "Sebastian wanted me to show you this place if you turned down Hap's offer to drive cows. This is where he wants to bring your mama. Left things unfinished here when you boys went off to war so he could go back and look out for her and your sisters."

They unsaddled and fed their horses. Lev noted signs of his father's imprint on the place as he gathered firewood and knew that he should have recognized it as Sebastian's without asking. The little canyon was shaped like God's own pine box coffin with the creek as a rope handle on each end. Bellies full from Hap's generosity and stretched on their bedrolls by the fire, Lev examined the hills and cliffs that surrounded them. They made for a feeling of being protected, but Lev felt watched, too. "Do you call them mountains? Highest I ever saw."

McCulloch rolled a cigarette and lighted it before answering. "You can call them anything you like. Guess they mountains in Texas, but puny compared to the Rockies. We're more below the earth than they are above it."

"How deep or how high?"

"Probably no more than two, three hundred feet from here to the highest points."

"Papa has a reason for most things he does. Expect he picked this place because it's out of sight. Any other way in or out except the way we came?"

McCulloch pointed toward the southwest corner of the canyon. He waited for Lev to squint and study the rocky hills. The gap was almost invisible unless you knew it was there. "There's lots of ways to approach the place, but that's the only one to come up easy and horseback. Only place to drive cattle or horses in or out is the way we came."

"What about the painted trees I saw coming in? Trail markers?"

McCulloch shook his head. "Indians. That's why they call that creek Palo Pinto. Spanish for painted post, I heard."

"Always wondered how Indians got paint."

McCulloch picked up a handful of dirt. "They make up a concoction of this red clay, leaves, bird shit, throw in a little charcoal. Boil it all up with some type of dead animal for the fat. Wild plums for red, berries for blue."

Lev studied the God-sized four-sided deep oven they were in. He had trouble locating the path they had followed. He studied the bald, steep bluffs on the southwest and wondered how a man could approach or leave on horseback. Rocks, cactus, hills, cedars, rattlers. Bleached driftwood revealed that the creek had been out of its banks. Its only value seemed to be as a place to hide. "How would a man make a living here?"

"Only way your papa knows. Cattle and horses. There's pasture outside this little canyon. Not too good, but good enough. A bite of grass here is worth ten times as much as a bite back home. Stray cattle left over from the war running all over these hills and plains." He took a stick and stirred the fire. "Course, your daddy favors horses. He built that corral and barn before the dugout."

In spite of himself, Lev began to like the place. The air was still light and he could imagine water running in the creek. "What does a man do for water in a drought like this?"

"Me and your papa used mules and a couple of slaves to build that little dam and waterway to capture overrun from the creek. When we first saw it, the creek was full and running blue. Pretty."

"Good idea, but it won't feed many cattle for long."

"The Brazos ain't so far away that cows can't reach it. And we dug a gyp water well just behind that cabin. Bad to the taste, but it will keep a man from dying of thirst."

"I been looking up at the hills. A man could get within two hundred yards of us and not be seen."

McCulloch stretched out on his bedroll to indicate his impatience with the questions. "I expect so. But if he sticks up his head or gets closer, you can kill him."

Stretched out on his bedroll with his saddle for a pillow, Lev listened to McCulloch softly snore. He watched the break in the hills and tried to hear water running until he fell asleep.

20

LEV FELT LIKE AN ALMOST UNWELCOME appendage when they rode back into Rachael's yard a few days later. It was early afternoon, and he was surprised when Sebastian did not appear to ask about the horse sale. There was no sign of Boy, either. McCulloch explained that Sebastian was usually gone during daylight and returned at night. Lev was dejected when Rachael told him that Hy and Hester were also gone. Resourceful Hester had found a widow just outside of Dresden whose husband had not returned from the war. There was a small run-down cabin on the edge of the place where she and her husband had lived before building a newer house. She had no objection to Hy pasturing a few horses on the two-hundred-acre place, as long as he tended to her own stock and her corn and cotton crops. Lev's loneliness compounded his despair.

Refusing to come inside, McCulloch sat on a stump in the yard to consume the biscuits cold from breakfast and beans cold from dinner that Rachael brought from the house on tin plates. Lev squatted by the stump and spooned his beans. McCulloch left before Lev was finished, anxious to ride to Sebastian's camp. In late afternoon, Lev built a fire outside and heated water for a bath. Minnie and Rachael brought him lye soap, towels, quilts and dry clothes scavenged from days before the war. Heating the water over an open flame reminded him of how Olivia had looked standing in firelight, hair still wet, washing his clothes.

He was sitting on a porch step, shirtless with a towel draped carelessly across his shoulders when he felt a wet nose against his hand. Boy had appeared almost soundlessly. Lev looked up to see the old man approaching. He had wanted more time to think before facing his father. He was buttoning the last button on an old shirt that seemed a little snug when Sebastian dismounted. "Hear you made a fair trade on them sorry horses."

"I reckon. Kinda got rusty on what horses are worth."

"Them was a good sale at any price. Likely to get you hung here if you kept 'em."

"Things that bad?"

"Worse. I rode some while you were gone, picking up things here and there. Feller in Dallas told me there's more than thirty thousand Yankee soldiers in Texas already. More on the way."

"Damn." Lev tucked in his shirt. "Why?"

"To keep us in our place. Even that loud-mouthed, prissy-assed Custer is down in Austin, saying they gonna stay till they're sure we're good and whipped. We're under something called Presidential Reconstruction. Andrew Johnson already appointed himself a Texas governor. We don't get no say in it."

"Who's the governor?"

"Andrew Hamilton—a damned Unionist." Sebastian fished in his pocket and read from a crumpled sheet of paper. "They've set up something called the Bureau of Refugees, Freedmen, and Abandoned Lands."

"What's that supposed to do?"

"Sounds like it's to take over our land and make sure we treat these freed slaves right. Hell, the damn slaves don't know come here from sic 'em about making a living or surviving on their own." Sebastian sat on the porch step and looked at his son as if expecting some sort of verbal solution. He did not get one. "Bad enough we got to worry about Texas slaves, but they're coming in by the droves from the states east of here."

The peaceful feeling that came over Lev while he was bathing under the stars left him, replaced with the futility of years of fighting. Sebastian was breathing hard and Lev noticed the smell of whiskey. His father was getting old. Sebastian seemed to notice sympathy in Lev's look. He could not abide sympathy. "Hell, boy. They're saying you boys can't even vote unless you take some kind of damned oath of loyalty to Yankees. If you take the oath, you'll have to lie ... and this a free country."

Sebastian stood and shook himself as if he had been wallowing in dirt—as if he wanted to rid himself of the impending calamity that was rolling toward him like a stampede. "You take to that country out there?"

Lev smiled. "I did. Man can see where he's going."

"I like it, too." Sebastian pulled at the top of an ear—something he did when broaching a subject not comfortable to him. "You think you could talk your mama into moving out there?"

"Why would she want to do that?"

Sebastian remounted. "We all gonna have to either move or fight. If we fight, we'll lose ... and they'll hang us." He turned and rode back toward his camp.

Lev watched the old man until he disappeared into the trees. He was skeptical of what he had said. It could not be that bad. Sure, there would be tension, but if they abided by the law and stayed out of sight as much as possible, they could survive here. He only wanted isolation, anyway. He would stay out of town and out of their way.

He wrapped the guns in oilcloth, hid them under piles of straw in the barn and bedded down beside them. It was warm in the barn, so he kept the door open to let in the breeze and to make him feel safer. He was surprised to see Boy lying just outside the open barn door. Sebastian must have given him permission to stay. He invited him in to sleep on the hay.

Lev laid back on the soft soogan and a feather pillow that Minnie had brought him from the house. He could see just enough sky through the open door and cracks in the barn roof and could hear whippoorwills calling. Papa Jim and Mama Armelia Rivers had believed that birds talked to people ... if people listened. As a boy, he loved crows and imagined that he could hear messages in their caws. Lev tried to decipher a message from the whippoorwills as he drifted off.

He was up at first light and gone before breakfast. The bath and his first good night's sleep in days had cleared his head, or maybe the birds had really talked to him. He had a plan.

As he drew close to Dresden, his determination faltered. He saw the neatly painted sign before he was ready. Dentist/ Barber/Apothecary hung over a barber pole and two doors. The bullet moved a little as he peeked into the window. The room was different than he remembered. A tall-backed rocking chair sat in front of a large mirror, its rockers nailed to the floor, a chair-cloth draped across its back. Lev ran his gaze over the counter under the mirror, touching with his sight the large shaving mug, straight razors, and the hanging razor strop. The door to the apothecary was closed, and the barber/dentist shop door was held open by a small buggy tether. The smell of shaving soap, talcum and lilac water drifted through the cracked door. He motioned for Boy to lie down just between the doors. The hinges creaked as Lev pushed it back. The sound brought her through the apothecary door.

Lev removed his hat and held it against his chest as if for protection. She smiled, but he thought he saw apprehension in her expression. They stood in silence for long seconds until they were both uncomfortable. She was in a dress that dusted the wood floor with each step, unruly hair pulled back, hands clasped in front. "I heard you were back."

"Word gets around quick, I guess."

"Not so quick. I hear you've been home for weeks."

"Not exactly." Lev pointed four fingers in a vague westerly direction. "Here one day, gone the next ...out west delivering some ... goods to some people."

"I see. Well, it's good to see you."

"Good to see you, too." He waved his arms expansively around the shop and toward the apothecary door. "Looks like you've got everything here a man could need."

Her fixed smiled widened a little. "The apothecary stuff belongs to Doc Robinson. He says the barbershop and dentist work is all mine to keep."

"You get to do any doctoring?"

"A little, but mostly only when he needs another pair of hands or when he's away." She absently picked up the chair-cloth to refold it and he took it as an invitation. He hung his hat on a corner hall tree and started for the chair.

She suppressed a grin as he turned his back to sit down. "You figure you're gonna need that gun?"

He looked at her, unbuckled the gunbelt, and hung it just beneath his hat before returning to the chair. He sensed her closeness as she ran her hand along the back of the chair. "Shave and haircut? You could use both."

Lev had deigned not to shave two weeks of beard that morning without admitting to himself why. Without waiting for an answer, she popped the chair-cloth and let it drift easily across him. She pinned it around his neck and touched his bearded cheek and ran her fingers through his long hair. He was glad that he had washed it only last night. The light touch of her fingers on his forehead reminded him of the first time she had dressed and bandaged his wound. He closed his eyes and was surprised as she draped a warm, wet cloth across his face. "I usually do it the other way around, but I think a shave first this time." He had had a real barbershop shave once before, but there had been no warm water. He felt the hair on his arms stand up as the ivory-handled brush clinked against the shaving mug as she stroked the bristles against the cake of soap inside.

He kept his eyes closed when she removed the wet cloth, allowing himself to imagine the expression on her face, the sun filtering through the front windows to rest on the back of her neck as she touched the bristles to his face. The sunlight allowed him to see her form, even tiny strands of unruly hair, like particles of dust, on the back of her neck. He drifted, allowing each stroke of the sharp razor to wash over him like waves of serenity. The scraping sounds against his beard sounded like the smooth stroke of a bow across fiddle strings. She wiped the remaining soap from his face and ran a comb through his wet mustache, tweaking the ends with fingers lightly coated with wax. Olivia's movements seemed calculated and slow, but the shave was over much too soon.

He opened his eyes briefly as she ran a wet comb through his hair. She clicked the scissors above his head and smiled at him before cutting the first strands and letting them fall to the floor. He sensed she was done when she put both hands just above his ears and positioned his head for an approving look in the mirror. He was staring at the reflected image of the fingers, not his hair, when he saw a familiar form limp by on the street outside. Boy growled and yelped once.

21

OLIVIA'S FINGERS GREW COLD AND TENSE AS she dropped them to her sides. Lev opened his eyes wider, as if awakening from a pleasant dream and walking into a nightmare. The air in the room changed, an odor of sulfur overpowering the clean smell of barbering. The hairless mongrel pushed a snout against the door and slithered into the room. Filson leaned against the doorframe. Lev was shocked to see the bartender from Rusk. Filson had long since found seclusion in the recesses of his memory. He seemed like an evil specter arisen from the death of a previous life.

Lev gripped both chair arms as the chair-cloth draped over him turned from a comforter to a prison. Filson sauntered away from the barbershop door, one foot showing a slight limp, and leaned against the door to the apothecary. "Mister Rivers, I believe."

Lev looked down and felt a small twinge of pleasure as he imagined missing toes in the booted foot. Lev glanced at Olivia's frozen face and returned Filson's glare without reply.

Filson eased a little closer to Olivia as he spoke to Lev. "Tonsorial work or dentistry today? Our lovely Olivia does either with deft hands, you know. I always enjoyed her shaves."

Lev felt a coldness replace the warm, almost floating cloud of serenity as he moved his left hand outside the sheet and let it rest on the chair arm. Under the chair-cloth, his right automatically reached across his waist to where his pistol should have been. He did not look at the Colt and holster that Olivia had suggested he hang on the hall tree.

Lev cringed and gritted his teeth as the dog's nose touched the back of his hand. The creature showed his teeth and seemed to be taunting him. Filson moved between Lev and the mirror. "Get back, Slick. As I recall, Mister Rivers don't cotton to dogs being inside."

Lev wondered what was keeping Boy quiet as the big dog moved closer to his master. His skin crawled as Filson reached down to stroke Slick. "Been looking for you and your brother for quite a while. Figured you'd turn up to sniff around Olivia sooner or later." He was wearing a light wool coat, and Lev figured he had to be sweating. He saw the handle of a belly gun lurking behind the coat.

"Well, you found me. What is it you want?" He moved his right hand slightly under the sheet, hoping Filson would think he was touching the butt of a pistol.

Lev watched Filson's reflection as he moved behind him and touched the gunbelt on the hall tree. "I got papers being drawn up for your arrest. Robbing and shooting a man's against the law." He took a step closer to the chair as his voice lost all pretense of politeness. "Confederate soldiers be damned now. Y'all gonna pay for what you did to me."

Lev's eyes narrowed and hardened as he looked at Olivia. She seemed transfixed, focused on something on the street outside—her expression blank. Lev turned his head toward Filson and raised his left hand toward him. "I'll see them papers."

"Told you they're being drawn up. No hurry."

Lev saw just enough of the hat brim at the edge of the apothecary door to recognize it. He took a deep breath. "The hell you say. You ain't much in Rusk and you're even less around here."

Filson smiled. "You'll find out better soon enough."

Lev looked toward the apothecary door. "You'll remember my brother, Hy."

Hy stepped into the shop and tossed a handgun to Lev just as Filson made a siccing motion with his hand that sent Slick snarling toward Lev. Lev threw the chair-cloth over the dog and caught the gun just in time to bring the barrel down on the big dog's skull. The dog yelped and fell back, fighting the cloth. Lev hit him again, this time with the gun handle. He stood and took a deep breath, aiming the cocked gun at the dog. A whimper, and it lay still. "Like hitting a damned anvil."

Hy's pistol barrel found a familiar home against Filson's forehead in three quick steps. He removed Filson's belly gun. "Seems like we been here once before. Shoulda kilt you back then, you son-of-a-bitch." Filson stared at the now still form of Slick under the chair-cloth.

Olivia came out of her trance, put her hand over her mouth and ran through the apothecary door. Lev took his gunbelt from the hall tree and buckled it on before putting his nose close to Filson's. "Sit down and take off your boots."

Filson seemed only slightly perturbed. "What the hell for?"

Hy slapped the back of Filson's head hard. "Damned if you ain't a slow learnin' bastard. That goddam surly mouth is likely to get you killed. Now do as my brother says."

Filson sat in the barber chair and removed his boots.

Lev took the boots and tossed them toward the door. "Now the socks."

Filson looked at each brother as he began to understand. He removed the sock from his good foot and hesitated as he pulled the other one. Lev and Hy stared at the missing middle toes and then at each other. Lev pointed his pistol at the foot. "Just wanted to be sure we killin' the right man." He turned toward Hy. "What are we gonna do with him?"

Hy looked at the straight razor. "Could just slit his damn

throat. Can't chance a gunshot."

Lev turned toward Olivia, standing in the doorway to the apothecary. "You got any ether in there?"

She returned in seconds with a bottle. Lev held the face cloth and turned his head as she poured the small bottle's contents onto the rag. Filson began to squirm. "I ain't breathin' that shit."

He stopped short as Hy held the razor to his throat. "Breathe or bleed. Don't make a tinker's damn difference to me."

They held the cloth over his nose until Filson's head went slack. Hy helped Lev throw Filson's big frame over his shoulder before wrapping the chair cloth around the dog and throwing it over his shoulder. "Damned if this stinking son-of-a-bitch is not heavier than Filson." They hauled them out the back door, around a horse corral and down to the creek, winding their way long the creek bed until they were behind the livery stable. They dumped Filson and his dog in some tall weeds. Hy shook out the chair-cloth and clucked at the bloodstains. He started to walk away, but stopped when Lev did not budge.

Lev stared at Filson's inert frame. "I was wrong."

"How so?"

"Should have let you kill him back in Rusk. We mighta got away with it with the war on."

"It ain't too late."

"Yes, it is. Even if I could shoot a man asleep, they'd hang us for sure."

Hy nodded. "Well, at least you killed that damn dog."

"That wasn't no dog. What I did is more akin to killing a snake."

Hy walked back toward the barbershop.

Lev took one last look before following. "How come you to be here? Couldn't have come at a better time, but I was surprised to see you."

"Been riding the widder-woman's horses in between looking

out for her farm crops. Broke two since you been gone. I brought 'em into town for shoes. Me and Captain Rutherford watched you ride into town. We was having a laugh at your expense when ..."

"What was you laughing at?"

"Well, I figured where you was heading when you rode in. We could see that haircut and shave through the window. Well, anyway, we stopped laughing when Filson walks up with that damn dog. I started over soon as the son-of-a-bitch smacked Boy over the head."

Lev jaw clenched. "He kill my dog?"

"I expect. He wasn't moving when I walked through that apothecary door."

Olivia was leaning over Boy when they returned. She had put one of her concocted salves on the small slit in his scalp and he was looking at her with gratitude. Lev stoked the dog's hip. "Looks like he may think more of you than he does me." They focused on the dog as Hy slipped out the door. Olivia's eyes were red. The dam had burst. Lev reluctantly pushed the chair-cloth toward her, but she recoiled.

"Burn it."

Lev looked around the room as if he might find a stove going on the warm day. His need to be rid of the bloody cloth became urgent. He walked outside, laid it on the wooden sidewalk and returned for Boy. "He able to travel, you think?"

"Let him ride with you till he's ready to walk. He'll ask to get down when he is."

Lev put Boy under his arm and looked at Olivia. "Forgot to pay you for the haircut and shave."

She flinched. "It's on the house."

"How about for the cloth?"

She put both hands on the counter and leaned into them. "Stop talking about money."

Lev was about to ask the fee for doctoring Boy, but thought

better of it. "Much obliged for taking care of the dog."

She handed him a small tin of ointment. "Put this on till it scabs over. Watch him for a few hours. He was pretty addled."

Lev again reached for coins, but his hand stuck in his pocket. He pointed four fingers in the direction of where they had deposited Slick and Filson. "We didn't kill him."

"Didn't figure you did."

"You think he's gonna blame you for what happened?"

"Why would he?"

Lev's expression showed frustration and confusion. "You welcome to stay at our place for a while ... or I could find Doc Robinson and see about somebody looking out for you."

"I've been alone for quite some time, Lev. I can still manage."

"I know, but has Filson been around?"

She looked deep into his eyes for what seemed a long time. "That's what you really want to know, isn't it?"

"I just hate to leave you here. Not knowing ... and all."

"Like I told you when you last rode off from this place, Lev. You will never know for sure."

22

LEV PICKED UP FILSON'S BOOTS AND SOCKS AS if they were contaminated, dropped them on the drop cloth and tied a knot in the ends. He draped the bundle across Butter's hips, careful not to get blood on his saddle. He sat Boy on the saddle and led the horse across the street to Captain Rutherford's blacksmith shop. Rutherford looked up from his forge as Lev took the bundle from Butter's hips. Hy was squatting on one knee nearby, holding the leads to two freshly shod horses. Boy put two front paws in Butter's mane and kept his seat in the saddle as if he had been born to ride. His ears began to perk again. Lev extended the bloody chair-cloth toward the blacksmith. "You got a place to burn this thing?"

Rutherford dropped it into a burn barrel. "Good riddance. Damn beast sullied up the air around here long enough."

Hy rose from his squat as Lev turned toward Butter. "Hold up. You're going the wrong way, but I'll ride aways with you. Pick up my horses on the way back."

Boy reluctantly gave up his seat as Lev swung a leg over his saddle and placed him across the pommel. Hy sniffed the air as he mounted the dun. "What's that sweet smell?"

Lev was confused for a few seconds before he realized the smell was coming from him. "Barbershop."

They were passing the last building in Dresden when a stringy-haired woman stepped into their path. She was grayer and her hair was thinner, but Lev recognized her from The Good Samaritan. "My name is Lydia ... Filson. You kill him?" Hope was in her voice. When Lev shook his head, her face screwed up like she might cry. "You at least kill the damn dog?"

She sighed with relief when Lev nodded. "He ain't what he seems, you know."

"How do you mean?" Hy asked.

"He's a slick talker ... especially with women."

"He ain't talking too sweet right now."

"He's got these soldiers around here thinking he's some kind of Yankee spy hero. He ain't nothing but a deserter ... from both sides." The brothers looked skeptical as Lydia drew closer to Butter. The mare's eyes widened. "He killed a man up along the Red River. Joined the Confederates so he could hide from the law. Then killed a man in Arkansas after he deserted. Joined the Yankees to hide again. Volunteered to spy for the North, came back to Texas and never left."

Lev was listening with great interest, but Hy chuckled. "Filson sure nuff gets around, don't he? How's a man wear so many stripes?"

Lydia's tone was derisive. "His name ain't Filson. It's Cullen Montgomery."

Hy raised his eyebrows. "That's a right smart of joining and deserting for one man. You still living with him?"

"No. He don't even know I'm around."

This hit a nerve with Lev. He leaned down to look directly into her eyes. "So why are you around? From what we saw back in Rusk, looks like you'd want to get away from him."

"I followed him here, hoping you boys would kill him. I want to spit on his grave so I can rest again." She waited, but the brothers did not respond. "He's got a powerful hate for the two of you."

Lev cradled Boy down in the crook of his arm until the dog's paws touched the ground, then pulled himself upright in the saddle. "We never took nothing more than two toes from the man when he tried to cheat us. Why does he hate us so much?"

"You still don't get it. It ain't the toes. It's the woman. You took his woman off. He never gives up on a woman. Gets real attached to things ... especially things he can't have."

Hy shook his head. "Still don't make no sense."

She stared at her almost-worn-out black lace-up high-tops. "I know what I'm saying. That man he killed in Arkansas was my daddy."

Hy stood in his stirrups and made a circle with his finger. "You run off with a man what killed your daddy?"

"I was already married to him." She read the look of disgust on their faces. "I wanted him. I was young, and, like I said, he was good-looking and a smooth talker."

Lev pointed a thumb back toward town. "Where's he staying?"

She pointed in the general direction of his thumb. "He ain't staying with her, if that's what you mean. Got a little cabin in the timber about a mile outside of town. You can't miss it."

Lev looked toward the spot where they had dropped Filson. "Wasn't planning on visiting."

"He killed her daddy, too, you know."

"Olivia's daddy? The doctor? How?"

"Poisoned him gradually. The old man was a drunk. Took a drop of strychnine with his whiskey. Didn't notice when Filson doubled the dose."

"A doctor took rat poison on purpose?"

Her face darkened a shade. "Thought it helped him with womenfolk. If you know what I mean."

"Why did Filson want to kill him?"

"Old Doc didn't mind drinking with Filson, but he knew what he was. Would never have stood for Olivia having anything to do with him. Filson wanted Olivia and he always gets what he wants."

"When it comes to women, seems like he does." Lev squeezed Butter and rode past her.

She called after them, desperation in her voice. "You'll have to kill him, you know. He won't stop at nothing till he kills you or sees you hanged." She began to trot with Boy alongside the horses. "You gonna need me to tell my story when you kill him. Otherwise, they liable to hang you for it."

Hy held up the dun and turned toward her. "Supposing we do, where can we find you?"

"I got a job in the courthouse in Dallas."

"Doing what?"

"Cleaning up."

23

IT WAS ALMOST A MONTH BEFORE THEY CAME. Lev had settled into the slave quarters cabin. He rebuilt the old corral and made himself a pen without corners. He broke a few horses for Sebastian, took the money and invested it into a couple of green ones for himself. He was working one in the pen when they arrived. They rode up in the front yard from the east. Lev was afoot, his hand holding only a rope. He shamed himself as he thought of the guns he had left in the cabin. Rattle and Wade Monroe seemed relaxed and unthreatening. When Filson rode in from the south, Lev knew why. Now it was three against one.

Lev looked around for a weapon, but saw the uselessness of it as a fourth rider rode in from the north, leading Hy's dun. Hy's hands were tied to the saddle horn. A sickening, heavy feeling filled Lev when he recognized Anderson Bonner. A tin badge sagged from Bonner's black muslin shirt as he put a pistol barrel to Hy's temple. Hy's eyes were cold and narrow, but sent no message. Filson opened two buttons on his shirt and withdrew folded papers. "You wanted papers, Rivers. Now I got 'em. You and your brother are under arrest for murder and robbery. Saddle one of them nags."

Lev studied his options and found them wanting. "Have to walk over to the other pen to get my riding horse." Rattle kept his gun trained on him as he saddled and bridled Butter, looking for an excuse to take revenge. Butter pinned her ears at the sight of Rattle's blue uniform and Lev had to calm her. Rachael stood on the porch, helpless, as they rode away. She vowed to never let Boy leave with Sebastian again. The dog would have warned them in time.

Hy and Lev remained wordless all the way to the county seat. Outside the courthouse in Corsicana, their hands were untied and they were shoved through the front door to a small office. With barely room to stand, the room grew hot quickly, and Lev began to sweat. A young Yankee lieutenant walked into the room followed by a man about Sebastian's age. They stopped behind a small table and the men shuffled to face them.

The soldier sat and leaned back in the chair. The old man stood beside him and looked at the men before him, tugging his chest-length gray beard. His eyes lighted with recognition as he saw Lev and Hy, but he said nothing. The brothers followed his lead.

Wordlessly, the lieutenant reached out a hand toward Filson. Filson handed him the warrant and began describing the charges. The lieutenant held up his hand to stop him. "I can read."

He perused the papers for several minutes before looking at Lev and Hy. "I understand you were Confederate soldiers. Which outfit?"

Lev took the question. "Nineteenth Texas Cavalry. Colonel Parson's brigade."

The soldier frowned. "Horse soldiers. I recall some stories about Parsons' men and their horsemanship."

Hy sensed an opportunity. "What outfit you with?"

The lieutenant seemed impatient with the question. "I'm from Ohio." He turned to Filson. "You say these men robbed you at gunpoint and tried to kill you?"

"That's right. Stole a horse from a man named Luther Hathaway and likely killed him, too."

Hy started to speak, but the old man's eyes told him to keep shut and let the soldier continue. "When and where?

"In Rusk, about a year or so ago."

"How did they try to kill you?"

"Shot me."

"Where?"

"Sir?"

"It's a simple question, Filson. Where did they shoot you?"

"In the foot. Still crippled from it. Blew two of my toes plumb off. " He pointed at Hy. "Son-of-a-bitch whacked me with his pistol, too. Cost me two molars. Still can't hear out of one ear real good."

Lev and Hy kept their silence while a flicker of a smile crossed the old man's bearded face. Wade saw it. "What's old Crawford doing here? He don't carry no sway around here no more."

The lieutenant grimaced. "Judge Willis Crawford has held about every elected or appointed office in this county at one time or another. I admire his advice and his honesty. He knows everybody and people around here respect him." The lieutenant paused as if anxious for Wade or Filson to reply. "Now, this proceeding will go a lot faster if we ask the questions. Understood?"

Judge Crawford took a step forward. "What did these two boys take from you in this robbery?"

Filson stiffened. "Had me a roadhouse and saloon over in Rusk. They robbed it."

"Got any witnesses?"

"Room was full of witnesses."

"What did these two boys take?"

"Walked out without paying a bill for a bottle of whiskey."

"And what did you charge for this whiskey?"

"Prime whiskey goes for twenty dollars a barrel."

"They steal a barrel?"

The old judge put his palms on the desk and leaned forward. "Two toes, two dollars, and two teeth is what I hear is at stake here. And all this took place in Cherokee County."

The lieutenant examined the papers again. "What's this about a dog?"

"They killed my dog, too. And you're forgetting about Hathaway and his horse. The horse they stole is just outside."

Judge Crawford looked around the room at dog level, hoping not to see Slick. "When you say dog, do you mean that stinking swamp creature that followed you around town? Thought about shooting it myself. Damn public nuisance, Lieutenant."

The lieutenant laid the papers on his desk and put both hands over them. "Filson, we got much more serious business than this in these hard times. People getting killed right and left, violence between freedmen and whites. You might want to take your case to Cherokee County. Doubt you could get a jury in Ellis County to convict these two boys. As for the horse theft, I know the story about the horse and Hathaway. Coroner over there in Cherokee County said the man's heart likely gave out from the exertion of a bowel movement. He was not shot."

Filson's expression hardened. "Can I keep 'em in your jail till I can get papers drawn up over there?"

The lieutenant shook his head. "No. We can't feed and guard the prisoners we have now—much less ones that are not going to be tried here."

Judge Crawford walked around the desk and cut the ropes tied around Hy's hands. Wade reached for the knife. "You can't do that."

Hy stepped between the judge and Wade as the old man sawed Lev's ropes. "The hell he can't."

Filson turned to the lieutenant. "I aim to take these boys back to Rusk to stand trial there."

The young officer rose and spoke with bored resignation in his voice. "Cherokee County is under military jurisdiction just like Ellis. You'll find the same conditions there."

"I doubt it."

The lieutenant's face reddened. "A word of advice, Filson. Our provisional government is temporary. We're here to reconstruct the South. You and your men were given authority to stop violence, not settle old grievances. Either way, these papers are no good here and these men are free to go."

Hy pulled his gun from Anderson Bonner's waistband. Filson leaned over the desk and put his face close to the Lieutenant's. "What about weapons? Johnny Rebs ain't supposed to be owning no weapons. I know these boys stole horses and weapons."

"Then that's what you should have sworn out papers for, Mister Filson." He reached out a hand to Hy. "I'll take that pistol." Hy handed over his Colt, butt first.

The crowded, smelly room had been working on Lev since they entered. As he turned to leave, Wade Monroe stood in the doorway. Lev, face dark, stared at his old friend until he stepped aside. Hy followed his brother out to the courthouse porch. Filson shoved past Wade and Bonner to catch up. He pointed a fist at Hy as he stepped off the porch and untied the dun. "This ain't over."

It was enough to ignite the fire that had been building in Lev. He touched Filson's chest with a finger. "It is over, Filson. It's done." He paused, searching for words to express his anger and frustration. "You see me coming from now on, best to get away."

Bonner moved behind Lev, standing close enough for Lev to feel the buttons on his shirt. Lev turned to face him, wrinkling his nose. "You was wearing them same clothes the first time I saw you. Ever think of washing 'em?"

Bonner reached for his pistol, but the barrel of Filson's pistol across his face dropped him to his knees. Filson put a finger on his forehead. "You stupid enough to kill an unarmed man right here in front of the law?" He turned back toward Lev. "Excuse the nigger." He tipped his hat and smiled. "Another time."

Bonner stood and stepped back from Filson, his rheumy eyes ablaze with red as Hy and Lev rode away.

Lev knew that his mother had been left alone, so they broke into a long trot. Rachael and the buckboard were gone when they arrived. They were letting their horses rest before going after her when she returned, Sebastian and McCulloch not far behind.

Lev helped his mother down from the buckboard. She surprised him with a hug. "Thought you boys were in real trouble this time. What happened?"

When Lev and Hy mentioned Judge Crawford, Rachael looked toward her husband. "He came around often during the war to visit with your daddy and ask after you boys. Good thing he was there."

Sebastian wanted more credit for his influence with Judge Crawford, but took the crumbs Rachael was willing to scatter. "You think this thing with this Filson is all done, then? I been hearing a lot about him. He's in good with the Yankee military government. Got himself appointed some kind of military enforcer for several counties around here, I heard. Claims to work directly for the governor."

Lev felt the bullet poking him. "Looks like we might be done with Filson. He found out today we been around this part of the country long enough to still have a few friends. Hate to admit it, but that Yankee lieutenant seemed reasonable, too."

Sebastian watched Rachael climb the porch steps and go into the house to start supper. "I hear he's sweet on a Southern widow. Maybe she taught him some Texas ways. You boys ever talk to your mama about moving out west?"

Hy's eyebrows arched. "Don't see any reason for us to go now. Filson can't touch us for that thing up in Cherokee County and the only thing he's got here is killing a wild animal needed killing."

Sebastian shook his head. "It ain't just Filson and Wade, though I don't think they're done with you. It's worse than you think and not likely to improve." Lev and Hy looked at each other, doubt in their eyes.

Sebastian recognized their skepticism. "I'm worried about

you boys, but more so for the womenfolk. We got a powder keg of problems about to explode. Some of these people wearing badges are rotten to the core. Even the best of the people in charge have got it in for Confederates. You combine that with these freedmen looking to take revenge for slavery ..." Sebastian stopped, sensing the futility of his argument. Lev and Hy had won a victory, and they wanted no more talk of bad times ahead. Hy replaced his confiscated pistol with one of the stolen ones.

24

LEV KEPT TO HIMSELF AS MUCH AS POSSIBLE after the arrest. Conflicts with Filson and the law made him wary of every stranger, every sound—always expecting trouble. He could not think or make plans for the future. He made the slave shack into adequate living quarters for himself, but felt foolish taking meals with his mother. A man needed a family—his own table. Having Filson's charges rejected by Judge Crawford and the young lieutenant should have made him feel free again, but it did not. The prospect of being pulled back into violence unnerved him. Killing the dog had made his hands shake. He had broached the subject with Rachael, but she did not seem to understand and wanted no talk of further violence. "Trust in the Lord," she had said.

The morning after the arrest, he walked along Chambers Creek toward the spot where his father and McCulloch had camped during the years he and his brothers had been away at war. The old cabin had crumbled and part of the roof had collapsed, closing the entrance. He wanted to talk to his father, but Sebastian and McCulloch were in Red Oak. As Lev walked away, he heard the caws of crows. Shading his eyes, he found the black flock soaring above. He sat down in a meadow and listened to them call, answering the sounds of morning in woods devoid of any human sound other than Lev's breathing. He lay back in the dry grass, closed his eyes and let the sun's warmth caress him. He tried to return to his grandparents' old cabin, to the floor beside Papa Jim's chair. He had not tried to slow his heartbeat since the war ended. He was reminded of the bullet, but it did not hurt.

He did not sleep, but drifted as his heartbeat slowed. His mind went back and he heard the sound of his Choctaw grandmother's voice. "You're running from yourself, Son, running from the person you had to become during the war."

The caw of a single crow brought him back. He sat up, shaded his eyes, and found the blue-black bird, alone, drifting effortlessly on the rising warm air, an outline in black against the yellow of the sun and blue of the sky. The crow circled him twice, doing maneuvers in the warming air as if performing, drifting in a general direction, beckoning Lev to follow. As Lev walked deeper into the meadow, the crow flew higher, almost straight up, and then drifted down faster, swooping gracefully down to land beside its mate. The two birds pecked at acorns only a few yards from where Lev stood. He knew they were aware of his presence, but made no effort to fly away. Lev stopped as the crow lifted its head to watch him. He had his sign.

He was at her home by dusk. The old log house looked lonely and welcoming as it sat in the dusk of twilight, the last rays of the day's sun peeking over its roof. She came to the door in her apron. When she saw him, she lifted the apron to wipe her hands, hoping he would not notice the slight tremor. She stepped out on the porch instead of inviting him in. His rehearsed speech left him. "Your papa home?"

"He will be here about dark, I imagine. Why?" the reply came out as a hoarse whisper.

He had counted on Ransom House being at home, though there was little reason to expect it. Recognizing that he was at a loss for words, she put a hand under his elbow and guided him down the steps and across the yard to a brush arbor. Ransom had notched two stumps and dropped a rough-hewn board across them.

It was a crude job, and the seat they took was rough and splintery. Lev smiled as he sat on the board. "Looks like your papa is about as handy with tools as mine is. I'll come by one day and plane this down smooth for you."

She pushed back an invisible hair from her cheek. "That would be nice. It provides a nice shade in the summer."

They looked out across the yard and down the trail that led to it for an uncomfortable period of time. Lev cleared his throat. "Mary Ann, I came to see your papa, but I came to see you, too."

"My feelings would have been hurt if you hadn't."

"By all rights, my business with your papa ought to come first."

She studied his expression, looking for answers in his eyes. "Can I ask what you came to see him about?"

Lev rose and looked toward Corsicana as if he could see it. "Guess you been hearing about our troubles with this bunch running things now."

"Some."

Lev was irritated at her refusal to help him along with the conversation. Surely she knew why he was there. "I been uncivilized for a long time, Mary Ann. Not fit to be around decent folks."

"You're the only one that sees yourself that way." Sensing that she had said the wrong thing, she continued. "You did your duty, Lev, and we're all proud of you for it."

"The thing is ..." His voice trailed off.

"Go ahead and say it."

"I kinda took natural to it ... this uncivilized behavior. The life and all."

"What makes you say that?"

He sat down and reached for her hand. "I ain't told this to anybody before, but I think about it some. I dream about it."

"You mean killing?"

His eyes slanted. "This feller Filson ... I dreamed of killing him more than once." He hesitated. "You need to know that I nearly killed one of the men that tried to rob me and Hy on our way home from the war."

She squeezed his hand with both of hers. "You were just protecting what was rightfully yours."

"That's part of it. The thing is, I think I may have really wanted to kill him. Don't think I would kill somebody for no reason, but this dreaming about it ..."

"I can't imagine what you and the other boys went through, but I imagine it will take a while to get past it. The Lev that I knew before the war will come back. Mama always said you and Alfred was the gentlest of the Rivers boys."

Lev looked at her as if she were speaking in tongues. "If they would just let us go on about our business. But they keep after us, won't let us be."

She took her hands away from his and folded them into her lap. "Is that what you wanted to speak to Papa about?"

"Some of it. I want to own up to the things I have done, what I have become, before I ask him if I can ask for your hand in marriage." He looked away from her, not ready to see her response before he got it all said. "Wanted to tell him that it looks like this trouble with the Yankee law might be behind us." Turning, he saw her wince as if he had pricked her finger with a pin. "I ought not to have brought it up with you before asking him. It ain't respectful."

"We won't mention to Papa that you talked to me first. But your trouble won't be with him—it will be with me."

He felt the need to take a deep breath, but could not seem to draw it. He had taken her for granted. Hester had led him to believe that Mary Ann was his for the asking. Humiliated, he stood and put on his hat. "I am sorry I made a useless trip. I should have known I ain't fit for a woman as good and kind as you are."

She stood and faced him, their chests almost touching. He could feel her breath, smell the oven from their wood stove in her hair. She put both hands on his chest. "I want to give you what you need. I know I can bring you back from that dark place where you been ... but I need to hear the words."

"I know I'm no good at this, but I thought I had seen the signs in your eyes when we kissed them times before."

She made a tent with her hands, intertwined her fingers and slid them back and forth. "Lev, I've been waiting for this moment for four years. Longer. I've been waiting since we were children. Wanting you, needing you, thinking I had lost you."

"What changed?"

"You know what changed. I need for you to be sure."

"What can I say?"

She coaxed him with her eyes. "When I was eighteen, I would have thrown myself into your arms and said yes before you finished asking. But I ain't eighteen anymore. I been watching, learning. Watching your mama and papa and mine. What went wrong, what went right, what they say, what they do, how they touch. You don't look at me the way Papa looks at Mama and you ain't got the words."

Lev did not understand. He beseeched her with his eyes. He wanted her more than he had ever imagined. "What do I have to do to convince you?"

"You need to convince yourself."

Lev walked toward the hitching rail. She called after him. "You leaving without asking Papa? I hear his wagon coming." She trotted toward him and faced him. "You ask his permission, then go home and think for a few days. Talk it over with Hester. She has a way of looking into your heart."

"Already said what was in my heart. It's your heart that ain't made up its mind." Mary Ann smiled as Lev walked toward Ransom House, hat in his hand.

A week later, Hester kissed Hy goodbye before joining Lev on the wagon's spring seat. She had asked Hy to stay home. Mary Ann might be intimidated if both brothers came. She had worked on Lev for the better part of two days, questioning him about his feelings for Olivia and for Mary Ann. Hester flinched at the answer but seemed to accept it as raw and honest. "I can't go where Filson done been. I need me a pure woman." He assured her his delay in asking for Mary Ann's hand had not been caused by Olivia, but by his doubts about being civilized enough to share a bed with a gentlewoman like Mary Ann.

Hester began working on the marriage quilt she had started more than a year ago, intending to finish the binding before they reached Mary Ann's. Her fingers bled from pricks made each time the wagon lurched or dropped into a low spot in the trail. She spoke loud enough to be heard over the wagon's creaking and the horse's plodding steps. "Hy settled down just fine. Course, he never looks at things as deep as you. A wife and children made him forget the killing soon enough. Mary Ann can do that for you, too."

"I see that in her eyes. But it ain't me that needs convincing."

"What you boys did had to be done. That's all there is to it. It's over."

She seemed to be talking about Hy, not him.

"Hy tells me he loves me, Lev—not very often, but sometimes. Did you tell Mary Ann that you love her?"

It seemed to Lev that he had, but he could not recall his exact words. "Maybe not in those words, but she knew what I meant."

Lev almost bounced down from the wagon when he saw Mary Ann on the porch. He ushered Mary Ann to the brush arbor, seated her on the rough bench and paced in front of her, reciting his plans for their life together. He told her about what he had done and what he wanted to do to the slave shack and asked if she would mind living there. Without waiting for an answer, he launched into his work with horses and his plans to acquire land, more horses and cattle. She sat quietly and listened. When he finally paused, Mary Ann looked toward the porch. Hester had taken a chair there.

Lev followed her look and took both her hands to return her eyes to him. "I love you, Mary Ann. Your folks have given us their blessing. Would you do me the honor of being my wife?"

25

THE FIRST SIGNS OF AN EARLY FALL SHOOK THE leaves on sycamores as they entered the Corsicana square on September 30, 1865. Lev had figured to be married in a judge's chambers in Ennis or the courthouse in Waxahachie, but Ransom House exercised a father's prerogative and chose the family church in Navarro County as a proper location for his daughter's wedding. The chosen preacher, a vocal opponent of Northern aggression both behind the pulpit and on the streets of Corsicana and Ennis, was dragged to death two days before the wedding. His church was burned. When the House family began talk of postponing the wedding, Lev took control. Judge Crawford would marry them in the Navarro County courthouse.

Mary Ann sat beside her mother on the buggy seat as her father threw down a buggy tether. Lev stepped off Butter and tied the reins to the tether. She adjusted a vanilla white dress that came to her ankles, hoping that Lev would not notice her worn shoes. The dress contrasted with her dark skin and as she smiled, Lev felt something right about it all. He helped her down and the House family and Rivers family regarded each other awkwardly.

Sebastian, Hy, and McCulloch sat their horses beside the Rivers wagon, Rachael and Hester on the spring seat. On the northwest corner of the square, headquarters of the Union Occupation Troops, the Stars and Stripes rippled slightly in the north breeze where the Lone Star flag had hung before the war. A half-dozen Yankee soldiers lingered outside headquarters, returning Sebastian's venomous stare. Lev rubbed his wrists, recalling the last trip he had made to Corsicana with his hands tied.

Judge Crawford stood inside the district courtroom with a white-haired Presbyterian minister. Rachael took a deep breath of relief when he introduced the minister. At least it would be a Christian wedding. The judge tried to conceal the old preacher's dizzy spells by holding a hand under his elbow for support. With trembling voice, the minister coached Lev and Mary Ann through their vows before Lev began to feel the walls closing in.

Outside the courthouse, Mary Ann hugged Hester and her parents and took a seat beside Rachael on the Rivers' wagon. Without hesitation, she picked up the reins of the buggy as if they were the controls to her new life and pointed the buggy horse toward her new home. Lev rode alongside, occasionally urging the old wagon horse along with a slap from Butter's reins. Mary Ann smiled. "You in a hurry?" Rachael stared straight ahead and remained silent until Sebastian and McCulloch pulled off at their abandoned cabin and camp by the creek.

Mary Ann stopped the wagon in front of Rachael's porch. Lev hesitated, unsure whether to help his mother or his new wife down from the wagon. Mary Ann solved the problem by tying the reins to the brake handle, jumping off the spring seat and helping her new mother-in-law down. Rachael paused on the first porch step and turned to face her son's new wife. Her arms reached out as if she were poking them through glass, breaking an invisible barrier as she touched both of Mary Ann's shoulders and pulled her to her.

Lev felt an unfamiliar current of emotion moving through him as he saw his mother and bride embrace. He was surprised at the similarity between the two women—almost the same height, size and skin coloring. Only Mary Ann's black hair stood in sharp contrast to Rachael's gray. Rachael whispered into her ear. "I welcome you as my daughter and vow to treat you like my own child. My house is yours. Why not let me sleep out in that shack while you and Lev take my bed?"

Mary Ann's face warmed. She smiled as she looked at an inquisitive Lev, who was trying to overhear the whispers. "I am deeply grateful." She gestured toward the slave shack. "But that's Lev's home and it's going to be ours. I want us to spend our first night together there."

Lev finally dismounted as his mother closed the door to her house. He stood beside his bride, watching the closed door. She poked him with an elbow. "You gonna leave that old horse harnessed all night?" She reached into the wagon bed and removed her cloth bag.

Lev reached for it. "I'll take that."

"You take the harness off the wagon horse, and I'll unsaddle Butter."

"No, I'll take care of the horses. You go on inside our house and wait for me."

"I want us to go in at the same time."

Lev understood. "You bring that bag so you'll have something to sit on in the barn and I'll take care of both horses. No use both of us getting sweaty." He had taken a bath that morning, but was worried about trail dust and horse sweat. His hand trembled as he unbuckled the harness.

Horses bedded down, they held hands as they made their way in the crisp darkness to their little shack. Lev opened the door and carried her inside, trying to remember where things were in the dark. Wishing he had risked leaving a lamp burning, he put her down gently on the bed. Fire-starting had been his job since he was a small boy, so Lev took pride in his ability with flint, steel and tinder. He had seen men use lucifers during the war, but had never actually used one himself. Kindling and seasoned wood had been carefully selected and placed in the stove. His first breath blown on the tinder brought a small flicker that warmed their minds, if not their bodies. He had whittled a long twig for lighting the lamp, and they were soon bathed in warm light.

His work accomplished, Lev felt awkward, unsure of what to do next. Sensing this, Mary Ann rose from the bed and took his hand in hers. They held them together over the warming wood stove. She touched his face with her warmed hand, causing him to take a deep breath and hold it until she spoke. "We will be good together."

Lev looked longingly toward the bed, then around the room, realizing for the first time that there was only one chair. He pulled off his hat, hung it on a peg on the mantle he had carved for a future fireplace, and took her in his arms. The journey home had not harmed her freshness. She smelled just as she had when they spoke their vows—of soap that hinted of honeysuckle. He felt his mustache brush her lips slightly and wondered if it bothered her— wondered why it had never occurred to him during previous kisses. She met his lips with tenderness, if not eagerness, holding her body slightly away from his. He touched her elbow and she moved closer, putting the other hand on his cheek. He pulled his shirt over his head and she gently stroked the scar on his chest. It was silent in the cabin and something seemed to have silenced the birds and creatures of night. Only the crackling of the warming fire interrupted the sounds of their lovemaking.

He rose twice during the night to stoke the fire and add wood. The little stove had done its job, allowing him to stand comfortably naked in the room, observing his new bride. Her black hair swept across the pillow, and he recalled how she had removed the pins and let it fall. The vanilla-white dress had been carefully folded and draped across the foot rail of the bed. He could not remember when she had had done that, only how his mouth had become dry when he saw how beautiful her body looked in the lamplight. He had been surprised when she had stayed his hand as he started to extinguish the small lamp. She had even cracked one of the small stove lids to emit light from the fire. She had pulled her nightgown from her cloth bag, but never put it on. It lay beside her wedding dress. Lev smiled as he realized how she had coaxed him, letting him think that he was in charge, when she actually was. He sensed Hester's influence on her little sister. As he eased back into bed, he was overcome with the touch and smell of her. He had never been in bed with a woman before, never had a wife. He felt a sense of peace as he listened to her soft breathing.

26

<hr>

THE ONE ROOM SHACK HAD BECOME CROWDED by the time Mary Ann told him she was pregnant. She had brought more of her own things from home, including a rocking chair, and added things that Lev had not seen a need for before the marriage. Afterward, he lay beside her in the dark listening to the sound of her breathing, making plans for the addition to their family. The next morning, he began gathering materials for adding a lean-to room to the cabin. Rachael watched him from her kitchen window awhile before walking over. "Lev, I wish you wouldn't waste your money and time on this old shack. There's a better place to build a cabin for your family on the east side of this place. Your father has always said it was a better home site than this one. He's witched for water over there and says you can dig yourself a well. You could build a new corral, Mary Ann could have a garden."

"I doubt Papa still holds that opinion. He still wants us all to move west."

Rachael's expression hardened. "We haven't even seen your daddy in weeks. I hear he's down in Louisiana."

Rachael always seemed to know where her husband was and Lev wondered how. "What's he doing down there?"

"What he always does. Trading cattle or horses or land. Never comes out with nothing, just swaps one worthless thing for another. Never gets ahead."

<hr>

"I been hearing some things that make me think Papa might be right. Even some talk that they might divide Texas into two or three states. Papa says we would be better off out west if that happens."

Rachael turned to walk back to her house, and then turned back. "You can't run away from yourself. This place is my family place. It's got nothing to do with Sebastian Rivers. None of us are going west."

Lev had been leaning toward following Sebastian's advice and moving west until Mary Ann's pregnancy. Mention of his father brought a strange, empty feeling to his stomach. He had seen him only twice since the wedding—both times by accident. It was strange to run into your father unexpectedly. Lev felt disloyal for ignoring Sebastian's entreaties to head west, choosing instead to live in a shack in his mother's yard. He put down the drawknife he was using and drew a sleeve across his brow to wipe away sweat. "That may be so, Mama, but Mary Ann and me are saving up for our own place. I can't afford to build a house on this one."

"Why not buy this place?"

Lev had considered that possibility and dismissed it. His three older brothers would have first choice if she ever decided to sell. Besides, he could never get anyone to loan him that much money. "I was thinking on starting out with a little place. Figured one of the other boys would want this one."

"Jacob and Arch are already settled. They want you to have this one." She paused and studied his face for a reaction. "Providing, of course, that you agree to take care of me in my old age."

He wondered when she had talked it over with Jacob and Arch. It meant she was serious. "What about Hy?"

"Figured you and him could go in partners. I'll make the price fair. If I die before you pay me, the paper will go to all my children and you can pay the others."

"You discuss this with Hy and Hester?"

"With Hester. She wants her and Hy to move in and live with me. We got used to each other during the war. Mary Ann, I think, wants her privacy. You boys can work out the details between yourselves about the houses."

They did. They gave Rachael a note for the land and buildings. Hy agreed to help Lev build a new cabin and corrals in exchange for Lev's share of Rachael's house, the shack, barn and corrals. Lev and Hy were laying notched logs on the final wall to the new cabin when Sebastian and McCulloch appeared in the meadow. Hy looked up and waved to them. "Wonder how long they been watching?"

Lev motioned them forward. "Not long enough to break a sweat." He felt a little uncomfortable as they approached. He and Hy had purchased the land without consulting their father. Building a house meant that they had permanently rejected the idea of going west. Lev had always kept that option open. Until now.

Sebastian stayed in his saddle as he silently surveyed the site and the partially built cabin. "You chose well. Always tried to get your mama to build here, but she wanted to stay in her daddy's old house."

There was defeat in his voice. Lev sensed it. "Step down and set a spell. We ain't got much to offer in the way of food or drink. How about a glass of cool well water?"

Sebastian and McCulloch seemed not to hear the offer as they moved away from the house and toward the new corral. They studied the two horses inside. Lev and Hy stood on a rail and joined the scrutiny. Sebastian spoke to Lev without taking his eyes off the horses. "Looks like you picked up a few things about judging horseflesh. You in the market to sell these two?"

Sebastian's voice seemed hoarse, weak, almost a whisper. Lev moved closer to hear better. "Already sold. Buyer hired me to put a little better handle on 'em. I'll have 'em finished out by the end of the week." Lev looked closely at Sebastian. The old man's face was flushed and his eyes were bloodshot. Lev thought whiskey at first, but this was different. Sebastian had never been able to handle his liquor and the effect of more than one drink was pronounced and immediate. "I hear you been down in swamp country."

"Been lots of places."

Lev decided to break an unspoken rule with his father and probe into his affairs. "You do any good down there? Me and Hy didn't like it."

Sebastian smiled in McCulloch's direction. "McCulloch didn't take to it much, either. Mosquitoes bigger'n horse flies."

A long silence followed. Lev had opened the door, but without further comment or compliment on the house under construction, Sebastian nodded to McCulloch and they turned to ride away. He stopped as Hy stood in front of his horse. "Wouldn't hurt if you was to tell us where you was ever once in a while. Might need you. God forbid, you might even need us."

Sebastian looked down at his son for a long time before answering. "We been looking for a safe place to take this family when the time comes. I warned you boys, but you won't listen. The carpetbaggers and Yankee soldiers and coloreds are taking over Texas. Folks like us are at the bottom rung of the ladder now—worse off than slaves before the war. At least they had somebody to house and feed 'em."

Lev felt defensive. "We been making out all right. We mostly stay out here and keep our heads down when we go to town. Military and State Police pretty much leave us alone."

Sebastian looked off into the distance and shook his head. "Never thought I'd see the day when a son of mine would be satisfied to just keep his goddamned head down. What kind of life is that? I aim to keep my head up till they bury me."

Lev felt his face warm and his temper rising. "Hell, your solution is to run away. How's that keeping your head up?"

Sebastian finally dismounted. Lev had seen him do it thousands of times. All of his motions around horses, on and off, were always smooth and fluid. But something was different. Something had been lost. Lev stiffened as Sebastian walked closer and put a finger on his chest. "Look, boy. You and the other boys went off and gave those sons-of-bitches the best you had. There was just too many of 'em. They whipped us and they still got us under their thumb. Man don't recognize that ain't a hero, he's a damn fool." Sebastian looked at the framed house and pointed a hand west. "The only chance for any of us who took sides with the South during the war is to start over out west. I'd rather deal with heathen savages than a bunch of ignorant fools with badges they ain't qualified to wear and bankers and lawyers out to take your land." Sebastian was remounting as he spilled out the final words. He took a deep breath as he settled into the saddle and touched the mare's neck with a rein. The exertion seemed to tire him.

Lev and Hy watched their father ride away. Lev wanted to call him back—settle the argument once and for all. Make amends. Who knew when he would see the old man again? Did he know that he would have another grandchild in the winter? "You think Papa looked bad?"

"Just getting old. This military rule is scalding him pretty bad."

27

TWO DAYS BEFORE CHRISTMAS, MARY ANN gave birth to a boy. Rachael served as midwife. When Lev was finally allowed to hold his first-born, he told his mother that they had decided to name him Alfred Sebastian. Rachael's eyes filled as she stared at her new grandson. "It's almost like I've been given my baby son back. He even looks like Alfred." She touched the baby's check with her own and whispered, "Welcome back, Little Alfred."

Lev sat in Mary Ann's chair and rocked the baby. The smell of a freshly-cut cedar Christmas tree mingled with the bark from new log walls made pungent by the warmth of the fire from the stone fireplace he and his brothers had built. Even Sebastian had returned to lend his advice to the project, but had left again without saying goodbye. Lev wanted the old man to see his new grandson. He felt serenity not experienced since he lay at the feet of his Papa Jim as a small boy. He was proud to be able to offer his mother a separate bedroom when she decided to stay over through Christmas day.

Hy and Hester had made the move to Rachael's house and arrived Christmas morning with Otho and Kat and Christmas dinner. Mary Ann apologized for not being more help, promising to do better next year. Otho and Kat pored and poked curious fingers into Alfred's crib, evoking laughter from everyone. Lev felt like a man—a husband, a father, a man in his own house on Christmas day. Sebastian's presence would have made him feel complete. Lev wondered if the old man was staying away because he had been wrong. President Andrew Johnson had begun returning control of local and state governments to civil authorities. Things were returning to normal.

Unusually warm and humid spring weather had Lev's nerves on edge when he saw them riding up in the wagon. He was not in the mood to be caught doing women's work in the garden. Hy, dressed in his Sunday best, smiled as he stepped down from the spring seat and helped all the women and children down. Lev was irritated that his brother had not mentioned attending church with the womenfolk. He felt left out. He had intended to go himself one of these Sundays, but work always interfered.

Hy brought news from church. "Looks like Papa was right after all. Word is that Congress is stepping back in. Military rule is coming back. They're already removing our elected officials and replacing them with carpetbaggers and lapdogs." Lev felt the bullet nudge him for the first time in months.

Mary Ann was startled when Lev sat upright in bed that night. She put a hand on his back and found it wet with sweat. "Are you sick?"

"No, just a bad dream."

"What about?"

Lev thought a minute. "Can't recall." But he could. He laid back and tried to reconstruct it. The woman's thinning, graying red hair seemed to swarm his face and cut off his air. Her voice cut his nerves as efficiently as a razor. She had warned him about something, but he could not recall her words. He lay back and stared at the ceiling. Moonlight outlined a small sparrow as it flew though the open bedroom window. Lev always hung his gun and holster on the bedpost, and the tiny bird flew along the ceiling before perching on the handle of his Colt. The sparrow looked directly at Lev and then Mary Ann. It flew out the window as Lev moved. He took a deep breath. Armelia, his Choctaw grandmother, would have said that the bird entering and leaving the house was a sign of death. Sebastian, her son, did not believe in such things. Lev tried not to. He walked to the baby's crib and put a hand on Little Alfred's chest. The baby's soft breathing was comforting.

Lev and Hy were headed out with a string of horses the next morning when they met McCulloch driving a mule-drawn wagon. Lev somehow knew that Sebastian was in the wagon bed long before they reached it. McCulloch kept his eyes ahead but nodded backward toward Sebastian's inert form. "Your papa is in a bad way. Been sick for quite a while."

Lev could not recall ever having seen his father in a prone position, not even in bed. He stepped off of Butter and onto the wagon bed. Sebastian's face was swollen, bruised and yellowed. He was surely dead. Lev looked up to McCulloch on the spring seat, heat flaring in his eyes. "What the hell happened to him? If he's been sick, why didn't you tell us?"

McCulloch never turned back to look at Lev. "I don't do nothing your daddy asks me not to. I owe him a lot. Been trying to get him well, but he went into town a few days ago and didn't come back all night. I found him lying in the barn the next morning, looking like he looks now."

Lev stood. "Why the hell didn't you go with him?"

"He looks after me, Lev. Not the other way around. I'm getting too old to go everywhere your papa goes."

Hy leaned over and touched Lev's shoulder. "Take it easy. It ain't McCulloch's fault." He turned toward McCulloch. "You know who did the beating?"

"Only words to come out of his mouth since I found him said something about somebody not letting him vote."

Lev remounted Butter. "Godamighty. Get him to the house."

They heard her before they entered the meadow in front of Rachael's house. She was running down the dirt path, emitting a wail unlike anything Lev or Hy had ever heard from their mother. Lev's jaw dropped as he saw the frantic look on her face. His first thought was that something had happened to Hester, Mary Ann or one of the children. He urged Butter toward her. "What's wrong, Mama?"

She ran past him without answering and did not stop until she reached the tailgate of the wagon. McCulloch, alarmed, reined in the mules as Rachael threw herself onto the bed. She curled up beside her husband and cradled him in her arms. McCulloch turned and clucked the horse along. When they reached the house, Lev crawled on the wagon and gently pulled her arms away and put his hands under his father's shoulders. "He's dead," Rachael wailed. "I dreamed it last night and saw it this morning."

"No, he ain't, Mama. But he will be if we don't get him in the house and tended to."

Lev and Hy lifted their father gently from the wagon. Lev felt a strange sensation in his stomach as the warmth of his father's head pressed against it. His head swam and he thought his knees might buckle as he sensed helplessness in a man who had shown only strength in his life. He could not escape the thought that he was carrying his father through the door he had been barred from walking through for many years. Composure returned, Rachael held the door open. Hester held her children's hands as they watched their grandfather being carried inside.

Hy and Lev hesitated at the bedroom door, but Rachael pulled back the covers on her bed. Back in charge, she removed his boots. "You boys go on out now and bring me a pail of fresh water from the well." They stepped out of the room and she closed the door behind them.

When they came back with the water, Sebastian had been

stripped. His lower body was covered with a sheet. Lev and Hy stared. Neither could remember having seen their father without a shirt. The dark copper color of his hands, face and neck contrasted sharply with the paleness of his arms and chest. His ribs showed, but his chest was firm and the muscles in his arms were long and ropey. Rachael dipped a washrag into the cool water and began to bathe him. The sight made Lev's stomach turn. He had seen his grandmother prepare Papa Jim's body using the same ritual motions. He paced. "I'm going for a doctor."

Hy pulled his arm back as he stepped on the porch. "I best go with you. We don't know who did this and they may be waiting somewhere along the road or in town."

Lev was already mounted when he replied, leaving no room for argument. "I'll be on the lookout. You have to stay here with the women. Send McCulloch to get Mary Ann and Little Alfred and bring them up here."

Lev silently apologized to a winded Butter as he wound his reins around a tree limb in back of Dr. Robinson's office. From his corral, Sheep nickered a greeting to Butter. The back door to the office was open, but nobody was inside. He reluctantly stepped through the door leading the to the apothecary. Olivia was hovering over a mortar, grinding some powdery concoction with a pestle. She looked up when he entered, then returned to her grinding.

Lev looked around the room. "Doc Robinson about?"

"Don't expect him back until late this afternoon."

"Papa's been hurt. Looks like he may be sick, too."

She hesitated only a second before opening her bag. "Sheep is out back. Saddle him for me. How bad hurt and how is he sick?"

Lev explained Sebastian's symptoms and injuries on the way back. He felt a need to explain why he had brought Olivia instead of the doctor when they walked into the house, but there was no time. She was greeted warmly by Mary Ann and Hester and led to Sebastian by Rachael. Olivia stopped at the foot of the bed and studied him. She whispered to Rachael. "Has he said anything about what happened to him?"

"Not yet."

Lev stepped closer. "Said something to McCulloch about not being allowed to vote. I expect he put up a fight. McCulloch says he can't hear out of his right ear."

"How long has he been sick?"

Lev looked at his father. "We don't really know. I thought he looked a little off his feed a few weeks back, but he won't stay put long enough ... "

Olivia pulled back one of Sebastian's eyelids and leaned down to look closely. It was dark in the room and she asked for a lighted lamp. She pulled back the covers. She heard Rachael breathe deeply as Olivia put her hand on his bare chest and drew the lamplight over his exposed skin. She pulled the sheet back over him, touched Sebastian's forehead and straightened. They followed her out of the room and all the way to the porch. "He'll get over the beating. He may have a broken rib or a slight concussion, but I see no signs of internal bleeding."

Hy interrupted. "Why don't he wake up?"

"It's the body's way of recovering from injury. He's in sort of a shock."

Rachael spoke barely above a whisper. "Why is he yellow?"

Olivia hesitated. "I'm not a doctor, as you know, but I have seen this before. I believe he has yellow fever."

Considering her previous hysteria, Rachael took the news she had expected with composure. She had seen yellow fever before, too. Lev and Hy stepped back as if Olivia had slapped them. "What can we do?"

Olivia looked into each of their eyes before speaking. "Keep him comfortable."

Each knew that Sebastian had been handed a death sentence, but they asked questions, clinging to any possible mistake or hope. Olivia answered only what they asked, hoping that some of the things she had witnessed would not happen to Sebastian—black vomit, bleeding into the skin, delirium, coma.

Lev followed her to her horse. "How long?"

"I think a week or ten days. I left laudanum for his pain. Don't give him any more than you have to." She mounted Sheep and reached to touch Lev's shoulder. "I hope I'm wrong. I'll send Dr. Robinson out as soon as he can come."

"Much obliged."

"Come and get me when he gets worse."

Hy accompanied her back to town.

28

SHE LAY BESIDE HIM THE NEXT MORNING, waiting. Sebastian opened his eyes and looked directly into Rachael's. His eyes showed fear, confusion, and then surprise. His voice was hoarse and weak. "Thought for a minute I had died and gone to heaven. Been trying to get back into your bed so long it seems like a dream."

She smiled, then her face wrinkled with despair. "How can you ever forgive me?"

"All I need is for you to forgive me. You were right all along. I led the wrong kind of life."

"And I punished you far too long for it." She cradled his head in her arms and pulled him to her breasts. His hair was damp and his skin was warm. He pulled back, but she held him with surprising strength. His voice was muffled. "You need to get away from me. I know what I got. Told McCulloch not to bring me around the family."

"I don't ever intend to leave you again."

The other children were there by dark. Sebastian had seemed to gain strength in the morning as Rachael tended to him, but drifted in and out of consciousness in the afternoon. They propped him up with pillows and they each had their turn at the door. Minnie's new husband, Ben Parks, had to take her in his arms to keep her from hugging her father. When he saw his pending death reflected in his children's expressions, he sought to comfort them, but his voice could barely be heard. His sons gently questioned him about the beating, but he refused to name the people responsible and exacted promises from each of them to seek no revenge. "The beating was nothing. This yellow death is what's killing me. What are you gonna do, take revenge on God for that?"

He demanded that they move him into the slave shack to limit the contamination of the house. Rachael would not have it and told him it was too late, anyway. Lev and Hy ignored his request to stay away. They had been exposed, and they took turns helping their mother care for him. As he worsened, he sent Rachael to fetch them both. Hats at their breasts, they stood reverently at the foot of his bed, listening to the rattling sound of his breath, waiting for what they were sure would be their father's last instructions. The wait was painful and long, as Sebastian seemed to be summoning the strength to speak. When he finally did, his voice seemed to be coming from somewhere else, as if the sickness had manifested itself into something that could speak from inside his body. The voice was strong, but strained and of a deeper timbre than Sebastian's former voice.

"You boys were right. Keep your heads down and stay peaceful. Let this beating thing go. You see where violence took me." He paused and swallowed hard. "The Rivers have lost enough lives to it. Your mama can't take no more and don't you make her." He sighed deeply, hoarsely as he focused on Lev. "If it gets to where they won't leave you alone, go to the place McCulloch showed you out west."

Lev and Hy waited, wondering if he was finished. His eyes closed and it seemed to take all the force of his being to open them. The voice came again. "I aim to die in my sleep tonight. Bury me quick out by Alfred. Burn everything I touched." They turned to leave, but he called them back. "If I ain't dead by morning, take me down by the creek and leave me my revolver."

The brothers moved to the side of the bed. Lev held his hat

and squinted his eyes as if squinting could stop them from filling. The sight of the old man in his weakened state made him bend his hat brim to the point of breaking. He looked away, through the thin curtains of the open window, trying desperately to transport himself and his father to an earlier place, a better time. His voice was strained as he spoke to Sebastian's closed eyes. "Papa, you been a good man that all of us looked up to our whole lives." Hy nodded assent to his brother's words, but his face contorted and he was unable to speak. Sebastian opened one eye and seemed to smile.

Arch and Jacob went to fetch Dr. Robinson, but came back with Olivia, a coffin, and a circuit preacher. Sebastian was dead by the time they arrived. Rachael would not allow anybody to touch the body other than her. When she felt Sebastian's body was prepared properly, she called Lev and Hy to lift him into the coffin and nail it shut. The four sons lifted the coffin to their shoulders and carried it to the small plot where they had dug their father's grave. They used ropes to lower Sebastian into the ground beside Alfred.

The family stood beside the grave, listening to the welcome sound made by wind as it crossed the small mound of dirt and seemed to swirl inside the grave. McCulloch, as was his custom, stood a few feet back from the family. The tremble in his hands, like a slow-moving dark shadow, had traveled up one arm to his head and neck. Little Alfred turned loose of Mary Ann's hand and waddled toward the old man. Lev and Mary Ann watched their young son take McCulloch's trembling hand and place it on top of his head. The trembling eased. Neither had fully realized the strength of the bond formed between Little Alfred and McCulloch until now.

There seemed to be a collective realization that no plans had been made beyond this point. The finality of Sebastian's death seemed to freeze the small family in time. The young preacher was reluctant to take charge. Rachael, standing ramrod straight, nodded toward Otho. "Hand your Uncle Lev his fiddle and bow." With surprise in his eyes, Lev took them, but instead of putting the fiddle to his shoulder and chin, he let both rest under his arm, as if he were trying to remember how to play. He stood frozen for a few seconds, then lifted them and began to play. Rachael's eyes began to fill as he played the refrain she knew he would. Sebastian had called it "The Funeral Dirge" and she had asked him never to play it. Her husband had always laughed. He had shown Lev how to play it, but Lev did not like it and never played it again until today. The sound seemed to stop the wind, silence the leaves in the trees, and still their hearts.

When he was finished, the young preacher stumbled through a prayer and began a eulogy for a man he had never met. Fortified with scant information about Sebastian, he launched into a sermon of hellfire and damnation. His voice rose and his fervor grew until he caught Lev's withering glance. The young man stopped preaching, but launched into a prayer that seemed directed toward a sinful congregation where only God was allowed to listen. Rachael cleared her throat and brought it to a conclusion by pronouncing amen in a voice marbled with grief and stress.

The sons and sons-in-law picked up their shovels, but Rachael's voice stopped them. "Something should be said about Asbury Sebastian Rivers. He was always more of a man than I gave him credit for. May God forgive me for not forgiving him his faults. One of you children ought to say a final farewell to your daddy … maybe speak a word to The Lord about receiving him into His bosom."

They looked at each other, then at the mound of dirt that would soon cover their father's coffin. Minnie and Obedience focused on Lev. Lev looked toward his older brothers and found them staring at their boots. He stepped forward a half step and moved his hat an arm's length away from his chest as if he were sending his father away with Godspeed. "This good man set a horse as well as any man I ever saw." Lev sensed his mother's displeasure at this awkward start. "Taught us children everything he could. Never raised a hand to any of us what didn't have it coming. Never made me ashamed to be called Rivers. Always been proud. If there's a heaven, he's going." Rachael was not satisfied and the part about questioning heaven left her disturbed, but she gave tacit approval by tossing a handful of dirt into the grave.

When the grave was filled and the dirt rounded, Boy lay on the grave, his head nestled between his paws. A great sob came to Little Alfred's throat. He did not understand the enormity of what was happening, but Boy's lying on the grave signaled something permanent and terrible in his young consciousness. His tears broke the dam that Otho had been holding and Kat soon followed her brother and cousin as they joined Boy on the grave.

With Alfred sobbing and shedding great tears on his shoulder, Lev walked back toward the house beside his mother, "Mama, how did you know Papa was in that wagon that day before you even saw him?"

"I always knew when your papa was near. That's why I stood out on the porch all those many nights, holding that lantern. Knew he was close by." She squinted as she looked toward the sky. "I promised myself I would never forgive him when William was killed. God forgive me for keeping that promise."

It was awkward when Jacob, Arch, Minnie and Obedience drove guiltily away with their families. Rachael stood in the yard, Mary Ann holding one of her arms, Hester the other. She watched until the rest of her family was out of sight. "I wish Lucy and James could have been here. Lucy don't even know her papa's dead." Eliza Jane's face quickly replaced Lucy's in Rachael's mind. She had banished the child as she had banished her husband. In his last hours, Sebastian had asked her to forgive their daughter for marrying that Taylor boy. Rachael wondered where Eliza Jane was and contemplated how one evil act had caused Eliza to lose a husband and Rachael to lose a son and her marriage.

She spent that night in the bed where Sebastian had died, making it clear that she wanted to be alone. She slept on clean sheets, but would not allow them to burn the sheets he had lain on. Not yet. McCullough quietly prepared his bed in the old horse barn. Lev and Mary Ann slept with Little Alfred in the small shack where they had spent their first night together and allowed Hy's family to stay in their new cabin.

Hy rode back to the house well before sunup. Lev had a fire built in the yard and coffee boiling. He handed his brother a cup and poured. Hy blew and sipped. "Been up most of the night. So what are you figuring we got to do?"

Lev sat back on his haunches. "It's too warm most mornings for a fire, but it feels good today somehow." The fire burned steadily, unfazed by any stirring of air in the pre-dawn stillness.

Hy's question had been ignored. "We gonna keep our promise to Papa?"

"I expect we have to, till something makes us break it. Papa said not to take revenge, but he also said to hold our heads up. Hard to do both. We'll wait for a sign."

Hy looked at him, trying to figure if he was talking superstitious signs. His brother's body was there, but his mind had left. Hy knew the look—Lev wanted to be alone. He walked off toward the graveyard to have a private conversation with Sebastian.

Lev remained on his haunches, sipping coffee, until he grew tired, then eased back into a cross-legged position, still staring into the flames, letting his heart rest, letting Papa Jim and Grandma Armelia advise him. His Choctaw grandmother had said she tried to see the wind when she had a difficult decision to make. Lev asked to see the wind. A light breeze fanned the small flames, breaking the stillness. The wind was cool, too cool for summer. The flames stirred a little more, then tiny sparks floated skyward. A swirling circle of smoke drifted up from the embers and floated toward the tree line. When Lev finally looked up from his reverie, the wisps of smoke made a transparent outline of his father's body. The face was clear, the expression definite. The apparition looked directly into Lev's eyes before drifting away.

29

THE MOUND ON SEBASTIAN RIVERS' GRAVE had not had time to level when they buried Rachael beside her husband, son and brothers. Dr. Robinson said she might have died of yellow fever, but there had been no definite symptoms. Olivia said she had died of a broken heart. The family stood beside the two fresh graves in awkward, empty silence. Minnie, sensing that Lev had used up all his words at their father's service, told old stories about Rachael standing on the porch with a lantern or a candle, waiting for Sebastian. Now they were together forever.

They burned or cleaned everything she or Sebastian had ever touched. And waited. When no more symptoms came, Dr. Robinson pronounced the house safe and Hester and Hy and their children moved back in.

People avoided the Rivers when they went into town, fearful of the fever and of retribution. Lev and Hy felt watched. In Corsicana and Dresden, Union soldiers followed them; state militia or enforcers for the Freedmen's Bureau, usually in the form of Anderson Bonner and his troops, seemed to show up wherever they were. A badge had given Bonner a license to kill whites and he used it, seldom bringing in a prisoner alive.

Wade Monroe and Rattle watched from afar and seemed to be coordinating an organized watch of the Rivers family. When Hy and Lev encountered Wade on the sidewalk, they asked about the beating Sebastian had received as a sick old man trying to exercise his rights. Monroe professed innocence and ignorance of the event. Hy let him know their intent. "Best you help us find out who done it. Else we'll be coming for you." Wade stood defiantly in their path, shaking his head as if he were sad for their ignorance. A small crowd gathered across the street and shopkeepers started stepping onto board sidewalks or the dirt street. Wade looked at the crowd, waved his arms in a gesture of defeat, and walked around them.

Texas smoldered under the weight of reconstruction politics. Court cases, from property disputes to killings, weighed heavily against Confederate sympathizers, especially former soldiers. The heavy boot of the Union and carpetbaggers continued to harass and humiliate them, leaving them feeling disenfranchised, cheated because they had fought for a cause they still believed in. Imagined injustices combined with real ones to create an atmosphere of distrust of all authority and fanned the smoldering embers of violence. Sebastian's warnings combined with those from John Henry Brown and dominated the Rivers brothers' thoughts.

Word finally reached Eliza Collins, Sebastian's sister, that her brother and his wife had died. Lev and Hy discovered their aunt and her husband James standing at the foot of Rachael's and Sebastian's graves one afternoon. Over supper that evening, James, a sometimes lawman, discussed the powder keg of violence that Texas had become under Northern domination. He told the story of fifteen-year-old John Wesley Hardin, a friend of their son's. John Wesley, spurred by violence, hatred, and perceived and real oppression, had killed his first man, a former slave.

By the time the mounds on Rachael's and Sebastian's graves had leveled, Lev and Hy had traded and trained their way into a string of quality horses. But horses of all kinds, quality or not, were cheap in Ellis and Navarro counties because of drought. The military had already requisitioned two of Hy's best mares for less than half their value.

Hester had an arm full of kindling as she paused at the horse lot. "We spend more money feeding horses than we do feeding ourselves."

Lev was holding a young colt's rope halter while Hy rubbed and slapped a blanket over its back, sides, stomach and legs. Lev looked over the horse's withers at his brother's wife and smiled. "We know we got too many, but we can't sell 'em for what they're bringing now."

"McCulloch says they're selling good in Dallas. It ain't that far."

Hy moved away from the colt and walked toward Hester. "How is it that you and that old man know what horses are bringing in Dallas?"

"Stands to reason that they are."

Hy's expression grew serious as he looked toward Lev. "We thought about taking a string or two up to Dallas, but we might be gone more than a week."

"So? What's a week if you can put food on the table and lay in a little for winter? You boys got fine horses, we should get a fine price." They stared at their boots as she waited for their answer. "So what's the real reason you're not going?"

Lev rubbed the colt's face and neck once more before pulling off the halter. He coiled the lead rope and walked toward them. "The trail to Dallas is plagued with thieves and hooligans. Both of us would need to go to handle the horses and keep 'em from being stolen."

"And you're afraid to leave us helpless womenfolk home alone."

Hy nodded. "Any reason why we shouldn't be?"

"We have McCulloch." She smiled as Boy sat beside her. "And Boy, of course."

"McCulloch is a good man, but it's got to where I have to shake him awake of a morning. Shakes way too bad to hit anything with a gun."

Hester was persistent. "Mary Ann and I can put our families together and stay in one house. We shoot about as good as either one of you." Still no response. "Rather be shot than starve to death." Her expression changed to serious. "Take the horses."

They cleaned and oiled all the hidden guns and let the women and McCulloch test fire them. Boy strained against the small rope leash Lev had put around his neck to hold him until they could ride away. Since Sebastian's death, the dog was accustomed to going everywhere with Lev. They had traveled what seemed like a mile or so when Lev heard the howl of a dog that sounded like Boy. He turned Butter, prepared to discipline Boy and send him back home, but there was no sign of the small dog. Hy said he had not heard anything. Lev reluctantly turned back toward Dallas, but the howl had unnerved him.

They made the trip to Dallas safely and were watering their horses at a public horse trough downtown when Lev looked down the street into the rising sun. The man approaching was bathed in the sun's rays and the glare kept Lev from focusing, but he thought he recognized the gait. He shielded his eyes and tried to recall. The hair was a little grayer and had been trimmed, the lines around his eyes had grown deeper, but the voice was unmistakably John Henry Brown. "I believe I recognize two of the saddled horses, but not the young ones. You boys ain't taken up horse thieving, have you?"

Hy's shoulders rolled with laughter and they shook the hand of their old commander. "Me and Lev talked of you plenty of times, sir. Always thinking you was in Mexico, and here you are in Texas."

"Just passing through, gentlemen. I am on my way East, representing my adopted country of Mexico."

Lev looked up and down the street. "If there's a saloon

around here, we'd feel honored to buy you a drink."

"I would be honored to partake with two fine soldiers and horsemen, but I also represent the Evangelical Church in Mexico and no longer partake. I only wish I had the time to sit down for some coffee. I'm afraid, however, that my small caravan is heading north to a distant railway station, and we must abide by a strict schedule." He pointed down the street toward a buggy and buckboard. "One day soon, I'll be able to catch a train here. Now, I regret I must go." He extended a hand to each of them and turned toward the waiting buggy. He walked a few steps before turning back. "Men, I owe you a debt of gratitude." Lev and Hy did not understand, but asked no questions.

The old man pulled off his hat and ran a finger along its sweatband. "I'll soon enter my sixth decade on this earth and time is catching up with me. I admit I was feeling melancholy and suffering from a bout of homesickness when I saw you boys ride up." He looked upward as if seeking divine inspiration. "Seeing the way you boys still sit your horses and leading a fine string gave me renewed vigor and energy. Made me hope that our Southern boys can be whole again. Thank you for that." He turned and walked away.

———

They had been gone almost a week when Little Alfred and Otho watched as McCulloch sprawled over the side of a horse trough. Otho managed to pull his head out of the water before running to fetch his mother and aunt. McCulloch looked up at them with helpless, frightened eyes that seemed unable to focus. Alfred began to cry. The old man tried to speak but could not. One side of his body was already drawn and lifeless. Hester cradled his head in her lap while Mary Ann harnessed the wagon horse. Otho and Kat held the old horse while the sisters loaded him into the wagon bed. Hester climbed onto the spring seat and took the reins without speaking. As she lifted them, she turned toward Mary Ann. "Best I take him alone. You stay here with the kids. Keep a close watch. Boy will warn you. Shoot first and ask questions later."

Mary Ann was surprised at her own composure. She felt no fear. "You go on. Don't let the dark catch you on the trail. You stay in town with Olivia if it gets too late." She looked into the wagon bed and put a hand on McCulloch's chest. "Good Friend, you hang on. Doc Robinson will fix you up." Tears surprised her as they rolled down her cheek. She had not realized how fond she had become of the old man. She comforted a sobbing Little Alfred as they rode away. Lev was right—the boy was taking on the looks and personality of his namesake.

There was little that Dr. Robinson and Olivia could do. They kept McCulloch as comfortable as possible and administered a little laudanum for pain. It was noon when the hand Hester was holding changed. Dr. Robinson came back into the room as if he had sensed the death. He pulled the sheet over McCulloch's head. "This old man was ready to meet his maker. Not the kind of man who wants to live as a cripple."

A wave of sadness and fatigue washed over Hester as Olivia put a hand on her shoulder. She felt an urgent need to get back to her sister and her children. She wished that Hy were home. "Does the blacksmith shop still keep pine boxes?"

Olivia nodded.

It was twilight when they loaded McCulloch and his pine box onto the wagon bed. Hester was already on the spring seat. Captain Rutherford, the blacksmith, Dr. Robinson and Olivia pleaded with her to spend the night, but she felt an urgent need to be home. "Much obliged for putting your charges on account. We'll be in to settle up when Hy and Lev get back with money from their horses."

Both men nodded as Captain Rutherford spoke. "No hurry."

The night was very warm and the soft wind felt good on

her face as she rounded the bend and entered the last leg of her trip home, Hester's favorite part. The road had been etched out of the earth by horses, wagons and regular creek flooding, giving the soft sand the consistency that she imagined an ocean beach might have. Post oaks and elms stood as sentinels on each side of the road, spreading their branches across to meet each other and provide shade. Hester had always felt protected by the giant trees. She and Hy had shared many peaceful and loving times walking barefoot on the soft sand. The road was cut so deep that people walking the road could not see over the sides, making it seem even more private. She smiled at the memories.

She was startled at the sight of a huge root that had jutted through the dirt wall. In the dark, it looked like a predator. She smiled at her edginess as she looked up at the tree. It was leaning precariously over the road. She stopped the wagon. "Well, big fella, you're gonna fall over this road one of these days. Make sure you don't fall on me or mine."

"Who you talking to?" The deep voice made Hester's words hang in her throat. The dark outline left no mistake. A man afoot was holding her wagon horse's bit. Her breath and spit caught in her throat and she could only utter an unintelligible grunt as she tried to keep from choking. She reached for the rifle leaned beside her. Boy, asleep under the porch, perked his ears at the muffled cry followed by a gunshot.

30

OTHO WAS THE FIRST TO SEE THE WAGON WITH its pine box cargo stopped in front of the house. Mary Ann rushed out to the sound of his cry. She found her rifle, put all the kids in the wagon bed beside the coffin, and headed back down the trail. Hester was unconscious when Mary Ann found her pushed under a protruding tree root. Her dress was torn and blood had dried on the corners of her mouth. Otho sobbed, but he was strong enough to help Mary Ann put his mother into the bed of the wagon. Kat screamed until Mary Ann had to slap her. Little Alfred sat quietly staring at the pine box.

At the house, Mary Ann shushed the children and sent each on an errand of some kind—a bucket of water, rags, salve. Hester began to rouse when the cool wet rag touched her face. She stared at Mary Ann as if she did not recognize her. Her eyes darted from side to side as if checking for predators. Finally, she settled on Otho's kind, inquiring eyes and Kat's frightened eyes. "Mama is all right, babies." She turned to Mary Ann. "Let's get me cleaned up. I expect our men any time and I don't want Hy to find me like this."

Mary Ann saw them coming up the road just as she helped Hester down from the wagon at the house. They looked liked two avenging angels, with Captain Rutherford riding his gray and Olivia on Sheep. Olivia stopped Sheep a few feet away when she saw Hester struggle to stand beside Mary Ann. She drew tall in the saddle, took a deep breath, and then ducked her head as if she were trying to hide it under her arm like a sleeping hen. She shot the blacksmith a knowing, miserable look. Captain Rutherford looked at McCulloch's coffin, still in the wagon. "You were right. We should have come with her. You all take care of Hester. I'll take care of Old McCulloch."

The ground was so hard that Rutherford had to use a pickaxe and a shovel to dig the grave. Even with Mary Ann's and Olivia's help, it took most of the day. It was twilight when they slipped ropes under the coffin to lower it. McCulloch had grown even thinner the last few months, so the coffin was light. Mary Ann stood beside Olivia on one side and the big blacksmith held a rope in each hand on the other. He was about to slide the coffin over the grave when Hester walked stiffly and painfully into the yard. "What about Boy?"

Mary Ann's voice trembled. "You should stay in bed, Hester."

Hester put her hand over her mouth as her eyes narrowed and tears welled again. "He tried to protect me last night." She looked toward Olivia. "Did nobody see him on the road?"

Mary Ann walked to the barn and returned with a bundle in her arms. She had wrapped the dog in the only thing she could find in the dark, an old pair of holey longhandles. Hester was almost fierce as she took Boy's body from her. She carried it into the house and returned with the dog wrapped in a quilt. She laid him gently on top of McCulloch's coffin. Mary Ann flinched, but did not speak, as she stared at the quilt—one their mother had made.

———————————

Hy and Lev were in high spirits, pockets filled with money, as they traveled up the sandy road toward home. They squeezed Butter and the dun into long trots, slowing only when they saw the new grave. When Boy did not greet them, they left the horses ground tied as they ran into the house, each breathing sighs of relief as the first sight of their families. Hester was better, but she was still sore and had been unable to cover the bruising on both cheeks and the blue-black color of the skin around her eyes. Both sides of her mouth had scabbed over. Hy barely noticed until he took her in his arms. There was a slight hesitation, almost a shiver, as he touched her. Hester had always been a wife who folded herself fully into his embrace. He pulled her back and took it all in. "What the hell happened?"

Hester and Mary Ann had spent two days discussing their plans. Hester was adamant that neither Hy nor Lev would be told. Mary Ann insisted that they had to know. Too many people know besides us. Besides, that heathen has to pay for what he did, she had said. Hester replied that their daddy had said revenge belonged to God. Hy would kill or be killed if he knew, and Union law would take him away forever if he killed. Either way, I lose my husband, she had said. So she decided to lie.

As she looked into Hy's eyes and he into hers, she made up a story, but by nightfall, her determination faltered. She took him over to the shack and sat him down. Hy looked into her eyes and studied her face. He had felt it in her hand, now he saw it in her eyes. "You say you and me are one. I feel what you feel. That story you told me about them bruises on your face don't make no sense. You always been a woman don't keep secrets from her man. Tell me what really happened."

Still she hesitated. He smoothed her hair with tentative fingers. "Been gone a long time. I missed you." She shivered at his touch and drew that deep breath of disgust that she had drawn only once before. It caught in her throat again. For minutes, she could not utter a word. Hy touched the bruises around her mouth and eyes and knew for certain. He drew her to his breast and felt the rise and fall of her sobbing. He struggled to remain calm as he stroked her hair. "Who hurt you?"

The story poured out. His eyes inflamed with pity and flooded with tears at first. He could not come to grips with what had happened, blamed himself for not being there to protect her. He took her into his arms and promised to never leave her again. Mary Ann knocked on the door and told them that Otho and Kat were asleep in their beds and not to worry about them. They crawled into the bed at the shack and Hester put her head on Hy's chest. It was well past midnight when her breathing became rhythmic and she turned on her side. He eased out of the bed and waited until he was outside to put on his boots. Hy walked at first, and then ran along the bank of Chambers Creek until he was out of breath. He wrapped his arms around a live oak, butted his head against its bark, raised his fists skyward. "God damn you to hell, you son-of-a-bitch."

Lev rocked on the porch. He had never gone to bed, had watched his brother come out of the house and walk toward the creek. When he heard the guttural scream, he stopped rocking and waited. He checked the barn and made sure that the dun was still there before going to bed.

In the morning, they made a circle around the graves, men, women and children, holding hands for a respectable time. Little Alfred held his tears—death had become almost commonplace for him and he sensed its inevitability. Lev reached down and touched the mound of dirt. "So Boy's in there with McCulloch?"

Lev had no words to speak over McCulloch or his dog on this day. "We'll come back soon and do a proper service for the old man and Boy."

They walked away with no general direction or purpose. Hester seemed grateful as Mary Ann finally took charge, herding the women and children into the house to put away breakfast and prepare for dinner.

Outside, Hy began to pace. He stared wild-eyed at his brother as if he were a stranger. "You were right. This all started when I shot a man in the foot over two dollars. Shoulda just rode off and left it alone." He pulled off his hat and tugged at his hair as if he were trying to pull it out. "Who would have thought it would come to this? My Hester bore the brunt for what I done."

Lev shook his head. "No, I was the one that was wrong. I should have let you kill him then. Vermin like that are a stench and plague on the earth. Got to be stopped sooner, rather than later. Might have killed him and got by with it in wartime."

Hy pointed toward the house. "Think you can go in the house and get my rifle and pistol without Hester seeing you? I'll saddle the dun."

Lev touched his arm, and Hy recoiled like a rattlesnake. Lev studied his brother's wild look. "What are you aiming to do?"

"What has to be done."

"Did he rape her? Mary Ann said she wouldn't tell her."

Hy stared off into the distance, his hand clinching and unclinching, his voice menacing. "You need the words? He slammed her down in the wagon bed beside McCulloch's coffin and took her."

Lev stared at his boots.

Hy's voice broke. "He hurt my Hester. You stay with the women. I'll be back as soon as I can."

"Hy, I know how you feel, but we can't go into this thing half-cocked. Everything is against us now. We have to make plans."

Hy looked at his brother as if he did not know him. "You got no notion at all about how I feel. My guts are on fire. I got to do something now or burn up inside."

"Let me ride and get Arch or Jacob to stay with the women. I'll go with you and cover your back."

Hy nodded. "All right, but let me go for Arch and Jacob. You get the guns."

The guns were not in the house. Lev ran outside, but Hy and the dun were gone.

31

THREE DAYS LATER, LEV WAS DRAWING WATER from the well before dawn when he saw a movement by the hitching rail. He pulled his Colt and tried to adjust his eyes to the dark. He was not wearing a shirt, but he never went unarmed anymore. With nothing to duck behind, he crouched and tried to focus on what his ears had told him. The dun switched his tail and nickered lowly. Butter answered with a whinny from the horse lot. Lev recognized Hy, slumped in his saddle. Gone for three days, he and the dun were gaunt and wet with sweat. Hy looked sick. Lev put a hand on his brother's boot top and was answered with a pistol barrel next to his ear.

"Easy Hy, it's me."

Hy eased the hammer forward and took his finger off the trigger. His voice was hoarse. "I couldn't find the bastard. They're hiding him. Sent me on two or three wild chases, then into an ambush."

The scent of a cornered coyote lingered in the heavy air. Lev looked around for any sign of movement. "You get hurt?"

"No, thanks to the dun, they couldn't catch me."

A lamplight flickered from a window and Hester stepped out on the porch. "Hy? Is that you?"

Hy stepped off his horse as she ran to him. He took her in his arms and they held each other as Lev led the dun toward the barn, feeling that things might be all right again. Hy had breakfast and slept around the clock. He and Hester worked in the garden the next day. He stayed close to Hester, Otho and Kat with what seemed like contentment for more than a month. Hester, for her part, was healing in the companionship, soothing her wounds, trying to forget. Hy tried to push it out of his mind, to rationalize—not to forgive, just to stifle the rage. But the dreams grew in intensity—dreams where he discovered Filson attacking his wife—dreams of protecting her and the various ways he would punish her attacker.

Captain Rutherford told them of horses for sale on a small ranch near Waxahachie. Both of them could not go, of course, and Hy would not leave Hester's side. Lev returned in three days with two yearling fillies, only broke to lead.

Hy leaned over the corral rail, watching Lev let the young horses get acquainted with the smell and feel of him. Afterward, the brothers walked toward the house. Lev was looking forward to finally taking Mary Ann and Little Alfred home. Hy stopped him before they entered the house. "I need you to take the women and kids to Arch or Jacob's."

"Why?"

Hy looked at his brother for a long time. "It's eating my guts out."

Lev sighed and looked away, accepting the inevitable. "What about after it's done?"

"I head west. You bring Hester and the kids out to me when it dies down a little."

Lev looked skyward. "We'll both take 'em to Jacob's. Hester won't let you go off without her."

They took them to Jacob's the next morning, telling them it was just a surprise visit. The children played together that night and the adults watched, carefully avoiding discussion of the specter that hung over them. Just before dawn, Hy was holding a bucket of water under the dun's nose when Lev led Butter out of Jacob's small shed. Hy poured two cups of oats into a small trough. "Where you going?"

"With you."

"We can't both get mixed up in this. One of us has got to take care of the women and kids ... in case."

Hy took a saddle and blanket down from the corral rail. Lev followed suit. He smoothed his blanket and threw on Butter's saddle. "You know damn well you're betting on a busted flush going alone. They'll kill you. Then I'll have to go after 'em, anyway. Best to up the odds now, while we can."

Saddle cinched and ready, Hy checked his pistol, keeping his eyes down as he spoke. "It ain't your fight."

Lev froze with the latigo cinch in his hand. The barn was silent until a squirrel barked in a tree limb outside. Lev stared, waiting for Hy's eyes to level with his. "You say that to me? After all we been through?"

Hy grabbed a handful of mane and stepped into the stirrup. Hester and Mary Ann stood on the porch with Jacob as their husbands paused in front of the house. The women begged only with their eyes, never giving voice to their pleas as they watched their men ride away.

They had no plan for escape or for dealing with the consequences of what they intended to do. They just needed to right a wrong and things would then take care of themselves. They searched for days. Everyone seemed to be protecting Filson. When searching did not work, they left word in public places that they were looking for him—inviting him to meet them—trying to shame him into coming out of hiding. Wade Monroe stopped them outside the military camp in Corsicana. "You boys getting in over your head."

Lev and Hy sat their horses in silence until Wade continued. "Word's out you're looking for Filson. Don't make me no never-mind if the son-of-a-bitch lives or dies, but he's connected to this Union bunch. They'll hang you for sure."

They stared at Wade with dead eyes and spoke at the same time with the same words. "Much obliged for the warning." They camped by Filson's house for two nights and saw no sign. They gave up. On the way back to Jacob's, they stopped to water their horses in a mudhole. Hy watched the dun nuzzle the water after he had drunk his fill. "If we kill him, we'll likely have to leave this country and never come back."

Lev stood by Butter with his arms on the saddle seat. "I think we need to move out west, anyway. Should have taken Papa's advice in the beginning and none of this would have happened. Got no taste for this country anymore."

Hy mounted. "I remember some about living out west, but you don't know nothing. We don't even know if Papa had a place out there."

Lev eased Butter forward. "He did. I saw it. Think I can find it again."

They made plans all the way to Jacob's, deciding that they could not sell the land and houses. It had been part of their mother's family for too long—and too many of their own were buried there. The women studied their faces when they returned, but asked no questions. They loaded the wagons and headed home the next morning.

Lev waited until they were in bed at home to tell Mary Ann. She sat up. "We can't leave this place. Your mama will turn over in her grave."

"We aim to keep the place. Arch and Jacob and the girls can look after it till we get back."

"Get back? You know what moving around the country with no rhyme or reason did to your mama and papa. You gonna turn into Sebastian ... a man with no roots or home?"

Lev was glad it was too dark for her to see his expression.

He had not expected resistance. "You know we can't stay in this country after what happened to Hester."

"Have you asked Hester about leaving our mama and papa and our homes? You and Hy think it's all right to pull us up by the roots without even asking."

"I am asking."

The tone in Lev's voice made a chill run down her spine. She put her hand on his chest and turned to face him. "We're gonna be on the run from the law when we leave, ain't we? I knew you and Hy would not let this thing rest."

"We ain't done nothing against the law, but don't think for a minute that Hy can let it rest as long as we are in this country. Out west, he might forget." Lev turned on his side and feigned sleep.

Hy and Lev sent the children outside after breakfast and delayed feeding the stock so that they could linger over their coffee. The news of moving turned the kitchen into a funeral parlor. Mary Ann asked again why they had to leave. Lev hesitated as he looked at Hy, hoping his brother would come up with a valid reason. Hy did not disappoint. "We hear that General Canby is removing all our elected officials unless they take that damned oath. Yankees ain't gonna ever take their boots off our necks. I expect they'll be coming for our property or one of us any day."

Hester did not accept the explanation. "You both been griping about these things since the war. Why are they intolerable all of a sudden?"

Lev pointed three fingers at Mary Ann. "Now they're talking about dividing up Texas into three states. This part is gonna be called Lincoln. I ain't living anywhere named Lincoln."

When Mary Ann saw Hester's expression, she knew that further argument was useless. Hester needed to start again somewhere else. She pulled at her apron as she stood. "Well then, it's done. We're going to go to our new home. Hester, let's start our packing." She put her hand on Lev's shoulder. "I want to see Mama and Papa once before we go."

Lev watched Hy leave with the women and children at dawn on a cool, crisp morning. They had decided that Hy would take Hester and Mary Ann to visit Ransom and Edeline House while Lev made preparations to leave. His spirits lifted a little with pride as he worked the young horses one final time. On the spur of the moment, he decided to take them into Dresden and offer them to Captain Rutherford for resale rather then worry with them on the trip west. He needed traveling money, and the daylight trip to Dresden should be safe enough.

He was putting the fillies through their paces on Dresden's Main Street for the admiring eyes of Captain Rutherford when Olivia walked out of her apothecary shop. She shielded her eyes to watch as Lev made a filly roll over on her haunches and then collect herself for a sliding stop. Lev pretended not to notice that she was watching. He and the blacksmith had just settled on a price when Olivia approached. She had dark circles under her eyes and Lev noticed bruises on her hands and neck. Her tone was flat, almost nasal as she spoke. "Wade and his bunch got all sorts of traps set for you boys here and in Corsicana. They want you to try and kill Filson so they can kill you."

"So we found." He hesitated. "You know we're heading out soon."

She shook her head. "I had not heard. Is Hy all right with that ... leaving the man alive, I mean?"

The remark stung a little. "Guess neither one of us is all right with Filson or Montgomery or whatever his name is breathing the same air as decent people." He interpreted her look as one of disappointment tinged with disgust for anyone who would let a man get away with what Filson had done. "Whole town and the military are protecting him. We'll likely be hung if we kill him."

"When will Hy be back?"

"Tomorrow, without fail."

"I know where Filson will be tomorrow night."

A familiar flame flickered in Lev's chest as he looked into Olivia's eyes. "How you know that?"

Her eyes flashed with anger. "Go ahead. Spit it out. You been wanting to ask the question all these years now. You want to hear the plain of it?"

Lev's mixture of anger and sense of betrayal confused him, warmed his face. Rutherford walked away to keep from hearing more. "If you know where he is, just tell us."

"I'll do better than that. I'll deliver him to you."

"How do you propose to do that?"

She looked away. "I would kill him myself if I knew I could. I tried it once, so he's wary."

"So you want us to do it?"

"He has to be stopped."

"You can't get mixed up in this. Just tell me where to find him."

"You out of your head? How will I know that unless I'm there? He moves around and usually has two or three of his henchmen with him. He's got enemies all over Texas and Arkansas."

Lev felt his heart racing and anger rising. "So you gonna just tell him to put himself in our hands and he'll follow along like a whipped pup?"

Olivia was not deterred by his sarcasm. "There's a little smokehouse in the woods down by the creek behind his cabin."

"We watched his cabin for several nights. No sign of him."

Olivia stared, her eyes certain.

Lev broke the silence. "Anybody guard him?"

"Maybe Anderson Bonner. But he hates him almost as much as you do."

"I doubt that."

Lev paced as he felt the flicker again.

There was sadness and finality in Olivia's eyes. "I'll handle

Bonner. You just arrive after dark. I'll pass a light by the window if I can. If not, you just come in at midnight. Come in quick. I'll make sure the door is unlocked."

Lev considered his boots for a long time before he looked into her eyes. "You know this could be bad. Stay out of it."

Olivia pretended to study both the fillies. "I'm already in it way further than you can ever know." She looked across to her apothecary and barbershop with cloudy, expressionless eyes. "No need to worry about me. I've made arrangements for myself after it's done."

"Which window?" The simple question caused pain to shoot through his chest. He imagined the bullet moving so vividly that he looked down, expecting to see a growing bloodstain on his shirt.

"There's just one, and it's on the west."

So she's been in the cabin before. "If we do this, we'll all have to leave this country. You need to go with us. Head straight to our house after it's done. We'll leave from there."

Olivia tugged at the lace on her collar and walked away.

32

HY'S SUPPRESSED RAGE STUCK ITS HEAD above the water like a deadly water moccasin when Lev told him what Olivia had said. They harnessed the wagon horse, saddled Butter and the dun, and told Hester and Mary Ann to finish their packing. Mary Ann wanted to know why the rush. Lev shrugged off the question. "We been talking for weeks. Time to head west."

With vague explanations of going into town to get some farrier work done by Captain Rutherford and settle accounts with him and Doc Robinson, they told Hester and Mary Ann to gather the children into one room and made sure that weapons were loaded and ready. They tried to appease the women's protests, but left little room for argument about their plan to made the trip to Dresden before they headed west. Ordering the children to stay inside, Hester and Mary Ann ran outside in time to catch their husbands as they were mounting to leave. Hy and Lev made it plain they wanted no words to be spoken, but kissed their wives good-bye.

Using back roads, alleys, and the cover of trees, they arrived in Dresden just after dark. They put their horses in Olivia's lot with Sheep and walked along the creek bank. Their faces and hands were scratched and bleeding from thorns and limbs when they finally saw the smokehouse. Curling bois d'arc limbs and vines covered everything but the door and window to the small building. They had never even noticed the smokehouse on their previous vigils. The June night was warm, and the air was heavy and still. It was easy to stay out of sight, but difficult to see the door to the small building. They settled on a position that provided a partial view and sat on the grass behind a hedge of green thorny vines.

Hours passed in almost perfect, sweaty stillness before a whisper of wind drifted down like a soft mist, sighing its way through tree leaves, thorns and brambles. Lev imagined that it was God's exhaled breath, expressing disappointment in the deeds of his prodigal children, yet surrendering to what they were about to do. The breeze carried Olivia's voice to them as she walked down a narrow pathway with Filson. Lev's heartbeat quickened as he turned on his side to focus. Hearing her voice reminded him of the night in Rusk when he had seen her profile outlined by firelight as she washed their clothes.

The stirring of leaves drowned her exact words, but the sound of her voice caressed the scar on Lev's chest and pushed against the bullet lodged somewhere behind it. He could once again feel the hair on her arms tickling the hair under his. Hy leveled his rifle and pointed it at Filson. Lev put a hand on the barrel and pushed it down. Olivia was standing too close. As they lingered outside the door to the cabin, Olivia moved away from Filson as if signaling them to shoot him. Lev was impatient for Hy to pull the trigger, to end the years of agony that Filson had brought to their lives. When Hy released the hammer, Lev whispered. "If you lost your stomach for this, we can still walk away ... move west. I'll never bring it up again."

Hy turned toward his brother in the dark. "Lost my stomach? I ain't lost nothing. I just want the vermin to see it coming, who brought it ... and why." Hy turned back to his stomach and considered the small smokehouse. "I dreamed more'n once about cutting out his balls and stuffing 'em down his goddam throat. But the laws would go down just as hard on us for that as killing him. And we would still have to look at him."

Olivia turned to face them when Filson opened the door. Lev could not see her eyes, but he felt her pleading gaze.

Lev and Hy passed hours of agony. They had begun to wonder if Filson had killed her when a light flickered a few minutes before midnight. They rose and walked forward quietly and quickly. They stopped when they saw the dark outline of Anderson Bonner step out of the shadows. He stared at them for a few seconds, nodded, and then walked away.

Lev could smell Olivia's honeysuckle scent as Hy reached for the door latch. The door opened before he touched it. Olivia had blown out the candle and was waiting with her hand on the latch. She did not want its sound to stir Filson. Lev's eyes and throat constricted when he saw her. Her dark outline revealed that she stood naked, holding her clothes in the crook of her arm. Sparse moonlight from the window revealed chill bumps on her breasts and arms. Lev felt his body turn warmer than was justified by the warm night, his mind weaving softly between lust, anger, jealousy, and pity. He reached a tentative hand toward her. She stepped back, carefully avoiding looking into his eyes.

Hy walked quickly to the bed and leveled his pistol at Filson. Lev whispered to Olivia. "Get out. Now. Wait for us at home."

She stepped into her dress and tucked her bloomers under her arm. The stirring of the dress fabric brought the sweet smell of lilac water and stale talcum powder mixed with the scent of sex as Filson stirred in the bed. The smells brought burning acid to Lev's throat. He swallowed hard.

Filson looked first at the gun, then Olivia. "You bitch. I'll see you pay for this. You'll regret ..." Hy's pistol barrel swept gracefully but hard across Filson's face, stilling his threats, bringing blood to his lips, and breaking a tooth. He ran his tongue across the jagged tooth and spat blood on the floor.

Hy kept his pistol leveled. "How about talking that shit to me, you cowardly bastard. Your days of hurting women are goddam done."

Olivia looked at Lev with pleading eyes before walking through the door. Lev closed it behind her. Filson watched Olivia leave and spat out more blood. "You aim to kill an unarmed man?"

Hy looked at Filson's pistol, hanging on a ladderback chair next to the bed. "Go ahead and arm yourself if you feelin' lucky." When Filson did not budge, Hy smiled briefly before his eyes narrowed and his jaw clenched. "Take that excuse and tell it to the devil. You think I give a good goddamn whether you're armed or not? I reckon I'll give you the same chance you gave my wife."

Filson's eyes reflected more confusion than fear. It was as if he could not fathom the wild anger he felt emanating from the two men. "Your wife?" He leaned back on the pillow as if gathering his thoughts. "Yes, I do recall now. A comely woman. What was her name again?"

Their ears rung and their eyes stung from gun smoke when the shot rang out in the small room. Filson wrenched back, then forward to grab his knee as if his hands might stem the blood or mitigate the pain. "Goddamn you to hell. That's twice you shot me."

Hy pointed his pistol toward the ceiling. "Reckon you won't be needing that knee from now on, anyway." Hy absorbed the fear that had come to Filson's eyes the way a man dying from thirst drinks from a cool, bubbling spring.

Lev put a hand on his pistol grip, still resting in its holster on his left hip. "We got to go. Send the son-of-a-bitch to hell or I will."

Hy's eyes were blank as he turned toward Lev. He seemed to be in a trance as he allowed the pistol to lower until it was pointing at the foot of the bed. His visions of long torture to Filson had lost their appeal. Filson's head came up from the pillow as he propped himself on two elbows. The pain seemed to have abated. Shock, probably. "Hester, wasn't it?"

Hy jerked the pistol up and fired two shots into Filson's heart as quickly as he could pull back the hammer and pull the trigger. Filson's body jerked back and quivered. Smoke filled the room, burning their eyes, as Lev saw a small black spider making its way up the bedspread toward Filson. The room was so quiet that Lev imagined he could hear the spider crawl. It crossed the pillow just as a death rattle escaped from Filson's lungs and his eyes locked open in death's stare. The spider crawled across his face.

Filson's heart had pumped just enough to make a large bloodstain on his nightshirt before his eyes rolled back. Hy watched the cotton shirt slowly absorb the blood. "He ought not to have said her name."

Lev sighed deeply. His mouth was dry. "I reckon, by God, he won't ever say it again."

For a few seconds, Hy breathed huge gulps of air as if he were taking sustenance from Filson's death, replenishing what Filson had taken from his wife and from his own soul. But the replenishment seemed to fade away, leaving him empty. Hy holstered the Colt as if the handle had suddenly become hot. "Well, it's done. Let's go."

33

WORDS WERE OF NO USE ON THE WAY HOME. Lev was surprised and impatient when Hy dismounted at the graveyard instead of going directly to the house. He wondered if his brother had crossed sanity's bridge when he knelt by his parents' grave. Lev rode beside him, but did not dismount. Hy picked up a handful of dust and let it run through his fingers. "It don't feel like I thought it would." He rose and looked up at Lev. "Still, I couldn't let him go on breathing the same air as my Hester."

Lev's voice was filled with bitterness. "Had to be done. Less said about it now, the better." He looked back toward Dresden. "No sign of Olivia."

Hester and Mary Ann were ready when their men returned and had no questions as Lev and Hy carried their sleeping children to the wagons. The spattering of blood on Hy's shirt was telling, but they pretended not to notice. The men seemed especially gentle as they covered the children with quilts. The only delay came when Mary Ann ran to the family graveyard. She pushed dirt from between Sebastian and Rachael's graves into the small flower sack she had brought along for this purpose. Lev took it from her and put it in under the spring seat. He helped her into the wagon and smiled as he handed her the reins. The old plow and wagon horses had been traded and both wagons were pulled by teams now—one sorrel team and one gray. Both teams could run.

When the wagons were loaded, Lev hesitated as he looked down the trail toward Dresden. Hy stood in his stirrups as if he could see farther than Lev. "She said she would be all right. Said she had plans for after, didn't she?" Lev signaled for them to pull away.

Wishing for McCulloch or Sebastian, Lev led the way and Hy followed the wagons, riding back along the trail occasionally to see if they were followed. They traveled a meandering path heading generally west for three days, trying to pass through the country without being seen. After a week, they stopped worrying about being followed and started worrying about Kiowas. When they reached the Brazos, Lev saw two crows flying north along the banks of the river and followed.

They traveled slowly, often stopping well before dark to let the children rest. Lev and Hy knew that tracking and sense of direction had been gifts bestowed on their father and other brothers—that they had been given fighting and horsemanship as recompense. It took two weeks to find Palo Pinto Creek and Sebastian's homestead.

Lev held up a hand to stop the wagons and consider the place again with different eyes. The land was rocky with sparse grass and seemed ill-suited for raising stock or farming, but almost ideal for hiding. It seemed as if Sebastian knew they would be coming, knew they would be on the run. There was a meadow with rocky hills and cliffs on four sides, a small log shack, a dugout, even a corral with a lean-to shed that could be repaired with a few cedar posts and rails. He had chosen well.

Lev and Mary Ann stood outside and considered the dugout. Lev had heard his father talk about soddies before, but Mary Ann had never seen one. The dugout was mostly underground with a sod roof, short log walls, and a barrel chimney snuggled against the hill. He squeezed her arm. "Kinda reminds me of our honeymoon shack."

Mary Ann frowned at the comparison. "Makes me feel crowded just looking at it."

Spiders and other vermin scattered as they leaned down to enter the only door. Mary Ann was pleased that it had a wooden floor. The ceiling, however, was infested with wasp and dirt dauber nests and spider webs. She imagined spiders dropping on her face during the night. "I can stand the spiders, but I won't abide rattlesnakes, and I hear they're all over the place out here. I won't sleep on this floor with snakes crawling around."

Hy and Hester stepped out of the small cabin. He lifted his arms and seemed to take in the small valley completely. "Maybe we're supposed to be here. Remember that night you saw Papa come out of that fire? He was heading this way."

Lev was not so sure. "Don't know if we got any legal right, but we can make a good argument to anybody who tries to run us off. McCulloch says Papa filed all the papers. We got some claim, at least."

For days, the women unpacked and set up camp as Lev and Hy took turns traveling in a circle around their camp, looking for other settlers, sources of supplies, and possible danger. There were a few scattered settlers along the Brazos, but none closer than a day's ride.

Hy and Hester took the log cabin and Lev and Mary Ann took the dugout. It was late for a garden, but the women had brought seed and starters and planted one anyway. They did not know what would grow in the arid soil and what would not. They slept in the wagons until Lev and Hy could construct bed frames and slats from cedar trees and repair or replace holes in the roofs and walls. By the time Hester and Mary Ann spread the bedding they had brought in the wagon over the bed frames and cleaned the houses, it was cool enough to move inside. Lev and Hy broke colts for a neighbor in exchange for an old milk cow and a few chickens. They hunted and fished for the remainder of their food. Game was prevalent and generally easy to kill—a good thing, because hunting and fishing required more patience than either brother had.

Lev remained vigilant, watching the hills and the creek banks every day for strangers. He never saw an Indian within a day's ride of their secluded canyon. Hy had always been blessed with the ability to put unpleasant events in boxes and keep them closed. He used that ability with the killing. They mourned the fact that they might never see the rest of the family again, but were also relieved that it seemed they were not being pursued. Lev and Hy began to flourish in their freedom.

———————

Almost two years passed without real news from the outside world. They heard a few things from neighbors, but not much. The entire family was picnicking by the Brazos when a rider stopped from a respectable distance and helloed the camp, waving his hat for permission to enter. The young boy looked half cowboy and half farmer and appeared to be about nineteen or twenty, too young to be traveling the country alone. He was taller than Hy or Lev, but slight with red hair. They fed him fresh fish and onions and hot coffee and peppered him with questions. He said he was on his way to Fort Worth, intending to join a cattle drive going up the Chisholm Trail. He had been told that the Fort Worth settlement had fallen on hard times during the war, dropping to less than two hundred people, but was recovering because of cattle drives up the Chisholm. They milked the boy like a fresh cow for information of the outside world. He told them that Texas had been readmitted to the union. He turned toward the children. "Any of these younguns born during the war?"

Hester touched the heads of Otho and Kat. "Both of these."

The young cowboy waited until the children were out of hearing, then told them that Governor E. J. Davis had supported a law that would have bastardized children by nullifying all contracts made during the war, including marriage. He apologized for his language. The redheaded stranger told them that felons and Confederate veterans were the only ones not allowed to vote under the new government and that Governor Davis had asked the legislature to ban firearms. The Rivers shared meaningful glances, shook their heads and felt redeemed in their decision to leave Yankee tyranny behind.

When the boy mounted to leave the next morning, the women and children patted his legs as if he were one of their own, begging him to stay another night or even to settle permanently beside them. The boy could not read, but when he produced a newspaper from Austin from his saddlebags, Lev and Hy realized how hungry their wives had become for news of the outside world. When the young man saw Hester caress the paper and almost weep, he produced two more, saying that he had intended to spread them along the trail to folks who might be interested, but he was unlikely to find anyone who would enjoy them as much as this family named Rivers.

When Hy and Mary Ann finished with the papers, Lev focused on an editorial declaring "...we have never known such a flagrant abuse of power, such an open and bold violation of the rights of liberty and property of citizens..." The rest of the article attacked Yankee rule and the establishment of a state police force made up predominantly of colored lawmen, most of them former slaves. He also read about Jack Helm and state policemen who routinely killed prisoners instead of taking them in to stand trial. His blood grew cold as he read of thousands of arrests by these new state police.

In the coming days, Lev imagined seeing state policeman on every horse he encountered, behind every tree, on every hilltop. They had decided weeks before that Hy would travel to Fort Worth to sell four horses they had raised from weanlings and trained.

Hy looked forward to his second trip to Fort Worth. He took great pride in his abilities as a horse trader. Lev was helping him load a packhorse for the trip, warily watching the hills around the canyon, when Hy changed his mind. "You're making me nervous as a whore in church. Why don't you go to Fort Worth in my place? Take a break from all this."

Lev had not considered the possibility, but surprised Hy by agreeing at once. He had not seen civilization in almost two years. He made good time and was there in less than four days. Hy had always claimed the trip took a week. Lev negotiated a cheap price for one night's boarding for himself and his horses in a livery stable. The owner offered him use of an empty horse trough behind the horse stalls, a small mirror, and a bar of soap. It was dark by the time he hauled cold water to the trough and bathed. There was a lantern in the hall, but he decided it was too dangerous to light it with all the straw on the floor. In the dark hall of the livery, he shaved using his fingers to feel for whiskers. He soaked his clothes in the left over water, hung them across a stall rail and put on his only clean outfit. Mary Ann had given him a good haircut before leaving home, so he felt presentable as he found a wooden bench to sit on in a dark spot just outside. He leaned back against the livery door to see without being seen, but fell asleep in a few minutes.

He was awakened by gunfire. He buckled his gunbelt and peered down the street. Lights were coming from buildings on both sides of the street about two hundred yards from the livery stable. He returned to the bench and watched. He heard the sounds of revelry and another gunshot, but could see nothing but flickering lights and a moving shadow or two. Hy had told him about Hell's Half Acre—this must be it. Lev decided that potential horse buyers would likely frequent the place. A drunken buyer is likely to pay more for his stock than a sober one. Besides, Lev was curious.

As he drew closer to the lights, he heard the sounds of running horses and had to jump back to avoid being run over by three horses and riders racing down the middle of the street. He stopped to peer inside a circle of men watching one gamecock slaughter another. Outside a saloon next to the cockfight, he realized why Hy had said the round trip took two weeks. His brother loved saloons. He stepped into the saloon, eased to a corner table and sat down to watch.

A long bar ran most of the length of the back wall. Without meaning to, he caught a rare glimpse of himself in the bar mirror and wished he had paid more attention to his appearance. The room was loud and smoky, and Lev found it easy to remain inconspicuous. He watched a woman transfer a cigarette rolled with old newspaper from a cowboy's mouth to her own before drinking the last of his shot of whiskey and banging the counter for another.

The customers were mostly young, mostly cowboys, mostly armed, mostly drunk. They created so much demand on the bartender and the women that nobody approached Lev to sell him either food or drink. He watched it all with wide-eyed fascination. The young cowboys toyed with their guns and knives, making threatening gestures and occasionally firing their pistols. They made Lev aware of his age and his past. He thought of the revolver and knife on his hips, feeling confident that he knew how to use them, but hoping he would never use them again. Fatigue soon made the drunks boring to him and he rose to leave. He was half out of his seat when he felt her hand on his arm.

She sat down at the table without invitation. "What's your hurry, Cowboy?" She could not have been more than twenty. She was pretty in a mousy sort of way, with a thin face and light eyelashes. Her hair was the color of Hy's dun. It was thin and stringy and needed washing. But her eyes were deep and full of sorrow.

"Past my bedtime."

"Taking anybody to bed with you?"

Lev smiled. "Guess I'll go it alone."

"You look like a seasoned drover. We ain't seen many real cowboys in here for more'n a week. Just these boys. They say they waiting on a herd to come through, but they just hanging around. They claim to be cowboys, but mostly just swampers or carpenters and such."

Lev looked around the room. She seemed to be right. "I hear they're expecting a herd any day. You'll see real cowboys then."

She put an elbow on the table and rested her chin in her palm. Her eyes were inquisitive, searching. "You remind me of somebody."

"That right?"

She seemed embarrassed all of a sudden and stood. "I ain't gonna say who."

Lev stood as she walked away. As he stepped outside, the light from the saloon windows illuminated a street sign he had not seen before. Rusk, it said. A bad sign. He looked back toward the saloon, fully expecting to see a sign that said Good Samaritan, but there was no sign on the saloon. He hurried back to check on his horses and tack.

Lev showed what his horses could do on Rusk Street the next morning. He conferred with stockmen until he got a handle on horse prices. As Jacob Collins, his maternal grandfather's name, he sold his small remuda for a good price. He bought three more skinny colts and pocketed the rest. He lingered for two days, listening to talk about a railroad that would make Fort Worth a major player in the cattle industry. He watched the largest herd of cattle he had ever seen arrive in the stockyards. Nobody seemed to recognize him and there was little presence of law and no state police. He picked up some supplies at the new general store and prepared to leave.

He felt guilty for staying to watch the cowboys celebrate that night and the herd leave the next morning, and for how he envied those drovers as they headed north. The melancholy feeling stayed with him as he turned toward home. A sense of foreboding made him feel worse as he traveled. He was sure that bad news awaited him back on Palo Pinto Creek. He watched for owls and vultures all the way home, but saw no bad signs.

Worry was replaced with ebullience as Little Alfred, six now, looked up from the creek where he was fishing as Lev entered the arroyo that led to their small compound. Lev's travels had put a new face on the place, as he saw with refreshed eyes the porches they had added on the log cabin and dugout, the restored corral and the lean-to that had been converted to a barn. Hy had even made some progress on their new house in his absence.

The family gathered around a campfire that night to hear his stories of Fort Worth. Hy could not contain his enthusiasm as he heard about the large herd of cattle heading north. "We could gather us up a pretty good herd running wild around here if we put our minds to it."

34

"THEY AIN'T COMING, LEV. IT'S BEEN MORE than four years. People got bigger fish to fry than you and me. Besides, I'm the one did the killing." Hy had just returned from a trip to Dallas. He had used his real name in trading horses and a few steers for supplies and two 1866 Winchester rifles. He and Lev had ridden out to check their cattle and stopped on the banks of the Brazos to let their horses water.

Lev remained cautious. "We agreed that we would wait till we were sure. We haven't heard from anybody back home that we can trust to know what's happening." He followed his brother along the riverbank as he walked and led his horse. "Our brothers and sisters don't even know where we are and you go into one of the biggest settlements in Texas and start telling everybody your name. Damned foolish, Hy."

Hy pointed in the direction of their small herd "We done branded and bred our way to a respectable herd of cattle. We need to sell 'em."

"We take more than fifty head into Fort Worth, we'll draw attention."

"Hell, we both been to Dallas and Fort Worth and didn't create no stir at all."

"We went in like family men for supplies or to take a few

horses. Going in with a pretty big herd is different. We never used our real names before either."

Hy saw no need to add to Lev's concern by telling him he had always used his real name in all transactions and conversations. Made him ashamed to deny something he felt he had a right to. "You forgetting I got four kids and you got two to feed?" Dallas Matilda was three and Lane Arthur was one. Lev and Mary Ann's second child, Ellen Agnes, was two.

"They're fat and healthy enough, I reckon. All the more reason to stay close to home and out of sight."

"We're able to eat off the land well enough, but how about supplies? We need money for lumber to finish the house and build a horse barn if we aim to handle more horses. Merchants not as willing to trade as they used to be. They want money."

Lev knew his brother was right, but resisted driving the cattle to market until Hy mentioned the possibility of taking the women and children with them. "I'd a damn sight druther leave the place unattended than our families." It took almost a month to prepare for the trip. They fashioned wood wagon bows and borrowed an old wagon cover from a neighbor. The neighbor's wife had made it from spun linen and the husband had treated it with linseed oil for their trip west. It smelled of mildew and was rotten in places, but they figured it would serve to keep most of the rain off themselves and their supplies. They put Otho, Kat, and Little Alfred on horses and the other children in the wagon.

The weather had turned cool enough to make the children's noses red when they left in midmorning with the herd. Lev was nervous about leaving the place, but was more concerned about losing the cattle en route to Fort Worth. While Lev saw a stampede coming around every bend, Hy saw the trip as a great adventure and regaled the children with stories about what awaited them in the huge settlement called Fort Worth.

Lev's apprehension did not ease until they watered their

horses and cattle at the confluence of the West and Clear Forks of the Trinity River. He and Hy looked for signs of the arrival of the Texas and Pacific railroad in Fort Worth. There were none. Lev and the children kept the cattle from straying while Hy went into the settlement. He asked an old man sitting on a board fence, "Any herds coming through here that you know of?"

The old man shook his head. "Herds done tailed off quite a bit. Ain't you heard about the cattle market? Steers ain't bringing enough to pay the expense of driving 'em to Kansas."

"How you know that?"

"Cattlemen pass through here going to Kansas and coming back. Cattle that used to bring fifteen dollars a head are half that at the railheads now. Means they ain't worth shit here."

"Know anyplace where we could hold a little herd while we look for a buyer?"

The old man took off his hat and scratched his gray head. "You asking the wrong man. There's a few empty pens, but I don't own none of 'em." He pointed to a building down the street. "Might try in there. If there's any buyers for what you brung, they likely to be over there, too."

Hy read the sign. "Tidball, Van Zandt and Company. What kinda place is that?"

"They buy and sell cattle and such. Loan money, too. Likely as not, they probably own these pens."

Hy tried the door of the building and found it locked. A man in a brown wool suit stepped outside a dry goods store and hailed him. "Ain't open yet. Ready for business in a month or two. Can I help you?"

Hy walked close enough to shake hands with a man about his own age. "Hy Rivers."

"Major Van Zandt." He pointed a thumb over his shoulder. "I own this dry-goods store and am a partner in that business you was trying to get into."

Hy connected the sign to the name. "Feller sits on a fence rail over there said somebody around here might tell me where I could put about fifty head of cattle till I can find a buyer."

The man smiled. "That could be a long time, friend. Did he tell you that the cattle market had plunged?"

"He mighta mentioned that. Me and my brother ain't looking to get rich. Just sell for enough to take us through the winter."

Van Zandt pointed to the pens. "I can authorize you to go ahead and put your herd in those pens. I'll even see if I can find somebody to take them off your hands."

"Fair enough."

The cattle penned, Hy walked in the general direction of Hell's Half Acre. Lev leaned against the corral, coring an apple for Little Alfred while he watched a man walk down the board sidewalk. Otho sat on the fence rail beside Lev as the man crossed the dusty street with the morning sun at his back. He stopped in front of Lev. "K. M. Van Zandt. People around here call me Major."

"Lev Rivers." Lev cringed a little as his name sneaked out. But he knew Hy had already used it.

"Hy's brother, I presume."

Lev acknowledged with his eyes.

"Mister Rivers, as your brother may have told you, I am not a cattle buyer, but I pride myself on recognizing good stock when I see them. Mind if I walk through your herd?"

Lev shrugged. "Help yourself."

The man climbed the fence and walked through the herd, pushing cattle aside to make his way. He stopped frequently to watch the mixed herd mill. Unconcerned about what was happening to his shiny boots, he walked back to where Lev was leaning his elbows over the top rail. "All branded, I see. Mostly mavericks and wild ones left from the war?"

"Started out with range cattle running loose. We caught and branded 'em as we found 'em. Then we culled and raised what you see here. We left a few for beef and starting over. We mostly deal in broke horses. Cattle is a sideline."

"As I said, I am not a cattle buyer. However, I have sent messengers to people who are. I expect one or two might arrive in a week or so."

"A week? Hell, we got a place to get back to. Had hoped to leave sooner than that. We stay that long, we'll have to move the cattle back and forth from the Trinity for water and grass."

Van Zandt put a foot on the bottom rail. "Yes, sir, I expect you will." They both looked out over the milling herd. "Look, Lev. May I call you Lev?" Lev nodded.

"I almost never trade in cattle. I lend money and sell dry goods. However, I have been known to take a calculated risk once in a while. Would you be insulted if I made an offer for the cattle?"

"Don't reckon I got to take it if I don't like it."

"I'll take them all at three dollars a head, calves and all."

Otho looked down at Little Alfred and winked as Lev wrinkled his forehead and flinched, turned his back and walked off a few feet. Van Zandt followed him. "I know that's cheaper than what you expected, but the bottom has dropped out of the market and I don't know if I'll be able to sell them at all."

Lev climbed the fence and walked through the cattle, acting as if Van Zandt had offered to purchase his children for a paltry sum. He pointed out the qualities of various steers and heifers. "The bull ain't here, but these cows are out of good stock."

Van Zandt nodded. "I am sure they are. I do not question the quality of your herd, sir. And I warn you that I intend to offer them to a buyer at four dollars a head."

Lev had been skeptical at first, but the man seemed sincere. He knelt to one knee and tossed clods at a steer's hooves. "So you gonna take a dollar premium for the risk of the herd not selling?"

Van Zandt smiled. "I admire a man who understands business, sir. I may not sell them at all or I may have to sell them at less than I paid you. All the while, I will have to hire men to feed the cattle and transfer them back and forth to grass and water."

"Course, you're pretty sure you're gonna get four a head."

"I expect to get four, I'll ask four-fifty."

Lev frowned. "Have to talk it over with Hy. How long's the offer good?"

Van Zandt turned to walk away. "Close of business today. When I get home, I will be honor-bound to tell my wife of my gamble and she is a conservative woman."

People recognized Hy when he and Lev looked for buyers in Hell's Half Acre. He carried on conversations with people he seemed familiar with, but found no cattle buyers. At six o'clock, they walked into the dry-goods store with Hester, Mary Ann and all the children and asked for an extension until noon the next day. Van Zandt, smiling at Little Alfred, Lane and Ellen, granted it. "I will leave the offer open till noon."

Lev indicated the rest of his family with a wave of his hand. "We'll need to leave as soon as them cows are sold, and one way or another, you know they'll be sold by noon. If you would extend us some credit against that sale, we'd be much obliged. Save us from loading up and leaving late tomorrow."

Van Zandt walked to the counter, spoke to a clerk and returned to Lev. "Pick out what you need and he'll make a list."

They stocked up on supplies and dry goods and went back to the wagon. Lev and Hy were up at dawn, talking to everyone on the street and in every business in the settlement. No interested cattle buyers. At noon, they settled with Van Zandt and headed home.

As a precaution, Lev always rode a half-mile or so in front of the wagon and Hy rode the same distance behind. Almost two days out of Fort Worth, Butter began to shake her head and walk sideways. The unusual behavior irritated Lev and he was about to discipline her when he saw a wild boar rooting in a bog. A bad sign.

The bullet stung him a little, but Lev had almost forgotten the boar when they turned down the canyon toward home. They were un-harnessing the team and unloading the wagon when he saw a white owl sitting round-eyed on the porch of the dugout. He pulled his new Winchester from its scabbard.

Mary Ann put a hand on the rifle barrel. "What's got into you? That owl ain't doing no harm." Lev did not tell her what his grandmother had said about owls in the daytime.

35

LEV HAD FORGOTTEN THE OWL AND THE WILD boar by spring. His new colt had broken his first real sweat as he stopped on the ledge above the canyon, Lev's favorite spot. Two scrub oaks that seemed to grow out of solid rock offered scant shade and slight cover for him to see without being seen. It was one of the only spots on the hills where cedars did not block the view. The sight of their little compound from above usually calmed him, made him feel safe. It took a moment for the white wooly animal tied to a hitching rail in front of the horse corral to register. Sheep. Olivia.

Lev eased down into the canyon on the sure-footed young horse, thinking about the owl, the boar, and the last time he had seen Olivia. Why had she come? How had she found them? He took his time unsaddling and feeding the colt, hoping that Hy would emerge to tell him whatever bad news Olivia had brought. Outside the barn, he felt watched and scanned the horizon and hills for signs of who might be watching. He returned to the barn for his rifle.

Lev was pleased as he entered their small cabin and saw it through Olivia's eyes. She was having coffee at the kitchen table with Mary Ann and Hester. He stood mute in the kitchen doorway, his rifle across his chest. Olivia examined him the same way that he inspected horses, the way she had looked him over that first time in Rusk. Mary Ann studied her husband's expression. The silence finally got to Hester. "Well, where are your manners, Lev Rivers?"

Lev hung the Winchester on a rack above the outside door and removed his hat, feeling conscious of his changed appearance since Olivia had seem him last. The sun had darkened and reddened his complexion, made the lines in his face deeper. He knew a fine film of dust had settled on his face and clothes and that he smelled of a wet saddle blanket. "How do you do, Olivia? It has been a long time, for a fact." Without meaning to, he thought of the last time he had seen her, pulling on her dress, the smell of death in the small cabin.

Olivia smiled. "I do fine, thank you. You still carrying a bullet around inside you?"

Lev put a hand on the old wound. "I reckon. And what brings you to these parts?"

Her smile disappeared. "My husband is a trapper and hunter. Mostly East. He wanted to see the western country."

Lev stiffened slightly. "Husband. I was not aware you were married."

"Less than a year. Name's Jack LeDoux. Cajun fellow. Talks a little funny, but he'll do, I guess."

"We ran across a few Creole folks in Louisiana during the war."

Hy walked in the back door and spoke to Lev. "See you finally got here." He turned toward Olivia. "I see what you mean about that husband of yours. Didn't see hide nor hair of him. Can't you call him in?"

Olivia smiled. "He'll come when he's ready. We can all feel safer with him out there, I reckon."

Lev threw his leg over the back of a chair and eased down into his customary seat at the head of the table. He sat as if the chair were on fire. Hy dropped his hat on the table and sat at the other end.

Olivia took a deep breath as she ran her index finger back and forth through her coffee cup handle. "I bring news. I'm sorry it is not good."

Lev rose a little out of his seat. "Maybe it would be best if me and Hy hear this by ourselves."

Mary Ann put a hand on his. "Sit down, Lev. We been dancing around what happened back home long enough. Me and Hester ain't exactly stupid." She turned toward Olivia. "Go ahead."

Olivia put both hands on the table and studied them. "I guess you all were like me. I thought the thing with Filson had gone away. Most people around Ellis and Navarro counties just said good riddance. There was some talk by Union men and politicians about bringing killers to justice and all that, but everybody figured it was just talk."

Lev sucked in his breath as she paused. With his eyes, he urged her to get on with it. Olivia's face crinkled a little and her eyes glistened. "Then it raised its ugly head in the spring."

Hy nervously rolled the brim of his hat. "How come?"

"Lydia Filson, that's why." Olivia's lips puckered as if she had bitten into a green persimmon. "You'll recall that she was his wife. Well, she came back to town. She was all floozied up and said she came back to p ... er ... spit on her dead husband's grave."

Hester drummed her fingers on the table. The talk of Lydia Filson made her face warm. "I recall seeing her once."

Olivia frowned and seemed impatient with the question. "Seems she runs a whore ... a house of ill-repute in Dallas."

Lev drummed his fingers. "Go on. Get to it." Recognizing his tone sounded harsh, he amended. "If you're a mind to."

Olivia took a deep breath. "The long and short of it is that you boys were both indicted for murder in Dallas County in March."

Hy's chair fell backward as he jumped to his feet. "Damn. Are you sure?"

"Can't be absolutely sure because it was a sealed indictment.

But Jack, my husband, knows some people and Wade Monroe is telling it all over."

Mary Ann put her hands on her mouth to stifle a whimper. "Good Lord. How can that be—after all this time?"

Olivia shook her head. "Nobody knows for sure why. Only thing I know is that Lydia stirred up the pot. Bragged in the saloon and around town that she knew who did it and wanted to find you two so she could offer her thanks. Like the fool she is, she got a snootful and kept asking folks if they knew where you got off to. Said she would be glad to pay you for shooting the s.o.b. All the talk must have gotten to some of the laws."

Hester shook her head. "Has to be more than that. How do they know who did it?"

Olivia stared at her hands. "I don't know, but they say Anderson Bonner testified in front of the grand jury."

Hy stood and looked out the window. "We never made much secret of it. Still don't make no sense after all this time."

"I admit that, but if you consider the politics and all."

"What's politics got to do with us?"

"With reconstruction ending, the military is losing its power. Reconstruction lawyers and judges getting thrown out. I expect they wanted to get one last drop of revenge on Confederate soldiers before they leave. Filson's case embarrassed them, especially the military. One of their own killed right under their noses."

Mary Ann wrung her hands on the table. "Won't the new folks help us out? I mean, if the Confederates and Democrats are coming back into power ... they're Southerners."

Olivia put her hand over Mary Ann's. "Maybe. Some people say the Yankees are tightening down because of what Jesse and Frank James are doing. There's pressure to tighten down on anybody who seems to keep re-fighting the Civil War."

Hy turned away from the window and looked at Lev. "We never robbed no trains or banks. Never took nothing that wasn't ours, except when somebody was trying to rob us."

Olivia nodded. "I know that, but right now, there is a warrant out for your arrest and Jack says that Texas Rangers have you and Lev on a list of wanted fugitives."

Lev stood. "Texas Rangers ... looking for us?"

"And Jack says they have a base camp less than a day's ride from here."

Hy looked at his brother. "The hell you say. We ain't seen nothing of a Ranger camp around here."

Olivia shrugged. "Jack says it's down in a valley not far from here on a branch off this creek that runs by your place. He knows a Ranger or two. Most Rangers carry around little books that list wanted fugitives and you boys are on those lists."

Lev's voice was weak with despair. "Texas Rangers after us. Imagine that. Texans after us."

Hester reached to touch Hy's trembling hand. "I imagine it ain't personal. They don't know nothing about the why's and what-for's."

Mary Ann stood and pressed nervous hands against her apron as if it might fall. "Hester, we best start supper. We got company."

When Olivia stepped into the yard the next morning after breakfast, Jack LeDoux seemed to appear out of nowhere. Lev led a saddled Sheep from the barn and was startled to see him. Olivia introduced them. "Lev, I would like for you to meet my husband, Jack LeDoux." Jack wore a soft-brimmed cloth hat at a rakish angle. His skin was swarthy, eyes black, gaze piercing. His expression changed from cock-sure and threatening to friendly when he showed a fine set of white teeth as he smiled. He appeared to be at least a decade older than Olivia.

Lev reached up a hand to him. "Welcome. Appreciate you bringing Olivia to warn us."

"It was her wanted to come." He turned to Olivia. "We best be on our way." His accent reminded Lev of his time in the Louisiana swamps.

Olivia mounted as the whole Rivers family came into the yard. She rode close to Hester and Mary Ann. "You didn't ask, but I imagine you are wondering why your husbands and not me." She held up her hand to still the protesting shaking of their heads. "The answer is, I don't know. Maybe because I'm a woman. Maybe Doc Robinson ..." They nodded and she turned to follow LeDoux out of the draw. She turned Sheep and trotted back. "One thing, though. They won't find me to testify against you. Even if they do, I won't."

Lev watched them leave. "If that Creole can find us, then the Rangers sure as hell can."

36

LEV AND HY RODE OUT, SLUMPED IN THEIR saddles, soon after Olivia and LeDoux left. Both knew where they were going, but did not speak of it. They needed time to think. They followed the Leon River until they saw a string of tents strung haphazardly in a small valley along the riverbank. Half a dozen horses were strung out on a rope line between two mesquite trees. Three men were dragging logs into the campsite. Lev and Hy moved out of sight and dismounted to watch. They were close enough to hear the sound of their voices, but could not make out the words. There were no women or children, only young men. No ordinary campsite.

Hy rationalized the camp as a good sign. "Hell, if they was after us, they would have already come. Setting up housekeeping right in our back yard means they don't know or care a tinker's damn about us."

Lev's eyes squinted as he watched. "You know what this really means."

"What?"

"Means we got to move farther west."

Hy studied the sky for several minutes. His face darkened. "You remember our pledge?"

"What pledge is that?"

"About prisons and doctors." Silence. "If they catch me and

---

they ain't no chance for me to get away, you shoot me before you shoot them. I can't stand the thought of no prison. Can't stay in the house for long periods, much less get locked up behind bars."

When Lev did not acknowledge him or reply, Hy pointed two fingers at his brother. "I'm telling you I won't make it locked up."

There was little discussion and no argument as they began preparing the wagons for a trip. The women knew it was inevitable, and the children thought they were going to Fort Worth again. They planned to head north, away from the Rangers and west toward a less settled country. They had heard of rich grazing in the Panhandle. Comanches were said to be a problem, but widely scattered.

Not sure what settlements, if any, would be found along the trail, Lev took a packhorse and risked a trip into Palo Pinto for ammunition and supplies. Bringing his bounty home, he rounded a curve in the trail and approached his favorite spot overlooking their compound. The hair on the back of his neck stood up as he saw two turkey vultures swoop down the canyon wall toward his house. Noise from the packhorse and his cargo seem to pierce his eardrums.

He dismounted and stood between the two scrub oaks. The dun was saddled and tied in his customary place by the hitching rail, but a long-jawed horse stood ground-tied in the yard between Hy's house and the horse barn. It had a halter type headstall with wide brow and nosebands and large ring bits. The horse looked tired and bored, as if it were used to being left standing for long periods. It was well and efficiently saddled, with a large square blanket-pad, a double-rigged and well-used saddle with wide wooden stirrups. A thin bedroll was tied behind the cantle. The rifle scabbard was empty. Lev had seen the horse before.

He pulled his rifle from his scabbard and lay down between the two trees, rested the barrel of the Winchester between two rocks, and waited. The setting sun had cast its daily shadow over the compound when the door finally opened. Hy looked up as he came out the door. Lev was almost ready to stand and wave when he noticed that Hy's hands were tied behind his back. A man followed him with a rifle. The man wore a small felt hat and sported a fastidious mustache and a jaunty blue neck rag flopped over a wool vest. He walked stiffly and formally, his rifle slung loosely over the crook in his arm, his other hand resting on the butt of a holstered Colt. He seemed solicitous as he helped Hy to mount the dun, but malevolent when he tied Hy's ankles to the stirrups with rawhide string. When the Ranger mounted his horse, he touched his hat, and the women and children flooded into the yard as if it had been a signal. Hester and Mary Ann were crying but seemed to hold their emotions in check to keep from upsetting the children. Otho stared at the Ranger with death in his eyes.

Lev leveled the Winchester, relieved that Hy had talked him into trading for the newer gun, pulled back the hammer, sighted between the Ranger's shoulder blades, and fingered the trigger until a movement to the south revealed another rider sitting on the opposite ledge. Of course, the Ranger had not come alone. Lev wondered how many there were and whether they were surrounding him as he lay there. He looked behind him and to all sides but saw only the one other Ranger. When he turned back, Hy had turned the dun to face Lev and was looking up. Lev sighted again, this time on the middle of his brother's chest. The bullet in his chest throbbed. He tried to recall Hy's exact words and what he had promised. What would happen next if he were to pull the trigger? The children would see their father and uncle die, see Lev run for his own life. Hester would rush to her fallen husband, looking up to see where the shot had come from. Would she ever understand? Could he kill Hy and then kill both Rangers? Could he kill both Rangers before they could kill him or Hy? What if there were more? He moved his sight away from Hy to the Ranger and massaged the trigger until they were out of the canyon.

He rolled over on his back and looked up at the darkening sky, feeling like a coward for breaking a promise to Hy. He lifted himself up, tied Butter and the packhorse to the scrub oaks, and eased down the rocky ledge. He had only gone a few yards before he stumbled in the dark and caused rocks to cascade down the hill. He found a large rock to lie behind and waited for reaction to his clumsy noise. A coyote howled from close to where the second Ranger had been on the opposite ledge. Lev saw two dark shadows that could only be horsemen near the top of the ridge. Of course, they had been waiting for the other brother to show. He scrambled back up, untied both horses, mounted Butter and slapped the packhorse down the trail toward home. He pointed Butter north.

37

<hr>

HY GAVE GRUDGING RESPECT TO THE RANGER who decided to take him to Dallas alone. He was firm and emotionless, unfailingly polite, and the most cautious man Hy had ever seen. He did not sleep until Hy had been securely roped to a big tree trunk with a thirty-foot rope. The Ranger always apologized when he unwrapped the rope the next morning. Hy was allowed to sleep an extra hour with only his feet and hands tied while the Ranger cooked breakfast. He was fed well and treated courteously, but the Ranger did not want to make conversation, especially about why Hy had killed a military man.

Hy tried to shame him for taking him away from a wife and children who needed protection. The Ranger studied on Hy's situation for a full day's ride before he made any reply. "Don't they have family that will come and collect 'em?"

Hy shook his head. "Their family don't even know where we were. You forget we been hiding?"

It was another day before the Ranger replied. "We'll try to look in on your family from time to time. We sometimes kill more game than we need."

The man's tranquility wore on Hy, especially when he peacefully read his Bible each night before drifting off to sleep, leaving Hy hogtied to a tree. Finding that the man was a Confederate veteran, Hy spoke fondly of the Confederate cause and how he and

<hr>

his family had been abused by Yankees and carpetbaggers. The man was apolitical. Hy could not bear to tell him why he had really killed Filson. He sensed it would have made no difference, anyway. He looked for any opportunity to escape, but the Ranger left none.

It was night when they rode into Dallas and Hy got his first somber look at gas lamps illuminating the street and the signs of businesses. He had developed a toothache the first day on the trail and the pain had become worse with each step the dun took. When the gas lamps illuminated a small shingle with a drawing of a tooth and "Holliday-Dentist", he started to ask the Ranger to stop, but knew it would do no good. They crossed the Texas and Pacific railroad tracks and Hy almost fell off when the dun ran sideways at the sound of a train engine letting off steam. They rode in a light mist that created droplets off their hat brims. They finally stopped in front of a board and batten building that gave no hint of its function.

The Ranger silently followed as the jailer led Hy down a long dark hall and locked him in a cell. His face and countenance remained expressionless as he asked Hy to put his hands through the bars. He efficiently removed the ropes that bound Hy's wrists, coiled the small rope and hung it on the butt of his pistol.

Hy managed a crooked grin. "Not a man to waste any motion or task, are you?" The Ranger walked back down the hall without answering. Hy lay down on the cot in the dark cell and tried to recall how his worst fear had come true. He was running his tongue across his swollen gums when a man appeared at his cell door with a tin cup full of coffee. The man wore a wool suit with a vest that stretched tight against a well-fed paunch. His trouser legs were too long and had been dragged through muddy streets and across splintered floors. The man pulled up a chair, sat down with his coffee cup and crossed his legs. Hy noticed lace-up, high-topped shoes that had not seen a brush, shine rag, or shoe polish in their long lives. The visitor slurped his coffee and ran a finger under an ample mustache to collect the drippings. Hy involuntarily swallowed as he imagined having his own cup of coffee.

"H. H. Sneed, Mister Rivers. Do you have representation?"

Hy did not know what he meant, and his expression showed it.

The man tried again. "I mean are you represented by counsel?"

"Reckon not."

"The charge against you is murder, sir. I am at your service, and you will need my help."

"What's it gonna cost?" Hy's surprise arrest inside his own horse barn had caused him to leave home without as much as a coin.

"Depends on the facts of the case and the length of the trial. No way to know for sure."

"When and where is this trial gonna take place?"

"Next door, in the district courtroom of the Fourteenth District. I expect it will take place before the week is out. We can try to delay it if you like, but it won't do us any good."

"Not in Ellis County?"

"No, a change of venue was requested to assure you receive a fair trial."

"Who requested that?"

"It is a rather queer set of circumstances, Mister Rivers. All of that judicial maneuvering was done when the Rangers telegraphed to announce your capture. If you are not represented by counsel, I expect that the prosecuting attorneys in Ellis County somehow arranged to have your case transferred to Dallas in order to make it easier to secure a conviction."

"Thought it was so I could get a fair trial."

"That is usually the reason for a change in venue, but the law often works in strange ways."

Hy had expected a friendly jury back in Ellis County. He slumped back on the jail cot. "Don't reckon I'll be needing your services, Mister Sneed. Seems I left home on such short notice I forgot to bring along any cash. Besides, I figure I got little chance in a town full of strangers. Maybe you could just bring me a pistol instead."

Sneed stood and leaned a shoulder against the cell bars. "Poor lawyers are used to poor clients, Mister Rivers. Perhaps we could make a trade."

"Got nothing to trade."

"Perhaps not, sir, but I am an admirer of good horseflesh and could not avoid noticing the dun you rode in on."

Hy's eyes narrowed at first and Sneed began to think his client was capable of murder. He took a few steps down the hall before Hy called him back. "S'pose it's possible to get me a dentist thrown in on the deal?"

"I don't catch your drift."

"Worst toothache I ever had. Tried to dig it out myself, but not much luck without pliers."

"Assuming that the saddle is part of the bargain, I might be able to manage a dentist."

Hy looked in the general direction of the hitching rail where he had left the dun, ashamed that he had been unable to bed him down with a full belly. He had not even asked where his horse was stabled. Lev would never have done that. "That's been a fine horse that served me well. My brother grows right fond of all his animals. Never been sentimental about one myself ... until the dun."

"Doc Holliday is the only dentist I know that might work on a man locked up for a killing. He's a man been known to use a knife and pistol better than his dental equipment."

"Saw the sign when I rode into town. It's just a tooth-pulling. I ain't particular who does it."

Holliday arrived just before sunset the day before Hy's trial. He carried a small valise and a strong smell of whiskey and smoke. It smelled good to Hy. Like freedom. The dentist stared at him for a few seconds before speaking. "Which tooth?"

Hy put a tongue in his swollen cheek. "Last one on the top. Right side."

Holliday looked toward the jailer's office down the hall. "I wouldn't ordinarily leave a poker game to do dental work, but they tell me they gonna try you for killing some bastard what attacked your wife."

Hy nodded.

"They took my weapons but, (he patted the valise), I can kill a man seven ways from Sunday with what I got in here. Nothing against you, Mister Rivers, but I need your word that you ain't gonna give me no trouble if I step into that cell. Don't want to have to kill a man who's already got too much trouble."

"I got nothing against you. Ain't prone to kill people without reason ... at least not until you pull this damn tooth."

"Fair enough. The extraction will hurt, but not for long. They won't let me give you any whiskey, either." Holliday hollered for the jailer to open the cell door and bring a bucket of water.

Minutes later, Holliday dropped the bloody tooth into Hy's shirt pocket. "A souvenir. Rub on it during the trial. Might bring you luck."

Hy thought of his superstitious brother. "Might just do that. Much obliged. Assume that lawyer paid you." He swashed a dipperful of water around in his mouth and spit the bloody remainder in the corner of his cell.

Holliday closed the valise and stood. He lingered in the hall after the jailer had locked the cell door. "You ever hear of John Neely Bryan?"

"Can't say as I have."

"Well, he built that log cabin just down the street. First building around here. Folks say he founded this town. He was postmaster, owned a general store, ran a ferry across the Trinity. That sort of thing."

Hy did not see what this had to do with him, but was glad for the conversation. "Well, it's a big place, all right. How many people you reckon?"

Holliday pulled a cigar from his vest pocket, handed it to Hy, struck a match, and lighted it for him. It was the second cigar Hy had ever smoked, and it tasted sweet and good. Freedom again. "Much obliged."

"Way too many. They say more than seven thousand." Holliday pondered his cigar. "Thing is, this Bryan feller shot a man for insulting his wife. Might want to mention that to Sneed in case he don't know it. Maybe he could use it during the trial. Might help with the jury. John Neely Bryan is sort of old and slow-witted now, but he's still a local hero."

"Much obliged. I'll mention it."

Holliday lighted his own cigar and continued to linger. Hy hated to ask the next question. "Did they let this John Neely Bryan off?"

"Don't know the exact details, but he left town after the shooting and stayed gone six years. Gave the feller he shot time to completely recover."

Hy's face fell. "Man I shot won't be recovering."

Doc Holliday put out a hand, and Hy reached through the bars to shake it. The dentist started back down the long hall. He turned for a final word. "Never shot a man with the idea that he might recover. Damn poor job of shooting on Bryan's part, if you ask me."

The trial took a full day. Hy was impressed with Sneed's rhetorical skills that portrayed him as a brave man defending his wife's honor, but E. G. Bowers and George Aldridge, the prosecuting attorneys, painted a picture of an unarmed military officer being shot while in his bed. Wade Monroe led a parade of witnesses, some reluctant, that told of Hy's public promises to kill the man who had insulted his wife. Hy refused to deny the killing and only allowed Sneed to accuse Filson of insult and ravage. He drew the line when Sneed wanted to say rape in an open courtroom. The less said about his Hester, the better. Judge Hare recessed a full day in order to prepare a written charge to the jury. Hy rubbed the pulled tooth all the way back to his cell.

Back in his jail cell, Hy poked at a supper of cold beans and salt pork while Sneed explained what his options were. He assumed a guilty verdict. The only real question was whether they would find Hy guilty of murder or manslaughter and whether the judge felt favorably disposed toward him.

Hy put down his spoon and stared at his lawyer. "What's the difference?"

Sneed stiffened and took a deep breath. "First degree murder, you could be hung or get life. Second degree, no less than five, manslaughter, two to five years."

"I mean what's the difference in what you call it? I killed a son-of-a-bitch that needed killing. How can people lock up a man for that?"

"The judge will likely instruct the jury to decide your punishment based on when, why and how you did it."

Hy held his blank look.

Sneed had come to admire his client's pragmatic and clear view of right and wrong. Hy was not to be confused by shades of gray. "It comes down to this, Hy. If you had killed the man while he was in the act of, uh ... ravishing your wife, then it would clearly be manslaughter. Seeing as how you had time after he did it to consider the impact of what you were about to do, the jury may be inclined to find you guilty of murder."

"You mean if a man catches another man attacking his wife, it's all right to kill him right then, but if he don't catch him right then and kills him for it later, he gets punished more?"

"I'm afraid you have reached to the heart of it."

Hy studied Sneed's face for a long time, walked to the back

of his cell and faced the wall. Emotion welled and collided with his sense of honor, right and wrong. "I kilt the son-of-a-bitch as soon as I could."

38

GUILTY OF SECOND-DEGREE MURDER. EIGHT years in the state penitentiary at Huntsville. Hy felt both the contents and the outside of his stomach roll over as the verdict was read the next day. He tossed the tooth on the floor and stepped on it. Hester's moan from the back of the courtroom startled him. He had not known she was there. The agony of having her see him as a convicted prisoner washed over him like scalding water as he turned to find her. He had been able to keep his emotions intact, almost dead, during the ordeal until now. He felt anger at Lev for allowing her to come, anger at the jury for convicting him, anger at the witnesses who had come forward, but nothing compared to the agony of being humiliated in front of his wife.

He met her loving eyes before looking to see if any of the children were there. She had mercifully left them at home. She came forward and he was allowed to take her in his arms for a few seconds before they led him back to his cell. "Kiss my babies and don't tell 'em their Papa's in prison. And tell Lev not to be caught alive. I'd rather be dead than to be going where I'm going. They'll do the same to him if they get the chance."

A beautiful spring sunrise greeted Hy as he was led out of the jail the next morning. He was chain-shackled to a Negro and loaded on a wagon bed with two other similarly shackled prisoners. Two shotgun-armed deputies stood on the bed and balanced themselves at the front and back as a third deputy put reins to a two-horse team. Hy wondered if they were going to make the trip to Huntsville by wagon. He tried to keep his mind blank, but it worked on options for escape without his permission. His options depleted as they unloaded at the train station and disappeared completely when they were shackled to a railing in a freight car.

The Negro moved as far away from Hy as his chains would allow. "They tells me you as likely to slit my throat as not."

Hy turned to face his fellow prisoner. The man's face was half smile, half terror-stricken. "They'd be right."

"Say they gonna hang you for killin' a man."

"Suppose you're taking the trip to Huntsville for your health."

"Dallas burned down a few years back. Ever time they's a fire since then, they pick out a colored man to blame. My turn."

Tired of talking, Hy turned away.

They made the day-long trip standing up. Hy had been denied permission to visit the outhouse that morning and soon felt an urgent call of nature. He was told to wait, but when he said he could not, a deputy hooked another chain to the shackle around his waist, rolled open a side door and let him urinate out the door. He leaned against the chain, knowing that this would be the first of many personal humiliations he would suffer. He hoped that the chain would slip from the guard's hands. He would gladly take his chances in a fall from a moving train. The wind in his face and the countryside rolling by drained him of any hope and made him angry for not appreciating his freedom when he had it.

For most of his life, Hy had been able to put aside negative images or unhappy thoughts. During the war, the aftermath of battles seldom stayed with him more than a day. Even after killing Filson, the excitement of seeing new country washed away his trepidations like soft snow on a windswept plain. Standing against the rail, he tried to make his mind blank, but it kept mentally calculating eight years into days and hours. Without a pencil, he figured Otho would be twenty-two—Kat nineteen—marrying age. Their childhoods would be gone.

Inside the two-foot-thick brick walls of Huntsville prison, Hy was fed two cold biscuits, molasses and coffee before he was allowed to bathe. Naked, every fiber of his being resisted as he was rudely examined for identifying marks and scars. He was measured and weighed and recorded at five-nine, one-sixty-five. Standing in front of a stain-covered and deeply scratched wooden desk in his newly issued underwear, brogan shoes and dingy muslin shirt and pants, Hy was asked about marital status, tobacco use and his former occupation by a surly employee sitting behind a filthy desk. Hy grunted his answers, incoherent enough not to care about the accuracy of his replies. The surly interviewer noted his temperament as being sullen, recorded his complexion, eye and hair color in a journal. Hy flinched when the attendant consulted paperwork brought by the deputies and wrote murder under the offense column in the ledger. He sighed deeply when he saw the man write eight years in the sentence column and 1882 in the release date column. The man handed him a piece of paper. "You read?"

Hy's voice was weak and hoarse. "Prisoner number three-three-eight-three, wheelwright shop."

After the interview, he was taken to the prison barbershop where he was shaved and given a haircut. He stood passively in the blacksmith shop as an iron band was fitted around his ankle and attached to a ball and chain. Hy picked up the ball and followed a guard through the prison yard and up the stairs to a second floor cell. Other prisoners, some dressed in stripes and others in the same uniform Hy was issued, stared at the new inmate. The guard unlocked the ball's chain from outside the cell. "Your cellmate will be Emmett Day. He'll be along after supper. He gets to work late in the saddle shop sometimes."

Hy looked around his new home as he listened to the guard

lock the cell door. Two stacked wooden bunks with cornshuck mattresses, a slopjar underneath, a mottled-gray tin pitcher and basin with rust spots on a small table, a picture of a man and his family tacked to the wall with a rusty nail. He leaned back against the wall and slid down with his face in his hands. He had tried to chase his family's images from his brain, tried to empty his mind of thoughts. Now, he was truly alone. His mother's voice whispered in his ear, her shamed face played upon his mind. Rachael had urged him to repent, to get right with the Lord, attend church and be baptized. Now, it was too late. He wanted to talk to God, to ask for help, but was ashamed. A man did not turn to God after he was in trouble. He turned to God before he needed Him.

39

HE HAD NOT KEPT TRACK OF THE DAYS SINCE Hy's capture, but it seemed to have rained at least a little each day. Palo Pinto Creek had overflowed twice, but Sebastian had planned his buildings in harmony with the creek's flow and none were flooded. Lev found a small cave just as he began to feel he would never be dry again. The weeks had brought only pain and despair—no comfort, no plan, no signs. He had tried to see the image of his father, tried to imagine having McCulloch guide him. He needed help desperately, but none appeared.

He knew the supplies he had sent down on the packhorse had to be running low. The family could not move back to East Texas without him, and he could not go along without being caught. The Rangers would know the minute they started packing to leave. He decided to stay and feed them by hunting and fishing. He was a poor hunter and fisherman and knew it, but he now had to get better at both and he would have to do it without bringing attention to himself.

Lev's belly groaned as he watched the home light from his rock ledge. Always skinny, his ribs now seemed to be expanding through his skin. His chest was tender to the touch and his shirt scraped against chafed nipples with each labored breath. It was the weakness that frightened him more than anything else. He needed to be prepared at all times for fight or flight, and he was not.

On some days, he was so dizzy he could not stand. He could smell himself, especially the mustache that had grown completely over his mouth. He tried to make a mental note to wash in the Brazos before dawn, but knew he might forget. Hunger was affecting his vision and his thinking. He watched Mary Ann or Hester's shadow, he could not tell which, blow out the lamp. His wife and children had moved to Hy and Hester's slightly bigger house.

Hester and Mary Ann were practical, frugal and resourceful women. Lev rode methodical circles around the small gorge they called home, each circle wider than the previous one. Riding calmed him, helped him to focus on the tasks that lay before him. Ashamed for not paying more attention before, he looked at the land with new eyes, trying to mentally mark other homesteader land, hiding places, good campsites, good hunting and fishing. He rode the same circles for days, always on the lookout for Rangers. He began to be able to see, to read signs, inside the cedars.

Hester left once in the wagon, leaving Mary Ann alone with all the children. Disturbed, Lev had followed her for a few hours, intending to ask why she was leaving and where she was going, but the sight of other riders kept him away. Someone else was following her. He turned back in time to reach his hiding place on the rock cliff before dark. Hester returned in a few days with a heifer tied to the wagon and a few hens and a new rooster in a wooden pen.

Brief moments of acceptance of his situation, even reconciliation, finally began to appear. A grim sort of pride began to emerge for having survived in the wild without being captured. He had cursed himself many times for not paying more attention to his father's teachings about living in harmony with the land and surviving with the elements rather than against them. He used his voice only to hum softly or whisper to himself and began to play games with his mind, imagining himself as a predatory animal, usually a wolf. Lev's human form floated above and behind the animal, following and learning how to stalk, capture or kill its prey.

The imaginings caused concern that he might become a danger to his family—that he might be losing his grip on reality. But fright and anger began to succumb to determination. He felt confident that he could overcome anything or anyone that might try to kill or capture him. He was even able to leave the occasional wild turkey or rabbit on the porch of their house. He kept intending to leave a stringer of fish, but could not catch them at night.

After the first offering of fresh game, Mary Ann walked out on the porch with her lantern or a candle each night after the children were asleep. She had remembered. Lev had become Sebastian, and Mary Ann was becoming Rachael. Hester sometimes came with her, but most nights, Mary Ann came alone. She always sat her small light on the porch railing and dropped into her father's rocking chair. She rocked, scaling the walls of the canyon with her eyes. She moved her head along with her gaze, so that Lev would know that she was looking for him in the dark without seeing her eyes. Lev lay on his stomach watching, always reminded of the nights his mother had gone to the porch with her lantern ... nights when she knew that his father was watching. He felt a closer kinship to his father than he had ever felt when Sebastian was alive. Sebastian even began to whisper warnings and advice to him. How had his parents stayed apart all those years?

Lev's most tender senses had been dulled by the shock of being rudely separated from his family and the bare necessities of life. But when Mary Ann walked out that first night, he felt those senses start to return and they grew sharper with each passing day. He desired his wife in a way that he had never experienced when he could touch her at will. The desire was physical and emotional. She had been a part of his mind and body and the forced separation seemed more unbearable each day. He dreamed often of invisible hands that delved bloodlessly into his chest, pushing apart his ribs and withdrawing Mary Ann. He imagined that the terrible hands belonged to God until a vision of Rachael shamed him. He awoke from the dreams, wondering if he had shouted loud enough to give away his position, wondering if the bullet had caused the pain and the dream.

Butter had been a welcome and necessary companion, but Lev had been forced to abandon his principle of never doing work afoot that can be done horseback. Butter was often left in dark cedar thickets or in the shadows of rocks while Lev hunted, fished, or simply traversed the countryside like a coyote. The horse was too loud and too visible for such travel. He had managed to pilfer some corn from neighbors' cribs, but never enough to sustain the mare. Without proper feed, Lev turned her loose to forage for long periods. Butter always returned to the last spot where Lev had been or trotted toward the sound of his soft whistle. Forced to steal from neighbors, Lev always chose the poorest tools or oldest supplies, hoping that their owners would not miss them.

Using cedar limbs hacked with primitive tools he found at old campsites along the riverbanks, Lev built rough lean-tos against different sides of the hills surrounding his former home, trying to blend them into the environment. He alternated between these shelters each night, careful to avoid leaving a trail. He searched his memory for details that would allow him to build traps, finally settling on ideas that came to him during his sleep. Lev believed that Sebastian gave him help in his dreams. Crude things usually involving some sort of string or rope and cedar cages bound together by strings of bark, the traps rarely worked at first because he did not know where to put them or how to use them. After months of learning to sit in silence and observe, he began to enjoy limited success catching rabbits.

The sound of gunfire on a clear day could be heard for miles, so he saved his ammunition for only the best game—turkeys, prairie chickens, or a rare wild hog. Stray cattle were becoming scarce, the meat was difficult to transport and carcasses were hard to dispose of. Too much waste. Lev waited until the first frost to rope one.

Butter tripped the wild steer and Lev dismounted to cut its throat. They dragged it into a small mesquite thicket where Lev butchered it, keeping only a day's supply of meat for himself. He skinned the cow and laid the hide across Butter's hips, bloody side up. The horse raised only slight objection. Lev cut the carcass in two, tied small ropes to the legs and draped it across the hide.

He washed in Palo Pinto Creek and returned to the hill above the house to wait. He watched Mary Ann until she went inside. After he was satisfied she was asleep, he crept down the trail with his bounty. Delivering such a bounty was worth the risk of traveling horseback down the hillside. As he placed it on the porch, he felt good about himself for the first time in months—almost good enough to risk going inside. From the porch, he imagined that he could smell her, hear her breathing. He did hear Lane's asthmatic cough. Back on the hill, he watched Hester and Mary Ann discover the bounty at sunrise. Both glanced up as if they knew where he was before efficiently beginning the process of preserving the meat. He kept the hide, hoping to make a coat from it, but could never get it to soften enough. He used it as a ground tarpaulin for sleeping.

Lev tried to convince himself that the Rangers believed he had abandoned his family to avoid capture. There had been no sign of law except the men who followed Hester's wagon. He returned to their camp near the Leon River and was disappointed to see it taking on an air of permanence with a small tent general store, more canvas bunkhouses, an office, a log barn and a few scattered adjoining campsites that seemed to belong to civilians.

His desire to see his family almost overpowered his caution as the weather turned colder. Without the homemade calendar that Hester kept, he sensed more than knew that Christmas was near. He did not know that it was Christmas Eve when a rider came down the hillside trail and stopped in front of the house. Some sort of carcass was draped across the neck of his horse. Lev recognized the horse and the Ranger. Same stirrups, same hat, same vest. The man sat his horse politely until Hester came out on the porch. She stood with unwelcoming hands on her hips until the Ranger dismounted and placed the carcass on the porch near her feet. Lev watched him tip his hat and ride away. Lev levered a cartridge into the chamber and put the rifle's sight on the Ranger until he was out of the canyon.

The next night, Lev was waiting in the dark shadows by the side of the house when Mary Ann walked out on the porch with a lighted candle. He watched her scan the hills for a few seconds, drinking in her presence before whispering. "Is it Christmas?"

She flinched only slightly as she turned toward the sound of his voice. She wet her fingers and pinched out the candle flame. "I sensed you were near. Yes, it is Christmas. Come to me."

The light from the extinguished flame seemed to linger as he took her in his arms. They held each other almost to the point of pain before he put her face in his hands and met the lips he had so long desired with his own. Recalling the dreams of having her pulled from him with deep pain, he held her tightly as he whispered into her ear. Each whispered the same words. "Are you all right?" They laughed a little as he pulled her to arms' length to look into her eyes. Suddenly aware that they were standing in the light from a three-quarter moon, he pulled her closer to the house and into the darkness. "Kids asleep?"

"Yes, and the fire is not out yet. Come to my bed."

40

HY FIGURED THAT HIS CELLMATE, EMMETT DAY, saved his life. One of only a few prisoners as old as Hy at thirty-nine, he was also a Confederate soldier convicted of murder by a reconstruction court. His name was stenciled on the back of his cheap shirt with a silver-dollar-sized red dot underneath that meant he was in for life. In spite of this, he spoke regularly of reuniting with his family. Incarcerated for five years before Hy arrived, Day had pulled himself from the depths of depression to hope by planning escape. He was proficient with his hands and possessed an almost uncanny ability to figure how things worked. When there was a need for anything that could be made with available materials, prisoners and guards alike came to Emmett Day. Using these talents, he had wangled jobs in the wheelwright, blacksmith, saddle, carpenter, tailor and boot shops.

Hy only pretended to listen to Emmett's ranting about escape at first. He could see no logic in it because there seemed to be almost no chance of success. Even if Emmett's schemes worked, Hy had no desire to spend the rest of his life being hunted. He tried to see his life with Hester and the children as in the past. Thinking of them was torture. There was no future. Death was the only logical escape. It was only when Hy realized that attempting escape was a way to accomplish death that he began to listen in earnest to Emmett's plans.

In the open yard and away from prying ears, Emmett pointed in the four directions around the prison and started reciting details of all the rooms. Using a small, sharpened stick pilfered from the carpenter shop, he drew a complete diagram of the prison in the sand. Hy found new respect for his cellmate and soon discovered that listening to Emmett's plans kept his mind off his plight and lifted his spirits. That night in the cell, Emmett showed Hy how he had filed off the brads that held the shackles of his ball and chain and replaced them with a bolt and tap that could easily be removed—a product of his time in the blacksmith shop. Hy was impressed. The hope was hollow, but it was better than no hope at all. A month later, Hy's brads had also been filed off and replaced. Being killed while escaping seemed better than killing himself.

They had selected a date for invading the armory and stealing guns for escape when Hy heard about convicts being leased out to the railroad. He asked to be part of the crew. Anything was better than being inside prison walls. Emmett was wary, but agreed with Hy that escape might be easier on the outside. He talked his way onto the convict train to stay with Hy. Shackled and waiting to climb aboard the boxcar, they watched another group of shackled prisoners unload from an adjacent car. Emmett poked Hy with his elbow. "Well, I'll be damned."

Hy followed Emmett's gaze. "See somebody in that bunch you recognize?"

Emmett looked toward a burly, tall Indian with long hair. Everything about the man was broad, especially his face, nose, and shoulders. "That's Satanta. Kiowa chief. He and Chief Big Tree were pardoned outta here about a year ago."

"Pardoned? Looks like he's chained same as us."

"They were in for eight counts of murder. Wagon train. Sentenced to hang. Damned Governor Davis turned 'em loose to try to appease the Kiowa. Guess Satanta went back to his old habits. Too bad. He's like a caged animal in that hellhole. He'd gnaw his own arm off if it was caught in a bear trap."

Satanta was out of hearing range but stopped abruptly as if he knew he was being watched. He held up the chained line and turned toward Emmett. He stared until a guard pushed a rifle butt between his shoulder blades. Hy and Emmett watched the Indian pull himself to full height, regally ignoring the guard who had shoved him.

Emmett smiled. "Watch how he moves. Toe to heel. Never seen such a big man move so light. Like his moccasins never touch the ground, left foot almost stepping into the right track. Wouldn't want the man tracking me."

It was almost dark when the convict train stopped. None of the convicts had been fed since leaving Huntsville, so Emmett and Hy expected to be fed and bedded down before beginning work the following day. They were pushed out the boxcar doors so fast that many stumbled and fell. They looked up at a cloudy sky that threatened rain. Chains rattled and caught on vines and underbrush as they marched a half-hour through heavily wooded bottomland where alarmed and curious birds and other creatures of the woods heard the strange clinks of connecting chains being removed. The prisoners' hands were freed and filled with axes. As the men hefted the axes, guards holding shotguns with pistol holsters strapped to their waists warned about the speed of an ax versus the speed of shotgun pellets.

They began clearing the trees and brush away from the railway. Sebastian had taught his sons how to use an ax, and Hy soon had chips flying from a perfectly forming inverted V in a tree trunk. He glanced at Emmett long enough to note that he had finally found one thing he did better than his friend. The smell of his sweat mixed with the freshly-cut wood and sap and the stagnant odor of soil that had seen too little sun. The sounds and smells he had hated as a boy brought back poignant memories.

Well past normal bedtime back at the prison, the crew was

herded to a trestle. Gum logs had been stacked beside and under the trestle to form a pit. Hy, Emmett, and the other convicts were handed a small sack and pushed through a hole in the logs to slide or stumble down into the pit. Inside the sacks, they found cold slabs of bacon and burned cold cornbread. Another inmate tended large coffee pots over open fires in the center of the pit. Hy stared at his cold supper and looked forward to the coffee. He took a sip from his cup and looked down at the brew. Emmett grimaced. "I've had it before. It's brewed with burned cornbread crust."

They slept on cots under the trestle, guarded from above by two prison guards and two railroad overseers. Hy and Emmett soon learned that many of their fellow crewmembers were from crank's row, the prison term for a row of cells that housed insane prisoners. One crank prisoner fancied himself a coyote. His howls brought a chorus of braying jackasses, bobwhite quails, whippoorwills, and the shrill scream of a hawk from mocking cranks. Emmett pushed his bunk close to Hy's. "These crazy bastards have turned into animals out here in the woods. Never heard anybody could make sounds like that."

Hy lay with his hands behind his head, trying to see stars through the cracks in the trestle. Being outdoors made him almost forget he was a prisoner. "First one that comes close to my cot is gonna get his damn neck snapped like a chicken." They took turns guarding and trying to sleep. At dawn, they lined up to receive tin plates from one prisoner, large mounds of dough from a second, sorghum syrup from a third, and cups of cornbread coffee from a fourth. Hy stared at the dough. "What is this?"

Emmett cut his with a tin spoon and took a bite. "They call 'em duffers. Big piece of dough they let rise like a biscuit. It's a cross between biscuit and light bread." Hy barely had time to use his finger to lap up the last of the syrup before they were lined up to return to work. Clouds covered the sky and mist fell as Hy's crew headed down the railway. Wet ax handles flying from inexperienced hands made the work dangerous, but did not stop it.

Clouds broke mid-morning and Emmett paused long enough to wipe his brow with a shirtsleeve when the sun was high in the sky. They heard the familiar sounds of wagon harness and trace chains as a mule-drawn wagon approached. "John Henry is coming."

Hy released deeply held frustration and anger with each swing of the ax. John Henry brought back pleasant memories of his old commanding officer. The war seemed almost hospitable compared to his current situation and he wondered if John Henry Brown was still in Mexico—wished he had taken his advice and moved there himself. "Who's John Henry?"

"That's what they call the dinner wagon."

The wagon bed was lined with more Johnnie-sacks filled with sandwiches made from leftover duffers and salt pork. A trusty walked among them with a water pail and dipper. After the meal, they folded the sacks and handed them to another trusty for reuse.

The routine continued for several weeks and the nighttime howling by cranks began to take its toll on Emmett. Used to sleeping outdoors amid the sounds of nature, Hy adapted better, but one of the prison guards did not. He threatened and cursed the howlers every night. They stopped until he walked away, and then began a new chorus. The harried guard soon began to pull at his hair and threatened to shoot one howling crank.

When a new train arrived, the guard's demeanor changed. Always irritable and threatening, the guard seemed almost jovial as he walked among the prisoners at supper that night. Hy watched as the guard slapped something against his leg. "What's he slapping against his leg?"

Emmett looked up from his supper of beans and hog head. He stared at the guard until he turned, revealing a hickory handle in his hand about two feet long. Two leather straps about four inches wide and three feet long were attached to the handle. The guard was popping the leather straps against each other and his leg. "Looks like the train brought him a bat. I used to make those in the boot shop using sole or harness leather. Saw Satanta take thirty-nine lashes with one once. That's the limit they're allowed to give us."

Hy nodded. "I imagine the howling will stop tonight."

"Either that or the cranks will have a real reason for hollering."

The howling did stop. Hy and Emmett's crew ate their breakfast the next morning and watched as guards herded the old crew aboard the train to be shipped back to Huntsville. Emmett drained the last of his cornbread coffee. He was getting used to it. "Hear tell they got five men less to take back."

"How come?"

"Who knows? Guards may have killed one or two. The rest probably died from overwork or scurvy. Some of our boys got dysentery now."

Hy looked at Emmett and rolled his almost empty stomach. He had been experiencing dizzy spells for a few days and felt weak. One of the cranks had laid down yesterday and refused to get up. He was missing this morning. "Guess I owe you an apology."

"How's that?"

"Taking a job of work on this damn leased crew ain't been my best idea. How much longer you figure we got?"

"I heard one of the guards say a crew stays about six months unless too many of 'em die. Means we got about three months left."

41

HESTER HAD PRETENDED NOT TO HEAR WHEN Lev came into the small house and entered Mary Ann's bed. She wept silently. Well before dawn, she felt Lev's presence in her room and his hand on her shoulder. Lev's wild smell brought to mind a mixture of wet pecan shells and a freshly used saddle. Not a repulsive smell, just unfamiliar and unnerving. Barefoot, they treaded softly to keep from disturbing Otho, Kat, Dallas, and Lane. Lev sensed more than saw that Otho might have been awake. Outside, Hester whispered details of Hy's trial and sentence and delivered Hy's message. Lev studied Hester's features in the sparse moonlight. She had aged some since he had seen her last. Her beauty had always been expressed in freshness and cheerfulness more than features. Both were gone, leaving behind a sadness and tiredness that made him want to take her into his arms. "Hester, during the war, me and Hy promised to kill the other one if it looked like one of us was gonna be captured or sent to a hospital. Hy made me repeat that promise when we heard Rangers was looking for us."

The words made the new lines in her face grow deeper, her full eyes to spill over. "And could you do that?"

Lev shook his head. "When the time came, I was a coward."

She touched his arm. "I'm grateful for that. Guess it's selfish, but those kids in there are living for the day he'll come back. That's what keeps me going."

"Eight years. They'll be near grown by then."

"They don't know about the eight years."

Lev hugged her and returned to his wife's bed. He pulled away from Mary Ann's arms just before dawn, feeling pain almost as severe as in his dreams, then kneeled beside the pallet where Alfred and Ellen slept. He listened to their innocent breathing, trying to absorb the sights and smells of them, breathe their breaths, without touching. It was too dangerous for them to know that their father lived in the hills. Little Alfred would surely try to find him and might be followed. Mary Ann touched his shoulder and kissed his neck as he rose to depart.

He retreated quickly and silently to a small cave he had found less than two miles from the house. Lev had watched the cave for days after discovering it, afraid that it was home to bears, before finally entering. Outside the cave, he wrapped himself in the ragged quilt he had brought from the house and luxuriated in the warmth of another layer of clothing and the wool coat he had longed for since the first norther had found him without a home. At first light, he checked the cave for varmints before spreading his bedroll inside the circle made by his horsehair rope in the cool dampness of the cave. He had become a nocturnal animal, moving at night and sleeping during the day, but sleep did not visit him this day.

Inside the cave, Lev tried to absorb the impact of eight years removed from a man's life. It seemed like a lifetime. He had never considered the length of a prison sentence for his brother, only that he would either be hanged or turned loose. Hy would never last eight years locked up. Maybe he should have shot him like he promised. What would Hy be like when he returned? Would he try to escape? When he returned, would it be Lev's turn to take his punishment for a crime neither of them saw as unjust? Could he stand eight years of confinement after eight years of living life in the wilds?

It was early fall when Lev found a honey tree with wild berries nearby. Gathering both in a log he had carved to serve as a bowl, he returned to his lookout above the valley to wait for dark. He had been there less than an hour when he saw the Ranger making his way down the hill. Hester and Mary Ann had told him that many of the Rangers had gone west to fight Indians. The sisters also told Lev about the fugitive list book the Ranger carried—his black book. Hester had shivered when she read *in prison* written beside Hy's name.

Mary Ann said the book described Lev as 5'11" and 165 pounds, an incessant smoker with light blue eyes. Lev had laughed softly. "I could walk right by a Ranger looking for a feller who fit that description." Lev's eyes were a soft chocolate brown. Although he liked to smoke, he seldom had tobacco. The Ranger always politely asked the women about Lev's whereabouts and urged them to arrange his surrender before more violence occurred. They did not answer.

Lev dipped a finger into the wild honey and sucked on a piece of honeycomb as the Ranger neared the house. Hester came out on the porch to greet him. She no longer put her hands on her hips or affected hostile gestures when conversing with the lawman. Lev was bothered by their familiarity. She accepted the basket he offered and seemed to be grateful. He buried deeper behind the rocks when the Ranger looked in his direction. He kept his head down until he heard gunfire. He peered over the rocks and saw Otho struggling with Hester and the Ranger over a rifle. Lev levered a cartridge into the chamber and leveled his Winchester, waiting for a good shot. This decision was easy. He would kill the Ranger this time. He was likely alone and Lev could not allow him to hurt the boy or take him away. There would be no more Rivers taken alive.

Mary Ann, her pregnancy visible under her apron, came out on the porch and ran to help Hester control her son. The other children followed. Alfred clenched his fists, wanting to help his cousin, knowing he could not. Ellen began to cry. Lev was in his stirrup when he heard another shot. Hester had Otho's rifle pointed toward the sky. The Ranger held a fighting Otho with both hands, pushed him to the ground and tied his hands behind him. He took the rifle from Hester, who seemed to be pleading with him. The Ranger finally released Otho and allowed Hester to take him inside.

Mary Ann came out to talk with the Ranger as he emptied the rifle and handed it to her. Lev strained to make out the words, but heard only the wind. She walked alongside his horse all the way to Palo Pinto Creek, making pleading gestures. Lev was about to go down the hill when she finally gave up. He anxiously watched his pregnant wife make the walk back.

The night was moonless and pitch dark, so Lev sensed Hester before he heard the first sliding rocks and knew that she was coming up the hill. She was out of breath when Lev reached out a hand and pulled her over the rocks onto the trail. "What happened?"

Hester drew two deep breaths. "Did you see Otho try to shoot the Ranger?"

"I was watching. What got into the boy?"

"He's had murder in his heart for that Ranger ever since he took his daddy off to prison." She put a hand to her forehead. "You know Otho. Such a sweet boy to be ruined by all this."

"Did he just let him go?"

"No. Says he can't. He told us he'll give us a day to say goodbye and pack him some things. Says he's bringing a horse when he comes back for Otho tomorrow."

"That don't make no sense."

"We think he's using Otho to get you to come down. Guess he got tired of waiting for the baby to come. Think he figured that would bring you down for sure."

Lev counted the months. The baby had to be at least three

months away. "He figures to capture me when I come down to help with the baby?"

"That's what we think. But Otho gave him an opportunity. We think he left him here to give us time to tell you what happened."

"What makes him think I won't just kill him from up here when he comes?"

"He knows you've had plenty of chances before. Figures you know that killing a Ranger is like stirring up a bed of ants. You're likely to get stung."

"He'll probably bring help this time, too, but I can't let him take Otho off to jail."

"Mary Ann and I think he's short-handed back at headquarters and won't try to wrestle with you and Otho at the same time. We think he just wants you."

Lev's heart sank a little as he tried to make out the expression on her face in the darkness. "You're saying you want me to go in Otho's place? That if I go, he'll leave Otho alone?"

Hester shook her head enough to make her wiry hair jiggle. "No. We can't take a chance on that. We want to send Otho home to Mama and Papa. He's fifteen now and shouldn't be a burden to them."

Lev thought for a while before nodding. "I doubt that the Rangers will follow a boy all that way."

"It's you they want."

"He should already be gone. Put him on that old wagon horse he rides all the time and send him on. Can he find his way?"

"I drew him a map."

"You just come up to tell me that?"

"And to tell you not to come down when it's time for the baby."

"Been there for the first two. I reckon nobody's gonna keep me away from this one. Besides, the Ranger don't know when it's coming. Likely he won't be here."

Hester put both hands on Lev's chest. "He watches more

than you think. He's a patient and stubborn man. Think with your head and not your heart, Lev." She tried to gauge his reaction in the dark, but could not. "This is what Mary Ann wants. She will be fine."

Hester did not understand the humiliation he felt when he was kept from doing what he considered his responsibility as a husband and father—and his right. "Plenty of time to think on it, but you wave the lantern if it comes at night or have the kids make some kind of noise I can hear during the day. Not a gunshot."

Otho was gone well before daylight. Lev was almost grateful that it was too dark in the canyon to see the boy ride off. He traveled afoot on the highest points on the hills above the trails all day, waiting for the Ranger to arrive. He never came that day or the next, or the next. Lev returned to hunting, trying to escape his feeling that the Ranger's not coming for Otho was a bad sign.

He had almost lost faith in signs other than those left by the animals he stalked. Crows seemed to fly their normal patterns, not noticing or speaking to the man that had blended himself into their environment. He had neither seen nor heard messages from his grandmother. His father's transparent, smoky visage had appeared in dreams, but left no instructions. His mother's messages were mostly admonitions in his sleep. He still placed a rope around his bed to ward off snakes and slept facing south, still dreamed often and wondered if the screams in his dreams were imagined or real. Had the spirits left him because he slept during the day? He usually slept fitfully, always with one hand on his rifle. After Otho escaped, he began having rude awakenings with the sense that something bad had just happened. He began to imagine that these were signals that Otho had been killed or captured or that Hy had died in prison or been killed trying to escape.

Lev's sense of looming misfortune haunted him. The dreams worsened, the bullet seemed to move, and the rude awakenings increased in intensity. He imagined his insides being twisted like the strands of a rope, each day drawing them tighter and tighter.

The pain of the tightening caused him to walk in a sideways fashion, one hand on his stomach. The pain in his stomach was mild, however, compared to the headaches. A humming went on in his head most days. It came with sharp pain that worked its way through his temples and out his eyes, causing him to see something akin to heat waves on the peripheries. He had begun to dream constantly and to talk incoherently as if he had made up some language that was all his own.

In September, three months after Otho left, Hester came to the porch on an unusually warm and windy night and waved her lantern instead of setting it on the porch rail—a sign that the baby was near. Lev had not seen the Ranger since the day Otho had tried to kill him, but still felt his presence like a looming, murky specter. He nervously checked the hills for movement as Hester looked up in his general direction. He undressed Butter and turned her loose to graze before heading down the mountain. A fierce anger seemed to work through him as he descended. At the edge of the yard, he stopped behind a rock to check for movement again. In peripheral vision sharpened by living in the wild, he saw Hester holding something above her head. A white bundle. He crouched and watched. When she went back inside, he waited and watched. Finally, he arose and walked boldly through the yard in the moonlight, daring anyone or anything to stop him.

They named the boy William Ransom: William for Lev's brother—killed in a jail cell after killing Eliza Jane's husband, and Ransom, for Mary Ann's father. Each wondered if Ransom House was still alive and would ever see his namesake grandson. Lev wanted to lie beside his wife and new son, but knew that he was not fit for her bed. It had been too cold to bathe in the river and his smell and appearance had become obvious to him when seen through the eyes and expressions of the children. They were afraid of him, so he lay in the floor and coaxed William Ransom into gripping his finger.

Lev felt the twisted rope begin to relax, the humming to diminish. The smell of wood smoke and cedar emanating from him seemed to fill the room. It seemed strange to him that he never noticed it in the cave or outside. He lay on the floor beside the bed until he heard the rhythmic breathing of his wife and their children, and then crept outside to sleep under the house. He could no longer abide spending the whole night with a roof over his head. On the third day, Lev sensed a threatening presence. His head began to hum again, the bullet ached and the rope began to tighten. He returned to the hills.

42

HY STEPPED OFF THE PRISON SCALE BACK IN
Huntsville, twenty-five pounds lighter for his time working on the
railroad. Emmett had lost almost thirty, but could stand the loss
better than Hy. Both looked better than the cranks who returned with
them. The bat had taken something away from them. The beatings
had stopped the night-howling, but it also turned the cranks into
creatures without spirits. Watching them stumble through the days
like wandering spirits, many wetting and soiling their pants, sank
Hy to the depths of misery. He began to imagine himself as one of
them. His mind continually worked on ways to escape, but Emmett
rejected every plan. Their positions had reversed. Their chances for
escape had been no better outdoors than they had been inside the
walls of Huntsville Prison.

Carrying replacement balls and chains down the center hall
toward the open yard and the cells, Hy and Emmett stopped at
the sight of the big Kiowa chief standing on a wooden barrel in
the center hall. Satanta's arms were folded, his stance erect and
authoritarian as if he were presiding over a tribal council. Another
Indian, not nearly as regal, sat atop the carpenter horse, a long,
beveled two-by-six supported by four plank legs. The Indian was
astride the two-by-six with the beveled edge up, his toes barely
touching the floor. Emmett turned to the guard behind them. "What
did these boys do?"

The guard looked up at Satanta. "Ain't sure. They was there when I came in this morning. The chief lives in a world of his own. Probably refused an order or talked when he shoulda been listening."

Hy looked up at Satanta's steady eyes and could not help but admire the dignity and defiance he saw in his expression. He doubted if talking had gotten the chief into his predicament. "How long they got to stay up there?"

"Ain't no concern of mine or yours, but I hear they're serving twelve hours. Should be about up, I imagine." He looked critically at Hy and Emmett. "You boys get slim rations out there in the wilderness?"

Emmett smiled. "The food was tasty and plenty of it."

The guard chuckled. He liked Emmett. "Figured we'd have to put you boys on Crank Row when you come back."

There were lots of things that needed fixing, so Emmett managed to swap fixing things for getting back their old cell. They had left drawings on the back of woodwork, and tools in the walls of that cell. He soon had their riveted balls and chains converted to bolts and taps and began to plan again.

They had not seen Satanta for weeks when they came across him in the prison yard, sitting with his legs crossed beneath him, palms facing up. Hy thought he was asleep with his eyes open. Emmett asked him why he had been brought back after being pardoned. The chief looked at them as if they were children. Finally, he told them that he had to steal to feed his people, that they were starving on the reservation. Satanta's regal nature in the face of continual degradation inspired Hy—made him aspire to reach deep within himself for hope that he had not known since his first night in the Dallas jail. He did not know what he hoped for, but he began searching within himself to achieve the serenity that Satanta seemed to have achieved. Hy realized for the first time that he had never been totally at peace, even when he was free. Maybe a man could slow his heartbeat. Being caged forced him to seek the tranquil state his grandmother had taught.

Sensing their admiration for him and enjoying it, Satanta gradually opened up to Hy and Emmett, telling them stories of Chiefs Big Tree, Sitting Bear, and Little Mountain. Hy was particularly amused when Satanta spoke of their shared hatred for Generals Custer, Sherman, and Sheridan. Custer was dead, but Satanta felt an intense animosity toward Sheridan and described him as a cursed man destined to find himself on the shaft of Satanta's lance. "If they hang me or kill me in here, my people will avenge me. Sheridan will be the first to die."

Hy studied the chief. He figured them to be close to the same age, but Satanta seemed to have lived many lives. "What happened to Big Tree? Emmett says he was in here with you before."

"They took him to the guardhouse in Fort Sill. Did not want us together."

"I'm in for eight years. Lost count on the railroad, but think I know I'm working on three about now. How long you in for?"

Hy regretted the question as soon as it left his lips. Satanta looked deeply into his eyes for several seconds before answering. "I will be free soon."

Emmett looked at Hy and shook his head.

43

LEV HAD STUDIED HESTER'S CALENDAR WHEN William Ransom was born. Back in the hills, he began scratching a calendar of his own on the cave wall. He devised a system to mark off the days, weeks and years. He studied it every morning, trying to stop the humming long enough to concentrate, to see how long he had lived like an animal and how much time was left.

He awoke often from dream-filled sleep that had been interrupted often by sudden sensations of danger or the sense that something terrible was happening in a faraway place to someone he loved. The rope that his guts had become tightened and the headaches and humming returned. Squatting like a coiled rattlesnake, he studied the cave calendar carefully before making another mark. He counted 1,109 days—three years that Hy had lived as a prisoner and he had lived as an animal. About eighteen hundred days to go—two hundred fifty nine weeks—fifty-nine months—almost five years. He pulled at his hair and beard, tying to hold himself together.

He squatted at the cave opening and waited for the sun to go a little farther behind the hill before positioning for his nightly vigil. Butter stood behind the two scrub oaks a few feet away. Lev had resumed the verbal communication with Butter that he and Handler had practiced before the war. He had found that sitting with his legs beneath him and hanging his head would stop the buzzing and offer a measure of comfort from the rope inside him. With practice, he had developed the ability to drop into a restful stupor and awaken refreshed—something he could never achieve when he tried to sleep normally after his daily hunt. He was awakened by Butter's approach. She came toward Lev in a fast walk. Lev felt a sense of danger, not faraway danger to someone else, but immediate, lurking danger.

He awoke looking into the tender eyes of his son. Ten-year-old Alfred squatted beside his father, whispering words that were unintelligible to Lev. Lev managed a smile for the boy before terror struck. Alfred fell back as his father sprang to his feet in one catlike move. Butter flinched at the sudden movement just as the first hint of sunrise illuminated the canyon walls. Lev reached for his knife and found it missing as he felt, then saw, two people rushing him. His agility left him as quickly as it had arrived, and the humming in his head intensified to the point of explosion as he fell forward in the dirt.

Her palms were pressed hard against his shoulders. "No quick moves, Lev. You're safe, but you can't move. You'll start the bleeding again."

Lev looked into Mary Ann's eyes, searching for answers to the questions forming like the rapid firing of a gun. He looked around, trying to remember where he was and how he got there. He did not want to admit his confusion to his wife or the children. They all stared at him as if he were a wild animal.

"We had to cut you open a little. You been out of your head

awhile. " Mary Ann gently rubbed a wet cloth across his forehead. "You remember anything yet?"

"Cut me? Why?" Moving his lips brought pain. Fever blisters covered his lips and part of his nose.

Mary Ann reached into an apron pocket and produced a small fragment of gray lead. "This thing worked its way to your back. Got festered. Poisoned your blood. Me and Hester had to tie you up so we could cut it out."

Lev opened his hand and she laid the lead on his palm and smiled. "You fought us like a wildcat."

Lev looked around and knew that he was in the horse barn. The women had made a mattress by sewing old blankets and stuffing them with hay. "How did I get here?"

"Little Alfred found you in the yard before sunup a few days back. Guess you passed out and fell off your horse. Would have taken you in the house, but you wouldn't let us. You thought you had yellow fever. Said the kids would get it."

Lev tried in vain to recall these events, but could only see his father's yellow body dying in bed back home. He could not recall mounting Butter or riding down the hill.

She saw the fear, the unknowing, in his eyes. "Probably safer here, anyway."

Lev noticed that the pain from the bullet was gone, replaced with a soreness on his back just below his shoulder. It felt good to be free of it. Maybe the buzzing in his head would leave too. As he looked at his smiling wife, the memory of Olivia nursing his wound seemed like another lifetime, like someone else's memory. His desire to hold Mary Ann made him suddenly self-aware. "I smell like a goat."

"We bathed you the best we could, but had to nearly kill ourselves and you to get it done."

When the women and children hauled water and heated it for a bath, Lev was reluctant. He had grown accustomed to the filth and smell; they had become a sort of protection. A covering of dust and grime made him warmer at night and his wild smell made him a better hunter. The thought of sitting naked in a tub, even inside the barn, made him feel vulnerable. When he relented and eased himself down into the tub, his nakedness protected, Hester came into the yard, carrying clean underclothes and wool pants. His socks, worn threadbare and full of holes, were thrown into the fire and replaced with a pair the women had darned. As he watched Hester and Mary Ann work, he recalled the night in Rusk, when Olivia had washed his and Hy's clothes. He tried to link the events from that time in the distant past to his situation today, but could not. Could not even recall the events that had them to this point of desperation. He had been someone, some thing, different then and he and Hy had been free.

Refreshed and calmed by the bath and the strange feel of clothes he could barely remember as his own, Lev leaned against the barn and peered into the fire. He cautioned himself against comfort—worried that the children would be in danger now that they knew where and how he lived. Hester put a wrinkled newspaper in his lap and a small glass of clear whiskey in his hand. Lev sipped, surprised by a taste he had all but forgotten. Hester poured some bear fat into the barn lantern and lighted it so that he could see better. She put her finger on the article she wanted him to read.

"Where did you get this newspaper?"

"The Ranger leaves us one sometimes. We run into rail-splitters and cedar-hackers that can read once in a while, too."

Lev looked at Hester and then at his wife. Resentment boiled up. How could they consort with a man who clearly intended to kill or imprison him?

Hester read his thoughts. "I think the man took a liking to Hy when he took him to Dallas. You know how your brother is. Think the Ranger feels guilty about taking him off and leaving us alone out here."

"Guilty? He don't give a damn about this family. He's just using you to try and catch me." Little Alfred flinched at the anger in his father's voice.

Mary Ann stepped forward with hands on her hips. "You think we haven't thought about that—that it is ever far from our minds when we converse with the man?"

Hester nodded. "We're not stupid, Lev. I really think he is a man just doing his job. He's our sworn enemy, but one with a conscience."

Mary Ann folded her arms across her chest. "Just read the paper."

Lev looked down at the article from the Dallas Herald. He moved the paper closer to the lantern and read. "Says here Major John Henry Brown might be a delegate to the constitutional convention." He looked up to find the date. "More'n two years ago. I expect that's over and done with."

The women fixed him with quizzical and exasperated expressions. Mary Ann gave their feelings voice. "Isn't he yours and Hy's old commander?"

"I expect so. He was into politics before the war. Went to Mexico for a while."

Hester kneeled and placed a cautious hand on Lev's knee. "We been hearing and reading a little about Confederate soldiers sent to prison during Reconstruction being pardoned."

"More Ranger talk."

Hester rose and clasped her hands in front of her apron. "We want you to go to Dallas and find him. Take me with you. I'll beg him to help my Hy."

The request seemed to strike Lev dumb. He looked up at the stars before concentrating on the dirt around him. He was at another place, another time. "Hy and me just seen him once since the war. That trip to Dallas. Doubt he would even remember me." He stroked his whiskers and ran a hand through his long hair. "Especially the way I look now."

Mary Ann pulled a pair of scissors from her apron. "We're gonna make you look like you used to."

Lev looked at the scissors. The women exchanged worried glances as his eyes glazed and he seemed to drift. He knew that no amount of bathing or scissoring would make him like he once was. "You two forgetting that I am a wanted man? John Henry is a man that abides the law. He might call the sheriff to arrest me on sight." He could tell that they had not considered this.

He argued against it, stating his fears of leaving them alone. What would happen if Kiowas came? How would they eat? They listened patiently, then took him into the old dugout. There, stacked on neat shelves and hung from the ceiling, candlelight revealed an adequate larder. Strips of beef and venison hung from the ceiling, cured beef sat on the shelves, smoked and covered with brine. Elm and hackberry bark tied with cedar bark strips and rawhide kept dirt off the food. Cured hides lined the walls. The women said they were saving the rabbit skins to make the children coats. Behind the house, Hester showed him stacks of cedar rails and posts, ready for fencing.

"Who split them rails?"

Mary Ann smiled. "We did. Hester more than me. People drop by pretty regular to buy from us."

Lev wanted to know how they could have done all this without his seeing, but realized that there were several hours during the day when he was asleep or away hunting. All this time, he had thought that they could not survive without him. He felt inadequate, unneeded, misled.

He succumbed to a haircut and shave before bedtime. Little Alfred and Ellen watched with wide eyes as their father was transformed from wild creature into someone they vaguely remembered. When Mary Ann held the mirror for Lev to see, he recalled the shaves and haircuts that Olivia had given him and

Hy. The face that stared back from the mirror was a stranger, just like it had been then. Lev wondered how many faces, how many strangers, he would see in the mirror before he could come home a free man.

He lay beside Mary Ann that night, baby William Ransom between them, Little Alfred and Ellen asleep on and under quilts beside the bed. Lev lay flat on his back, staring at the dark ceiling, listening to their breathing, listening for sounds of danger. Mary Ann seemed content to caress his clean face and leave a hand on his chest. Just as his eyes were about to close, he felt the baby stir and heard sounds of nursing. Little Alfred pretended to be asleep, but Ellen boldly put her elbows on the side of the bed and stared at the wild man that was her father. Lev looked into her eyes and felt a strange peace come over him. He remembered how to slow down his heartbeat. The humming had stopped. The headaches had not returned. He remembered the bullet was gone. He touched her cheek and slept.

They had won the argument, but Lev refused to take Hester. Mary Ann and the children could not be left alone. Lev was up before first light and had Butter saddled when the women appeared in the barn door with cold biscuits slabbed with bacon and molasses. They ate standing inside the barn, the awkward silence interrupted only by the sounds of chewing and swallowing and a rooster crowing. Lev had intended to be gone before daylight, but was still in the yard as the first rays of sun traveled down the valley floor and cast diamond reflections off the water in the creek.

He was reluctant to leave, unsure of his journey. The sisters handed him a little paper money, a handful of coins, and a knapsack filled with beef strips, a small skillet, and more biscuits. He had pulled on the pair of new leggings cured and stitched by the women. Suddenly nervous about being exposed, he mounted quickly and scanned the hills with his eyes. Mary Ann held Ransom up to him, her face a mixture of disappointment and worry. "I been calling him Rance."

"Rance it is." Little Alfred had secreted himself in the barn and watched through a crack as his father snuggled and kissed his baby brother and handed him down to his mother.

Lev touched the brim of his hat and pointed Butter north. A few yards away, the horse suddenly stopped and rolled on his haunches to face the women. Lev stepped down as Mary Ann handed the baby to Hester and ran to him. Lev took her in his arms and kissed her. She whispered words of gratitude and asked him to just do the best he could. She did not expect a miracle. He thought of Little Alfred and Ellen, but considered it best to leave them asleep. He tipped his hat in Hester's direction, remounted and rode away. Mary Ann was surprised when Alfred came out of the barn and ran after his father. She caught him and held his arms as Lev rode into the cedars, disappearing a little with each step. In two of Little Alfred's deep breaths, his father was gone, a ghost once again. Mary Ann put her hands on his shoulders and gave him an affectionate squeeze. "Your Papa's just doing what he has to do."

Lev never looked back to see the houses and barns slip from view, never knew that the people he loved most kept watching for movement in the cedars until he was over the first hill and headed northeast.

44

AS THE SUN REACHED ITS ZENITH, LEV DECIDED to walk. Walking had become more natural than riding and seemed much safer. He spent much of the first day walking in the cedar breaks, scrub oaks, and thorny mesquites parallel to, but several yards away from Butter until he recognized the foolishness of sending a saddled horse along a trail without a rider. When he finally took to the saddle in open prairie, he began to get a sense of the man he had once been. Butter moved across the prairie as if she had found herself, too, glad to do what she was born to do.

The horse's hooves were sore when they reached Dallas and Lev rebuked himself for failing to shoe her before leaving. He felt like a wild animal again as people on the streets of Dallas seemed to gawk at him. He found the blacksmith shop he remembered from previous trips and tried to engage the smithy in conversation that might lead to John Henry Brown. But the man seemed unwilling or unable to shoe a horse and talk at the same time. Also unaccustomed to conversation, Lev managed to inquire about boarding after the last shoe was nailed. The farrier seemed suspicious of Lev's desire to sleep in a livery stable, but they finally came to terms. Lev had intended to sleep on the banks of the Trinity, but found it much more populated than on his last visit. The livery stable seemed more private.

For three days, he walked the streets of Dallas, hoping to

pass John Henry Brown. The sight of so many people disoriented him and he cursed himself for thinking he would simply run into his old commander on the street or in a general store. He blamed Hester and Mary Ann for sending him on a fool's errand. For the better part of three years, most of his spoken words had been uttered to a horse, and these Dallas people appeared as predators who spoke a foreign language. Engaging in conversation with anyone other than Butter seemed unnatural to him. When he did approach strangers to inquire about John Henry Brown, they scurried away without answering. Lev wondered if he had lapsed into some type of language that only his family and his horse could understand.

The confidence he had found within himself in the wilds seemed to turn on him in this new environment. He forgot to shave and bathe and gradually began patrolling the alleys and dark corners off the main streets, eventually finding a sheltered area between two buildings that reminded him of his cave. He slept with Butter in the livery at night, but crouched in the alley during the day. He started scratching a new calendar on the wooden wall. He had been in Dallas a week when she followed him to the alley one morning.

"Excuse me." Lev was crouched, so she bent at the waist to better see his face. She seemed ready to flee in case the strange man leapt from his crouch.

Lev looked up at her, realized that his crouch was threatening, and rose. "Ma'am?"

"Excuse me, but I have seen you on the streets the last few days and you look familiar. You move like someone I once knew."

Lev looked behind him at the blocked alleyway that he had thought of as his cave. She stood in the only way out. He studied her face. "I reckon I do." It sounded foolish, but he could think of nothing else to say to this woman who looked more worn out than old.

"My name is Lydia."

Lev's expression did not change.

She tried again. "Lydia Filson?" She could tell that the name did not register. "You look a lot like one of the Rivers brothers." She studied him intently. "I am sure of it."

Lev tensed.

She held up both arms defensively. "I mean you no harm. I owe you a lot ... probably my life. Sooner or later my former husband would have killed me, or me him."

Lev's arms hung stiffly by his side as he examined her. The hair was still thin, now totally gray. She was heavier, the beginnings of a wattle shaking under her chin. When she spoke, the skin under her upper arms quivered with each gesture. She continued to talk, but he did not hear what she said. The noise of her voice started to make his head hum again. He knew who she was, but said nothing.

"Olivia blamed me when they indicted you boys. Weren't my fault, but she blamed me just the same. She's more to blame than me. Stole my husband and got this whole thing started in the first place."

Olivia's name caused him to flinch slightly. She saw it and knew she was right about who he was. "Anyway, seems to me you ain't in jail, anyway."

He straightened and stepped closer to her face. "No, but my brother is."

His closeness, the wild smell, frightened her. "Now looka here. I might be able to help you. I know my way around Dallas. Might find you a place to sleep and a good meal."

When he did not respond, she shrugged and turned to walk away. She was almost to the street when he touched her arm. "You say you know this town?"

She waved her arms expansively. "I clean the courthouse and most of the other official buildings. Got two nigger women work for me."

"Thought you ran a cathouse."

She smiled a bitter smile. "Did till the refined women in this town shut me down."

"I'm looking for a man named John Henry Brown."

She smiled, and for a brief moment, he saw something in her that might have attracted Filson to her in the long past.

Lev followed her up the outside stairway of a board and strip building. He hesitated when she used a maid's key to open the door on the landing. He looked through the opening down a long narrow hall. The thought of being upstairs and inside made him feel trapped. She seemed to recognize his wariness and her expression turned sympathetic. "You been hiding a long time, ain't you?" Unfazed by his lack of response, she patted his arm. "You just wait out here where there ain't no roof to bother you and I'll see if I can find the Honorable Mister Brown." She ducked inside the door briefly before sticking her head back out. "He writes books, you know. Served in the Texas legislature, too." She seemed unsatisfied when Lev did not seem impressed. "I know most of the big dogs in Dallas. Clean their offices. They talk to me, but I don't never tell what they say."

Lev considered his escape routes, figuring he could jump from the railing without breaking a leg if John Henry Brown or the woman returned with the law. The wait seemed long and he noticed hunger pains, noticed that the old rope was beginning to tighten, but it was only a few minutes before John Henry Brown appeared on the landing. He was bald on top and the hair on the sides had turned almost white. An unruly mustache, long chin whiskers and craggy brows would have confirmed his identity to Lev, and the kind, intense eyes made the rope relax. He remembered again that the bullet was gone, replaced with a sudden feeling of well-being.

Major Brown offered his hand and held Lev's in a strong grip as he looked into his eyes as if searching for the young soldier he had known. "Well, sir. It has been a mighty long time. Lydia said you were Hy, but you must be Lev."

"You have a good memory for names and faces, sir."

"A gift from God. It is fine to see you, my old friend." Brown looked into Lev's eyes until Lev became aware of how he must look, how he must smell.

John Henry Brown gave no indication that he noticed. "My wife always packs a meal adequate for two men. Pardon my saying so, but it looks as if you have missed a few meals. I would be pleased to share my plain repast with you."

Lev shook his head and instantly regretted it. It was impolite to refuse such an offer. And he was hungry. "Well, Major, I don't know if I am fit for polite company anymore, but I would be pleased to join you if I won't put you out or keep you from a full meal." Lev felt satisfaction at having strung together a long sentence that seemed to come out all right.

Finished with his dinner, Lev sat in the oak straight-backed chair across from John Henry's desk. He had eaten too fast and imagined that the sounds he made as he chewed and swallowed were like those made by a feral sow. He had been hungry, but was pleased when the meal was over. Time to get down to business. John Henry neatly folded the paper sack for re-use, placed it in a leather pouch, and put both hands flat on his desk. "I fear I owe you an apology, Lev. I have heard that you and Hy had troubles, but I did not know how to find you. I confess I should have tried harder."

Heartened by those words, Lev launched into his story. He knew few details of Hy's trial and did not mention the killing of Filson. He told only of the plight of Hester and Mary Ann—that they had sent him to ask for help. "A fool's errand, I imagine, but they mentioned pardons." He wished he had not said it. A pardon seemed only a foolish man's dream and he doubted if such an undertaking was within the purview of his old commander.

John Henry listened with those kind eyes. "Tell me about the killing."

Lev flinched. "I know I may have put you at risk by coming here. Reckon I'm still a wanted man. I am sorry for that, but am a desperate man pleading for his family. It's a hard thing." With that, Lev launched into the story of how Filson was killed.

John Henry held up a hand. "Go back further. I want to know how it all began. How you came to kill this Filson."

"All the way back to the war days?"

"All the way. Try not to leave anything out. Especially as it relates to your service in the Confederacy."

Lev took off his hat and deliberated silently for a few seconds. Going back that far in his memory seemed an impossible journey. With the advantage of hindsight, the choices he and Hy had made now seemed foolish. "Well, sir, I got shot in the Red River Campaign up in Yellow Bayou. I was serving in Burford's Nineteenth Texas and we had joined Colonel Parson's Brigade ... "

Lev took him through Rusk, Texas, The Good Samaritan Inn, shooting Filson in the foot, Olivia following them when they escaped, Filson showing up in Ellis County, their arrest by Filson, the beating of Sebastian and the subsequent death of Sebastian and Rachael.

John Henry Brown waited patiently as Lev paused. "I ain't denying anything about Filson being shot. Me and Hy figured it had to be done." He skipped to the details of the shooting and their flight west.

"I understood that Hy's wife might have been insulted or injured."

Lev looked down at the floor, Hy's voice whispering to him. "Yes, sir. I reckon she was."

"You're sure that Filson was the man who did this?"

"I would have to call our Hester a liar if I was not."

"Was that brought out at trial?"

"I was not there, but I understand not."

"Did Hester testify?"

"Hy would not allow that, I am sure. Hester said they made a big to-do about when Filson was killed. Said if he had been killed in the act of attacking her, sentence might have been lighter. That make sense to you?"

John Henry smiled a wan smile. "No."

"We killed him as soon as we found out where he was."

"Do you know the woman who cleans this building?"

"She was Filson's wife. Said his name was not really Filson, though, but Cullen Montgomery. Said he killed her own daddy."

John Henry's eyes widened. "You mean I have been seeing this woman for months, unaware of her connection to you?"

Lev shrugged, as puzzled as John Henry Brown.

John Henry stood and looked down the hall before closing the door. He put a hand on Lev's shoulder before returning to his chair. "The woman is a repulsive pest, so I have steadfastly ignored her attempts at conversation. She did mention that her former husband was a spy for both sides in the war. I didn't believe it."

"She told us the same thing."

"Was he?"

"Only thing I know is that he had Union connections. Had clout with Yankee soldiers and carpetbaggers."

"If we can get proof that he spied for both sides or even fought on both sides, it will help our case."

Lev was confused. "That ain't why we killed him."

Major Brown studied Lev's gaunt frame and open expression. "You are a man without guile, Lev Rivers. I admire that."

Lev did not know what guile was, so he remained silent.

John Henry intertwined his fingers and laid both hands on his desk. "Many of our fine soldiers were wrongly convicted during Reconstruction. It has been my mission and the mission of many former Confederate officers to right these wrongs." He stood and removed a framed certificate on the wall, hesitating as he held it in his hand. "Can you read?"

"I can ... if the words ain't too big."

Lev studied the words.

If I had foreseen the use those people designed to make of their victory, there would have been no surrender at Appomattox Courthouse; no sir, not by me. Had I foreseen these results of subjugation, I would have preferred to die at Appomattox, with my brave men, with my sword in my right hand.

General Robert E. Lee.

Surprised by the force of the words, Lev read them again before returning the framed document to his commander.

John Henry hung it on its nail with reverence, stepped back and regarded it again before returning to his chair. "You will recall that I told you there would be hell to pay in Texas after the war."

"Me and Hy rehashed that bit of advice many times." Lev looked down at the floor with his elbows on his knees and shook his hat. "Never imagined that my brother would be in prison and me only a mistake away."

"I fear that you and others like you were caught between two factions. The Yankees wanted revenge, of course. Loyal Southerners wanted our old South back. Robbing trains and banks, lynchings, and violence of all kinds had to be reduced to show that we did not need northern control—that we could govern ourselves."

"Me and Hy ain't thieves. Never held nothing against the colored."

"All were painted with the same brush. Powerful people felt that you had to serve as an example of what happens when people take the law into their own hands."

"Weren't no law to avenge Hester."

John Henry gave up. "How long do you intend to stay in Dallas?"

"I came to see you. Unless you need me for something, I plan to retrieve my horse as soon as I set foot off those stairs. Left my family unprotected."

"You wouldn't still be riding that Yankee horse, would you?"

Lev smiled. "I would. She's still a fine animal. Sorry to see her getting long in the tooth."

"She seemed to have a big heart when you rode her to Palmito Ranch. Parson said the horse you lost seemed to know why he was fighting."

"My daddy always said it wasn't right for a man to own two horses as good as Butter and Handler."

John Henry's expression turned serious again. "How long have you been scouting?"

"Near as I can tell, three years."

John Henry shook his head and pulled on his beard. "And your wife and family as well as Hy's have been without a husband and father all that time? Alone on the prairie?"

"I been watching from the hills most every day. Seen the light from our cabin every night." Defiance came into his voice. "I see to it."

"That's no life for a Cavalry soldier. Of course, it's worse for your brother. How aggressively are they pursuing you?"

"Hard to tell. One Ranger, mostly. Same one that arrested Hy."

"Don't take this the wrong way, Lev, but it would help if you surrendered. I can offer you protection until we can do something for you and maybe Hy."

Lev rose and put on his hat. "No, sir. I don't see any way me and my brother can take a chance on being in prison at the same time. There's the women and babies to look after. We done lost Hy's oldest. Had to send him back to Ellis County, but we still don't know if he made it."

John Henry gestured for Lev to return to his chair. "How can I reach you if I have news to depart?"

Lev could think of no safe way he could be contacted.

"It's a difficult request, I am sure, but can you draw a map to your place?"

Lev studied his old commander for an uncomfortably long time before asking for a pencil and paper. He touched the lead to his tongue, drew a map, and placed it on the desk. "Never been much on maps or tracking. A weakness that has caused me lots of misery."

John Henry studied the map and compared it to a Texas map on the wall. "Not much near you. No wonder they can't find you." He pointed at Palo Pinto with a thumbnail. "You know people there?"

"A few. Trained a few horses for folks before we had to hide."

"If you can get to the post office there, I know the postmaster, James Dillahunty. If he's not still the postmaster, he'll probably still own the general store."

Lev nodded, thinking that his commander did not realize the dangers of going into Palo Pinto. "Know him by sight."

"Good. He can be trusted. I will write Dillahunty right away with instructions. You just need to warn the women not to shoot him if he approaches their home." John Henry paced and tapped his forehead with a pencil as he devised a plan. "When I send a message, I will put a sealed letter to you inside a bigger package to him. He will open only his package and read my instructions. If my message is urgent, he will deliver it personally." John Henry returned to his seat as he noticed the doubt in Lev's expression. "Unopened, of course. If not urgent, he will hold it for two weeks. Perhaps one of the women could check every two weeks at the post office or general store. If it is not picked up within two weeks, he will deliver it anyway."

"Rangers know the Rivers name. How we gonna ask for a letter for me without attracting attention?"

"Fair enough. I will address your letter to William Parsons. You can ask for it by that name."

Lev thought the whole scheme seemed foolhardy, but he decided not to look a gift horse in the mouth. "I think we can arrange to be on the lookout for Mister Dillahunty." He rose and pulled his hat down. "Don't know how we can check the general store or post office without raising too much suspicion, but we will figure out something."

John Henry put pressure on the desk with both hands, as if he had trouble rising from his chair. When he finally did, he shook Lev's hand. "I promise nothing but my best efforts, sir. I will immediately write letters and speak to like-minded former Confederates on your brother's behalf." He hesitated. "Your dilemma, of course, will be more difficult if Texas Rangers have you on their wanted list."

They shook hands and Lev stepped through the door. John Henry stepped out on the landing as Lev descended the stairs.

Lev turned and waited.

"I need time. Stay away from the Ranger."

Lev looked toward the horizon as if he were considering the wisdom of that admonition before turning and taking the steps two at a time.

45

HE RODE HOME WITH A LIGHTER HEART. Butter glided across ground as if she were showing off her new shoes. Lev ignored the tiny circle of vultures that seemed to hover above his home, figuring that his sense of direction had failed him again. He smiled. They probably only seemed to be circling in the general vicinity of home. Miles away, most likely. He had to stop paying attention to signs. Most of the bad ones had turned out to be wrong. Sure enough, the vultures were gone when he reached the canyon.

It was late afternoon when he moved to his usual position of vigil behind the scrub oaks. He looked down on their small home. Quiet. Just before dusk, a low rumbling came from Butter's throat as her ears perked and pointed toward Palo Pinto Creek. Lev saw them then. Two riders watered their horses in the creek.

Lev whispered to Butter. "Damn. We recognize them old boys, don't we." Wade Monroe and Rattle were unmistakable. Rattle was still wearing the blue uniform of a Yankee soldier. Lev wondered if it was the same one or if he had stolen several. The sight of these two figures from his past brought a strange sort of relief to Lev, as if they were coming to bring him the freedom he once had—to return him to a past life when he had been a mere man who moved freely among friends as well as enemies.

Wade and Rattle, of course, had to be counted as enemies,

not friends. Lev moved Butter back behind the trees and crawled along the trail to get a better look. He watched them ride within range of his rifle, trying to determine how they could have found them and why they had come.

He relaxed a little, confident that he could kill them both before they put his family in danger. His visit with John Henry Brown had left him feeling strangely serene, so he decided to wait. Killing anybody now might ruin Hy's chances at a parole. Maybe they would ask about him and then leave. Maybe they brought news of Otho or his brothers. He could see that Wade was still sporting a badge of some sort. The women could truthfully tell them that Lev was gone. He scanned the hills to see if the two men were alone and saw nothing.

It was foolhardy to ride right up to the house, but Wade and Rattle did. They stopped in the yard and waited. Neither dismounted to knock on the door. Lev tensed and cursed himself for not killing both men before they reached the house as he saw Little Alfred and Ellen peek around the corner of the porch. Wade looked at them and made a rough gesture toward the house, saying something Lev could not hear. Ellen ran inside. Little Alfred, fists clinched, stiffly watched the intruders. No sign of the other children. Mary Ann and Hester stepped out on the porch as Wade dismounted.

Lev watched as Wade spoke to the women for what seemed like a long time. Hester pointed a finger east as if inviting them to go back where they had come from. Both sisters seemed agitated and angry. When Mary Ann poked a finger into Wade's chest, he slapped her. She dropped to her knees from the blow. Lev sucked in his breath as he stifled a shout. The sound came out as a growl. Hester quickly came to her sister's defense and Little Alfred made a sound like a dying rabbit as he rushed to protect his mother. Lev's rope tightened, and the humming returned. *Too dangerous to shoot them from here now.* He saw wavy lines in his peripheral vision as he ran toward Butter.

Lev tied the reins loosely across the mare's neck, pointed her down the hill, and whispered, "Hope the sight of blue still pisses you off." He slapped the horse on her hip and sent her down.

Watching from the south canyon wall, the Ranger watched the cedar breaks come alive as the copper mare charged down the hill. He dismounted and walked from his hiding place for a better look. The horse appeared to be riderless, but he figured Lev was somehow hanging to the opposite side. People had told him that the man could ride like a Comanche. He watched for a leg or a hat to appear above or below the horse, but saw none. The mare seemed unfazed by the steep decline and cedar limbs as she jumped boulders as if they were small streams running at full speed. Rocks and dust spewed from the hillside and fell toward the house. The Ranger put a foot on a large rock by the trail, his rifle held in the crook of his arm, too absorbed in what he was watching to take action. He decided that Lev could not possibly be attached to the horse and began scouring the area for signs, finally sighting something that looked like a big wolf moving through the cedars just beyond and behind the horse. By the time he could raise and sight his rifle, it was too late.

Butter seemed to know her mission. Her squeal reminded Lev of Handler when he lay dying. She slid full force into the back of Rattle's mount, causing the horse to stumble to his knees and come up bucking. Rattle dropped his rifle and grabbed for the saddle horn.

Wade saw an animal approaching as a reflection in Hester's eyes and turned just as the hickory stick struck the front of his knee, bending it grotesquely backward. His scream drowned the sound of bone cracking. Wade dropped to his good knee just as the stick struck him in the face.

Lev felt facial bones cracking, saw blood well up in Wade's right eye. He was crouched and waiting when Rattle's horse finally unloaded him. Rattle was struggling to his feet when Butter's front hoof caught him between his shoulder blades. He fell face-forward into the dirt. Adrenalin at full force, Lev pulled his Winchester from Butter's saddle scabbard and levered a cartridge into the chamber.

Mary Ann put a hand on his arm. The wild animal scent emanating from her husband matched the look in his eyes. "Don't kill 'em, Lev. Not unless we have to."

Lev felt the Ranger watching him before he saw him. Holding the rifle, he walked away from his family toward the hill where the lawman sat mounted. Kill or be killed—Lev was ready for it to be over. The Ranger moved out of sight.

Hester and Mary Ann helped him to throw each man over his mount. Lev ran ropes through the stirrups and tied their hands to their feet under the horses' bellies like slaughtered and gutted buffaloes lashed to panniers. He found a catch rope in the barn, ran it under the horses' tails, around their necks, and back around the limp frames of the two men to keep them from going forward or backward. As he tied the reins around the horses' necks, Wade opened his good eye. "Don't do it. These damn horses likely to kill us before we can get loose."

Lev hesitated, trying not to remember when the man had been his best friend. Wade struggled with his tied hands and feet, causing the horse to squeal and kick up its hind feet. His voice cracked. "We was friends once."

Lev looked east, as if trying to remember the two men who had been friends in a different time and place, then slapped the horses and yelled "hyaaa." Wade's and Rattle's heads bounced as the horses felt the ropes under their tails and began to buck as they ran east.

Mary Ann's breath was ragged as she watched her husband walk back toward them. He traveled in a sort of crooked, light, floating motion that reminded her of the coyotes she had seen boldly cross the yard on their way to try and kill one of their laying hens. The wild smell of her husband had stayed in her nostrils. She had welcomed the sight of him, but the savagery of his attack on Wade and Rattle unnerved her. He had seemed to enjoy it. It was efficient. She was sure he would have killed them both as easily as she had wrung the neck of a pullet early that morning. She rubbed her throbbing check and cut lip as she watched Wade and Rattle being carried away. "They may be dead before they can get off those horses."

"Probably shoulda killed 'em right here, but burying a man as big as Wade takes a lot out of a man." Silence. Lev looked toward the hills. "Ranger sent 'em. He seen 'em go, reckon it's his job to cut 'em loose." He looked up toward the Ranger once more.

"The Ranger didn't send 'em, Lev. Wade came of his own accord."

"Looking for me?"

"No, he thought you ran off and left us. He came looking for Hester. Seems his wife died."

The thought of Wade taking Hester made Lev's skin crawl. "What the hell made him think she would just go off with him?"

Hester answered. "Lev, you don't understand Wade Monroe. Never have. He always gets whatever woman he wants. Never accepted that I would prefer a man with Hy's looks to his own."

"I understand the son-of-a-bitch hit my wife."

Hester's eyes smiled, though her lips remained firm. "Because she told him he wasn't worth the shit off Hy's boots."

46

HY WATCHED EMMETT READ THE LETTER FOR what seemed to be the tenth time. It had come more than a week ago, but Emmett would not speak of its contents. He had dropped more weight from an already lean frame and his color had turned to ashen gray. He awoke each morning with a hacking cough and Hy had seen blood in his spittle more than once. Emmett flinched as if he had been stuck with a knife when Hy asked about the letter's contents.

Plans for escape had not been discussed since it arrived. Hy had tried to interest Emmett in their old plans, but he rejected them all, saying they would take too long. He finally admitted that they had been only unlikely dreams—dreams that gave them both enough hope to make it through a day.

Hy tried in vain to connect the decline in his friend's health to the letter, but it did not fit, because Emmett's physical decline had started when they were still working on the railroad. He said it felt as if he had a tapeworm eating his guts. "Think I'm coughing up my lungs."

Hy tried to substitute for Emmett in his various duties, but he was a poor craftsman and thus inadequate in doing the things that Emmett found easy—the work that prisoners and guards found valuable. To a man, prison guards and officials liked Emmett and showed concern for his declining health. Hy hated his own weakness—hated that he pitied himself more than Emmett—did not see how he could survive in prison without him.

From the moment he was locked in the Dallas County Jail, Hy's normal cheerful outlook, the attitude about life that had sustained him during the war, through killing Filson and becoming a fugitive, forsook him without apology or explanation. He needed Emmett to live. Emmett had made prison life bearable, had taken Hy's mind off of ways to end his life. A man who had hope in the face of a life sentence was inspiring and Emmett was one of the few men alive who could listen to and understand Hy's despair at being deprived of everything he valued in life.

Two weeks after the letter arrived, Hy, uninvited, followed his cellmate to the prison yard. Emmett headed directly for Satanta. The Chief was squatted and leaned against the barrel, as if defying the guards to make him stand on it again, as if he had subdued this instrument of torture. He sang softly in words they could not understand. A guard leaned against the yard wall, swatting a bat against his leg as if he were swatting flies. Emmett squatted beside the chief, waiting for him to stop chanting. When he finally paused, Emmett spoke slowly and quietly. "Chief, you say you will be free soon."

Chief Satanta did not make eye contact, gave no indication that he had heard Emmett.

Emmett looked around the yard like a cornered cat. "I need your help. I have to get out of here and I have to get out now."

Hy wondered why Emmett believed the chief. He had placed his own faith in Emmett's knowledge of the prison layout and his skills. Hy admired Satanta's stubbornness and dignity in the face of cruel treatment, but saw his talk of freedom as just talk.

The chief looked across the yard, still avoiding eye contact. Emmett tried again, his voice breaking this time. "My little boy has died, my wife is sick. I need to get to my family."

Satanta looked into Emmett's eyes and held his gaze. The eyes were red and pleading, but did not stray. Satanta was the first to look down. He shook his head. "I cannot help you. You are not of The People. Only a chief of The People can will himself free."

"I'm sick. I don't want to die in this hellhole."

Hy thought he recognized sympathy in Satanta's expression. "White people have their own God. He does not speak to me. I do not speak to Him. Go to your God if you need help."

Emmett walked to a corner of the yard, leaned against the wall and slid down as if he had no strength to go farther. Lev sat beside him. Arms draped across their knees, they sat in silence until it was almost time to go back to work. Emmett's breathing was labored. "You ever ask forgiveness for what you done?"

"Don't know that there was anyone to ask. Man I shot needed killing. Never saw any family. Only thing that loved him was a hairless creature he called Slick and my brother killed him."

"Man I killed was taking a horsewhip to his wife. Didn't start out to kill him, but he told me I'd have to kill him to make him stop. Kept right on whipping her. Guess he didn't think I would."

Hy had asked before, but this was the first time Emmett had discussed the crime that had put him in Huntsville. "Sounds like he needed killing, too."

"It was a spur of the moment thing. I was young and hotheaded. Should have left him be. Prosecutor at my trial said it was a family argument."

"You think you need forgiveness for keeping a woman from being horsewhipped?"

"Strange thing was, she tried to claw my eyes out when her husband died." Emmett turned to look at Hy. His eyes were pleading. "But it ain't her forgiveness I'm talking about, it's God's. I reckon He don't take kindly to any killing at all. I reckon He's punishing me for it now."

Such matters had always confused Hy. He tried to imagine

what his mother would say. He knew her views on killing during war, but could not imagine what they would be on killing Filson or killing a man that was horsewhipping his wife. "My papa would say that God put good men here to keep the bad ones from doing such things as horsewhipping and ravaging women." He had almost uttered rape, but checked himself.

Emmett seemed unmoved by Hy's explanation. "Just in case that ain't true, have you asked forgiveness?"

"I prayed plenty of times, asking to get out of this hellhole." Hy seemed embarrassed by this personal revelation. "He ain't never answered any of my prayers. Figure He wonders why I didn't do more praying when I wasn't in so much trouble."

Emmett Day spent most of that night on his knees beside his bunk, praying. Hy listened in agony, then prayed silently for his own forgiveness, asking his mother to intervene on his behalf. He found escape in sleep just before dawn. An hour later, Hy found his friend dead on the floor.

They buried Emmett at Peckerwood Hill, the prison graveyard, at twilight. Back in his cell, Hy, feeling like a thief, read the letter from Emmett's wife. Then he opened one of Hester's letters. He had not been able to read any of them and had never written to her. He had no address to write to, and feared that a general delivery letter would lead the law to Lev. There were only three letters. None had a return address, of course. The first was mailed in Dallas and was waiting for him when he arrived in Huntsville. She had written it the day he was sentenced. The other two were postmarked in Fort Worth. Hester had probably prevailed upon strangers passing through to mail them.

He cried when he read the letter from Emmett's wife and cried again when he read Hester's. He understood his friend's hopelessness. He could not find the words to write to Hester alone, so he wrote a letter to Hester and his children—a long letter telling them to try and forget him—to go back to Ellis County. He wanted to think of Hester back home, near her parents and his siblings. When he finally finished, he folded the letter and placed it with Hester's letters to him, resolving to find a way to get it to her without calling attention to Lev.

He barely functioned for several days. Waking and the daily routine of living seemed to physically hurt and exhaust him. He spoke only when spoken to, and did as he was told. The guards began to recognize a whipped dog and they treated him accordingly. He cowered at first, unwilling to resist. Satanta reproached him in the yard. "Your friend is dead. You shame him by acting like a cur dog. Stand up. Walk proudly."

The words stung. Hy reflexively straightened and stood as close as possible to Satanta's face. "I see how you stand proudly, Chief. Most of the time, you straddle the carpenter horse or stand on the damn barrel." Hy waved his arms like bird wings. "When are you going to fly over these walls and be free?"

Satanta met his gaze. "I am already free."

Two days later, Satanta faked a heart attack and was taken to the prison hospital. Singing the Kiowa death song, he jumped through the second story hospital window and landed on a brick wall below. Anxious to avoid unwanted publicity that might provoke violent reaction from his Kiowa followers, prison officials hurriedly buried him before dawn at Peckerwood Hill, his passing noted only by a lonely chant from a fellow Kiowa in the prison yard. Alone in his cell, Hy listened to the chant, admiring the courage of the Chief. Now there was nobody left to talk to.

The next morning, Satanta's Indian friend sat quietly on the spot where Satanta had landed, continuing his chant. Hy stood by him, patiently waiting for a break in the death song. There was none. A guard told Hy to move on. "He don't stop that soon, I'll put him on the barrel or the carpenter horse. See how good he can sing from there."

Hy looked at the guard, but spoke to the spot where Satanta

had fallen. "Said he was going to be free. Now I know what he meant."

A prison guard who had been friends with Emmett stopped at Hy's cell later that night. "Bad about Day. Satanta's jump is what got us in the papers, though. The Chief turned out to be pretty famous. May cost a few scalps. Redskins will blame all whites."

Hy was unsure of how to feel or what to say. He felt somehow responsible for the deaths of both Satanta and Emmett. Mostly, he felt self-pity at being abandoned.

The guard lingered. "Getting another prisoner soon that'll make folks forget the Indian."

Hy was not in the mood to talk, but humored the guard. He needed any kind of friend. "Another Chief?"

"Better."

Irritated at the guard's smugness, Hy did not reply.

"Mister John Wesley Hardin himself will be here soon enough, I reckon."

Hy straightened. "That right? I been told we're kin. He married a cousin."

The guard laughed in a mocking tone. "Well, bein' family and all, maybe the two of you can get shot together when you try to break out. We been told to be ready. Hardin will try a break, for sure. Get his ass killed if he tries it in here."

47

THE ENCOUNTER WITH WADE AND RATTLE AND
his unspoken challenge to the Ranger emboldened Lev, but if the
Ranger returned, it would probably be soon and he would bring
enough help to flush Lev out of the hills. He figured that the Ranger
had tired of the challenge and now must capture him to save face.
It had probably been an interesting game, stalking Lev like a deer,
but now it was over. The children knew that Lev was hiding in the
hills now, so he visited the house more often, always under the
cover of night. But Mary Ann and Hester did not know how to find
him. Lev had his escape planned if the Rangers came, and no
longer believed they could catch him. He had to remain free, at
least until he heard from John Henry Brown.

The children were not allowed to visit his hiding places,
but Lev had seen Alfred and Ellen look up to the hills too often.
Alfred seemed angry much of the time, and Lev feared the look of
desperation he saw growing in his son's eyes.

The women were heartened when Lev told them most of
what his old commander had said. Lev's spirits ebbed and flowed,
but he had difficulty believing that the major could actually exert
enough influence to free his brother or help him. Back in the hills,
he lost some of his sharpness and vigilance. Taking meals at home
and occasionally sleeping in his own bed softened him. Having
the children near brought tears to his eyes and he could not bring

himself to offer tenderness to them, for fear they would start to need something he might not be able to offer if he were captured, killed, or had to flee.

When the Ranger did not reappear, Lev was bothered. The hunt had kept him sharp, a contest of will between himself and the Ranger. The sober voice of reason and John Henry Brown's warning not to kill the Ranger or be killed by him was silenced. Keeping the women and children fed and protected had sustained him before, kept him focused. Doing it while being hunted kept him virile. He had grown accustomed to himself as a feral animal and liked it. Now that Mary Ann and Hester had shown him they were self-sustaining, the battle of wits with the Ranger was all he had left. Without it, he felt useless and insignificant, without purpose.

Lev started to hunt the Ranger. He rode to the Ranger camp and watched from behind trees, hoping to catch the lawman leaving, maybe follow him as he headed toward Lev's hills. Killing his pursuer would free him, restore his vitality and make him necessary to his family again. But the Ranger was nowhere to be found.

Six weeks after his visit with John Henry Brown, Lev rode Butter down Palo Pinto's only street. The sounds of dogs barking and chickens clucking and the smell of beef cooking assaulted his senses. But the sound of fiddle music filtered through it all and drew him like a fly to a spider web. Butter stopped and pointed her ears as if she appreciated the music, too. An old man sawed a tune that Lev thought he recognized, but could not put a name to. The music washed over him like rippling water, and he tried to recall when he had last heard music of any kind.

The old man stopped playing and held the fiddle out to Lev. "Care to take a turn, sir?"

Surprised, Lev shook his head. "No, thank you. Never could play."

The old man held the fiddle against his chest. "Old age claims certain advantages, my friend. I would never call a man a liar, but I know a fiddle player when I see one. You been looking at this fiddle like it was a comely woman."

Lev managed a crooked grin. "Reminds me of my daddy. He played."

The man returned the fiddle to his shoulder and cheek. "If you're a lover of music, there's a street dance tonight about where your horse is standing."

Street dance. Lev had not danced with Mary Ann since they waltzed on dirt when he got back from the war. "Thanks. I'll remember that." Feeling watched, Lev looked over his shoulder and saw a man with a badge stopped in the street behind him. The man smiled, nodded and kept walking.

The old man picked up on Lev's discomfort. "That's Sheriff Jim Owens. A man devoted to the Confederacy if I ever saw one."

Lev eased Butter toward the old general store that he had occasionally visited before Hy's capture, making no attempt to hide his identity. He looped Butter's reins over the hitching rail and leaned against a post on the board sidewalk. It felt good to be out in the open letting the Indian summer sun work on his tired muscles. He nodded without speaking to the first customers he saw, judging them to be dangerous or unlikely sources of information about Texas Rangers. As the sun reached its noon high, his wait was rewarded. A wagon came down the street driven by an approachable man dressed like a farmer in brogan shoes and overalls. His wife sat beside him on the wagon seat. Six children rode in the wagon bed. The farmer helped the smallest of the children down and followed his family as they entered the store. Lev leaned away from the post just enough to partially block the man's path.

The farmer took note of Lev for the first time and his expression changed from friendly to cautious. Lev tried to smile as he touched the man's arm, but it seemed the muscles in his face would not work right. Conversation with strangers, a skill he had never been good at, had completely abandoned him. He could not get his mouth to form words. When the man started to step around, Lev managed a sentence. "Sorry to bother you, sir, but I need information."

The farmer's smile returned. "I imagine you came to the wrong place, but I'll do what I can."

"Looking for a feller. Friend of mine." He wanted to take back the words as soon as he said them. He realized he did not even know the Ranger's name.

"What's his name?"

"Meant to say, a friend of mine sent me looking for him. Said he might be able to help me find work. Traveled so far, I done forgot his name."

The farmer stared, curiosity in his expression. His tone full of compassion, he spoke to Lev as if he were a small boy. "The name would help. What does he do?"

Lev knew it was too late to recover, so he started to step off the sidewalk. The man caught his arm. "I want to help."

Lev turned and the words tumbled out. "He's a Texas Ranger. Rides a jawboned horse with a roman nose. Rides with a halter and bridle, wide wood stirrups with flat bottoms." Lev saw no light in the man's eyes. "Carries a Winchester rifle, Colt pistol, and a Bowie knife." Still no light.

"Sir, you have just described virtually all of the Rangers in this area. They come and go, too. Sometime stay on scouts for as long as six months."

"This one has a mustache like mine, only trimmed. No beard. Fastidious dresser." Lev touched both hands to his chest. "Wool vest."

The light came on. "I've seen that feller. Don't know his name, though. Keeps to himself. All business-like. Don't see him around the saloons like some of the others. He might show up at this store if you wait long enough. Seen him pick up his mail here a time or two."

Lev looked inside the store and saw James Dillahunty sorting mail behind a small barred window. John Henry Brown's voice spoke to him. *Check every two weeks after a month.* Lev looked past the farmer and bent his fingers to count the days since he had seen John Henry. He had set aside any hope of hearing from him. False hope could make a man weak. He started around the farmer, headed toward Dillahunty.

The farmer put a hand on his arm. "Say, I don't know what I'm thinking. You being a stranger, you probably don't know where the Ranger camp is. You can just ride out there and find your man, or at least his whereabouts."

"Much obliged." Lev stepped around him without waiting for directions to the camp. The farmer shrugged and joined his family. Lev stared at the postmaster through the iron bars. "Package for William Parsons?"

Dillahunty looked up and scrutinized Lev, his eyes full of curiosity. He pushed a big envelope under the bars but placed a timid, white, slightly plump hand on top of it. Lev looked at the protruding veins on the man's soft hand and put his own scarred, copper-colored hand beside it. The back of his hand looked as if the skin had been drawn taught against the bone for tanning and been wrinkled by a too-hot sun. The postmaster looked at Lev again, noted his appearance and smell, the wild look in his eyes. "Mister, I don't mean to cause trouble, but I was told this package would be picked up by a woman."

"John Henry Brown tell you that?"

The postmaster smiled. "You know who sent it, I guess it's yours." He removed his hand and gave Lev a reluctant look. "If you're who I think you are, you might be knowing how I can deliver this one, too." He slid a smaller envelope under the cage. "I served Texas in the war, friend."

Lev studied the small envelope addressed to Hester Rivers, General Delivery, Palo Pinto, Texas. The handwriting looked familiar. He looked up long enough to address Dillahunty in a hoarse voice. "Much obliged. Might be able to deliver this one on my way back." He put both envelopes under his shirt and resisted the urge to tear them open as soon as he stepped outside. As he left the small settlement, the missives against his heart were like having the hand of John Henry Brown on his shoulder and Olivia's hand on his chest where the bullet had entered. He shuddered a little and rolled his shoulders as he considered the enormity of the mistake he had made by ignoring John Henry's advice to stay clear of the Ranger. He realized that he had become two parts, one wild animal and one human, and the non-reasoning animal was taking over.

Silently cautioning himself against optimism about the contents of either letter, he waited until he was in his cave to open them. He stared at both before opening Major Brown's. There was no greeting, no signature—nothing that would identify the addressee or the author of the message.

Have confirmed that Filson served for the Confederacy as well as Union forces under the name of Cullen Montgomery. True loyalty unknown, but have sworn oath of one Confederate officer that the man posed as a spy for the South and provided false information. Known to have deserted from Confederate army. Probably deserted from Union also, but no proof.

Have signed statement from Lydia Filson (Montgomery), his widow, that the man killed her father as she watched. She says that Montgomery also poisoned local physician in Rusk named Brand. Said a daughter named Olivia would testify to that. Also said that Filson took indecent advantage of Olivia when she was only a child.

This information has gained support for a pardon request from Dallas Mayor W. S. Cabell, clerks of county and district courts, City Attorney, and the Sheriff at the time of your brother's arrest. This is a fine beginning to our endeavor.

Prosecuting attorney George Aldridge and jury foreman at Hy's trial as well as several state representatives of my acquaintance will sign petition to Governor if we can get three additional forms.

One: Affidavit from wife (Hester) saying she was raped by Filson (Montgomery)

Two: Petition stating your brother's good character signed by citizens from Ellis County area, where the shooting occurred.

Three: Sworn affidavit from the poisoned doctor's daughter (Olivia Brand) saying that the man killed her father and raped her.

Gov. Hubbard leaves office this year. Must act before then. Will go to Governor without these things, but we will likely get only one chance. Having the final three will, I think, give us a fighting chance.

Send or deliver them to me at General Delivery, Dallas. I need them in time to make trip to Austin well before Christmas.

John Henry Brown enclosed a petition stating Hy's excellent qualities as a peaceable citizen, husband and father. It was written on a long piece of paper with spaces for twenty signatures. There was no affidavit for Hester or Olivia to sign. Lev read the petition twice, trying to keep his eyes and mind off the other letter. He read John Henry's letter three times, his hopes rising with the first paragraph and falling with the second in each reading. What month was it? Late September, he guessed. He had stopped maintaining his cave calendar when he went to Dallas. Was there time? Would Hester sign an affidavit in violation of Hy's wishes? How could he return to Ellis County for signatures without being arrested? And

Olivia. He had no idea where she was—could not even remember her husband's name. Daylight was fading and it was too hot for a fire as he opened the second letter.

48

HESTER LEFT THE LANTERN ON THE PORCH THAT night, signaling all was well. Lev entered the back door just before midnight and handed the letter from John Henry Brown to Mary Ann. She read it and ran to fetch Hester. Lev herded the gleeful sisters outside to keep their suppressed shouts of joy from waking the children. "I admit it's good news, but don't see how we can get the three things he wants."

Hester would have none of it. "Do you realize that my Hy could be home in time for Christmas?"

"Whoa. Back up a little. Them documents may be hard to come by and we have to get 'em to John Henry, then he has to take 'em to the governor before he leaves office."

Hester held the lantern close enough to read the letter for the third time. "I'll write the first one tonight."

Lev looked at Mary Ann as he spoke to Hester. "Hy won't have you saying it."

"Hy's got no say in it. I intend to do my letter and then start off tomorrow to get the other two."

Lev handed Hester the second letter. "You may already have the second one."

Dear Hester,
Trust this finds you and yours well. I am in my old place at

Dresden, but unable to perform my prior duties as a barber, dentist or dispenser of drugs. I find that Lev and I have something in common. I have a bullet lodged in my spine that cannot be removed. Sorry I did not show him more sympathy. I think of him each time it stabs me and fear I am not holding up as bravely as he has.

I write because of Hy. I think of him often. In a prison cell, partially because of me. In my current condition, I have found courage that shames my former self. I have taken a signed oath that I am the one that shot Filson and proud for having done it. Perhaps this could help Hy. It is in the possession of Dr. Robinson here in Dresden.

I hope you can forgive me for any part I played in your troubles.

Olivia

Hester read the letter again before handing it to Mary Ann. She looked at Lev with questioning eyes. "Will her oath help?"

"It ain't what Major Brown asked for. Me and Hy never denied the killing. Her confessing to it could do more harm than good."

Hester was undeterred. "No matter. Her letter says to me that she will sign the affidavit he wants if we can get to her in time."

"In time?"

Hester glanced at Mary Ann, still reading the letter for a second time, before answering Lev. "This is a letter from a dying woman."

Mary Ann finished reading. "And a woman without a husband, I would guess."

Lev took the letter from Mary Ann. "Didn't see no mention of her husband or dying."

Mary Ann shook her head impatiently. "She's back in Dresden, living where she used to, wanting to barber and dentist and conjure. No mention of her man."

Hester tucked both letters into the bosom of her dress. "I'll leave at first light."

Mary Ann took Lev's hand. "No, we'll all leave together." She stopped her husband before he could protest. "I want to see Mama and Papa. Show them Papa's namesake. They don't even know about Little Rance ... or Ellen, for that matter."

Lev agreed. "We'll be a long day's ride from Dallas if we get what we need. Could save more than two weeks in getting the paperwork to John Henry." Lev turned to look at the gap in the hills and thought of the Ranger. "We'll take both wagons. Pack everything we can. Anything left behind will likely be stole."

Hester smiled. "So you do think it's possible."

"Enough to try. Just remember the governor is likely to have hundreds of folks begging him just like us."

Hester hugged Lev. "We could have a Christmas tree and celebrate Christmas. These little ones have never seen a real Christmas celebration."

Lev readied for the trip without benefit of a lantern that might attract attention. He was still loading the wagons, horses, tack and feed when Mary Ann joined him in the barn. She helped him load a sack of corn and pull the dusty wagons into the yard for easier harnessing in the morning. It was almost too late to bother going to bed by the time they finished preparations. "You got provisions and clothes for the babies all ready?"

Lev marveled at the efficiency of the two sisters. They had shown their strength often enough, but he had never fully accepted it. Now, he was forced to acknowledge that they were almost self-sufficient and that he might need them more than they needed him. Standing beside his wife, he had feelings not experienced in years—a sense of change, of movement forward, of newness, of a purpose in life other than avoiding capture. Without meaning to, he allowed a glimmer of hope to enter his consciousness—the possibility that he and Hy could be free. When she took his hand to guide him toward the house, he felt a sense of elation and closeness that had been missing since his first day of hiding in the hills.

She nudged against his arm as they walked. "Our last night here, at least for a while. You sleep with me."

He lay beside her and allowed a sense of safety and contentment to creep into his soul. He felt almost safe enough to sleep soundly.

She spoke softly to keep from waking the children. "You called out for her, you know."

"Called out for who?"

"Olivia. The night we took out the bullet. You talked to her most of the night."

"Out of my head. Probably thought I was back in those first days when I got shot." He waited for a reply, but there was none. The sense of contentment gone, he slept for about an hour.

As he harnessed the second team, he recalled his repeated complaints to his brother about the foolishness of keeping two wagons and two teams. Now, he was pleased that Hy had talked him out of selling a wagon and team. Had Hy known the whole family would flee again?

Mary Ann and Hester and the six children filed outside just as he finished saddling Butter. Everyone except the babies carried a full burlap bag over each shoulder. Lev had tried for weeks to ignore Mary Ann's swelled stomach, but he brushed against it as he took the sacks from her shoulders. Weeks earlier, she had dismissed his questions and pulled his hand away when he touched her there. Little Alfred and Kat studied Lev as they helped him load, trying to reconcile the man they had seen attack Rattle and Wade with the man they saw now.

Lev felt like a new man as they entered shaded country. He stopped to pick up the first post oak acorns he saw and carried one in each pocket for good luck. The family's chances for good fortune seemed to increase with each mile traveled away from the Ranger. Lev rode behind the wagons as often as in front to be sure they were not being followed, dragging a switch full of leaves tied to Butter's tail to cover wagon and horse tracks. The trees and heavy air were a little stifling at first, but he began to see the trees and lower country as protection. Six days into the journey, they camped less than a day's ride from their old home place off Chambers Creek. Lev knew better, but he could not shake the feeling that his parents were waiting for him there. They had started appearing in his dreams again.

Hester washed supper dishes in water warmed over a campfire. "Mary Ann and me need to check on Otho and Mama and Papa first."

The children were asleep in the wagon and Lev was spread out on a bedroll. He rose to one elbow. "Know you want to see your boy and the folks, but do we have time for that?"

"It's on the way to Corsicana. We thought Sebastian's old friend, Judge Crawford, might help with the petition."

Lev was ashamed that he had not thought of that. He could not collect signatures without risk of being caught, so Judge Crawford was a smart choice. "Providing he's still alive, that's real good thinking."

Mary Ann touched his arm. "To save time, we thought you might sneak into Dresden and see what you can find out about Olivia while we go on to Papa's."

Lev hesitated, but could see that their minds were set. "I'll meet you on the Corsicana Square in three days. If I am not there, go back and wait at your folks."

Lev watched the women and children leave before daybreak. He was not comfortable with letting them fend for themselves, but they were armed and knew their way around this country. No Indians here, and he had heard that the thugs who terrorized the country after the war had been thinned out. He destroyed all signs of their camp and rode toward Dresden, comforted in the fact that the Ranger would choose to follow him rather than the wagons.

It was dusk as he studied the familiar little town from timber just behind the main street. He could not see the barbershop or Captain Rutherford's blacksmith shop from his vantage point. He pulled his hat low and rode behind the apothecary and returned up the alley behind the blacksmith shop. No familiar faces. No sign of life in Olivia's apothecary and he could not bring himself to knock on the back door. He turned toward Doc Robinson's home just outside of town. At Mary Ann's insistence, he had washed in the creek the night before and shaved. He felt presentable as he knocked on Robinson's door.

To his surprise, the doctor answered. Lev brushed his hat off his head and held it against his hip. "Evenin', Doc." Lev saw no recognition in the doctor's face. He tried again. "Lev Rivers, Doc. Don't mean to cause trouble for you, but I'm trying to find Olivia."

Belated recognition filled the doctor's eyes before they turned sad. "Olivia is in bad shape, Lev. I have a colored woman staying with her in her old place. Probably be a good idea not to disturb her."

"Yes sir." Lev pulled her letter from his buttoned shirt and let the doctor see the address in Olivia's handwriting. "She wrote Hester this here letter about my brother Hy."

The doctor sighed, but did not take the letter. "She insisted on having me write up that oath about killing Filson. Did you come for that?"

"Not exactly, but I do need to see her."

"I don't know why, but she has expressed a desire to see you before she dies. Olivia is a fine woman who seems to have made a habit of making poor choices in her men."

"She dying?"

"Yes. Her husband brought her to me in the back of a wagon. The bullet had done its work on her before I examined her. Lodged in her spine." Dr. Robinson's eyes started to cloud. "Can't be removed without killing her or crippling her. Lead poison has set in."

"Can I ask who shot her?"

"Her husband."

"Thought you said he brought her in."

"He did. They both claim it was an accident, but I have not seen the son-of-a-bitch since he brought her to my office. At worst, he is a murderer. At best, he has abandoned a fine woman and wife."

Lev looked away, his own eyes clouding now. "She able to converse?"

"Most of the time." The doctor looked past Lev and resignation crossed his face. "Just knock on the back door to the apothecary. Colored woman's name is Bitsy. Tell her I sent you. She'll let you in if you can call her name."

"Much obliged."

Lev was already in the saddle when the doctor gestured for him to wait. "Best watch yourself. Wade Monroe has sworn to kill you on sight. He was might near dead before he got away from the horse you tied him on."

49

THE SMELL OF OLIVIA'S POTIONS AND barbershop lilac water greeted Lev as he entered the building. The familiar fragrances were overshadowed slightly by a faint odor that Lev did not recognize. It reminded him of Filson's mongrel dog and the day he killed it in the barbershop. He was unnerved as Bitsy led him into the small room Olivia had taken as her bedroom.

Her head was propped on two pillows and she was awake, but barely. She smiled and he thought he saw a twinkle in her sad eyes when she saw him. Her wiry, rust-colored hair was longer than he remembered and lay against the pillows with a few unexpected strands of gray. A single candle provided the only light for her sallow face. There was darkness under her eyes and the skin across her cheeks seemed slack.

She had always seemed tomboyish to him, athletic and strong for a woman. Seeing her in this weak state made him not trust his voice. Bitsy pushed a chair against his legs and left the room. He touched Olivia's hand and eased into the chair.

"You came."

"Didn't you know I would?"

"Never figured the letter would reach Hester, much less you."

They passed nervous small talk for a few minutes, trying to avoid the gravity of the situation. Lev finally found a way to approach

---

it. "Hear you're trying to stay up with me and carry around a bullet for a few years."

"Never intended to do that, but I have a new appreciation for your suffering. Afraid I was too hard on you at the time."

"You saved my life."

She grimaced with the smile and shake of her head. "Not so. Do you still have the bullet?"

"I do. He reached into his pocket and withdrew the small piece of lead. "Worked its way out my back, just like you said it might. Liked to killed me leaving though."

She focused on the piece of lead. "How is Hester ... and Mary Ann?"

"Both fine. They're on their way to see about their folks and Hester's son, Otho. The boy got crossways with this Texas Ranger that arrested his daddy. Had to send him off to his grandparents."

She stared at him for a period, as if he were a cool drink of water and she was dying of thirst. "You did well in choosing your women ... and I did just as poorly at picking my men."

Lev did not know how to approach the subject of her husband and the shooting and decided to let it alone.

Her strength for conversation waning, Olivia seemed almost impatient to get to the reason for his visit. "About Hy. Can I help him?"

Lev wished for the letter from John Henry Brown so that he could read from it, but Hester had it. "We got an old Confederate officer that is trying to get him a pardon."

She smiled again. "Really?"

"A long shot, I reckon, but Hester and Mary Ann are out getting a petition signed saying good things about Hy."

"Is that all it's going to take?"

Lev rose from his chair and bounced his hat in his hand as he walked to the foot of her bed and back. He sat back down and ran a finger under his mustache.

Her giggle seemed to hurt her. "I know you, Lev Rivers. Spit it out."

"This feller, name being Major John Henry Brown, is pretty well connected in Dallas. Says an affidavit from you would be a lot of help."

"Why, sure. Told you I would swear to killing that weasel who called himself a man. Wish I had. Anything for you and Hy, my two favorite men ... other than Doc Robinson, of course. "

Lev's expression showed pain. "You see, there ain't no doubt about who shot him. Hy done admitted to that."

"Go on."

Lev tugged on an earlobe. "Well, Hester has to swear that Filson ... raped her. Major Brown says it would help if you did the same. Filson's wife says he poisoned your daddy, too. If either one of them things is true, it might help if you said so in writing. Only if it's true, of course." There, the words were out there ... between them—the ones that had kept them apart all these years.

Her lips smiled, but her eyes seemed to be somewhere else. She patted Lev's hand. "Ask Doc Robinson to get it drawn up. I'll sign it. Let's do it tomorrow."

Lev rose and pulled down his hat. "Tomorrow it is." He leaned down and kissed her forehead and wondered what had made him do it. When he rose, he knocked over the single candle. It was a bad sign and he righted it at once.

Lev was in Doc Robinson's yard at first light. At the doctor's insistence, he tied Butter to the buggy and rode beside him into Dresden. He explained about John Henry Brown on the way. Hy was impressed that Dr. Robinson knew about his old commander. They drank coffee together in his office as Lev tried his best to recall John Henry's exact words while Dr. Robinson wrote the affidavit. "I'll take it to Captain Rutherford first. We'll both sign as witnesses."

Doc had patients to see, so it was noon when they entered Olivia's room. The morning sunlight was not as kind to her as the candle had been. Her face and hair were grayer, the lines around her mouth deeper, and the circles under her eyes darker. Even her voice seemed weaker. Dr. Robinson propped her up with pillows and she read the document as if it were a history of her life, every word inflicting pain. She sighed and signed it at once. Lev felt selfish as he took the document from her, as if he were taking her last breath of life, her dignity.

Lev's voice cracked. "Much obliged, Olivia. Whether it works or not, Hy and me will never be able to repay you."

"Telling the truth is never too hard. Should have done it sooner." She held out a closed fist to him. "Open your hand." She dropped the rabbit's foot he had given her the first night they met into his open palm.

Dr. Robinson left them alone and Lev sat in the chair beside her bed until she drifted off to sleep. As he backed out of the room, he stepped into the barbershop and took himself back through the years, but gained no peace from it. He returned to the door of her room and leaned against the doorjamb, studying her as she slept, trying not to hear the slight gurgling sound she made as she breathed. The window shade near her bed fluttered and Lev felt the angel of death tease him. The closeness of death overwhelmed him with memories of the time he had kissed Olivia a few feet from where he stood, the war, the killing and hiding in the hills. He had not expected this from life and knew that she had not. It all seemed unfair and he dared not think of what might have been.

He stiffened in resistance to the melancholy that threatened to overcome him, realizing that neither he nor Hy could afford it now. He stuffed the affidavit inside his shirt and walked out onto Dresden's main street without thinking. He smelled the familiar smell of coals burning in a smithy's forge and looked across the street at Captain Rutherford shoeing a horse. He looked up and down the street before walking across.

He was shaking Rutherford's hand before he recognized the

horse. Rutherford saw his look of recognition. "Yep. Rattle's nag."

Lev turned to see Rattle running down the street. "Hell's bells."

The blacksmith pointed toward him. "He'll be going for Wade. He's still the law around here. You still wanted?"

Lev was already halfway across the street. He had left Butter standing behind the apothecary and headed for the alley beside the barbershop to reach her. Wade limped from behind two stacked barrels and stood in the middle of the path toward Butter, a rifle held in the crook of his right arm. Wade's right eye focused on Lev, but the left looked up and away; his left hand hung at an awkward angle; one leg seemed unable to bear his weight; his expression a mixture of surprise and hate. "Didn't believe it when they said you was back here." The voice had changed too, from mellifluous to guttural.

As if Hy and Sebastian were whispering instructions, Lev pulled his pistol and started toward Wade at a fast, but steady pace. Before Wade could lift the rifle and steady it with his bad hand, the barrel to Lev's pistol touched his forehead. There was a rank odor of fear-caused sweat as Lev glanced at the bad knee.

His voice filled with helpless rage to the point of breaking, Wade's thirst for revenge poured out. "Busted my knee for good with that damn stick. Put out my eye. Me and Rattle nearly got killed before we got away from them horses."

Lev tried to hold back the surge of pity for his former friend, but Wade saw his expression change and poured out the story in pain-filled anguish as if he were telling it to his mother. "They spooked and took us through them cedar breaks, and then mine fell down one of them rock hills and rolled over me. Rolled the saddle under his belly. Damn horse drug me and kicked me till he got tired. Limb damn near tore out my left eye." He took a deep breath to steady himself and focused a wish-for-death stare with his one good eye on Lev. Hate gave him strength and his voice came back strong, reminding Lev of the buzz a rattlesnake issues as a warning. "You goddam Rivers might near ruined my whole life and I aim to kill all of you before I'm through."

Lev studied him with resignation. He did not need this. Not now. "We was friends once. You changed that. You brought all that on yourself, Wade. Taking a hand to a man's wife likely to get any man killed."

Wade's bad eye widened as he tried to look at the pistol that still touched his forehead. The good eye scanned the street.

Lev felt, but did not see, Rattle lurking somewhere close. "Only reason you're still alive is I'm tired of killing. Promised my wife I was done with it."

"Better do it anyway. You still a wanted man. I can kill you and nobody will say a damn thing."

Lev stared at his old friend-turned-nemesis with despair and finality. He had papers that had to be delivered—papers that might help Hy. "Had business here. It's done. I'm leaving. Don't make me kill you on the way out."

Wade searched the street behind Lev for Rattle but he did not appear. "Piss on you, your old man, your mama, and piss on your bitch wife and her whore sister. Wish I'd hit the bitch harder." Lev reached across himself with the gun and swung the barrel hard against Wade's forehead, just above his good eye. Wade screamed with rage and pain as he dropped to his bad knee and fell over in the alley dirt. Lev walked around him, headed toward Butter.

50

HOW LONG HAD HE BEEN GONE? LEV HAD promised to meet them on the Corsicana Square at sunset in three days. The time with Olivia had seemed to span a lifetime but had taken only two of those three. Corsicana was less than a day's travel. He had time to camp once more at the old home place. Doc Robinson said the county had taken it for back taxes, but nobody would buy it because of fear of yellow fever.

The sinking sun warmed his back as he stood at the old family graveyard. A whippoorwill called early, the bird's way of letting him know that Sebastian, Rachael, Alfred, McCulloch, even Boy, knew he had returned. He stood at the graves, hat in hand, until a heavy tiredness and sadness made him sit down in the sand. His boots touched a flat board at the foot of Rachael's grave. The remnants of long-dead flowers drooped across the board like sentinels caught asleep. Lev brushed his hand across the board and flicked away the sand.

Someone had scratched a heart-shape with Mama and Papa inside it—beneath the heart, initials. L. E. had been scratched at the same time as the heart. E. J., scratched under the first set of initials, was deeper and had been done later. Lev rubbed the carvings as if to connect to his older sisters who had found their parents' graves. Lucy Elizabeth had probably come as soon as word reached her. Rachael had openly wished for Lucy when Sebastian died, but had not mentioned her estranged daughter, Eliza Jane. He wondered if Rachael knew of their visits—if Eliza Jane forgave in order to be forgiven.

There were lessons to be learned here, he knew, if he could just think clearly. Rachael had forgiven Sebastian, but only when it seemed too late. Now, Eliza Jane seemed to have forgiven her mother, but only through scratching on a board, not through words and caresses. He decided not to go into either house. He knew what happened inside abandoned houses and did not want to see it. He built a fire, hoping it would bring a visit from his father, but he drifted off to sleep disappointed.

Lev arrived in Corsicana just before sunset, hoping it was the third day. It was cool, but not uncomfortable in the shade as Lev stopped Butter in the alley. He saw his family waiting on the square. Mary Ann sat on the wagon seat, her bonnet off, black hair moving slightly in the easy breeze. She seemed to be soaking up the autumn sun. Little Rance sat in the wagon bed with Ellen; Little Alfred leaned against a wheel, and Hester, arms crossed, leaned against the hitching rail.

Lev watched them from the shadows and checked out the street. The encounter with Wade had brought back the feeling of being chased, but seeing his family sitting peacefully on a busy street calmed him. Gratitude and hope washed over him with the sun when he emerged from the alley. Little Alfred saw him first but resisted the urge to wave, wary that his father might still be hiding from the law. Judge Crawford, Kat, Dallas and Lane emerged from the general store just as he arrived.

Hester waved something that looked like paper toward him. "We have the signatures. Good, prominent people, thanks to Judge Crawford."

Mary Ann looked at her husband as he shook the judge's hand, patiently awaiting a report on his part of the mission. He smiled at the sisters as he pulled Olivia's affidavit from his saddlebag. "Guess the only question now is how to get the documents to Dallas the fastest way possible."

Mary Ann had not taken her eyes off her husband. "How was Olivia?"

Lev dismounted and reached both arms up to his wife and helped her down. He put his hands on her cheeks and kissed her full on the lips. Mary Ann drew in her breath with surprise. Lev had never kissed her in public before. Little Alfred and Ellen stood back, arms hung stiffly by their sides, waiting for their father's recognition. Lev dropped to one knee and opened his arms to them both. Ellen fell into the embrace while Alfred barely touched his father's shoulder.

Lev rose and put his arm across his wife's shoulders. He took a minute to look at them all before answering her question. "Olivia is hurt bad." He took a deep breath and smiled to keep his composure. "Doc says she won't make it a week. Gladly signed the paper, though. Reads just like John Henry wanted." He put his index finger on the document. "Doc and Captain Rutherford signed as witnesses."

Mary Ann took Olivia's affidavit from him and sat down on the sidewalk boards to read it. Tears in her eyes, she handed it to Hester. Lev watched Hester read, wondering if she was comparing Olivia's words and pain to her own. A young man approached and stood behind her as she finished. She wiped at her eyes before putting a hand on the man's taller shoulder. She nudged him toward Lev.

Recognition was slow in coming to Lev's tired eyes. "Otho? Is that you?"

The boy was almost eighteen and looked older. Already had a red beard and was carrying a pistol. Lev could see that the anger had not left him.

Lev was shaking Otho's hand when Rance extended his fingers, then hands, over the wagon bed toward his father. Lev pulled the boy from the wagon and into his arms, nuzzling his cheek while he spoke to Mary Ann. "Think he missed his papa." He held the boy high above him to study his face. "Did you get to see the man you're named for?"

Lev felt silence engulf the family as he watched his baby son. When he looked up, Mary Ann's and Hester's eyes were filled. Mary Ann told him. "Papa died almost a year before Rance here was born. Guess I somehow knew that when we named him Rance."

Lev kissed Rance's cheek. "He would have been proud. How's your mama?"

Mary Ann twisted her bonnet strings. "As well as can be expected. Hoping we can move back close to her again. Otho's been good to look out for her."

Otho stepped closer to Lev at the mention of his name. "You think all this paperwork is gonna help Papa? It don't, I aim to get him out."

Lev studied Otho's young face, too young for such rage. "I am beginning to believe it might. John Henry Brown is not a man without influence in Texas. Either way, it's a long shot we have to try."

"I aim to kill that Ranger for you and Papa, Uncle Lev. He won't never leave us alone if I don't."

Lev put a hand on the boy's shoulder. "You keep away from any law until we see if this works. You see what killing got me and your Pa." He turned back to Mary Ann. "See Arch and Jacob?"

She nodded. "They wanted to come today, but Judge here says they could be arrested just for talking to you. Law's been pestering them all this time because of the killing."

Lev turned toward the judge. "Why go after my brothers?"

"They figured Arch and Jacob knew your whereabouts."

Judge Crawford took Lev's arm and led him away from the others. "Captain Rutherford sent a rider to tell me about you running into Wade. Word is, you hurt him bad. Can't see out of his only good eye after you whacked him."

Lev felt momentary panic, and a trace of pity for Wade. "He's blind?"

"Looks like it. If he is, there'll likely be a posse come for you. I suggest you get on the road to Dallas with those papers."

Lev walked back to Mary Ann. "Wait for me at your mother's."

Otho extended a hand toward Lev. "Let me take the papers, Uncle Lev. You look all give out. Getting too old for this kinda riding."

Lev wondered if he looked that tired. Knew that he could outride the boy any day. Otho was hot-headed and did not know Major Brown. "It's a job for me, son. I could use a fresh horse, though. Butter's barely had a rest since leaving the West Country."

Judge Crawford pointed toward the hitching rail in front of the general store. "Take my gelding. Got him from your daddy just before his passing. Still sound and up to the trip. These ladies will give me a ride home, I imagine."

Lev looked at the horse, trying to recall his father astride him. "Much obliged. I'll see he's returned."

Hester went into the general store and returned with a burlap bag tied securely with twine. "Don't have to tell you that Hy's life is in this bag." Lev dropped the bag into a pocket of the cavalry saddlebags and turned as he took the rabbit's foot from his pocket and dropped it beside the papers. He tied all three leather straps and patted the pocket as he smiled at Hester.

The women filled the saddlebags on the judge's gelding with provisions from the wagon and corn for the horses. Hester stroked Lev's bearded cheek. "If I get my Hy back, we might even have a real Christmas for the kids this year. Your little ones never seen one and Kat don't even remember."

Lev took Mary Ann in his arms and whispered into her ear. "When I get back, we'll start living like people are supposed to."

Judge Crawford handed the gelding's reins up to Lev. "If Wade is blind, your best bet is to return out West after you deliver the papers. Still a lot of Union sentiment around here and lots of Yankees will be upset about Hy getting out, too. News about a possible parole has already got around." He patted Lev's leg like a father would. "I'll send word as soon as I know something."

"Send me a message in care of the postmaster in Palo Pinto. Secret's out by now, anyway. Or just send Otho. He knows the way."

Captain Rutherford, riding a lathered horse, met him just outside of town. "Doc Robinson says Wade's probably going to be blind the rest of his life."

Lev wished he had not expressed those tender feelings of hope to Mary Ann. Foolish wishing.

51

LEV RODE AS HARD AS HE FELT THE HORSES and he could endure. John Henry Brown was surprised to see him on the stairway landing with saddlebags on his shoulder. He studied the documents while Lev paced. Finally, he looked up. "Fine job, Lev. I could not have hoped for better. Beyond my expectations."

Lev took a seat. "You think we got a real chance at this thing?"

The major hesitated before answering. "These things are always a gamble, grant you, but I think we have a strong case. A former Confederate as governor in his final days in office gives us an advantage made in heaven. From reading these documents, this man belonged in hell and Hy did us all a favor by sending him on his way." John Henry Brown stood as he returned the documents to their pocket. "Is it acceptable if I borrow these saddlebags?"

Lev felt unexpected apprehension as he removed his remaining provisions from the opposite side of the bags. He felt the fur from the rabbit's foot and argued with himself whether to leave it with the papers or take it with him. He dropped it into his pocket. "A trip to Austin is long and dangerous. Thought I might go with you."

"I see you are apprehensive about turning over this precious cargo. If there were time, I would have the papers duplicated. As it is, Sheriff Jim Barkley has agreed to accompany me. I will guard them with my life."

Lev kept his eyes on the saddlebags as if he had not heard the reply. John Henry Brown walked around the desk and stood in front of Lev. "I understand your need to protect these documents and how hard it must have been to get them. But having you along with the sheriff would make things awkward. You're still a wanted man."

"Just so you understand that the document from Olivia Brand may be irreplaceable. She is in a bad way from a gunshot wound."

"I'm sorry. A great loss to you and your brother, from what I understand."

Lev looked toward the window without speaking.

"What are your plans? How may I contact you with news?"

"Judge Crawford advised me to head west again. Know too many people back home. Had a little run-in with the local law while I was getting the documents. Suppose I will take the judge's advice."

Major Brown returned to his seat. "I concur. Let me write you a letter. No guarantee, but it might help."

―――――――――――――

Lev was wary as he rode the gelding to his usual lookout point above the little canyon where they had lived for almost four years. Butter would follow without being led and the gelding would not, so Lev had ridden the judge's horse most of the way home. The mare seemed comfortable as she examined her old stomping grounds. She scanned the valley with alert ears, but did not twitch them. No nicker, snort or blow. She seemed bored as she lowered her head and searched for sparse grass. Lev unsaddled both horses and checked the cave for bears and varmints before storing the gear inside. A skunk walked by him in a hurry and sprayed the gelding on its way out. Nature had already begun to take back the cave.

He scanned the area for a week, following his old footfalls and hunting places. Late fall weather was kind. On a sunny morning, he saw a white owl on a limb of a scrub oak near the cave. It looked at him for a few seconds before taking flight. It flew in a circular pattern across the hills before dipping down over the house and barn, and then followed the creek out of the valley. Lev's breath was ragged, his voice soft as the feeling of loss washed over him. "Olivia."

Another week passed before he decided to visit Hester and Mary Ann's larder. He wondered if game was really scarce or if his hunting skills had returned to their former sorry state. Either way, Lev was almost out of food. He unsaddled both horses in the dark of the horse barn and crept to the dugout. Varmints had invaded the larder, but he was able to cut off a few strips of beef that had been left. He assumed all the chickens had been taken by predators, but found a few eggs in the nesting boxes. He tested a raw egg and found it fresh. His mouth watered as he imagined a pullet in a frying pan. When the much-smaller brood returned, he felt a sense of admiration for the survivors.

Dreams had convinced him that going into the house alone would bring ill fortune, so he slept around the clock in the barn. He had not slept that long since the women had removed the bullet.

For three warm and sunny days, he busied himself caring for tack and tending to the sore feet of the judge's gelding. He tried to stay inside the barn during daylight, but the unseasonable warmth of the sun made him bolder in his outdoor movements. Squawking brought him to the rescue of a pullet from a wild dog, but he arrived only soon enough to keep the dog from his meal. The sight of the dying pullet brought a strange feeling of empathy for the creature as Lev connected himself to the pullet and the dog to the Ranger. He noticed angry tears dropping onto her feathers as he finished the job the dog had started.

Lev built a fire under the lean-to, out of sight of the gap, boiled some water, and plucked the chicken. Spring-like thunder surprised him on a night that turned suddenly sultry. An unexplained feeling of well-being and good fortune came over him as he roasted the pullet on a spit and oven he fashioned from small sticks and stones. He would stay dry if it rained, was warm and was about to have a hot meal.

He had just broken a second egg in the skillet when a brisk breeze blew across the low fire, almost putting it out. A bad sign. He saw a moonlight shadow cross the smoldering embers. His free hand was the wrong one, so he dropped the skillet as he reached for the Colt.

"Keep still." The Ranger's rifle was cocked and at his shoulder, pointed at Lev's chest.

The wind whistled through the rocks and crevices on the south ridge, signaling a change in weather, but Lev felt trickles of sweat under his arms. He felt rage at having his moment of peace taken away—at being caught unprepared. They glared silently for a few seconds. Lev tried to appear calm as he picked the skillet out of the coals and assessed the damage to his eggs. He looked up at the Ranger. "About to have myself a little supper. Care to join me?"

A gust of wind whipped at the Ranger's hat and made it hard to hear his voice. "Had mine already. Though it was not as hot as yours." He relaxed the rifle only a little. "Throw that Colt away from you and I'll ease my grip on this trigger."

Lev set the skillet on a rock and eased the pistol from its holster. He took care as he placed it on a saddle blanket just at the end of his reach. "Just as soon not throw it. Man caught out here without a pistol can get himself killed." He returned to his skillet and looked up at the Ranger. "First time to see you this close."

"I expect."

"Coulda killed you more than once."

"Had a chance or two at you."

"What kept you from it?"

The question seemed to fluster the levelheaded lawman for an instant. "Asked myself that question. Guess taking your brother away from his family bothered me a little. A man to admire in different circumstances."

"What you got planned for me?"

"Got no plans beyond taking you in. Up to other folks after that."

"What made you go hard against me after all this time?"

"The women leaving, I guess. Guess your providing for them and the children mighta slowed me some without my realizing it."

Lev touched his hat brim. "Mind if I get something out of my hat?"

"You can take it off, but show it to me before reaching in."

Lev slowly removed his hat and turned it so the Ranger could look inside. He took the envelope out of the sweatband and handed it toward him.

"Drop it on the ground and move back." The Ranger drew his pistol and leaned his rifle against the barn before stepping closer to the firelight with the letter.

The envelope was addressed simply, Law Enforcement. He bent to his knees, opened it and read silently.

> *To whom it may concern,*
>
> *I consider Lev Rivers a friend. I commanded him on a mission during The War of Northern Invasion and he fought with distinction. Efforts are currently underway to pardon his brother for the crime he is accused of. If these efforts succeed, and I fully expect that they will, Lev will surely be exonerated at the time his brother is pardoned. Please take this into consideration.*
>
> *John Henry Brown, Esq.*

Lev watched as the Ranger let the letter soak in.

The Ranger stood and handed it back to Lev. "I have heard of John Henry Brown. Served in the Texas legislature, as I recall." He let the words drift away on the brisk wind that had allowed him to approach Lev without being heard. "But as far as I know, he has no authority in this matter."

Lev put the letter back in his hat and pulled it down. He pulled the overcooked eggs from the skillet with his Bowie knife and ate both of them in four bites. Appetite gone, he started on the chicken.

The Ranger allowed himself to sit back on his haunches and seemed to relax. "I hope your brother gets his pardon. Heard he killed that feller for attacking his wife. That true?"

Lev looked at him, but did not answer.

"And you helped him to do the deed?"

"I did."

"How long before you find out about the pardon?"

"Only thing for sure is that it needs to be done before Governor Hubbard leaves office. What time of year is it?"

"Just past Christmas."

Lev made an involuntary sound of disappointment—a clicking sound between his cheeks and gums. He had thought it was closer to the first half of December. "Expect to hear from somebody any day."

"I checked with Dillahunty for mail before I left. You didn't have any."

"I expect to get my news by messenger."

"Can't wait much longer than tomorrow noon without taking you back. Jailers like to be home with family this time of year."

Lev smiled bitterly. "Sure wouldn't want to spoil a man's time with his family."

The Ranger took a rope from his saddle. "Sorry, but I have to tie you up for the night."

52

HY ADDED HIS LETTER FROM HESTER TO THE stack, wishing she would stop writing, hoping she had gone home to East Texas. He had not opened a letter from her in two months. Too painful to read. The letters were filled with false hope and loving memories. Hope made a man weak, memories made him bitter. He had started crying when he read the letters and a man should never cry in prison.

He looked at his young cellmate. The man was as close to an animal as Hy had ever seen. He carried a constant smell of rank sweat and stale urine. He was loud, crude, and obnoxious. A man prisons were built for. Hy dreamed of choking him to death almost daily.

He could not chase away sentiment for Christmas, a holiday he barely noticed as a free man. Slim hopes for escape had been dashed when the guards checked his ball and chain after Emmett died. They found the same handiwork on Hy's ball and chain as on Emmett 's. They took him to the blacksmith shop and replaced the bolt and tap with permanent brads. He had to stand on the barrel for half a day as punishment.

Hy was shivering from cold and near-pneumonia when a guard came to his cell. The prison warden and an older gentleman who looked familiar to Hy followed the usually talkative prison guard. The gentleman seemed to come from the dark corners of Hy's past, but he could not match the face with a name.

53

THE RANGER TIED LEV'S HANDS AND FEET TO the bedposts of his own bed and slept the stormy night on the floor. Lev laid on the bare mattress, listened to the sounds of rain on the tin roof, and studied the cobwebs on the walls and furniture. Anger and despair brought the almost-forgotten rope and humming back.

At sunrise, they rekindled the embers from the night fire and cooked eggs and ham from Hester and Mary Ann's lauder. The rain had stopped, leaving behind a feeling of wet and chill when the wind shifted from southern gusts to an easterly breeze. No words passed between them until Lev had swallowed his last bite of ham. "Guess I owe you a debt of thanks for helping the women fill that dugout with cured meat."

The Ranger shook his head. "Not my doing. The women did most of it by themselves. Saw evidence that you added your own bounty, as well."

Lev rose and put his hands in his pocket to rub the post oak acorns, the rabbit's foot and the bullet remains for any kind of luck they might bring. "You say it's after Christmas?"

"I expect."

"Why kind of man would come out here so close to Christmas rather than staying with his family?"

"No family. Just doing my job. I been gone on a scout. Saw signs that you were back when I was on my way back to camp.

Figured you would come down to the house sooner or later."

"What signs?"

"Your gelding left a polecat scent. Followed it up to your cave and back down here." The Ranger stood and drained his coffee cup. "We need to be on our way."

Lev stalled for time. "How come you never came down here with a whole bunch of Rangers if you knew I was hiding in them hills?"

"My Captain never believed what I told him about you. Seemed unlikely to everybody but me that you could stay so close to home for so long with us camped less than a day's ride from here. The battalion had a good laugh at my expense."

Lev's face warmed at the notion of giving up his freedom so that the man could prove a point. "Guess you'll get the last laugh now."

The Ranger took no visible satisfaction in his victory.

"So why in hell couldn't you just leave it alone if your Captain could?"

"The job was given to me to do a long time ago. Wrote your name and your brother's in my book. I never shirk a task or leave one unfinished."

Lev studied the inscrutable expression on the Ranger's face and knew there was no need for further talk about why. Despair washed over him again. "Hester wanted Hy home for Christmas. Promised the women and kids a regular Christmas this year. Been a long time."

Lev inclined his head toward Palo Pinto Creek. "Been keeping my eye on a little cedar tree just off the creek over there. Figured I would cut it and bring it up here when they come in."

"Told you Christmas done past."

"Any law says a family can't celebrate late?"

The Ranger looked in the direction of the cedar tree. "Seems a foolish gesture, but get it done quick."

Tied hands slowed Lev's chopping of the tree, but it finally fell. The rapidly cooling north wind felt good when he started to sweat. He tied his rope to the tree trunk and Butter dragged it down the rocky ledge toward the house. He stopped at the creek and considered how to get across without getting the tree muddy. He dismounted and threw the prickly little cedar across his saddle. It fell off. Lev remounted and pulled the roped trunk high enough to keep it off the ground and out of the water. Butter was in the middle of the creek when Lev's arms and tied hands started to give out.

"Loop that around the middle." The Ranger was beside him, handing him one end of a rope. Lev managed to loop it and toss the end of the rope back to the Ranger. Lev dallied his rope, and the Ranger held both ends of his. His rifle was back in its scabbard, his pistol in its holster. They crossed the creek with the tree suspended between them and stopped at the porch.

Lev leaned the tree against the front door. He thought of writing a note, but had nothing to write with or on and nothing to say. "The gelding is borrowed. Can we take him with us? Maybe send word to the owner to pick him up?"

Lev took silence as assent and decided to ride the gelding and let Butter follow again. The Ranger watched as he switched saddles. When he was mounted, the Ranger tied his hands to the saddle horn before tying his feet to the stirrups with rawhide strips. "Sorry about the feet, but I have seen what you can do onboard a horse." They had just entered the gap when Butter stopped, turned, and nickered. Lev took great pride in the old mare's following without a lead rope and was embarrassed by her show of disrespect. Butter blew and snorted as her ears pointed toward the other end of the little canyon.

The creek water, still warm from the days before, had clashed with the cold air and released a smoky fog that gathered in the narrow entrance. The shifting wind brought the jangle of singletrees and the creak of wagons to Lev's ears. He saw slight movement behind the mist and felt something swell his chest and choke his breath. Two wagons eased through the smoky curtain before a wind gust blew the fog out of the canyon. He could barely make out the human forms, but he knew the horses. Hester rose a little from her seat on the front wagon and pointed toward the two men leaving the canyon through the gap. She gave a tentative wave toward Lev, but he could not reciprocate.

There beside Hester, driving the team, sat Lev's gaunt brother. Hy stopped the wagon and looked up at Lev and the Ranger. Hester's rifle lay in the wagon boot and Hy reached down to retrieve it. Hester restrained him without taking her eyes from the two riders on the hill. Otho fingered the butt of his rifle as he stopped beside the wagon. John Henry Brown, driving Mary Ann's wagon, pulled it even with Hy's. Mary Ann sat beside him, a bundle cradled in her arms.

The Ranger stiffened slightly in his saddle, his face showing slight curiosity, and maybe a little impatience with himself for not being already gone. The wind was now strong out of the north and a mixture of sleet and snow stung their eyes. The Ranger studied the scene and considered his options. He pulled his rifle and laid it across his pommel, then grunted a little as he signaled for Lev to lead the way back down the hillside toward the house. As if she knew what was happening, Butter left them in a dead run. The wagons started moving at the same time and arrived just ahead of Lev and the Ranger. Butter nudged the noses of the wagon horses and stared warily at Hy as if trying to connect the sickly-looking man with someone from her past. She was sticking her curious head over both wagon beds to be petted by the children as Lev and the Ranger arrived.

Lev and Mary Ann looked longingly at each other and the bundle in her arms. All other eyes focused on the Ranger. Mary Ann motioned toward Lev's tied hands. She spoke to Lev while looking at the Ranger with pleading eyes and demand in her voice. "Lev, you come here and help us down from this wagon. Take a look at your new son."

The Ranger moved forward and patiently untied the rawhide strips from his hands and feet. Hy wanted to get down and cut them, but Hester put a hand on his shoulder, wanting things to take their natural course. She knew the value of patience with this Ranger. Lev stepped down from the gelding and moved toward his wife, but the Ranger stopped him and retied his hands. With bound hands, his embrace of Mary Ann was awkward. She pulled back the quilt to allow him his first glimpse of the baby boy. "Born on the way here. If it's all right with you, I want to call him Willis, after Judge Crawford." She looked to where John Henry Brown sat in the wagon seat. "Wanted to name him John Henry Rivers, but the major said Willis is a better choice."

John Henry Brown smiled. "Held us up a little when Mary Ann decides to have a baby on the way. Wanted to make it by Christmas."

Still watching the Ranger, Hy stepped down from his wagon and helped Hester and the children down. Kate, Dallas and Lane sensed the tension and gathered like chicks around their mother and long-absent father. They had remained close to his side, as if he were a recovered treasure, since meeting him at the prison gate. Otho dismounted and stood beside his father, keeping a hand on the butt of his pistol, eyes full of fury. The reality of the pardon had not settled in Hy's mind and he figured the Ranger's presence meant it had all been a mistake. Freedom still seemed unnatural to him, but he managed a gesture that took Otho's hand from his pistol.

In pecking order, oldest to youngest, Arthur, Ellen and Rance presented themselves to their father for embrace and took another curious peek at their new brother and a timid look at their father's tied hands. The family then stood stiffly beside Hy's, presenting a united wall as they faced the Ranger. He returned their stares without flinching.

Lev looked away from his wife and children long enough to study his brother—free for the first time in four years. Lev could not remember seeing Hy without a pistol and Bowie knife on his hips and he looked almost naked in the light pants and shirt from Hester's needle. He was skinnier than he had been, even during the war.

Unsure of what to do next, Lev turned back to the baby. "The judge is a fine man to name a boy after." He touched the baby's cheek with a finger.

Hy moved behind his brother, drawn, gaunt and pale, and looked over his shoulder at his nephew. "Takes a good man to live in the wild and keep having younguns."

Lev's tied hands were clumsy as he took Hy's outstretched hand, his voice a hoarse whisper. "By God, I never would have believed it. A free man."

"I can't ever repay you."

"It was the women more than me ... and Major Brown."

"I expect you're right. We made fine choices in our women. Got better'n we deserve."

Lev heard himself chuckle. An unfamiliar sound.

Hy turned toward John Henry Brown. "I already tried to thank Major Brown, but can't find the words for that, either. Expect I'll go to my grave in his debt."

John Henry Brown carried his usual aura of self-assurance. "A small role, but a finer thing I have never done." He turned toward Mary Ann and pointed toward the baby. "We need to get this young man inside and warm. I've grown quite fond of him, even with the trouble he has already caused. And I could use some coffee."

Hester removed a sack of supplies from the wagon and followed Mary Ann and the baby to the house. She carefully moved the Christmas tree away from the door, held it erect and looked toward the Ranger before carrying it inside.

The wind had picked up and sleet was giving way to heavier

snow when John Henry Brown approached the Ranger, his hand extended. "Name's John Henry Brown. I have a copy of the pardon granted to Hiram Griffin Rivers by Governor Hubbard just a few days ago. The district attorney of Dallas County has given me his assurance that this will also result in the dismissal of the indictment against Lev Rivers."

The Ranger took the hand and the paperwork. The families waited with anguish while the Ranger, eyes burning, tried to read the blowing paper and keep an eye on his prisoner at the same time. Little Alfred, trying to conceal his shivering, closed and unclosed his fists as the Ranger read.

John Henry Brown turned toward Lev and spoke in a low voice. "I have also received word that Wade Monroe did not incur permanent damage from his unpleasant encounter with you. He will see out of one eye again. He has been urged by Judge Willis Crawford not to press charges."

Fire started and coffee on to boil, Willis down for a nap in a warm bed, Hester and Mary Ann returned to stand with their families in front of their home. Mary Ann stroked her empty arms and Hester brushed snow from her hair as they watched the Ranger read.

The usually confident lawman seemed confused, unsure of his duty. He looked up to see a wall of two families, all eyes on him. John Henry Brown saw his opening. "I respect and admire your devotion to duty, sir. If it will help in your decision, let me further note that Major James Barkley, sheriff at the time of Hy's arrest, the prosecuting attorney, and the jury foreman at Hy's trial all signed our petition for pardon."

The Ranger looked at Hester and Mary Ann, possible surrender in his expression. Hester's smile was pained. "I expect our larder has been taken by the bears and varmints, but we intend to have Christmas dinner soon as we get our supplies unloaded. Supper, too. You're welcome to join us."

The Ranger looked back through the gap toward Ranger camp. When he turned back, a wind gust bent the brim and almost took his hat. Snow was starting to accumulate on hats and shoulders.

John Henry Brown stepped forward. "It seems that God grows impatient with us, sir."

The Ranger turned in his saddle, opened his saddlebag, and tossed Lev's Bowie knife to him. Lev caught the knife with tied hands and held it for a moment, his eyes on the Ranger, unsure of this gesture. Hy stepped in front of him, took the knife, and cut the rawhide strips. When they fell, Hy turned back to the Ranger and extended a hand. "My Hester has invited you into our home for coffee and a meal. I would consider it a kindness if you accepted."

Still looking toward the gap, the Ranger dismounted and allowed Hy to lead him into the house. As Otho and Kat led the horses to the barn, Arthur remained beside his father, who seemed unable to move. Lev looked up to the west ridge, near the twin scrub oaks, toward his cave, then to the sky. For the first time since before the war, he did not sense danger. Little Alfred watched as his father pulled the rabbit's foot, the acorns and the bullet from his pocket. Lev seemed to be somewhere else as he studied them in his open palm. He tossed them up slightly and then closed his palm around them. He lifted Alfred's hand and dropped them into his son's open palm. Mary Ann appeared beside him and slipped her hand into his.

Epilogue

HIRAM (HY) GRIFFIN AND HESTER HAD ONE more child in 1880. Hy died in 1905 at the age of sixty-nine near Garland in Dallas County (the county where he was indicted for murder.) Hester died in 1929 at the age of ninety. I cannot confirm, but some records show she returned to West Texas and died near Throckmorton.

Mary Ann and Lev had twins two years after this story ends (1879) and named them Hiram Griffin and Hester after Hy and his wife. The boy twin was to be my grandfather. Lev and Mary Ann had a total of eight children. Lev died in 1918 at age seventy-six near Ranger in West Texas, a town named for the Texas Ranger camp established there. He was buried beside the Leon River with only an unmarked stone to identify his grave. Mary Ann died in Rowlett, a town near Dallas, in 1930 at age eighty-two.

An oil boom in Ranger in 1918 increased the population by ten-fold. Soon after Lev's death that year, Hiram (my grandfather) and his wife Eva left Ranger in a covered wagon with five children, including my father. As she had done every morning of his seven years, Minnie, Lev's sister, cooked my father biscuits the morning they left. She sent an extra two biscuits for the trail. Daddy would only eat biscuits cooked by Aunt Minnie. On the trail, he realized he might never see her again and kept the biscuits. I still have them.

The family traveled back across Texas to Delta County in

Northeast Texas. They moved back west a few times, but always returned to East Texas just like their grandmother Rachael had.

Afterword

THANK YOU FOR GETTING THIS FAR. MOST readers who have read my *Follow the Rivers Trilogy* have surmised that the Rivers family is based on my own. In those three novels, I changed or deleted a few stories or scenes that I knew to be true because editors and manuscript reviewers found them unbelievable. Truth is, indeed, stranger than fiction.

This fourth novel steps back a full century from the period of the other books, but is still based on family history. But I could do fewer interviews and could not work from memory on this one. In large part, I left the stories I believe to be true unchanged, even when I doubted them. All of the family characters are based on real people with only the surname changed to Rivers. I have confirmed most of the names and dates, but these facts are only as good as the sources I used.

The true stories and characters were more difficult to tell and describe than the fictionalized ones. My father, grandfather, uncles and aunts were consistent in telling that Uncle Hy had killed someone, but the reasons were always unclear and nobody seemed to know if he was ever punished. Oral history proclaimed that Lev had tried to prevent the shooting, but had become involved or been blamed for it and "scouted" for several years, always a fugitive, but able to see a light from the house every night. Nobody could say where Uncle Hy was during that time.

Notorious ancestors usually invoke more interest, and the wild stories about Uncle Hy and Great-grandfather Lev fascinated me for most of my life. I wanted to know the real story, but my curiosity was backed by only sporadic research. Interviews with my grandfather's twin sister, Hester, (daughter of Lev and Mary Ann) near her hundredth birthday renewed my interest. But it was an in-law who really stirred the coals. Rance (son of Lev and Mary Ann), only two when this story ends, married Beulah Pannell in 1912. He was thirty-seven and she was twenty-one. I interviewed Beulah in 1982 when she was ninety and found her to have a remarkable grasp of her husband's family history. I was able to confirm almost all of what she told me, but still she could not say why Hy had killed someone, whom he had killed, and whether he was ever punished.

Twenty-four years later, I met the retired warden of Huntsville Prison in Huntsville, Texas at a meeting of the East Texas Historical Association. Jim Willett had written a book called *Warden*. I bought a signed copy after his presentation. In retirement, Jim manages the Huntsville Prison Museum. He mailed me a copy of pages from the prison register (roll) for the period in question and there was Uncle Hy (spelled High). I am sure that a real historian or genealogist would have discovered this much sooner.

At the Cowboy Symposium in Lubbock in 2006, I met Dr. Len Ainsworth, the great grandson of Arch, Lev's and Hy's brother. Retired from Texas Tech, he was selling collectors' and antique books. He showed me a copy of *The Ainsworth-Collins Clan* by Shirley Insall Pieratt. I found Shirley in Austin and she told me about a book called *Fugitives From Justice*, a reproduction of Texas Ranger James Gillett's notebook. In that notebook, I found great-grandfather Lev Ainsworth, listed as a fugitive wanted for murder, indicted in *Dallas County*, September 1873. Hy was not listed. I had initially thought the killing occurred around Eastland County in West Texas and concentrated my research there to no avail. When I eventually found it had occurred in Ellis County in East Texas, I searched records there, again without result. I had been looking in the wrong counties. The killing had taken place in Ellis County, but there had been a change of venue. With this new information, I was able to find that Hy was tried and convicted in Dallas in March 1874. I found the judge's charge to the jury in an old article from *The Dallas Herald* and an article about the killing in the *Galveston Daily News*, referred to by some as Texas' oldest major newspaper.

The prison register also showed that Hy was pardoned in 1877 before serving his eight-year sentence for murder. I felt that readers would have trouble believing that, but I found the governor's proclamation and the pardon in the Texas State Archives and have reproduced them on the following pages, complete with the names of prominent citizens of the state. Further research has shown that such pardons were not that uncommon during the period after Reconstruction. Even John Wesley Hardin was pardoned in 1894. For your willing suspension of disbelief, I thank you. You can release it now. If you found this unbelievable, I do not blame you. So did I.

Some of the characters in this book are entirely fictional or fictionalized based on oral history. Even the real characters' actions, of course, had to be fictionalized to some extent in order to tell the story. I cannot prove the real reason Uncle Hy shot a man and the character of Filson is fictional, although he is based on a real person who committed crimes similar to the ones described in this book. The reason for the killing is based on oral family history, the judge's charge to the jury, and what is listed in the pardon and proclamation. I gave Hy motivations that he may or may not have had.

Reconstruction Texas was a turbulent and violent period, and people were sometimes killed for what might be considered minor offenses today. I tried not to judge these historical characters by the standards of today or to paint them all with the same brush of violence or ignorance. They lived in a different world that we can never completely understand. Political correctness not withstanding, people, characters and history are complex. We can only try to understand what they did and why they did it. I believe that we would need even more understanding from them if the situation were reversed.

I do know that Asbury Sebastian Ainsworth and Rachael Collins Ainsworth had five sons who served in the Confederate Army and that they qualify as a Texas First Family. I tried to stay true to history with John Henry Brown, but confess I do not know the details of his relationship with Hy and Lev, other than his name on the pardon paperwork. I believe that Doc Holliday was in Dallas at the time Uncle Hy was brought to Dallas for trial. I cheated a little on Chief Satanta. He was in prison with Hy, but made his death leap soon after Hy was released.

My father and his brother, like Hy and Lev, married sisters. And, oh yes, my middle initial stands for Hiram, so there is a little of Uncle Hy in me.

—Jim H. Ainsworth

PROCLAMATION LEADING TO PARDON FOR HIRAM AINSWORTH
signed by Richard B. Hubbard, Governor of Texas and former
commander of 22nd Texas Infantry.
Courtesy of the Texas State Archives.
(Note reference to petition submitted by John Henry Brown and
list of prominent citizens of Dallas and Ellis Counties. Petition was
also signed by the foreman of jury that convicted Hy and one of
the attorneys that prosecuted him.)

See pages 358 and 359

See pages 358 and 359

No. 1703.

Executive Office, State of Texas,
Austin, December 26, 1877.

The State of Texas,

vs.

Hiram Ainsworth   In Criminal Dist. Court, of Dallas County.

Convicted at the March Term,
1874 of "Murder," and sentenced to the Penitentiary for Eight years.

Whereas, it appears from statement
made in writing by Hon. John Henry Brown, that
the homicide for which this defendant was convicted and sentenced, was done in defence, as he believed, of the honor of his wife, to whom the deceased Reid C. Pryor had made dishonorable proposals, which being communicated to Ainsworth,
led to the killing; that subsequent to the killing
and before his arrest and trial, Ainsworth was a
peaceable citizen on the frontier, sober, industrious,
and kind to all, until his arrest about four years
later; that he had won the good will of all his
neighbors, and that since his incarceration in
the Penitentiary, (now about three years and
eight months,) his deportment has been most
exemplary; and that the wife of said Ainsworth
is a noble and true woman, and with her little
children, in desperation, from poverty, has settled
on a small piece of school land in Eastland
county, and is there now making rails, fencing and cultivating the soil to feed her little
children; and whereas the petition in behalf of

said Ainsworth is signed by Alex. Harwood, Esq., clerk of the County Court, Wm. A. Harwood, Esq., Clk. District Court, David W. Adams, Esq., Attorney; Jeff. Word, Jr., Attorney; Hon. W. L. Cabell, Mayor City of Dallas; Maj. James E. Barkley, Sheriff at time of conviction; L. T. Smith, Esq., Attorney; B. Gibbs, Esq., City Attorney; W. W. Peak, Esq., J.P.; W. H. Price, Esq.; C. T. S. Dake, Esq., W. B. Gano, Esq., M. Thevenet Esq., H. G. Nohny, Esq., D. A. Williams, Esq., John H. Cochran, Esq., and J. T. Downs, Esq., Representatives from Dallas County; Dr. J. S. Sizer, Foreman of the Jury who convicted him; and Geo. W. Aldridge, Esq., who assisted in the prosecution; and also by a large number of citizens of Ellis County (where the killing took place,) as is represented by Hon. J. H. Browe; therefore the premises considered, the convict having already served nearly half of the time for which he was sentenced, he will be granted a full pardon.

R. B. Hubbard
Governor.

GOVERNOR'S PARDON FOR HIRAM AINSWORTH ISSUED BY
Richard B. Hubbard, Governor of Texas.
Courtesy of the Texas State Archives.
(Note reference to W. L. Cabell, former Confederate General and
active leader of United Confederate Veterans, the first of three
generations of Cabell men to serve as Dallas Mayors.)

Hiram Ainsworth.   Pardon.

Proclamation.

By the Governor of the State of Texas.

To all to whom these presents shall come:

Whereas, at the March Term, 1874, in the Criminal Dist. Court of Dallas County, State of Texas, Hiram Ainsworth was convicted of "Murder", and sentenced to the Penitentiary for eight years:

Now, therefore, I, R. B. Hubbard, Governor of Texas, in consideration of the recommendation of Hon. John Henry Brown, Alex Harwood Esq., Clerk of the County Court, & Wm. A. Harwood, Clk. of the Dist. Court; Hon. W. L. Cabell, Mayor of Dallas; Hon. John H. Cochran and J. T. Downs, Representatives and of prominent citizens &c &c, do, by virtue of the authority vested in me by the Constitution and laws of this State, hereby grant to the said Hiram Ainsworth full pardon.

In Testimony Whereof, I have hereto signed my name and caused the Seal of State to be affixed, at the City of Austin, this 27th day of December, A. D. 1877.

L.S.

(signed)   R. B. Hubbard.
                    Governor.

By the Governor:
(signed) G. H. Bowman,
     Actg Secretary of State.

CPSIA information can be obtained at www.ICGtesting.com
Printed in the USA
BVOW08s2318170616

452387BV00001B/28/P

9 780865 347458